before the frost

Also by Henning Mankell

before
the frost

A LINDA WALLANDER MYSTERY

HENNING MANKELL

translated by Ebba Segerberg

THE NEW PRESS

NEW YORK
LONDON

© 2002 by Henning Mankell
English translation © 2005 by The New Press
All rights reserved.
No part of this book may be reproduced, in any form, without written permission from the publisher.

Requests for permission to reproduce selections from this book should be mailed to: Permissions Department, The New Press, 38 Greene Street, New York, NY 10013

Originally published as *Innan frosten* by Leopard Förlag, Stockholm, 2002
Published in the United States by The New Press, New York, 2005
Distributed by W. W. Norton & Company, Inc., New York

LIBRARY OF CONGRESS CATALOGING-IN-PUBLICATION DATA

Mankell, Henning, 1948–
    [Innan frosten. English]
    Before the frost / Henning Mankell ; translated by Ebba Segerberg.
    p. cm.
    ISBN 1-56584-835-7 (hc.)
    I. Segerberg, Ebba. II. Title.

PT9876.23.A49I5613 2005
839.73'74—dc22   2004055197

The New Press was established in 1990 as a not-for-profit alternative to the large, commercial publishing houses currently dominating the book publishing industry. The New Press operates in the public interest rather than for private gain, and is committed to publishing, in innovative ways, works of educational, cultural, and community value that are often deemed insufficiently profitable.

www.thenewpress.com

Book design by Kelly Too
Composition by Westchester Book Composition

Printed in the United States of America

10 9 8 7 6 5 4 3

before the frost

prologue

Jonestown, November 1978

His thoughts were like a shower of red-hot glowing needles, causing an almost unbearable pain. He tried desperately to remain calm, to think clearly. The worst thing was fear. The fear that Jim would unleash his dogs and hunt him down, like the terrified beast of prey he had become. Jim's dogs: they were what he was most afraid of. All through that long night of November 18, when he had run until he was exhausted and taken shelter among the decomposing roots of an upturned tree, he imagined he could hear them closing in.

Jim never lets anyone escape, he thought. *He seemed to be filled by an endless and divine source of love, but the man I have followed has turned out to be someone quite different. Unnoticed by us, he changed places with his shadow or with the devil, whom he was always warning us about. The devil of selfishness, who keeps us from serving God with obedience and submission. What appeared to be love turned into hate. I should have seen it earlier. Jim himself warned us about it time and time again. He gave us the truth, but not all at once. It came slowly, a creeping realization. But neither I nor anyone else wanted to hear it—the truth buried between the words. It was my own fault, because I didn't want to see it. In his sermons and in all his teachings he didn't just talk about the spiritual preparations we needed to undergo to ready ourselves for the Judgment Day ahead. He was also always telling us we had to be ready to die.*

He interrupted his thoughts and listened. Wasn't that the dogs barking? No, it was still only a sound inside of him, generated by his fear. He went back in his confused and terrified mind to the apocalyptic events in Jonestown. He needed to understand what had happened—Jim was their leader, shepherd, and pastor. They had followed him in the exodus from California when they could no longer stand persecution from the media and government authorities. In Guyana, they were going to realize their dreams of a life of peaceful coexistence with nature and one another in God. And at first they had experienced something very close to that. But then it changed. Could they have been as threatened here in Guyana as in California? Would they be safe anywhere? Perhaps it was only in death that they would find the kind of shelter they needed to construct the community they strove for. "I have seen far in my mind," Jim said. "I have seen much farther than before. The Day of Judgment is near at hand, and if we are not to perish in that terrible maelstrom we have to be ready to die. Only through physical death will we survive."

Suicide was the only answer. When Jim stood in the pulpit and mentioned it for the first time, there was nothing frightening about his words. First, parents were to give drinks laced with cyanide to their children, cyanide that Jim had stockpiled in plastic containers in a locked room at the back of his house. Then the adults would take the poison. Those who were overcome with doubt in the final moments would be assisted by Jim and his closest associates. If they ran out of poison, they had guns. Jim would make sure everyone was taken care of before he put the muzzle to his own head.

He lay under the tree, panting in the tropical heat. His ears strained to catch any sound of Jim's dogs, those huge red-eyed monsters that had inspired fear in all of them. Jim had told them that everyone in his congregation, everyone who had chosen to follow his path and come to Guyana, had no choice but to continue on the path laid out by God. The path that James Warren Jones had decided was the right one.

It had sounded so comforting. No one else would have been able to make words like death, suicide, cyanide, *and* weapons *sound so beautiful and soothing.*

He shivered. *Jim has walked around and inspected the dead,* he thought. *He knows I'm missing and he's going to send the dogs after me.* The thought clawed its way out of his mind: *the dead.* Tears began to run down his face. For the first time he took in the enormity of what had happened: Maria and the girl were dead, everyone was dead. But he did not want to believe it. Maria and he had talked about this in the small hours: Jim was no longer the same man they had once been drawn to, the one who promised them salvation and a meaningful life if they joined the People's Temple. Maria was the one who put her finger on it: "Jim's eyes have changed. He doesn't see us now. He looks past us and his eyes are cold, as if he wants nothing more to do with any of us."

They talked about running away together, but every morning they agreed that they couldn't abandon the path they had chosen. Jim would become his old self again. He was suffering some kind of crisis and it would soon be over; he was stronger than all of them. And without him they would never have had this brief experience of what seemed to them like heaven on earth.

There was one memory that stood out more clearly than any other. It was from that time when the drugs, alcohol, and guilt about leaving his little daughter had brought him close to ending it all. He wanted to throw himself in front of a truck or train and then it would be over and no one would miss him. During one of those last meandering walks through town, when he was saying goodbye to all the people who didn't care one way or another if he lived or died, he happened to pass by the People's Temple. "It was God's plan," Jim said later. "He had already decided that you would be among the chosen, one of the few to experience His mercy." He didn't know what had made him walk up those steps and enter the building that looked nothing like a church. He still didn't know what it was, even now as he lay among the roots of a tree waiting for Jim's dogs to find him and tear him limb from limb.

He knew he should be making good his escape, but he did not leave his hiding place. He had abandoned one child already; he was not going to abandon another. Maria and the girl were still back there with the others.

What had really happened? They had gotten up as usual that morning and gathered outside Jim's door. It remained closed, as it often had in the last days. They had therefore prayed without him, all 912 adults and 320 children. Then they had left for their various jobs. He would never have survived had he not been part of a team with the task of finding two runaway cows. When he said goodbye to Maria and her daughter, he had no inkling of the terror to come. It was only when he and the other men reached the far side of the ravine that he knew that something was terribly wrong.

They had stopped dead in their tracks at the first sound of gunshots and thought they heard human screams mingled with the chatter of the birds. They had looked at each other and then run back down toward the colony. He had become separated from the other men on the way back—possibly they had decided to flee rather than return. When he emerged from the shady forest and climbed the fence to the fruit orchards, everything was silent. Too silent. No one was there picking fruit. No one was to be seen. He ran toward the houses, sure that something disastrous had occurred. Jim must have come out of his house this day with hate, not love, blazing from his eyes.

He had a cramp in his side and slowly shifted position, straining not to make any noise. *What conclusion had Jim come to?* As he ran through the fruit orchards, he tried to do what Jim had always taught them: to put his life in God's hands. He prayed as he ran. *Please, God, let Maria and the child be safe.* But God had chosen not to hear him. In his desperation he started to believe that the shots he had heard from the ravine were the sounds of God and Jim taking aim at each other.

When he came rushing onto the dusty main street of Jonestown he half expected to catch the two of them in their duel. But God was nowhere to be seen. Jim Jones was there, the dogs barked like crazy in their cages, and there were bodies everywhere. He could see at once that they were all dead. It was as if they had been struck down by a giant fist from the sky. Jim Jones and the six brothers who were his personal assistants and bodyguards must have gone around and shot children trying to crawl away from their parents' corpses. He ran around among the dead looking for Maria and the child, but without success.

It was when he shouted Maria's name that he heard Jim calling him. He turned around and saw his pastor cocking a pistol at him. They were about twenty meters apart, and between them, outstretched on the burned brown earth, were the bodies of his friends, contorted in their death throes. Jim pulled the trigger, but missed. Before Jim had the chance to shoot again, he ran. He heard many shots being fired and he heard Jim roar in rage, but he had not been hit and he made his stumbling way across the bodies and kept running until it was dark. He didn't know if he was the only survivor. Where were Maria and the girl? Why was he the only one who was safe? Could one person escape the Day of Judgment? He didn't know, he only knew it was no dream. This was all too real.

At dawn, the heat began to rise like steam from the trees. That was when he finally realized that no dogs were coming. He crawled out from under the tree, shook his aching limbs, and stood up. He started back toward the colony. He was exhausted and extremely thirsty. Everything was still very quiet. *The dogs are dead,* he thought. *Jim must have meant it when he said no one would escape judgment. Not even the dogs.* He climbed over the fence and started to run. The first bodies he saw were those who had tried to escape. They had been shot in the back.

Then he stopped by the corpse of a familiar-looking man. Shaking, he turned the body face up. It was Jim. *His gaze has finally softened,* he thought. *And he's looking me straight in the eyes.* He had a sudden impulse to hit Jim, to kick him in the face. But he quelled this urge for violence and stood up. He was the only living soul among these dead, and he would not rest until he found Maria and the girl.

Maria had tried to run; she had fallen forward when they shot her in the back. The girl was in her arms. He bent over and cried. *Now there's nothing left for me,* he thought. *Jim has turned our paradise into a hell.*

He stayed with them until helicopters started circling over the area. He reminded himself of something Jim had told them shortly after they first came to Guyana, when life was still good: "The truth about a person can just as well be determined with the nose as with your eyes and ears," he said. "The devil hides inside people and the devil smells of sulfur. Whenever you catch a whiff of sulfur, raise the cross for protection."

He didn't know what the future held, if anything. He didn't want to think about it. He wondered if he would ever be able to fill the void that God and Jim Jones had left behind.

PART I

the darkest hour

1

The wind picked up shortly after nine o'clock on the evening of August 21, 2001. Small waves rippled across the surface of Marebo Lake, which lay in a valley to the south of the Rommele hills. The man waiting in the shadows next to the water stretched out his hand to determine the direction of the wind. *Almost due south,* he thought with satisfaction. He had chosen the right spot to put out food to attract the animals he would soon be sacrificing.

He sat down on the rock where he had spread out a sweater against the chill. It was a new moon, and no light penetrated the thick layer of clouds. *Dark enough for catching eels,* he thought. *That's what my Swedish playmate used to say when I was growing up. The eels start their migration in August. That's when they bump into the fishermen's traps and wander the length of the trap. And then the trap slams shut.*

His ears, always alert, picked up the sound of a car passing by some distance away. Apart from that, there was nothing. He took out a flashlight and directed the beam over the shoreline and water. He could tell that they were approaching. He spotted at least two white patches against the dark water. Soon there would be more.

He turned off the light and tested his mind—exactingly trained—by thinking of the time. *Three minutes past nine,* he thought. Then he lifted his arm and checked the display. Three minutes past nine—he was right, of course. In another thirty minutes it would all be over. He had learned that humans were not alone in their need for regularity. Even wild animals could be trained to respect time. It had taken him three months to prepare these animals for tonight's sacrifice. He had proceeded with patience and deliberation. He had made himself their friend.

He turned the flashlight back on. Now there were more white patches, and they were nearing the shore. He briefly illuminated the tempting meal of broken bread crusts that he had laid out on the ground, as well as the two gasoline containers. Then he turned the light off and waited.

When the time came he did exactly as he had planned. The swans had reached the shore and were pecking at the pieces of bread he had set out for them, either oblivious of his presence or simply used to him by now. He set the flashlight aside and put on his night-vision goggles. Altogether there were six swans, three couples. Two were lying down while the rest were cleaning their feathers or still combing the ground for bread.

Now. He got up, grabbed a can in each hand, and sprayed the swans with gasoline. Before they had a chance to fly away, he emptied what remained in each of the cans and set fire to a clump of dried grass among the swans. The burning gasoline caught one swan and immediately spread to the rest. In their agony they tried to fly away over the lake, but one by one plunged into the water like fireballs. He tried to fix the sight and sound of them in his memory: both the burning, screeching birds in the air and the image of hissing, smoking wings as they crashed into the lake. *Their dying screams sound like broken trumpets,* he thought. *That's how I will remember them.*

The whole thing was over in less than a minute. He was very pleased. It had gone according to plan, an auspicious beginning for what lay ahead.

He threw the two gasoline containers into the lake, tucked his sweater into his backpack, and shone the flashlight around the place to make sure he hadn't left anything behind. When he was convinced he had remembered everything he took a cell phone out of his coat pocket and dialed a number. He had bought the phone in Copenhagen a few days before.

When someone answered, he asked to be connected to the police. The conversation was brief. Then he threw the phone into the lake, put on his backpack, and walked away into the night.

The wind was blowing from the east now and was growing stronger.

2

It was the end of August and Linda Caroline Wallander was wondering if she took after her father in ways she hadn't already thought of, even though she was almost thirty years old and should know who she was by now. She had asked her father, had even tried to press him on it, but he seemed genuinely puzzled by her questions and brushed them aside by saying that she was most like her grandfather. These "who-am-I-like" conversations, as she called them, sometimes ended in fierce argument. They kindled quickly but also died away almost at once. She forgot about most of them and assumed that he did too.

But there had been one argument this summer that she had not been able to forget. It had been nothing, really. They had been talking about their differing memories of a holiday they took to the island of Bornholm when she was a little girl. For Linda there was more than this episode at stake; it was as if by reclaiming this memory she was on the verge of gaining access to a much larger part of her early life. She had been six, maybe seven years old, and both Mona and her father had been there. The idiotic argument had started over whether or not it had been windy that day. Her father claimed she had been seasick and thrown up all over his jacket. But Linda remembered the sea as blue and perfectly calm. They had only ever taken this one trip to Bornholm, so it couldn't have been a matter of mixing up several trips. Her mother had never liked boat rides and her father was surprised she had agreed to this one.

That evening, after the argument, Linda had had trouble falling asleep. She was due to start working at the Ystad police station in two months. She had graduated from the police academy in

Stockholm and had actually wanted to start working right away, but here she had nothing to do all summer, and her father couldn't keep her company, since he had used up most of his vacation time in May. That was when he thought he had bought a house and would need extra time for moving. He had the house under contract; it was in Svarte, just south of the highway, right next to the sea. But then the buyer changed her mind at the last minute. Perhaps it was because she couldn't stand entrusting her carefully tended roses and rhododendron bushes to a man who only talked about where he was going to put the kennel—when he finally bought a dog. She broke the contract, and her father's agent suggested he ask for compensation, but he chose not to. The whole episode was already over in his mind.

He kept looking for houses that cold and windy summer, but they were all either too expensive or just not the house he had been dreaming of all those years in the apartment on Mariagatan. He kept the apartment and asked himself if he was ever really going to move. When Linda graduated from the police academy, he drove up to Stockholm and helped her move her things to Ystad. She had arranged to rent an apartment starting in September. Until then she could have her old room back.

They started getting on each other's nerves almost immediately. Linda was impatient to start working and accused her father of not pulling strings hard enough at the station to get her a temporary position. But he said he had taken the matter up with Chief Lisa Holgersson. She would gladly have welcomed the extra manpower, but there was no room in the budget for more staff. Linda would not be able to start until the tenth of September, however much they might have wanted her to start earlier.

Linda spent the intervening time reacquainting herself with two old school friends. One day she ran into Zeba, or "Zebra," as they used to call her. She had dyed her black hair red and also cut it short, so Linda had not recognized her at first. Zeba's family came from Iran, and she and Linda had been in the same class until junior high. When they ran into each other on the street this July, Zeba was pushing a toddler in a stroller. They had stopped at a café and had coffee.

Zeba told her that she had trained as a bartender but that her pregnancy had put a stop to her work plans. The father was Marcus. Linda remembered him—the Marcus who loved exotic fruit and who had started his own plant nursery in Ystad at the age of nineteen. The relationship had ended quickly, but the child remained a fact. Zeba and Linda chatted for a long time, until the toddler started screaming so loudly and insistently that they had to leave. But they had kept in touch since that chance meeting, and Linda noticed that she felt less impatient with the hiatus in her life whenever she managed to build these bridges between her present and the past that she had known here.

As she was on her way home to Mariagatan after her meeting with Zeba, it suddenly started to rain. She took cover in a clothing store and—while she was waiting for the weather to clear up—she asked for the telephone directory and looked up Anna Westin's number. She felt a jolt inside when she found it. She and Anna had not had any contact for ten years now. The close friendship of their childhood years had ended abruptly at seventeen when they both fell in love with the same boy. Afterward, when the feelings of infatuation were long gone, they had tried to resuscitate the friendship, but it was never the same. Linda hadn't even thought about Anna very much for the last couple of years. But seeing Zeba again reminded her of her old friend, and she was happy to discover that Anna still lived in Ystad.

Linda called her that evening, and they met a few days later. The rest of the summer they often met several times a week, sometimes all three of them, but mostly just Anna and Linda. Anna lived on her own as well as she could on her student budget. She was studying medicine.

Linda thought Anna was even shyer now than when they were growing up. Anna's father had left when she was only five or six years old, and he had never been heard from again. Anna's mother lived out in the country in Löderup, not far from where Linda's grandfather had lived and painted his favorite, unchanging motifs. Anna seemed pleased that Linda had reestablished contact with her, but Linda soon realized she had to tread carefully around her. There was something vulnerable, almost secretive about Anna, and she didn't let Linda come too close.

Still, being with her old friends helped make Linda's summer go by, even though she was counting the days until she was allowed to pick up her uniform from Mrs. Lundberg in the stockroom.

Her father worked constantly all summer, handling a case of bank and post office robberies in the Ystad area. From time to time Linda would hear about this case that seemed like a well-planned series of attacks. When her father fell asleep at night, Linda would often sneak a look at his notebook and the case files he brought home. But whenever she asked him about the case directly, he would avoid answering. She wasn't a police officer yet. Her questions would have to go unanswered until September.

The days went by. One afternoon in August, her father came home and said that his real estate agent had called about a property by Mossby Beach. He wondered if she wanted to come and see it with him. She called and postponed a coffee date she had arranged with Zeba, and then her father picked her up in his Peugeot and they drove west. The sea was gray. Fall was on its way.

3

The house stood on a hill with a sweeping view of the ocean, but there was something bleak and dismal about it. The windows were boarded up, one of the drainpipes had come detached, and several roof shingles were missing. *This is not a place where my father could find peace,* Linda thought. *Here he'll be at the mercy of his inner demons. But what are they, anyway?* She began to list the chief sources of concern in his life, ranking them in her mind: first his loneliness, then the creeping tendency to put on weight and the stiffness in his joints. What else? She put the question aside for the moment and joined her father as he inspected the outside of the house. The wind blew slowly, almost thoughtfully, in some nearby beech trees. The sea lay far below them. Linda squinted and spotted a ship on the horizon.

Kurt Wallander looked at his daughter.

"You look like me when you squint like that," he said.

"Only then?"

They kept walking and came across the rotting remains of a leather couch behind the house. A field vole jumped out of the broken springs. Wallander looked around and shook his head.

"Remind me why I want to move to the country."

"I have no idea—why *do* you want to move to the country?"

"I've always dreamed of being able to roll out of bed and walk out the front door to take my morning piss, if you'll pardon my language."

She looked at him with amusement.

"Is that it?"

"Do I need a better reason than that? Come on, let's go."

"Let's walk around the house one more time."

This time she looked more closely at the place, as if she were the prospective buyer and her father the agent. She sniffed around like a dog.

"How much?"

"Four hundred thousand."

She raised her eyebrows.

"That's what it says," he said.

"You don't have that much money, do you?"

"No, but the bank has pre-approved my loan. I'm a trusted customer, a policeman who's always been as good as his word. I think I'm even disappointed I don't like this place. An abandoned house is as depressing as a lonely person."

They left. Linda read a sign on the side of the road. MOSSBY BEACH. He glanced at her.

"You want to go down there?"

"Yes. If you have time."

This was the place where she had first told him about her decision to become a police officer. She was done with her vague plans to refinish furniture, become an actress, as well as her extensive backpacking trips all over the world. It was a long time since she had broken up with her first love, a young man from Kenya who was studying medicine in Lund. He had finally returned to his homeland and she had stayed put. Linda had looked to her mother Mona to provide her with clues about how to live her own life, but all she saw in her mother was a woman who left everything half-done. Mona had wanted two children and only had one. She had thought that Kurt Wallander would be the great and only passion of her life, but she had divorced him and married a golf-playing retired banker in Malmö.

Eventually Linda had started looking more closely at her father, the detective chief inspector, the man who was always forgetting to pick her up at the airport when she came to visit. The one who never had time for her. She came to see that in spite of everything, now that her grandfather was dead, he was the one she was closest to. One morning, just after she had woken up, she had realized that what she wanted was to do what he did, be a police officer. She had kept her thoughts to herself for a year and only talked about it with her boyfriend at the time, but finally she became sure of it, broke up with her boyfriend, flew down to Skåne, took her father to this beach, and told him her news. He asked for a minute to digest what she had said, which made her suddenly anxious. Before she told him she was convinced he would be happy about her decision. Watching his broad back and his thinning hair blowing up in the wind, she prepared for a fight. But when he turned around and smiled at her, she knew.

They walked down to the beach. Linda poked her foot into some horse prints in the sand. Wallander looked at a seagull that hung almost motionless in the air.

"What are your thoughts now?" she asked.

"You mean, about the house?"

"I mean, about the fact that I'll soon be wearing a police uniform."

"It's hard for me even to imagine. It will probably be upsetting for me, though I don't feel that way now."

"Why upsetting?"

"I know what lies in store for you. It's not hard to put the uniform on, but then to walk out in public is another thing. You'll notice that everyone looks at you. You become the Police Officer, the one who is supposed to jump in and take care of any conflicts. I know what it feels like."

"I'm not afraid."

"I'm not talking about fear. I'm talking about the fact that from the first day you put on the uniform it will always be in your life."

She sensed he might be right.

"How do you think I'll do?"

"You did well at the academy. You'll do well here. It's up to you in the end."

They strolled along the beach. She told him she was about to go to Stockholm for a few days. Her graduating class was having a final party, a cadet ball, before everyone spread across the country to their new posts.

"We never had anything like that," Wallander said. "I didn't receive much of an education, either. I still wonder how they chose the applicants when I was young. I think they were interested in raw strength. You had to have some intelligence, of course. I do remember that I had quite a few beers with a friend after I graduated. Not in public, but at his place on South Förstadsgatan in Malmö."

He shook his head. Linda couldn't tell if the memory amused or pained him.

"I was still living at home," he said. "I thought Dad was going to keel over when I came home in my uniform."

"How come he hated it so much—you becoming a police officer?"

"I think I only figured it out after he died. He tricked me."

Linda stopped.

"Tricked you?"

He looked at her, smiling.

"What I think now is that it was actually fine with him that I chose to be a policeman. But instead of telling me straight out, it amused him to keep me on my toes. And he certainly managed to do that, as you know."

"You really believe that?"

"No one knew him better than I did. I know I'm right. He was a scoundrel through and through. A wonderful man, but a scoundrel. The only father I ever had."

They walked back to the car. The clouds were breaking up, and it was getting warmer. Wallander looked down at his watch when they were leaving.

"Are you in a hurry?" he asked.

"I'm in a hurry to start working, that's all. Why do you ask?"

"There's something I should look into. I'll tell you about it while we drive."

They turned onto the highway to Trelleborg and turned off by Charlottenlund Castle.

"I wanted to drive by since we were in the neighborhood."

"Drive by what?"

"Marebo Manor. Or more precisely, Marebo Lake."

The road was narrow and windy. Wallander told her about it in a somewhat disjointed and confusing way. She wondered if his written police reports were as disorganized as the summary she was getting.

Yesterday evening a man had called the Ystad police. He had not given them a name or location and he spoke with a strange accent. He had said that burning swans were flying over Marebo Lake. When the officer on duty had asked him for more details, the man hung up. The conversation was duly logged, but no one had followed up on it since there had been a serious assault case in Svarte that evening, as well as two robberies in central Ystad. The officer in charge had decided that it was most likely a prank call or a matter of hallucinations, but when Wallander later heard about it from his colleague Martinsson he decided it was so bizarre that there might be some truth to it.

"Setting fire to swans? Who would do anything like that?"

"A sadist. Someone who hates birds."

"Do you honestly think it happened?"

Wallander turned off onto a road leading to Marebo Lake and took his time before answering.

"They didn't teach you that at the academy? That policemen don't think anything? They only want to know. But they have to remain open to all possibilities, however unlikely. That includes something like a report about burning swans. It could turn out to be true."

Linda didn't ask any more questions. They parked the car in a small parking lot and walked down to the lake. Linda walked behind her father and felt as if she was already wearing a uniform.

They walked around the entire lake but found no trace of a dead swan. Neither of them noticed that someone was following their progress through the lens of a telescope.

4

Linda flew to Stockholm a few days later. Zeba had helped her make a dress for the cadet ball. It was light blue and cut low across her chest and back. The class organizers had rented a big room on Hornsgatan. All sixty-eight of them were there, even the prodigal son of the group who had not managed to hide his drinking problem. No one knew who had blown the whistle on him, so in a way they all felt responsible. Linda thought he was like their ghost; he would always be out there in the fall darkness with a deep-seated longing to be forgiven and taken back into the fold.

On this occasion, their last chance to say good-bye to each other and their teachers, Linda drank far too much wine. She wasn't a novice drinker by any means, and she could usually pace herself. This evening she knew she was drinking too much. She felt more impatient than ever to start working as she talked with student colleagues who had already taken the plunge. Her best friend from the academy, Mattias Olsson, had taken a job in Norrköping rather than return to his home in Sundsvall. He had already managed to distinguish himself by felling a bodybuilder who had taken too many steroids and run amuck.

There was dancing, speeches, and a relatively amusing song roasting the teachers. Linda's dress received many compliments. It would have been an altogether enjoyable evening if there hadn't been a TV set in the kitchen.

Someone heard on the late-night news that a police officer had been shot down on the outskirts of Enköping. This news quickly spread among the dancing, intoxicated cadets and their teachers. The music was turned off and the TV set brought out from the kitchen.

Afterward Linda thought it was as if everyone had been kicked in the stomach. The party was over. They sat there in their long gowns and dark suits and saw footage of the crime scene as well as images of the officer who had been murdered. It had been a cold-blooded killing that occurred while he and his partner tried to question the driver of a stolen car. Two men had jumped out of the car and opened fire on the policemen with automatic weapons. Their intention had clearly been to kill. No warning shot had been fired.

Everyone went home late that evening. Linda was on her way to her aunt Kristina's apartment when she stopped at Mariatorget and called her father. It was three o'clock in the morning and she could tell from his voice that he was barely awake. For some reason that made her furious. How could he sleep when a colleague had just been killed? That was also what she said to him.

"My not sleeping won't help anybody. Where are you?"

"On my way to Kristina's."

"You mean the party went on until now? What time is it?"

"Three. It ended when we heard the news."

She heard him breathing heavily, as if his body had still not decided to become fully awake.

"What's that noise in the background?"

"Traffic. I'm trying to catch a cab."

"Who's with you?"

"No one."

"Are you crazy? You can't run around alone in Stockholm at this hour!"

"I'm fine, I'm not a child. Sorry I woke you up."

She hung up on him. *This happens way too often,* she thought. *He has no idea how infuriating he is.*

She flagged down a taxi and was driven to Gärdet, where Kristina, her husband, and their eighteen-year-old son lived. Kristina had made up the sofa bed in the living room for her. The room was partly lit up from the streetlights outside. There was a photo of Linda and her father and mother in the bookcase. She remembered when the picture was taken; she was fourteen years old, it was sometime in the spring, and they had driven out to her grandfather's house in Löderup. Her dad had won the camera in an office raffle and then, when they were about to take a family picture, her grandfather had suddenly balked and locked himself in his studio. Her dad had been extremely upset and her mom had sulked. Linda was the one who tried to convince her grandfather to come out and be in the picture.

"I won't have my picture taken with those two people and their fake smiles when I know they're about to leave each other," he said.

She could remember to this day how that had hurt. Even though she knew how insensitive he could sometimes be, the words still felt like a slap in the face. When she had collected herself she asked him if what he had said was true, if he knew something she didn't.

"It won't help matters if you keep turning a blind eye," he said. "Go on. You're supposed to be in that picture. Maybe I'm wrong about all this."

Her grandfather was often wrong, but not this time. And he had refused to be in the picture, which they took with the self-timer on the camera. The following year—the last year her parents lived together—the tensions in their home only escalated.

That was the year she had tried to commit suicide. Twice. The first time, when she had slit her wrists, it was her dad who found her. She remembered how frightened he had looked. But the doctors must have reassured him, since he and her mother said very little about it. Most of what they communicated was through looks and eloquent silences. But it propelled her parents into the last series of violent disputes that finally persuaded Mona to pack her bags and leave.

Linda had often thought how remarkable it was that she hadn't felt responsibility for her parents' breakup. On the contrary, she felt that she had done them a favor and helped catapult them out of a marriage that in all but name had ended long before.

He didn't know about the second time.

That was the biggest secret she kept from her father. Sometimes she thought he must have heard about it, but in the end she remained convinced he had never found out. The second time she tried to kill herself it was for real.

She had been sixteen years old and had gone to stay with her mother in Malmö. It was a time of crushing defeats, the kind only a teenager can experience. She hated herself and her body, shunning the image she saw in the mirror while she also strangely enough welcomed the changes she was undergoing. The depression hit her out of nowhere, beginning as a set of symptoms too vague to take seriously. Suddenly it was a fact, and her mother had had absolutely no inkling of what was going on. What had shaken Linda the most was that Mona had said no when she pleaded to be allowed to move to Malmö. It wasn't that there was anything wrong with her dad; she just wanted to get out of Ystad. But Mona had been surprisingly cool.

Linda had left the apartment in a rage. It had been a day in early spring when there was still snow lying on the ground here and there. The wind blowing in from the sound had a sharp bite. She wandered along the city streets, not noticing where she was going. When she looked up she was on an overpass to the freeway. Without really knowing why, she climbed up onto the railing and stood there, swaying slightly. She looked down at the cars rushing past below with their sharp lights slicing the dark. She wasn't aware of how long she stood there. She felt no fear or self-pity; she simply waited for the cold and the fatigue spreading in her limbs to get her finally to step out into the void.

Suddenly there was someone by her side, speaking in careful, soothing tones. It was a woman with a round, childish face, perhaps not much older than Linda. She was wearing a police uniform and behind her there were two patrol cars with flashing lights. Only the officer with the childish face approached her. Linda sensed the presence of others farther back, but they had clearly delegated the responsibility of talking that crazy teenager out of jumping to this woman. She told Linda her name was Annika, that she wanted her to come down, that jumping into a void wouldn't solve anything. Linda started defending herself—how could Annika possibly understand anything about her problems? But Annika hadn't backed down, she had simply stayed calm, as if she had infinite patience. When Linda finally did climb down from the railing and start crying, from a sense of disappointment that was actually relief, Annika had started crying too. They hugged each other and stood there for a long time. Linda told her that she didn't want her father to hear about it. Not her mother either, for that matter, but especially not her dad. Annika had promised to keep it quiet, and she had been true to her word. Linda had thought about calling the Malmö police station to thank her many times, but she never got further than lifting the receiver.

She put the photograph back into the bookcase, thought briefly about the police officer who had been killed, and went to bed. She was woken up in the morning by Kristina getting ready for work. Kristina was her brother's opposite in almost every regard: tall, thin, with a pointed face and a shrill voice that Linda's dad made fun of behind her back. But Linda loved her aunt. There was something refreshingly uncomplicated about her, and in this way too she was her brother's opposite. From his perspective, life was nothing but a heap of dense problems, unsolvable in his private life, attacked with the force and fury of a ravenous bear in his work.

Linda took the bus to the airport shortly before nine in the hopes of catching a plane to Malmö. All of the morning headlines were about the murdered police officer. She got on a plane leaving at noon and called her dad when she got to Sturup.

"Did you have a good time?" he asked when he came to pick her up.

"What do you think?"

"How could I know? I wasn't there."

"But we talked on the phone last night—remember?"

"Of course I remember. You were rude and unpleasant."

"I was tired and upset. A police officer was murdered. No one was in a good mood after that."

He nodded but didn't say anything. He let her off when they got to Mariagatan.

"Have you found out anything more about this sadist?" she asked.

At first he didn't seem to understand what she was referring to.

"The bird hater? The burning swans?"

"Probably just a prank call. Quite a few people live around the lake and someone would have seen something if it wasn't."

———

Wallander drove back to the police station and Linda walked up to the apartment. Her father had left a note by the phone. It was a message from Anna, *Important. Call back soon.* Then her father had scribbled something she couldn't read. She called him at work.

"Why didn't you tell me Anna called?"

"I forgot."

"What have you written here—I can't read your handwriting."

"She sounded worried about something."

"How do you mean?"

"Just that. She sounded worried. You'd better call her."

Linda called but Anna's line was busy. When she tried again there was no answer. At seven o'clock in the evening, after she and her dad had eaten, she put on her coat and walked over to Anna's place. As soon as Anna opened the door Linda could see what her father had meant. Anna's expression was different. Her eyes darted around anxiously. She pulled Linda into the apartment and shut the door.

It was as if she were in a hurry to shut out the outside world.

5

Linda was reminded of Anna's mother, Henrietta. She was a thin woman with an angular, nervous way of moving, and Linda had always been a little afraid of her.

Linda remembered the first time she had played at Anna's house. She must have been around eight or nine. Anna was in another class at school and they had never been able to figure out exactly what had drawn them to each other. *It's as if there's an invisible force that brings people together. At least that's the way it was with us. We were inseparable—until we fell in love with the same guy, that is.*

Anna's father had never been present except in pale photographs. Henrietta had carefully wiped away all traces of him, as if she were telling her daughter that there was no possibility of his return. The few photos Anna owned were stashed away in a drawer, hidden under some socks and underwear. In the pictures he had long hair, glasses, and a reluctant stance, as if he hadn't really wanted to pose for the camera. Anna had showed her the pictures in the deepest confidence. When they became friends her father had already been gone for two years. Anna quietly rebelled against her mother's determination to keep the apartment free of all traces of him. One time Henrietta had gathered up what remained of his clothes and stuffed them in a garbage bag in the basement. Anna had snuck down there at night and rescued a shirt and some shoes that she hid under her bed. For Linda this mysterious father had been a figure of adventure. She had often wished that she and Anna could trade places, that she could exchange her quarreling parents for this man who had simply vanished one day like gray wisps of smoke against a blue sky.

They sat on the sofa and Anna leaned back so half of her face was in shadow.

"How was the ball?"

"We heard about the murdered police officer in the middle of it and that pretty much ended it right there. But my dress was a success. How is Henrietta?"

I know what she's doing, Linda thought. *Whenever Anna has anything important to talk about she can never come right out and say it. It always takes time.*

"Fine."

Anna shook her head at her own words.

"Fine—I don't know why I always say that. She's actually worse than ever. For the past two years she's been composing a requiem for herself. She calls it 'The Unnamed Mass' and she's thrown the whole thing in the fire at least twice. Both times she managed to salvage most of the papers, but her self-esteem is about as low as a person with only one tooth left."

"What does her music sound like?"

"I hardly even know. She's tried to hum it for me a couple of times—the very few times she's been convinced that what she was working on had value. But it doesn't sound like anything close to a melody to me. It's the kind of music that sounds more like screams, that pokes and hits you. I have no idea why anyone would ever listen to something like that. But at the same time I can't help admiring that she hasn't given up. Several times I've tried to persuade her to do other things in life. She's not even fifty yet. But every time she's reacted like an angry cat. It makes me wonder if she's crazy."

Anna interrupted herself at this point as if she were afraid of having said too much. Linda waited for her to continue.

"Have you ever had the feeling you were going crazy?"

"Only every single day."

Anna frowned.

"No, not like that. I'm not kidding."

Linda was immediately ashamed of her lighthearted comment.

"It happened to me once. You know all about that."

"You're thinking of when you slit your wrists. And then tried to jump off the overpass. But that's despair, Linda. It's not the same thing. Everyone has to face their despair at least once in their life. It's a rite of passage. If you never find yourself raging at the sea or the moon or your parents, you never really have the opportunity to grow up. The King and Queen of Contentment are damned in their own way. They've let their souls be numbed. Those of us who want to stay alive have to stay in touch with our sorrow and grief."

Linda had always envied Anna's fanciful way of expressing herself. *I would have had to sit down and write it all down if I were going to come up with anything like that,* she thought. *The King and Queen of Contentment.*

"In that case I guess I've never really been afraid of losing my mind," she said lightly.

Anna got up and walked over to the window. After a while she returned to the sofa. *We're much more like our parents than we think,* Linda thought. *I've seen Henrietta move in just the same way when she's anxious: get up, walk around, and then sit down again.*

"I thought I saw my father yesterday," Anna said. "On a street in Malmö."

Linda raised her eyebrows.

"Your father? You saw him on the street?"

"Yes."

Linda thought about it.

"But you've never even seen him—not really, I mean. You were so young when he left."

"I have pictures of him."

Linda did the math in her head.

"It's been twenty-five years since he left."

"Twenty-four."

"Twenty-four, then. How much do you think a person changes in twenty-four years? You can't know. All you know is that he must have changed."

"It was him. My mother told me about his gaze. I'm sure it was him. It must have been him."

"I didn't even know you were in Malmö yesterday. I thought you were going in to Lund, to study or whatever it is you do there."

Anna looked at her appraisingly.

"You don't believe me."

"You don't believe it yourself."

"It was my dad."

She took a deep breath.

"You're right; I had been in Lund. When I got as far as Malmö and had to change trains. There was a problem with the line. The train was cancelled. Suddenly I had two hours to kill until the next one. It put me in a terrible mood since I hate waiting. I walked into town, without any clear idea of what I was going to do, just to get rid of some of the unwanted, irritating time. Somewhere along the line I walked into a store and bought a pair of socks I didn't even need. As I was walking past the Saint Jörgen Hotel a woman had fallen down in the street. I didn't walk up close—I can't stand the sight of blood. Her skirt was bunched up, and I remember wondering why no one pulled it down for her. I was sure she was dead. A bunch of people had gathered to look, as if she were a dead creature washed up on the beach. I walked away, through the Triangle, and walked into the big hotel there in order to take their glass elevator up to the roof. That's something I always do when I'm in Malmö. It's like taking a glass balloon up into the sky. But this time I wasn't allowed to do it—now you have to operate the elevator with your room key. That was a blow. It felt as if someone had taken a toy away. I sat down in one of the plush armchairs in the lobby and looked out the window and was planning to stay there until it was time to walk back to the station.

"That's when I saw him. He was standing on the street. Now and then a gust of wind made the windowpane rattle. I looked up, and there he was on the sidewalk looking at me. Our eyes met and we stared at each other for about five seconds. Then he looked down and walked away. I was so shocked it didn't even occur to me to follow him. To be perfectly honest I still didn't believe I had really seen him. I thought it was a hallucination or a trick of the light. Sometimes you see someone and you think it's a person from your past, but it's really just a stranger. When I finally did run out and look around, he was gone. I felt a bit like an animal stalking its prey when I walked back to the train station—I tried to sniff out where he could be. I was so excited—upset, actually—that I hunted through the inner city and missed my train. He was nowhere to be found. But I was sure that it was him. He looked just like he did in the picture I have. And my mother once said he had a habit of first looking up before he said anything. I saw him make that exact gesture when he was standing on the sidewalk on the other side of the window. When he left all those years ago he had long hair and thick black-rimmed glasses; he doesn't look like that now. His hair is much shorter and his glasses are the kind without frames around the lenses.

"I called you because I needed to talk to someone about it. I thought I would go nuts otherwise. It *was* him, it *was* my father. And it wasn't just that I recognized him; he stopped on the sidewalk outside because he had recognized me."

Anna spoke with total conviction. Linda tried to remember what she had learned about eyewitness accounts—about the rate of accuracy in their reconstructions of events and the potential for embellishment. She also thought about what they had been taught about giving descriptions at the academy, and the computer exercises they had done. One assignment consisted of aging their own faces by twenty years. Linda had seen how she started looking more and more like her father, even a little like her grandfather. *Our ancestors survive somewhere in our faces,* she thought. *If you look like your mother as a child, you end up as your father when you age. When you no longer recognize your face it's because an unknown ancestor has taken up residence for a while.*

Linda found it hard to accept the idea that Anna had actually seen her father. He would hardly have recognized the grown woman his little girl had become, unless he had been secretly following her development all these years. Linda quickly thought through what she knew about the mysterious Erik Westin. Anna's parents had been very young when she was born. They had both grown up in big cities but been beguiled by the seventies' environmental movement—the so-called green wave—and had ended up in a collective out in the isolated countryside of Småland. Linda had a vague memory that Erik Westin was handy, that he specialized in making orthopedic sandals. But she had also heard Henrietta describe him as impossible, a hashish-smoking loser whose sole objective in life was to do as little as possible and who had no idea what it meant to take responsibility for a child. But what had made him leave? He had left no letter, nor any signs of extensive preparations. The police had looked for him at first, but there had never been any indication of crime and they eventually shelved the case.

Nonetheless, Westin's disappearance must have been carefully choreographed. He had taken his passport and what little money he had—most of it left over from selling their car, which had actually belonged to Henrietta. She was the only one with an income at the time, working as a night guard at a local hospital.

Erik Westin was there one day and gone the next. He had left on unannounced trips before, so Henrietta waited two weeks before contacting the police.

Linda also recalled that her own father had been involved in the subsequent investigation. There had been little to go on, since Westin had no record—no previous arrests or convictions, nor any history of mental illness, for that matter. A few months before he disappeared he had undergone a complete physical and been given a clean bill of health, aside from a little anemia.

Linda knew from police statistics that most missing persons eventually turn up again. Of those who didn't, the majority were suicides. Only a few were the victims of crime, buried in unknown places or decomposing at the bottom of a lake with weights attached to them.

"Have you told your mom?"

"Not yet."

"Why not?"

"I don't know. I suppose I'm still in shock."

"I'd say you're still not fully convinced it was him."

Anna looked at her with pleading eyes.

"I know it was. If it wasn't, my brain has suffered a major short-circuit. That's why I asked you if you've ever been afraid you were going crazy."

"But why would he come back now, after twenty-four years? Why would he turn up in Malmö and look at you through a hotel window—how did he know you were there?"

"I don't know."

Anna got up again, making the same journey to the window and back.

"Sometimes I wonder if he really disappeared at all. Maybe he just chose to make himself invisible."

"But why would he have done that?"

"Because he wasn't up to it, to life. I don't mean just his responsibilities for me or my mom. He was probably looking for something more. That search drove him away from us. Or perhaps he was only trying to get away from himself. There are people who dream about being like a snake, about changing their skin from time to time. But maybe he's been here all along, much closer than I realized."

"You wanted me to listen to you and then tell you what I thought. You say you're sure it was him, but I can't accept it. It's too close to a childhood fantasy, that he would suddenly turn back up in your life. I'm sorry, but twenty-four years is too long."

"I know it was him. It was my dad. I'm not wrong about this."

They had reached an impasse. Linda sensed that Anna wanted to be left alone now, just as she had earlier craved some company.

"I think you should tell your mom," Linda said as she got up to leave. "Tell her that you saw him, or someone you thought was him."

"You still don't believe me?"

"What I believe is neither here nor there. You're the only one who knows what you saw. But you have to admit it sounds farfetched. I'm not saying that I think you're making it up; obviously you have no reason to. I'm just saying it's very unusual for a person who's been gone as long as your dad has to turn up again, that's all. Sleep on it and we'll talk about it tomorrow. I can come by around five—is that good for you?"

"I know it was him."

Linda frowned. There was something in Anna's voice that sounded shrill and hollow. *Is she making it up after all?* Linda thought. *There's something that doesn't ring true in all of this. But why would she lie to me?*

Linda walked home through the deserted town. Some teenagers were standing in a group outside the movie theater on Stora Östergatan. She wondered if they could see her invisible uniform.

6

The following day Anna Westin disappeared without a trace. Linda immediately knew that something was wrong when she rang Anna's doorbell at five o'clock and no one answered. She rang the bell a few more times and shouted Anna's name through the mail slot, but still no one answered. After thirty minutes Linda took out a set of passkeys that a fellow student had given her. He had bought a collection of them on a trip to the United States and given them out to all his friends. In secret they had then spent a number of hours learning how to use them. By now Linda was proficient with any standard lock.

She picked Anna's lock without difficulty and walked in. She toured the empty, well-kept rooms. Nothing seemed amiss; the dishes were done and the dish towels hanging neatly on the rack. Anna was orderly by nature. What had happened? Linda sat down on the sofa in the same spot as the night before. *Anna believes she saw her father,* she thought. *And now she disappears herself. Of course these two events are connected—but how?* Linda sat for a long time, ostensibly trying to think it through, but in reality she was simply waiting for Anna to come back.

The day had started early for Linda. She had left for the police station at seven-thirty in order to meet with Martinsson, one of Kurt Wallander's oldest colleagues who happened to have been assigned to be her supervisor. They were not going to be working together, as Linda—like the other new recruits—would be assigned to a patrol car with experienced colleagues. But Martinsson was the senior officer she would turn to with questions should the need arise. Linda remembered him from when she was little. Martinsson had been a young man then. According to her father, Martinsson had often thought of quitting. Wallander had managed to talk him out of it on at least three occasions over the last ten years.

Linda had asked her father if he had had anything to do with Lisa Holgersson's decision to assign Martinsson as her mentor, but he vehemently denied any involvment. His intention was to stay as far away from any matters concerning her work as possible, he said. Linda had accepted this declaration with a grain of salt. If there was one thing she feared, it was precisely that he would interfere with her work. That was the reason she had hesitated so long before deciding to apply for work in Ystad. She thought about working in another area of the country, but this was where she had ended up. In retrospect it seemed fated.

Martinsson met her by the front desk and escorted her to his office. He had a picture of his smiling wife and their two children on his desk. Linda wondered whose picture she was going to have on hers. That decision was part of the everyday reality waiting for her. Martinsson started by talking about the two officers she was teamed up with.

"They're both fine officers," he said. "Ekman can give the impression of being a bit tired and worn-out, but no one has a better grasp of police work than he does. Sundin is his polar opposite and focuses on the little things. He still tickets people who cross against a red light. But he knows what it means to be a policeman. You'll be in good hands."

"What do they say about working with a woman?"

"If they have anything to say about that, ignore them. It's not how it was even ten years ago."

"And my father?"

"What about him?"

"What do they say about my being his daughter?"

Martinsson waited a moment before answering.

"There are probably one or two people in the station who would be happy to see you fall on your face. But you must have known that coming in."

Then they talked at length about the state of affairs in the Ystad police district. The "state of affairs" was something Linda had heard about at home from early childhood, as she played under the table with the sounds of clinking glass and the voice of her father and a colleague discussing the latest difficulties above her. She had never heard of a positive "state of affairs"; there was always something to lament. A substandard shipment of uniforms, detrimental changes in patrol cars or radio systems, a rise in crime statistics, poor recruitment numbers, and the like. In fact, this ongoing discussion about the "state of affairs," about how this day was different from the day before, seemed to be central to life on the force. *But it's not an art they taught us at the academy,* Linda thought. *I know a lot about how to break up a fight in the main square and very little about pronouncing judgments on the general state of affairs.*

They went to the lunchroom for a cup of coffee. Martinsson's assessment of the situation was fairly concise: there were too few officers working in the field.

"Crime has never paid as well as it does today, it seems. I've been researching this. To find a historical equivalent you have to look back as far as the fifteenth century, before Gustav Vasa pulled the nation together. In that time, the era of small city-states, there was widespread lawlessness and criminality just as there is today. We're not in the business of upholding law and order. We're just trying to keep this spread of lawlessness from getting any worse."

Martinsson followed her out into the reception area.

"I hope all this talk hasn't depressed you. We certainly don't need more demoralized police officers—in order to be a good police officer you'll need all the courage and faith you can muster. A cheerful disposition also helps."

"Like my dad?"

Martinsson smiled.

"Kurt Wallander is very good at his job," he said. "You know that. But he's not renowned for being the life of the party around here, as I'm also sure you've already figured out."

Before she left, he asked her about her reaction to the murdered officer. She told him about the cadet ball, the TV in the kitchen, and its effect on the festivities.

"It's always a blow," Martinsson said. "It affects all of us, as if we're suddenly surrounded by invisible guns out there aimed at our heads. Whenever a colleague is killed a lot of us think about leaving the force, but in the end most people choose to stay. And I'm one of them."

Linda left the station and walked to the apartment building in the eastern part of Ystad where Zeba lived. She thought about what Martinsson had told her—and what he had left out. That was something her father had drilled into her: always listen for what is left unsaid. That could prove to be the most important thing. But she didn't find anything like that in her conversation with Martinsson. *He strikes me as the simple and straightforward type,* she thought. *Not someone who tries to read people's invisible signals.*

She only stayed at Zeba's briefly because Zeba's boy had a stomach ache and cried the whole time. They decided to meet over the weekend when they would be able to have some peace and quiet to discuss the cadet ball and the success of Zeba's handiwork.

But the twenty-seventh of August did not go down in Linda's mind as the day she met with Martinsson, her mentor. It would be filed away in her mind as the day that Anna disappeared. After Linda had let herself into the apartment by picking the lock, she sat on the sofa and tried to recall Anna's voice telling her about the man who met her gaze through the hotel window and who bore a striking resemblance to her father. What was it she had really been trying to say? She had insisted that it was her father. That was like Anna—she sounded convincing even when she was claiming as facts things that were imagined or invented. But she was never late for an appointment, nor would she forget a date with a friend.

Linda walked through the apartment again, stopping in front of the bookcase by Anna's desk in the dining room. The books were mostly novels, she determined as she read the titles, as well as one or two travel guides. Not a single medical textbook. Linda frowned. The only thing even close to a textbook was a volume on common ailments, the kind of encyclopedia a lay person would have. *There's something missing,* she thought. *These don't look like the bookshelves of a medical student.*

She proceeded to the kitchen and took note of the refrigerator contents. There were the usual food items, a sense of future use suggested by an unopened carton of milk with a September 2 expiration date. Linda went back into the living room and returned to the question of why a medical student would have no textbooks in her bookcase. Did she keep them somewhere else? But that made no sense. She lived in Ystad, and she had often told Linda she did most of her studying here.

Linda waited. At seven o'clock she called her father, who answered with his mouth full.

"I thought you were coming home for dinner tonight," he grumbled.

Linda hesitated before answering. She was torn between wanting to tell him about Anna and saying nothing.

"Something came up."

"What is it?"

"Something personal."

Her father growled on the other end.

"I had a meeting with Martinsson today."

"I know."

"How do you know that?"

"He told me—only that you met. Nothing else. Don't worry."

Linda went back to the couch. At eight she called Zeba and asked her if she knew where Anna could be, but Zeba hadn't heard from Anna in several days. At nine o'clock, after she had helped herself to food from Anna's small pantry and fridge, she dialed Henrietta's number. The phone rang a number of times before Anna's mother answered. Linda tried to approach the subject as carefully as possible so as not to alarm the already fragile woman. Did she know if Anna was in Lund? Had she planned a trip to Malmö or Copenhagen? Linda asked the most harmless questions she could think of.

"I haven't talked to her since Thursday."

That's four days ago, Linda thought. *That means Anna never told her about the man she saw through the hotel window, even though they're close.*

"Why do you want to know where she is?"

"I called her and there was no answer."

She sensed a tinge of anxiety on the other end.

"But you don't call me every time Anna doesn't answer her phone."

Linda was prepared for this question.

"I had a sudden impulse to have her over for dinner tonight. That was all."

Linda steered the conversation over to her own life.

"Have you heard I'm going to start working here in Ystad?"

"Yes, Anna told me. But neither one of us understands why you would want to be a policewoman."

"If I'd gone on learning how to refinish furniture as planned, I'd always have tacks in my mouth. A life in law enforcement just seemed more entertaining."

A clock struck somewhere in Anna's apartment and Linda quickly ended the conversation. Then she thought it all through again. Anna wasn't a risk-taker. In contrast to Zeba and herself, Anna hated rollercoasters, was suspicious of strangers, and never climbed into a cab without looking the driver in the eye first. The simplest explanation was that Anna was still disconcerted by what she thought she had seen. She must have gone back to Malmö to look for the man she thought was her father. *This is the first time she's ever stood me up,* Linda thought. *But this is also the first time she's been convinced she saw her father walking down the street.*

Linda stayed in the apartment for several more hours.

By midnight Anna had still not returned.

Then she knew. There was no good explanation for Anna's absence. Something must have happened. But what?

7

When Linda got home shortly after midnight, she found her father asleep on the couch. He woke up at the sound of the closing door. Linda eyed the curve of his belly with disapproval.

"You're getting fatter," she said. "One day you're just going to pop. Not like an old troll who wanders out into the sunshine but like a balloon when it gets too full of air."

He pulled his robe tighter across his chest protectively.

"I do the best I can."

"No, you don't."

He sat up heavily.

"I'm too tired to have this conversation," he said. "When you walked in I was in the middle of a beautiful dream. Do you remember Baiba?"

"The one from Latvia? Are you still in touch with each other?"

"About once a year, no more. She's found someone else, a German engineer who works at the municipal waterworks in Riga. She sounds very much in love when she talks about him, the wonderful Herman from Lübeck. I'm surprised it doesn't drive me insane with jealousy."

"You were dreaming about her?"

He smiled.

"We had a child in the dream," he said. "A little boy who was building castles in the sand. An orchestra was playing in the distance and Baiba and I just stood there watching him. In my dream I thought, 'This is no dream, this is real' and I was incredibly happy."

"And you complain about having too many nightmares."

He wasn't listening.

"The door opened—that was you, of course—a car door. It was summer and very warm. The whole world was full of light like an overexposed picture. Everyone's face was white and without any shadows. It was beautiful. We were about to drive away when I woke up."

"I'm sorry."

He shrugged.

"It was just a dream."

Linda wanted to tell him about Anna, but her dad lumbered out into the kitchen and drank some water from the faucet. Linda followed him, and when he was done he stood up and looked at her, smoothing his hair down in the back.

"You were out late. It's none of my business, I know, but I have an idea you want me to ask you about it."

Linda told him. He leaned against the refrigerator with his arms crossed. *This is how I remember him from my childhood,* she thought. *This is how he always listened to me, like a giant. I used to think my dad was as big as a mountain. Daddy Mountain.*

He shook his head when she finished.

"That's not how it happens."

"What do you mean?"

"That's not how people disappear."

"But it's not like her. I've known her since I was seven. She's never been late for anything."

"However idiotic it sounds, some time has to be the first. Let's say she was preoccupied by the fact that she thought she had seen her father. It's not unlikely that she—as you suggested yourself—went back to look for him."

Linda nodded. He was right. There was no reason to assume anything else had happened.

Wallander sat down on the sofa.

"You'll learn that all events have their own logic. People kill each other, lie, break into houses, commit robberies, and sometimes they simply disappear. If you winch yourself far enough down the well—that's how I often think of my investigations—you'll find the explanation. It turns out that it was highly probable that such and such a person disappeared, that another robbed a bank. I'm not saying the unexpected never happens, but people are almost never right when they say 'I never would have believed that about her.' Think it over and scrape away the layers of exterior paint and you'll find other colors underneath, other answers."

He yawned and let his hands fall onto the table.

"Time for bed."

"No, let's stay here a few more minutes."

He looked at her intently.

"You still think something happened to your friend?"

"No, I'm sure you're right."

They sat quietly at the kitchen table. A gust of wind sent a branch scraping against the window.

"I've been dreaming a lot recently," he said. "Maybe because you're always waking me up in the middle of the night. That means I remember my dreams. Yesterday I had the strangest dream. I was walking around a cemetery. Suddenly I found myself in front of a row of headstones where I started recognizing the names. Stefan Fredman's name was among them."

Linda shivered.

"I remember that case. Didn't he break into this apartment?"

"I think so, but we were never able to prove it. He never told us."

"You went to his funeral. What happened?"

"He was sent to a psychiatric institution. One day he put on his war paint, climbed up on the roof, and threw himself off."

"How old was he?"

"Eighteen or nineteen."

The branch scraped against the window again.

"Who were the others? I mean on the headstones."

"A woman called Yvonne Ander. I even think the date on the stone was right, though it happened a long time ago."

"What did she do?"

"Do you remember that time when Ann-Britt Höglund was shot?"

"How could I forget? You left for Denmark after that happened and almost drank yourself to death."

"That's an extreme way of putting it."

"On the contrary, I think that's hitting the nail on the head. Anyway, I don't remember Yvonne Ander."

"She specialized in killing rapists, wife-beaters, men who had been abusive to women."

"That rings a bell."

"We found her in the end. Everyone thought she was a monster. But I thought she was one of the sanest people I had ever met."

"Is that one of the dangers of the profession?"

"What?"

"Do policemen fall in love with the female criminals they're hunting?"

He waved her insinuations away.

"Don't be stupid. I talked to her after she was brought in. She wrote me a letter before she committed suicide. What she told me was she thought the justice system was like a fishnet where the holes were too big. We don't catch, or choose not to catch, the perpetrators who really deserve to be caught."

"Who was she referring to specifically? The police?"

He shook his head.

"I don't know. Everyone. The laws we live by are supposed to reflect the opinions of society at large. But Yvonne Ander had a point. I'll never forget her."

"How long ago was that?"

"Five, six years."

The phone rang.

Wallander jumped and he and Linda exchanged glances. It was four o'clock in the morning. Wallander stretched his hand out for the kitchen phone. Linda worried for a moment that it was one of her friends, someone who didn't know she was staying with her dad. Linda tried to interpret who it could be from her father's terse questions. She decided it had to be from the station. Perhaps Martinsson, or even Höglund. Something had happened in the vicinity of Rydsgård. Wallander signaled for her to get him something to write with and she handed him the pencil and pad of paper lying on the windowsill. He made some notes with the phone pressed into the crook of his neck. She peered over his shoulder. *Rydsgård, turn off to Charlottenlund, Vik's farm.* That was close to the house on the hill they had looked at, the one her father wasn't going to buy. He wrote something else: *burned calf. Åkerblom.* Then a phone number. He hung up. Linda sat back down across from him.

"A burned calf? What's happened?"

"That's what I want to know."

He got up.

"I have to go out there."

"What about me?"

He hesitated.

"You can come along if you like."

"You were there for the start of this thing," he said as they got in the car. "You might as well come along for the rest."

"The start of what?"

"The report about burning swans."

"It's happened again?"

"Yes and no. Some bastard let a calf out of the barn, sprayed it with gasoline, and set it on fire. The farmer was the one who called the station. A patrol car was dispatched but I'd left instructions to be contacted if anything along these lines happened again. It sounds like a sadistic pervert."

Linda knew there was more.

"You're not telling me what you really think."

"No, I'm not."

He broke off the conversation. Linda started wondering why he had let her come along.

They turned off from the main highway and drove through the deserted village of Rydsgård, then south toward the sea. A patrol car was waiting at the entrance to the farm. Together the two cars made their way toward the main buildings at Vik's farm.

"Who am I?" Linda asked quickly.

"My daughter. No one will care. As long as you don't start pretending to be anything else—like a police officer, for instance."

They got out. The two officers from the other car came over and said hello. One was called Wahlberg, the other Ekman. Wahlberg had a bad cold and Linda wished she didn't have to shake his hand. Ekman smiled and leaned toward her as if he were shortsighted.

"I thought you were starting in a couple of weeks."

"She's just keeping me company," Wallander said. "What's happened out here?"

They walked down behind the farmhouse to a new-looking barn. The farmer was kneeling next to the burned animal. He was a young man close to Linda's age. *Farmers should be old,* she thought. *In my world there's no place for a farmer my own age.*

Wallander stretched out his hand and introduced himself.

"Tomas Åkerblom," the farmer said.

"This is my daughter. She happened to be with me."

As Tomas Åkerblom looked over at Linda, a light from the barn illuminated his face. She saw that his eyes were wet with tears.

"Who would do anything like this?" he asked in a shaky voice.

He stepped aside to let them see, as if displaying a macabre art installation. Linda had already picked up the smell of burned flesh. Now she saw the blackened body of the calf lying on its side in front of her. The eye socket closest to her was completely charred. Smoke still rose from the singed skin. The fumes were starting to make her nauseated and she took a step back. Wallander looked at her. She shook her head to indicate that she wasn't about to faint. He nodded and looked around at the others.

"Tell me what happened," he said.

Åkerblom started talking. He still sounded on the verge of tears.

"I had just gone to bed when I heard a sound. At first I thought I must have cried out in my sleep—that happens sometimes when I have a bad dream. Then I realized it came from the barn. The animals were braying and one of them sounded bad. I pulled the curtains away and saw fire. It was Apple—of course I couldn't identify him immediately, just that it was one of the calves. He ran straight into the wall of the barn. His whole body and head were consumed by flames. I couldn't really take it in. I pulled on a pair of old boots and ran down there. He had already collapsed when I reached him. His legs were twitching. I grabbed an old piece of tarp and tried to put out the rest of the fire, but he was already dead. It was horrible. I remember thinking, 'This isn't happening, this isn't happening.' Who would do something like this?"

"Did you see anything else?" Wallander asked.

"No, just what I told you."

"You said, 'Who would do something like this?' Why? Is there no way it could have been an accident?"

"You think a calf poured gasoline over his own head and lit a match? How likely is that?"

"Let's assume it was a deliberate attack. Did you see anyone when you pulled the curtain away from the window?"

Åkerblom thought hard before answering. Linda tried to anticipate her father's next question.

"I only saw the burning animal."

"What kind of person do you imagine did this?"

"An insane . . . a fucking lunatic."

Wallander nodded.

"That's all for now," he said. "Leave the animal as it is. Someone will be sent out in the morning to take pictures of it and the area."

They returned to their cars.

"What kind of crazy lunatic bastard . . ." Åkerblom muttered.

Wallander didn't answer him. Linda saw how tired he was. His forehead was deeply furrowed and he looked old. *He's worried,* she realized. *First there's the report about the swans, and then a young calf named Apple is burned alive.*

It was as if he read her mind. Wallander let his hand rest on the car door handle and turned to Åkerblom.

"Apple," he said. "That's an unusual name for an animal."

"I played table tennis when I was younger. I often name my animals after great Swedish champions. I have an ox by the name of Waldner."

Wallander nodded. Linda could see he was smiling. She knew he appreciated originality.

They drove back to Ystad.

"What do you think this is about?" Linda asked.

"The best-case scenario is a pervert who gets a kick out of hurting animals."

"And that's the best-case scenario?"

He hesitated.

"The worst case would be someone who won't stop at animals," he said.

8

When Linda woke up the next morning she was alone in the apartment. It was half past seven. The sound of her father slamming the front door must have woken her up. *He does that on purpose,* she thought and stretched out in bed. *He doesn't like me sleeping in.*

She got up and opened the window. It was a clear day, and the nice weather looked like it would continue. She thought about the events of the night, the still-smoking carcass and her father looking suddenly old and worn-out. *It's the anxiety,* she thought. *He can hide a lot from me, but not his anxiety.*

She ate breakfast and put on her clothes from yesterday, then changed her mind and tried on two other outfits before deciding what to wear. She called Anna. The answering machine picked up after five rings and she simply asked Anna to answer the phone if she was there. No reply. Linda walked out into the hall and looked at herself in the mirror. Was she still worried about Anna? *No,* she said to herself, *I'm not worried. Anna has her reasons. She's most likely chasing down that man she saw on the street, a man she thinks is her long-lost father.*

Linda went out for a walk and picked up a newspaper from a bench. She turned to the automobile section and looked at the ads for used cars. There was a Saab for 19,000. Her father had already promised to chip in 10,000, and she knew she wanted a car. But a Saab for 19,000? How long would it last?

She tucked the newspaper into her pocket and walked over to Anna's apartment. No one answered the door. After picking the lock again and letting herself in, she was suddenly struck by the feeling that someone had been there since she had left the place the night before. She froze and looked all around the hall—the coats hanging in their place, the shoes all in a row. Was anything different? She couldn't put her finger on it but was convinced there was something.

She continued into the living room and sat down on the sofa. *Dad would tell me to look for the impressions people have left behind in this room, of themselves and their dramatic interactions. But I see nothing, only the fact that Anna isn't here.*

After combing through the apartment twice, she convinced herself that Anna had not been home during the night. Nor anyone else, for that matter. The only things she saw were tiny, near-invisible traces she herself had left behind.

She went into Anna's bedroom and sat down at the little desk. She hesitated at first, but her curiosity got the better of her. She knew that Anna kept a diary—she had done so since she was little. Linda remembered an incident from middle school when Anna had been sitting in a corner writing in her journal. A boy pulled it out of her hands as a joke but she was so furious that she bit him on the shoulder, and everyone knew to leave the journal alone after that.

Linda pulled out the drawers in the desk. They were full of old diaries, thumbed, crammed with writing. The dates were written on the spines. Up until Anna was sixteen they were all red. After that they were all black.

Linda closed the drawers and looked through some papers lying on the desk. She found the journal Anna was currently keeping. *I'm only going to look at the last entry*, she thought, telling herself it was justified since she was motivated only by her concern for Anna's well-being. She opened the folder at the last entry, from the day that they were supposed to have met. Linda bent over the page; Anna's handwriting was cramped, as if she were trying to hide the words. Linda read the short text twice, first without understanding it, then with a growing sense of bafflement. The words Anna had written made no sense: *myth fear, myth fear, myth fear.* Was it a code?

Linda immediately broke her promise only to look at the last entry. She turned the page back and there she found regular text. Anna had written:

The Saxhausen textbook is a pedagogical disaster. Completely impossible to read and understand. How can textbooks like this be allowed? Future doctors will be scared off and turn to research, where there is also more money.

Further down the page she had noted:

Had lowgrade fever this morning. Weather clear but windy—

That part was true, Linda thought. She flipped the page to the last line and read it through again. She tried to imagine that she was Anna writing the words. There were no changes in the text, no words scratched out, no hesitations that she could tell. The handwriting looked even and firm.

Myth fear, myth fear, myth fear. I see that I have signed up for nineteen laundry days so far this year. My dream—to the extent I even have one right now—would be to work as an anonymous suburban general practitioner. Do northern towns even have suburbs?

That was where the entry ended. Not a word about the man she'd seen through the hotel window. Not a word or a hint. Nothing. *But isn't that exactly the kind of thing diaries are for?* Linda wondered.

She looked farther back in the book. From time to time her own name appeared. *Linda is a true friend,* she had written on July 20, in the middle of an entry about her mother. She and her mother had *argued over nothing* and later that evening she was planning *to go to Malmö to see a Russian movie.*

Linda sat with the journal for almost an hour, struggling with her conscience. She looked for entries about herself. She found *Linda can be so demanding* on August 4. *What did we do that day,* Linda wondered. She couldn't remember. It was a day like any other. Linda didn't even have an organizer right now; she scribbled appointments on scraps of paper and wrote phone numbers on her hands.

Finally she closed the diary. There was nothing there, just the strange words at the end. *It's not like her,* Linda thought. *The other entries are the work of a balanced mind. She doesn't have more problems than most people. But the last day, the day she thinks she just saw her father turn up on a street in Malmö after twenty-four years, she repeatedly writes the words "myth fear, myth fear." Why doesn't she write about her father? Why does she write something that doesn't make any sense?*

Linda felt her anxiety return. Had there perhaps been something to Anna's talk about losing her mind? Linda walked over to the window where Anna often stood during their conversations. The sun was reflected from a window in the building directly opposite, and she had to squint in order to see anything. Could Anna have suffered a temporary derangement? She thought she had seen her long-lost father—could this event have disconcerted her so violently that she lost her bearings and started behaving erratically?

Linda gave a start. There, in the parking lot behind the building, was Anna's car, the little red VW Golf. If she had left for a few days, the car should also be gone. Linda hurried down into the lot and felt the car doors. Locked. The car looked clean and shiny, which surprised her. *Anna's car tends to be dirty,* she thought. *Every time we go out her car is covered in dust. Now it's squeaky clean—even the hubcaps have been polished.*

She went back up to the apartment, sat down in the kitchen, and tried to come up with a plausible explanation. The only thing she knew for sure was that Anna had not stayed home to meet with Linda as they had arranged. It wasn't a misunderstanding; there was nothing wrong with Anna's memory. She had chosen not to stay home that day. Something else had come up that was more important to her, something for which she didn't need her car. Linda turned on the answering machine and listened to the messages but only heard her own bellowing of Anna's name. She let her gaze wander to the front door. *Someone rang the bell,* she thought. *Not me, not Zeba, not Henrietta.* Who else was there? Anna had broken up with her boyfriend in April, a guy Linda had never met called Måns Persson. He was also a student in Lund, studying electromagnetics, and he had turned out to be less faithful than

Anna would have liked. She had been deeply hurt by the breach in their relationship, and she had told Linda on several occasions that she was going to take her time before letting herself get that close to a man again.

Linda had also recently had a Måns Persson experience, a man she kicked out of her life in March. His name had been Ludwig and he seemed uniquely suited to that name. His personality was part emperor and part impresario. He and Linda had met at a pub when Linda had been out drinking with some student colleagues. Ludwig had been with another group and they had simply ended up squeezed in next to each other due to the lack of space. Ludwig was in the sanitation business; he operated a garbage truck and made his pride in his work seem like the most natural thing in the world. Linda had been attracted by his huge laugh, his happy eyes, and the fact that he never interrupted her when she talked, actually straining to catch every word although the noise around them had been deafening.

They had started seeing each other, and for a while Linda dared to think she had found a real man at last. But then, purely by accident, she heard from a friend of a friend that when Ludwig wasn't working or spending time with Linda, he was spending time with a young woman who ran a catering business in Vallentuna. They had had a heated confrontation. Ludwig pleaded with her, but Linda sent him packing and cried for a whole week. She hadn't thought about it in those terms, but perhaps she too was waiting to recover from the pain of this breakup before she let herself look for someone new. She knew that the rapid succession of boyfriends in her life worried her father, even though he never asked her about it.

Before leaving Anna's apartment, Linda went to the kitchen, where she had spotted the spare keys to the car in a drawer. In order to avoid having to pick the lock every time, she had pocketed a spare set of keys to the apartment usually stored in a box in the hallway. She had borrowed the car on a few other occasions. *It won't matter if I do it again,* Linda thought. *I'm just going to borrow the car and visit her mother.* She left a note saying what she had done and that she would be back in a couple of hours. She didn't write anything about being worried.

———

First Linda stopped by the apartment on Mariagatan and changed into cooler clothing, since it was getting very warm. Then she drove out of town, took the turnoff to Kåseberga, and parked in the harbor. The surface of the water was like a mirror, the only disturbance a dog swimming around next to the boats. An old man sitting on a bench outside the smoked-fish shop nodded kindly at her. Linda smiled in return but had no idea who he was. A retired colleague of her father's?

She got back into the car and continued on her way. Henrietta Westin lived in a house that seemed to crouch among the tall stands of trees posted like sentries on all sides. Linda had to turn around several times in order to find the right driveway. She finally pulled in next to a rusty harvester and parked the car. The heat outside made her remember the vacation she and Ludwig had taken to Greece before they broke up. She shook away those thoughts and started making her way through the massive trees. She stopped at the sound of an unusual noise, a furious hammering. Then she saw a woodpecker up on the right. *Maybe he has a part in her music,* she thought. *Anna has said her mother doesn't shy away from using any kind of noise. His input might very well be crucial to the percussion section.*

She left the woodpecker and walked past an old run-down vegetable garden that had clearly not been tended for many years. *What do I know about her?* Linda thought. *And what am I doing here?* She stopped and listened. At that particular moment, in the shade of the high trees, she was no longer worried about Anna. There was surely a reasonable explanation for why she was staying away. Linda turned and started walking back to the car.

The woodpecker had flown away. *Everything changes,* she thought. *People and woodpeckers, my dreams and all that time I thought I had but that keeps slipping out of my fingers despite my best attempts to keep it dammed up.* She pulled her invisible reins and came to a halt. Why was she walking away? Now that she had come this far in Anna's car, the least she could do was say hello to Henrietta. Without betraying her anxieties, without making pressing inquiries about Anna's whereabouts. *She might just be in Lund, and I don't have her number there. I'll ask Henrietta for it.*

She followed the path through the trees again and finally came to a half-timbered, whitewashed house covered in wild roses. A cat lay on the stone steps and studied her movements warily as Linda approached. A window was open and just as she bent down to stroke the cat, she heard noises from inside. *Henrietta's music,* she thought.

Then she stood up and caught her breath.

What she had heard wasn't music. It was the sound of a woman sobbing.

9

Somewhere inside the house a dog started to bark. Linda felt as though she had been caught in the act and quickly rang the doorbell. It took a while for Henrietta to open the door. When she did she was restraining an angry gray dog by the collar.

"She won't bite," Henrietta said. "Come in."

Linda never felt completely at ease in the presence of strange dogs and so she hesitated slightly before crossing the threshold. As soon as she did so the dog relaxed, as if Linda had crossed over into a no-barking zone. Henrietta let go of the dog. Linda hadn't remembered Henrietta so thin and frail. What was it Anna had said about her? That she wasn't even fifty years old. It was true that her face looked young, but her body looked much older even than fifty. The dog, Pathos, sniffed Linda's legs, then retreated to her basket and lay down.

Linda thought about the sobbing that she had heard through the window. There were no traces of tears on Henrietta's face. Linda looked past her into the rest of the house, but there was no sign of anyone else. Henrietta caught her gaze.

"Are you looking for Anna?"

"No."

Henrietta burst out laughing.

"Well, I'm stumped. First you call and then you drop by for a visit. What's happened? Is Anna still missing?"

Linda was taken aback by Henrietta's directness, but welcomed it.

"Yes."

Henrietta shrugged, then directed Linda into the big room—the result of many walls being removed—that served as both living room and studio.

"My guess is that Anna must be in Lund. She holes up there from time to time. The theoretical component of her studies is apparently very demanding, and Anna is no theoretician. I don't know who she takes after. Not me, not her father. Herself."

"Do you have a phone number for her in Lund?"

"No, I'm not even sure she has a phone there. She rents a room in a house and doesn't like to give out the address."

"Isn't that a bit odd?"

"Why? Anna is secretive by nature. If you don't leave her alone she can get very angry. Didn't you know that about her?"

"No. She doesn't have a cell phone either?"

"She's one of the few people who's still holding out," Henrietta said. "Even I have one. In fact, I don't see the need for the old-fashioned kind anymore. But that's neither here nor there. No, Anna doesn't have a cell phone."

Henrietta stopped as if she had suddenly thought of something. Linda looked around the room. Someone had been crying. It hadn't occurred to her that it might have been Anna until Henrietta asked her if that was what she was doing, looking for her here. *But it couldn't have been Anna,* she thought. *Why would she be crying? She's not a person who cries very much. Once when we were girls she fell off the jungle gym and hurt herself. She cried that time, but it's the only time I remember. Even when we both fell in love with Tomas I was the one who cried; she was just angry.*

Linda looked at Henrietta, who was standing in a beam of light in the middle of the polished wooden floor. She had an angular profile, just like Anna.

"I don't get visitors very often," she said suddenly, as if that was what had been foremost in her mind. "People avoid me just as I avoid them. I know they think I'm eccentric. That's what comes of living alone out in the country with only a greyhound for company, composing music no one wants to listen to. It doesn't help matters that I'm still legally married to the man who left me twenty-four years ago."

Linda sensed a tone of bitterness and loneliness in Henrietta's voice.

"What are you working on right now?"

"Please don't feel you have to make polite conversation. Why did you drop by? Was it really that you're still worried about Anna?"

"I borrowed her car. My grandfather used to live in these parts and I thought I would take a drive. I'm feeling a little bored these days."

"Until you get to put on your uniform?"

"Yes."

Henrietta brought out a coffeepot and cups and set them on the table.

"I don't understand why an attractive girl like you would choose to become a police officer. Breaking up fights on the street, that's what I imagine it to be. I know there must be other aspects to the job, but that's what always comes to mind."

She poured the coffee.

"But perhaps you're going to sit behind a desk," she added.

"No, I've been assigned to a patrol car and will probably be doing a lot of the work you would expect. Someone has to be prepared to jump into the fray."

Henrietta leaned to the side with her hand tucked under her chin.

"And that's what you're going to dedicate your life to?"

Her comments put Linda on the defensive, as if she were in danger of being contaminated by Henrietta's bitterness.

"I don't know what looks have got to do with it. I'm almost thirty and on good days I'm generally happy with how I look, but I've never dreamed of being Miss Sweden. But more to the point, what would happen to our society if there were no police? My dad is a policeman and I've never had any reason to be ashamed of him."

Henrietta shook her head.

"I didn't mean to hurt your feelings."

Linda still felt angry. She felt a need to strike back, though she couldn't really say why.

"I thought I heard the sound of someone crying in here when I walked up to your house."

Henrietta smiled.

"It's a recording I have. I'm working on a requiem and I mix my music with the sound of someone crying."

"I don't even know what a requiem is."

"A funeral mass. That's almost all I write these days."

Henrietta got up and walked over to the grand piano by the window, which overlooked open fields and then the rolling hills leading down to the sea. Next to the piano there was a table with a tape recorder as well as a synthesizer and other electronic equipment. Henrietta turned on the tape player. A woman's voice came on, wailing and sobbing. It was the one Linda had heard through the window. Her curiosity about this strange woman increased.

"Where did you get it?"

"This is from an American film. I often record the sound of crying from films I see, or from programs on the radio. I have a collection of forty-four crying voices so far, everything from a baby to a very old woman I recorded secretly at a rest home. Would you like to donate a sample to the archive sometime?"

"No, thanks."

Henrietta sat down at the piano and played a few haunting chords. Linda went and stood next to her, while Henrietta continued to play. The room was filled with a powerful surge of music which then faded into silence. Henrietta gestured for Linda to sit next to her on the piano bench.

"Tell me again why you came here. Seriously. I've never even felt you really liked me."

"When I was little I was afraid of you."

"Of me? No one is afraid of me!"

That's where you're wrong, Linda thought. *Anna was afraid of you too—sometimes she had nightmares about you.*

"It was an impulse, nothing more. I wonder where Anna is, but I'm not as worried as I was last night. You're probably right that she's in Lund."

Linda broke off.

"What is it you aren't saying? Should I be worried about her too?"

"Anna thought she saw her father on a street in Malmö a couple of days ago. I shouldn't be telling you this. You should hear it from her."

"Is that all?"

"That's not enough?"

Henrietta touched the keys as if sketching out a few more bars of music.

"Anna is always catching glimpses of her father. She's told me stories like this since she was a little girl."

Linda raised her eyebrows. Anna had never mentioned one of these sightings before, and Linda was sure she would have. When they were younger they told each other everything. Anna was one of the few people who Linda had told about standing on the edge of the overpass in Malmö. What Henrietta said didn't fit this picture.

"Anna is never going to relinquish her hope," Henrietta continued. "The hope that Erik will one day come back. Even that he is still alive."

"Why did he leave?"

"He left because he was disappointed."

"By what?"

"By life. He had such marvelous ambitions when he was younger. He seduced me with those dreams, if you must know. I had never met a man who had the kind of wonderful visions that Erik had. He was going to make a difference in the world, in our generation. He knew without a doubt that he had been put on this earth in order to do something on a grand scale. We met when he was sixteen and I was fifteen. Even as young as I was, I knew I had never met anyone like him; he radiated dreams and life force. At that time he was still looking for his niche—was it art, sports, politics, or another arena in which he was going to leave his mark? He had decided to give himself until the age of twenty to figure it out. I can't remember any self-doubt in him until then. But when he turned twenty he started to worry. There was a restlessness in him. Until then he had had all the time in the world. When I started making demands on him to help support the family after Anna was born, he would get impatient and scream at me. He had never done that before. That was when he started making his sandals; he was good with his hands. He called them 'sandals of indolence' as a kind of protest, I think, for the fact that they were taking up his valuable time. It was probably then that he started planning his disappearance or, should I say, escape. He wasn't running away from me or Anna, he was running away from himself, from his disappointment in life. I wonder if he managed it—I've never been able to ask him, of course. One day he was just gone. It took me by surprise. It was only in hindsight that I realized how carefully he must have planned it. I can forgive him the fact that he sold my car. What I'll never understand or accept is that he left Anna. They were so close. I know he loved her. I was never as important to him, or at least not after the first couple of years while I was still a part of his dreams. How could he leave her—how can a person's disappointment in life, stemming as it did from an unattainable dream, conceivably weigh more heavily than the most important person in his life? I think that must be a contributing factor to his death, at least to the fact that he never returned."

"I didn't think anyone knew what happened to him."

"He must be dead. He's been missing for twenty-four years. Where could he possibly be?"

"Anna's convinced she saw him."

"She sees him on every street corner. I've tried to talk her out of it and make her face the truth. No one knows what happened. But he has to be dead by now."

Henrietta paused. The greyhound sighed.

"What do you think happened?" Linda asked.

"I think he gave up—when he realized the dream was nothing more than that. And that the Anna he left behind was real. At that point it was too late. He would always have been plagued by his conscience."

Henrietta closed the lid over the piano keys with a thud and stood up.

"More coffee?"

"No, thanks. I have to get going."

Henrietta seemed anxious and Linda watched her closely. She grabbed Linda's arm and started to hum a melody that Linda recognized. Her voice alternated between high, shrill tones and softer, cleaner ones.

"Do you know that song?" she asked when she was finished.

"I recognize it, but I don't know what it is."

"*Buona Sera.*"

"Is it Spanish?"

"Italian. It means 'good night.' It was popular in the fifties. So many people today borrow or steal or vandalize old music. They make pop songs out of Bach. I do the reverse. I take songs like *Buona Sera* and turn them into classical music."

"How do you do that?"

"I break down the structure, change the rhythm, replace the guitar sound with a massive flood of violins. I turn a banal song about three minutes long into a symphony. When it's ready I'll play it for you. Then people will finally understand what I've been trying to do all these years."

Henrietta followed her out.

"Come back sometime."

Linda promised to do so, and then drove away. She saw storm clouds heaped up in the distance, out over the sea in the direction of Bornholm. Linda pulled over after a while and got out of the car. She had a sudden desire to smoke. She had quit smoking three years earlier but the desire still hit her from time to time, even if it was getting more rare.

There are some things mothers don't know about their daughters, she thought. *Henrietta doesn't know that Anna and I told each other everything during those years. If she had, she would never have told me about Anna always seeing her father on the street. There are a lot of things I'm not sure of, but I know Anna would have told me that.*

There was only one possible explanation. Henrietta had not been telling her the truth about Anna and her missing father.

10

She pulled back the curtains a little after five o'clock in the morning and looked at the thermometer. It was nine degrees Celsius, the sky clear with little or no wind. *What a wonderful day for an expedition,* she thought. She had prepared everything the night before and it didn't take her long to leave her apartment across from the old railway station in Skurup. Her forty-year-old Vespa was waiting for her in the yard under a custom-made cover. She was the original owner and, since she had taken such good care of it, it was still in mint condition. In fact, word of it had spread to the factory in Italy and she had received several solicitations over the years asking her if she would consider letting the company put it in their museum. In return, the company would supply her with a new Vespa every year.

Year after year she had declined the offer, intending to keep this Vespa that she had bought when she was twenty-two years old as long as she lived. She didn't care what happened to it after that. One of her four grandchildren might want it, but she wasn't about to write a will for the sake of an ancient Vespa.

She adjusted her backpack, strapped on her helmet, and kick-started the old machine. It instantly roared into life. Half an hour later she arrived at the small parking lot by Led Lake. She walked the Vespa in behind some bushes beside a large oak tree. A car drove past on the main road, then silence returned.

As she prepared to walk into the forest and become invisible to the outside world, she wondered if this wasn't the most satisfying way of expressing one's independence: by daring to abandon the well-trodden path. To step into the underbrush and vanish from the eyes of the world.

Her brother Håkan had taught her that there were two kinds of people in the world: the ones who always chose the shortest distance between two points, and the ones who looked for the scenic route where the curves, slopes, and vistas were to be found. They had played in the forests around Älmhult when they were growing up. After her father was severely injured by a fall from a telephone pole while repairing a phone line, they moved to Skåne. Her mother got a job at the Ystad Hospital. That was where she spent her adolescence and forgot all about exploring, until the day she stood outside the gates to Lund University and realized she had no idea what to do with her life. She turned to her childhood memories for inspiration.

It was a day during that first difficult fall semester when she had enrolled as a law student for lack of a more interesting alternative. She had cycled out toward Staffanstorp and found a small unpaved road by chance. She left her bike there and continued on foot until she reached the ruins of an old mill. That was when the idea had come to her—or rather—tore through her mind like a bolt of lightning. What was a path? Why does a path go to this side of a tree and not the other? Who was the first person to walk here?

She knew in that instant it would become her life's mission to chart old trails. She would become the protector and historian of old Swedish paths and walkways. She ran back to her bike, quit her law studies the same day, and started studying history and cultural geography. She had the good fortune to meet a sympathetic professor who appreciated the originality of her interests and supported her cause.

She started walking along the path that curved gracefully around Led Lake. The tall trees shaded her from the sun. She had mapped this particular path quite a while ago. It was a standard walking path that could be traced back to the 1930s, when Rannesholm Manor was owned by the Haverman family. One of the counts, Gustav Haverman, had been an enthusiastic runner and had cleared bushes and undergrowth away from the edge of the lake to establish this trail. *But a little further on,* she thought, *up ahead in this old forest where no one else sees anything but moss and stone, I am going to turn off from this trail and follow the path I found just a few days ago. I*

have no idea where it leads, but nothing is as tempting, as magical, as fol-
lowing an unknown path. I still hope that one day I'll find a path that is a
work of art. A path that has been created without a destination in mind,
just for its own sake.

She paused at the top of a hill to catch her breath, looking down
at the glassy surface of the lake between the trees. She was sixty-
three years old now and, according to her own calculations, she
needed five more years to complete her life's work: *The History of
Swedish Walkways.* In this book she would reveal that paths were
among the most important clues to ancient settlements and their
way of life. Paths were not laid out only for the simplest way of
getting from A to B. On the contrary, she had ample evidence for
the numerous religious and cultural factors that determined where
and how paths made their way across the landscape. Over the years
she had published regional studies and maps, but the conclusions
of her many years of research had yet to be set down in final form.

She slowed down when she found the spot. Where the un-
trained eye saw nothing but grass and moss growing at the edge of
the path she spotted the clear outline of a trail that had been out of
use for many years. She started climbing up the side of the hill,
looking carefully before she stepped. Last year she had broken a leg
when she fell exploring a trail to the south of Brösarp. The accident
had forced her to take a long rest, which stood out in her mind as a
particularly difficult time. Even though it had given her more time
to write, she had simply become restless and irritated, especially
without her husband to care for her. He had died shortly before the
accident occurred and had always been the one to take care of
things in the home. She had sold the house in Rydsgård after that
and moved to the little apartment in Skurup.

She pushed some branches aside and moved in under the trees.
Once she had read about a meadow in the forest that could only
be found by someone who had lost their way. To her mind this
captured some of the mystical dimension of human existence. If
only one dared to get lost, one could find the unexpected. There
was a whole other world beyond the highways and byways—if you
just dared to take the turnoff. *And I'm the caretaker of these old forgotten paths,* she thought. *Sleeping beauties waiting for someone to wake*

them from their slumber. If paths remain unused for too long, they die.

She was deep into the forest now, a long way from the main trail. She stopped and listened. A branch broke some distance away, then all was quiet. A bird flapped noisily and flew away. She walked on, hunched over the ground, moving very slowly. The path was nearly invisible. She had to search for its contours under the moss, the grass, and the fallen branches.

Soon she started feeling disappointed; this wasn't an old path. When she first saw it she had been hoping it was part of the ancient pilgrim's trail that was rumored to pass close to Led Lake. On the north side of the Rommele hills it was still visible. It disappeared around Led Lake only to pop up again northwest of Sturup. Sometimes she was tempted to think the pilgrims had used a tunnel, but she knew that was not their custom. They walked on trails and one day she hoped to find it. Unfortunately it wasn't going to be today. After a mere hundred meters she was convinced the path was newly established, no more than ten or twenty years old. She hoped to be able to say why it had been abandoned when she figured out where it led. She was about three hundred meters into the forest by now and the trees and the undergrowth stood so thick and close together it was almost impossible to make her way through them.

Suddenly she stopped and squatted. She saw something that confused her. She picked at the moss with her finger. She had seen something white lying there: a feather. A dove? she thought. But are there white forest doves? They were usually brown or blue. She stood up and continued studying the feather. Finally she realized it came from a swan. But how could it have turned up so deep in the forest? Swans came ashore from time to time but never this far inland, not in thick forest.

After only a few more steps she stopped again, this time because the ground in front of her was curiously flattened. Someone must have walked here only a few days ago. But where exactly did the prints start? She examined the area for ten minutes and decided someone had come out of the forest and only joined the path at this point. She continued on slowly. She was no longer as curious about the path as she had been when she thought it might be the old pilgrim trail. This path was probably simply an extension of the paths Count Haverman had put in to satisfy his outdoor tastes, but that had fallen out of use since his time. The prints she was following probably belonged to a hunter.

After another hundred meters she arrived at a shallow ravine, a crack in the earth covered by bushes and undergrowth. The path ran straight down into it. She removed her backpack, tucked a flashlight into her pocket, and carefully scooted down into the ravine. She started lifting up branches in order to get past them and saw to her surprise that several of them had been cut and placed here in order to conceal the entrance to the hollow. *Boys,* she thought. *Håkan and I often made forts in the forest.* She pressed on past the undergrowth and sure enough, there was a small hut. It was unusually large to be the work of children. She was reminded of a news item Håkan had shown her from a magazine, pictures of a shack in a forest that served as the hideout for a wanted criminal by the wonderful name of Beautiful Bengtsson. He had lived in his hideout for a long time and had only been found out by a person who stumbled upon it by accident.

She walked up for a closer look. The hut had been constructed out of planks of wood, with a sturdy aluminum roof. To the back it bordered a steep part of the ravine. She felt the handle of the door—it wasn't locked. She knocked and felt like an idiot. If someone was there they would have heard her by now. She started feeling more and more confused. Could someone be hiding out in the Rommele forest?

Warning bells started going off inside her head. At first she dismissed these. She was never one to get scared easily. She had run across unpleasant men in remote areas before and although it had sometimes frightened her, she had always managed to control her fears and put up a tough front. Nothing had ever happened, and nothing was going to happen today. But she couldn't help feeling she was ignoring common sense by investigating this hut on her own. Only someone who needed to hide from prying eyes would have chosen a place like this. On the other hand, she did not want to turn back without finding out what was in here. Her path had indeed had a destination. No one without her trained eyes would have spotted it. But the person who used the hut had not even followed the old path. That was strange. Was the old path she had found simply a backup, the way foxholes had more than one exit? Her curiosity got the better of her.

She opened the door to the hut and looked in. There were two small windows on either side, but they only let in a little light. She turned on the flashlight. There was a bed on one side and on the other side a small table with a chair, two gas lamps, and a camp stove. Who lived here? How long had it been empty? She leaned over and felt the blanket on the bed. It wasn't damp. *Someone has been here recently,* she thought. *In the last couple of days*. Again she thought she had better leave. The person who had stayed here was not the kind to welcome visitors.

She was about to turn and leave when the beam of her flashlight fell on a book lying on the ground next to the bed. She bent down. It was a copy of the Bible. She opened it and saw a name that had been scratched out. The book was well-thumbed and torn in places. Various verses had been underlined and annotated. She carefully put the book down where she had found it. She turned off the flashlight and immediately realized that something had changed. There was more light now than before. Someone must have opened the door. She turned, but it was too late. The blow to her face came with the force of a charging predator. She was plunged into a deep and bottomless darkness.

11

After her visit to Henrietta, Linda sat up in the apartment waiting for her father to come home. But by the time he softly pushed the front door open at two o'clock in the morning, she had already fallen asleep on the sofa with a blanket pulled up to her ears. When she woke a few hours later it was from a nightmare. She couldn't remember what she had dreamed, just that she felt as if she were being suffocated. Low snores rolled through the apartment, like breakers on the shore. Her father's bedside light was still on. He lay flat on his back, wrapped in his sheet, not unlike a large walrus comfortably stretched out on a rock. She leaned over and checked his breath between snores. Definitely alcohol.

She wondered who he could have been drinking with. The pants that lay on the ground were dirty as if he had walked through patches of mud. *He's been out in the country,* she thought. *That means a night of drinking with Sten Widén. They've sat out in the stables and shared a bottle of vodka.*

Widén was one of her dad's oldest friends, and now he was seriously ill. Her dad had a habit of talking about himself in the third person when it came to expressing something emotional and he had taken to saying: *When Sten dies Kurt Wallander will be a lonely man.* Widén had lung cancer. Linda was familiar with the story of how he had raised fine racing horses on the ranch by the ruins of Stjärnsund Castle. A few years ago he had sold the ranch, but just as the buyer was about to close on the deal, Widén had changed his mind and used the clause in the contract that allowed this. He had bought a few more horses and received his diagnosis shortly afterward. It had already been a year since then, a grace period given the severity of his condition. Now he was again selling his horses and his ranch. He had arranged a bed for himself at a hospice in Malmö. This time there was no backing out of the deal.

Linda went to her room, put on her pajamas, and climbed into bed. She lay in bed staring at the ceiling and reproached herself for being so hard on her dad. Why shouldn't he be allowed to enjoy a night of drinking with his best friend, especially since the friend happened to be dying? *I've always thought of Dad as a good friend to the few he has. It's only right that he stay up late drinking in the stables.* She felt like waking him up so she could apologize for her disapproval. But he wouldn't appreciate being woken up. *It's his day off tomorrow. Maybe we'll do something fun.*

Before she fell asleep she thought briefly about Henrietta and the fact that she hadn't been telling the truth. What was she hiding? Did she know where Anna was, or was there another reason? Linda curled up on her side and thought sleepily that soon she was going to miss having a boyfriend to cuddle up with. *But where am I going to find one in this town?* She pushed her thoughts aside and fell asleep.

Wallander shook her awake at nine o'clock. Linda jumped out of bed. Her dad didn't seem hung over. He was dressed and had even combed his hair.

"Breakfast," he said. "Time is ticking, life is fleeting."

Linda showered and dressed. Her dad was playing patience at the kitchen table when she came in and sat down.

"I suspect you were hanging out with Sten last night."

"Right."

"I also suspect you drank too much."

"Wrong. We drank way too much."

"How did you get home?"

"Taxi."

"How was he doing?"

"I wish I could be sure I'll face the end with the same equanimity. He simply says: you only have so many races in your life. You just have to try to win as many of them as you can."

"Do you think he's in pain?"

"I'm sure he is, but he doesn't say anything. He's like Rydberg."

"I don't really remember him."

"He was an old colleague of mine with a mole on his cheek. Anyway, he was the one who made a policeman out of me when I was young and didn't understand anything. He died much too early, but without a single word of complaint. He had also run his races and accepted the fact that his time was up."

"Who's going to be that kind of mentor to me?"

"I thought you had been assigned to Martinsson."

"Is he any good?"

"He's an excellent policeman."

"You know, I have memories of Martinsson from when I was a kid. I don't know how many times you came home angry about something he had done or said."

Wallander reached an impasse and gathered up his cards.

"I was the one who trained Martinsson, just as Rydberg trained me. Of course I probably came home and complained about him. He can be damned thick-headed. But once he gets something down, he never forgets it."

"So that makes you my mentor indirectly."

Wallander got up.

"I don't even know what that word means. Come on, we're leaving."

She looked at him with surprise.

"Is this something we talked about? Did I forget something?"

"We said we would go out—not where. It's going to be a beautiful day, and before you know it the fog will be here to stay. I hate the fog in Skåne. It creeps right into one's head. I can't think straight when it's gray and misty everywhere. But you're right that we have a goal today."

He sat down again and filled his cup with the last of the coffee before continuing.

"Hansson. Do you remember him?"

Linda shook her head.

"I didn't think you would. He's another one of my colleagues. Now he's about to sell his parents' house outside Tomelilla. His mother has been dead a long time, but his father turned a hundred and one before he went. According to Hansson he was clear-headed and mean-spirited to the end. But the house is up for sale and I want to take a look at it. If Hansson hasn't been exaggerating, it may just be what I'm looking for."

There was a breeze but it was warm. When they drove past a long caravan of well-polished vintage cars, Linda surprised her father by recognizing most of the models.

"Since when do you know about cars?'

"Since my last boyfriend, Magnus."

"I thought his name was Ludwig."

"You have to keep up, Dad. Anyway, isn't Tomelilla all wrong for you? I thought you wanted to sit on a bench with your faithful dog, looking out over the sea."

"I don't have that kind of money. I'll have to settle for the next-best thing."

"You could get a loan from Mom. Her golf-playing banker is pretty loaded."

"Never in a million years."

"I could borrow it for you."

"Never."

"No view of the sea for you, then."

Linda glanced at her father. Was he angry? She couldn't decide. But she realized this was also something they had in common, flare-ups of irritation, a tendency to be hurt by almost nothing. *Sometimes we are so close and other times it's like a crevasse has opened up between us. And then we have to build rickety bridges that usually manage to connect us again.*

He took a piece of folded paper from his pocket.

"Map," he said. "Give me the directions. We're going to get to the roundabout at the top of the page soon. I know we go in the direction of Kristianstad but you'll have to guide me from there."

"I'm going to trick you into Småland," she said and unfolded the paper. "Tingsryd? Does that sound good? We'll never find our way back from there."

The house was attractively situated on a little hill surrounded by a strip of forest, beyond which there were open fields and marshes. A bird—a kite, it looked like—was suspended in the air currents above the house, and in the distance there was the rising and falling sound of a tractor at work. Linda sat down on an old stone bench between some red-currant bushes. Her father squinted at the roof, tugged on the drainpipes, and tried to peer into the house. Then he disappeared around the other side.

As soon as he was gone, Linda started thinking about Henrietta. Now that some time had passed since the visit, her intuition had solidified into certainty: Henrietta had not been telling her the truth. She was hiding something about Anna. Linda dialed Anna's number on her cell phone and got the answering machine. She didn't leave a message. She put her phone away and walked around the house to find her father. He was pulling at an old water pump that squeaked and sprayed brown water into a bucket. He shook his head.

"If I could move this house next to the sea I'd take it in a minute," he said. "But there's just too much forest for my taste."

"What about living in a trailer?" Linda suggested. "Then you could camp on the beach. Lots of people would be happy to let you stay on their land."

"And why is that?"

"Who wouldn't want free police protection?"

He grimaced and walked back to the car. Linda followed. *He's not going to turn around,* she thought. *He's already put this place behind him.*

Linda watched the kite swoop over the fields and disappear over the horizon.

"What now?" he asked her.

Linda immediately thought of Anna. She realized she wanted most of all to talk to her father about it, about the worry she felt.

"I'd like to talk," she said. "But not here."

"I know just the place."

"Where?"

"You'll see."

They drove south, turning left toward Malmö and leaving the main road at a turnoff for Kade Lake. The forest around the lake was one of the most beautiful Linda had ever seen. She had had a feeling her dad was going to take her here. They had taken many walks here when she was younger, especially when she was about ten or eleven. She also had a vague memory of being here with her mom, but she could not remember the whole family coming together.

They left the car by a stack of timber. The huge logs gave off a fresh scent, as if they had been recently felled. They walked through the forest, on a path that led to the strange metal statue erected to the memory of the warrior king Charles XII, who was rumored to have visited Kade Lake in his day. Linda was about to start talking about Anna when her dad raised his hand. They had stopped in a narrow glen surrounded by tall trees.

"This is my cemetery," he said.

"Your what?"

"This is one of my secrets, maybe the biggest, and I'll probably regret telling you this tomorrow. I've assigned all the trees that you see here to the friends I've had who've died. Even your grandfather is here, my mother and my old relatives."

He pointed to a young oak.

"I've given this tree to Stefan Fredman, the desperate Indian. Even he belongs in my collection of the dead."

"What about the other one you talked about?"

"Yvonne Ander? She's over there."

He pointed to another oak with an extensive network of branches.

"I came here a week or so after your grandfather died. I felt as if I had completely lost my footing in life. You were much stronger than I was. I was sitting down at the station trying to figure out a brutal assault case. Ironically it was a young man who had half-killed his father with a sledgehammer. The boy lied about everything and suddenly I couldn't take it anymore. I halted the interrogation and came here, and that's when I felt that these trees had become gravestones for all the people I knew who had died. That I should come here to visit with them, not where they are actually buried. Whenever I'm here I feel a calm I don't feel anywhere else. I can hug the dead here without them seeing me."

"I won't tell anyone," she said. "Thanks for sharing it with me."

They lingered a while longer. Linda wanted to ask about the identity of a few more of the trees but she said nothing. The sun was shining through the leaves, but the wind picked up and it immediately became colder. Linda took a deep breath and launched into the topic of Anna's disappearance.

"It'll drive me up the wall if you shake your head at me and tell me I'm imagining things. But if you can explain to me exactly why I'm wrong, I promise I'll pay attention."

"There's something you'll find out when you become a police officer," he said. "The unexplainable almost never happens. Even a disappearance turns out to have a perfectly reasonable explanation. You'll learn to differentiate between the unexplained and the merely unexpected. The unexpected can look baffling until you have the necessary background information. This is generally the case with disappearances. You don't know what's happened to Anna and it's only natural that it would worry you, but my intuition tells me you should draw on the highest virtue of our profession."

"Patience?"

"Exactly."

"For how long?"

"A few more days. She'll have turned up by then, or at least been in touch."

"I'm still convinced her mother was lying to me."

"I'm not sure your mother and I always stuck to the truth when we were asked about you."

"I'll try to be patient, but I do feel like there's more to this. It's not right."

They returned to the car. It was past one o'clock and Linda suggested they stop for lunch somewhere. They chose a roadside restaurant with the funny name My Father's Hat. Wallander had a fleeting recollection of lunching with his father at this restaurant and ending up in a huge argument. He couldn't remember what their argument had been about.

They were drinking their coffee when a phone rang. Linda fumbled for hers but it turned out to be her father's. He answered, listened, and made a few notes on the back of the check.

"What was that?"

"Someone's been reported missing."

He put money on the table and tucked the bill into his pocket.

"What do you have to do now?" Linda asked. "Who's disappeared?"

"We'll go back to Ystad via Skurup. A widow by the name of

Birgitta Medberg has been reported missing. Her daughter is worried."

"What are the circumstances?"

"The caller wasn't sure. Apparently the woman is a historian interested in mapping old walkways and she often does extensive fieldwork, sometimes in very dense forest. An unusual occupation."

"So she may simply be lost?"

"My first thought. We'll soon find out."

Wallander called the daughter of Birgitta Medberg to tell her he was on his way, and then they drove to Skurup. The wind was blustery. It was nine minutes past three on August 29.

12

They stopped in front of a two-story brick building—*quintessentially Swedish*, Linda thought. *Wherever you go in this country the houses all look the same. The central square in Västerås could be replaced with the one in Örebro, and this Skurup apartment building could as easily be in Sollentuna.*

"Where have you ever seen a building like this before?" she asked her father when they stepped out of the car and he was fumbling with the keys. He glanced at the brick facade.

"Looks like the place you had in Sollentuna, before you moved to the dorms at the police academy."

"Good memory. So what do I do now?"

"Come with me. You can treat this as a warm-up exercise for real police work."

"Aren't you breaking some rules by doing this? No one should be present at an interrogation without relevant cause—something like that?"

"This isn't an interrogation session, it's a conversation. Let's hope it will simply serve to put someone's fears to rest."

"But still."

"No buts. I've been breaking rules since I first started working. According to Martinsson's calculations I should have been locked up for a minimum of four years for all the things I've done. But who cares, if you're doing a good job? That's one of the few points Nyberg and I can agree on."

"Nyberg? The head of forensics?"

"The one and only. He's retiring soon, and in one sense no one will be sorry to see him go. On the other hand, despite his terrible temper, maybe all of us will."

They crossed the street. A bike missing its back wheel was propped up against the wall. The frame was bent as if it had been the victim of a violent assault. They walked into the entry and read the names of the people who lived there.

"Birgitta Medberg. Her daughter's name is Vanya. From the phone call I would say she has a tendency to hysteria. She also has a very shrill voice."

"I am not hysterical!" a woman yelled from above. She was leaning over the railing of the staircase, watching them.

"Remind me to keep my voice down in stairwells," Wallander muttered.

They walked up to her landing.

"Just as I thought," Wallander said in a friendly voice to the hostile woman waiting for them. "The boys at the station are too young. They still can't tell the difference between hysteria and a normal level of concern."

The woman, Vanya, was in her forties, heavy, with yellow stains around the collar and cuffs of her blouse. Linda thought it was probably a long time since she had washed her hair. They walked into the apartment and Linda immediately recognized the strong scent that hung in the air. *Mom's perfume,* she thought. *The one she wears when she's upset or angry.* She had another she preferred when she was happy.

They were shown into the living room. Vanya dropped into an armchair and pointed her finger at Linda.

"Who is she?"

"An assistant," Wallander said in a firm voice. "Please tell us what happened, starting at the beginning."

Vanya told them in a nervous, jerky style. She seemed to have trouble finding the right words even though it was clear that she was not the kind of person who spoke in long sentences. Linda immediately understood her concern was genuine, and compared it to the way she felt about Anna.

Vanya told them that her mother was a cultural geographer whose principal work was tracing and mapping old roads and walkways in southern Sweden. She had been widowed for a year and had four grandchildren, of which two were Vanya's. On this particular day, Vanya and her daughters were supposed to have visited her at noon. Birgitta had planned to be out on one of her short excursions before then. But when Vanya arrived, Birgitta had not yet returned. Vanya waited for two hours, then called the police. Her mother would never have disappointed her grandchildren like this, she reasoned. Something must have happened.

When she finished her story, Linda tried to guess what question her father would ask first. Perhaps something along the lines of: "Where was she going?"

"Do you know where she was going this morning?" he asked.

"No," Vanya said.

"She has a car, I take it."

"Actually, she has a red Vespa. Forty years old."

"Really?"

"All Vespas used to be red, my mother tells me. She's in an association for owners of vintage mopeds and Vespas. The headquarters are in Staffanstorp, I think. I don't know why—why she wants to be with those people, I mean. But she seems to like them."

"You said she became a widow about a year ago. Did she show any signs of depression?"

"No. And if you think she's committed suicide you're wrong."

"I'm not saying she did. But sometimes even the people closest to us can be very good at hiding their feelings."

Linda stared at her father. He glanced briefly in her direction. *We have to talk,* she thought. *It was wrong of me not to tell him about the time I stood on the bridge and was going to jump. He thinks the only time was when I slashed my wrists.*

"She would never hurt herself. She would never do that to us."

"Is there anyone she may have gone to visit?"

Vanya had lit a cigarette. She had already managed to spill ash on her blouse and the floor.

"My mother is the old-fashioned type. She never drops in on someone without calling."

"Our colleagues have confirmed that she hasn't been admitted to any hospital in the area, and there are no reports of an accident. Does she have a medical condition we should know about? Does she have a cell phone?"

"My mother is a very healthy woman. She takes care of herself—not like me, though it's hard to get enough exercise when you're in the grocery business."

Vanya made a gesture of disgust at her own body.

"A cell phone?"

"She has one, but she keeps it turned off. My sister and I are always getting on her case about it."

There was a lull in the conversation. They heard the low sound of a radio or a TV coming from the apartment next door.

"So let's get this straight. You have no idea where she may have gone. Is there anyone who would have more specific information regarding her research? Is there a diary or working papers of some kind we could look at?"

"Not that I know of. And my mother works alone."

"Has this ever happened before?"

"That she's disappeared? Never."

Wallander took a notepad and a pen out of his coat pocket and asked Vanya for her full name, address, and telephone number. Linda noticed that he reacted to her last name, Jorner. He stopped writing and looked up.

"Your mother's surname is Medberg. Is Jorner your husband's name?"

"Yes, Hans Jorner. My mother's maiden name was Lundgren. Is this important?"

"Hans Jorner—any connection to the gravel company in Limhamn?"

"Yes, he's the youngest son of the company director. Why?"

"I'm curious, that's all."

Wallander stood up and Linda followed.

"Would you mind showing us around? Did she have a study?"

Vanya pointed to a door and then put her hand to her mouth to smother an attack of smoker's cough. They walked into a study where the walls were covered with maps. Stacks of papers and folders were neatly arranged on the desk.

"What was all that about Jorner?" Linda asked in a low voice.

"I'll tell you later. It's an unpleasant story."

"And what was it she said? She's a grocer?"

"Yes."

Linda leafed through a few papers. He stopped her immediately.

"You can come along, listen, and look to your heart's content. But don't touch anything."

"It was just a few papers."

Linda left the room in a huff. He was right, of course, but his tone was objectionable. She nodded politely to Vanya, who was still coughing, and left the apartment. As soon as she was down on the street she regretted her childish reaction.

Her father emerged ten minutes later.

"What did I do? Is there something wrong?"

"It's nothing. I've already forgotten about it."

Linda made an apologetic gesture. Wallander unlocked the car while the wind pulled and tugged at their clothing. They got into the car, but he didn't start the engine right away.

"You noticed my reaction when she said her name was Jorner," Wallander said and squeezed the steering wheel angrily. "When Kristina and I were little there were periods of time when no art buyers had been by for a while in their fancy cars. We had no money. At those times Mother had to go to work. She had no education, so the only available occupations were on the assembly line or housekeeping. She chose the latter and landed a position with the Jorners, though she came home each night. Old man Jorner—Hugo was his name—and his wife Tyra were terrible people. As far as they were concerned there had been no social change over the past fifty years. The world, in their eyes, was upper-class and lower-class and nothing in between. He was the worst.

"One time my mother came home completely devastated. Even your grandfather, who never talked to her much, wondered what had happened. I hid behind the sofa and will never forget what she told me. There had been a small dinner party at the Jorners', perhaps eight people. My mother served the food and, when the guests were ready for coffee, Hugo asked her to bring in a stool from the kitchen. They were all a bit tipsy at this point and when she came in with it he asked her to climb up on it. She did as he asked and then he said that from her present vantage point she should be able to see that she had forgotten to lay a coffee spoon for one of the guests. Then he dismissed her, and she heard how everyone laughed as she left the room.

"I still remember it word for word. When she had finished, she started crying and said she would never go back. My dad was so upset he was ready to grab the ax from the woodshed and smash Jorner's head. But she managed to calm him down. I'll never forget it. I was ten, maybe twelve years old. And now I meet one of his daughters-in-law."

He started up the car angrily.

"I've often wondered about my grandmother," Linda said. "I think what I wonder about her most was how anyone could stand to be married to my grandfather."

Wallander laughed.

"My mom always used to say that he did what she told him if she just rubbed him with a little salt. I never really understood that—I remember wondering how you could rub a person with salt. The secret was her patience. She had an infinite fund of patience."

Wallander stepped on the brake and swerved suddenly as a sporty convertible overtook them in a dangerous curve. He swore.

"I should pull them over."

"Why don't you?"

"My mind is on other things."

Linda looked over at her dad, who appeared tense.

"There's something about this missing woman that bothers me," he said. "I think Vanya Jorner was telling us the truth and I think her anxiety is genuine. My feeling is that Birgitta Medberg either became sick, or perhaps temporarily confused, or else something has happened to her."

"Like a crime?"

"I don't know. But I think my day off is over. I'll take you home."

"I'll come with you to the station. I'll walk from there."

Wallander parked in the police station garage, and Linda started walking home in the wind that had become surprisingly cold. It was four o'clock in the afternoon. She walked in the direction of Mariagatan but changed her mind and walked to Anna's apartment instead. She waited after ringing the doorbell, then walked in.

———

It only took her a few seconds to feel that something was different. This time she had no doubt: someone had been in the apartment since she was here last. She couldn't articulate how she knew this. Was anything missing? She scrutinized the living room walls and the bookcase. Nothing appeared to have changed.

She sat down in the chair that Anna preferred. Something *had* changed, she was sure of it. But what? She got up and stood by the window to view the room from a different angle. That was when she saw it. There used to be a large blue butterfly in a framed glass case hanging on the wall between a poster from a Berlin art exhibition and an old barometer. Now the butterfly was gone. Linda shook her head. Was she imagining things? No, she was sure she remembered it being here last time. Could Henrietta have come by and picked it up? On the face of it, it didn't make sense. She took off her coat and methodically walked through the entire apartment.

When she opened Anna's closet she knew immediately that someone had been there. Several items of clothing were missing, as well as a bag. Linda could tell because Anna often left the closet doors open. She sat down on the bed and tried to think. Her gaze fell on the journal lying on the desk. *Anna must have left it behind,* she thought, and then corrected herself: Anna would never have left it behind. Whoever it was who had been here it wasn't Anna. She could easily have taken the clothes, perhaps even the butterfly. But she would never have left her journal. Not in a million years.

13

Walking into an empty room was like dipping below the mirror-like surface of a still lake and sinking into the silent and alien underwater landscape. She tried to remember everything she had been taught. Rooms always bore the traces of what had happened in them. But had anything of note happened here? There were no bloodstains, no signs of a struggle, nothing. A framed butterfly was missing, as well as a bag and a few clothes. That was all. But even if it had been Anna who had stopped by to pick them up, she would have left the same number of traces as an intruder. All Linda had to do was find them. She walked through the apartment again but didn't see anything else.

Finally she stopped at the answering machine and played the messages. Anna's dentist had called to ask her to reschedule her annual checkup, "Mirre" had called from Lund to ask if Anna was going to go to Båstad or not, and then there was Linda's own booming voice asking Anna to pick up.

Linda grabbed the address book on the table and looked up the number of the dentist, Sivertsson.

"Dr. Sivertsson's office."

"My name is Linda Wallander. I'm returning Anna Westin's calls as she's out of town for the next few days. Would you mind telling me the exact day and time of her appointment?"

The receptionist put her on hold, then came back on the line.

"The tenth of September at nine o'clock."

"Thank you. She probably has it written down somewhere."

"I don't remember Anna ever missing an appointment."

Linda hung up and tried to find a phone number for Mirre. She

thought about her own overstuffed address book that she was con-
tinually forced to patch up with tape. Somehow she could never
bring herself to buy a new one; it stored too many memories. All
the crossed-out telephone numbers reminded her of markers in a
private graveyard. That led her thoughts away from Anna and to
the moment in the forest with her father. A tenderness for him
welled up inside her. She sensed what he had been like as a boy. *A
little kid with big thoughts, maybe too big for his own good. There's so
much I don't know about him,* she thought. *What I think I know often
turns out to be wrong. I used to think of him only as a big friendly man who
was not too sharp, but stubborn and with a pretty good intuition about the
world. I've always thought he was a good policeman. But now I suspect he's
much more sentimental than he appears, that he takes pleasure in the little
romantic coincidences of everyday life and hates the incomprehensible and
brutal reality he confronts through his work.*

Linda pulled up a chair and turned the pages of a book about
Alexander Fleming and the discovery of penicillin that Anna had
obviously been reading. It was in English, and it surprised her that
Anna was up to the challenge. They had talked about doing a language program in England when they were younger. Had Anna
gone and done it on her own? She put the book back and picked up
Anna's address book again. Every page was covered in numbers,
like a blackboard during a lecture on advanced mathematics. There
were scratched-out numbers and changes on every page. Linda
smiled nostalgically at a couple of her own old phone numbers, as
well as the names and numbers of two of her ex-boyfriends. *What
am I looking for? I guess I'm trying to find traces of Anna that would explain what's happened. But why would they be here?*

She kept going through the address book, still feeling that she
was trespassing on Anna's most private self. *I've climbed over her
fence,* she thought. *I'm doing it for her sake but it still feels wrong.*

Then something caught her eye. The word "Dad" appeared on
one page, written boldly in red. The phone number was nineteen
digits long, all ones and threes. *A number that doesn't exist,* Linda
thought. *A secret number to the unknown city where all missing persons go.*

She wanted to put the book away, but forced herself to look all
the way to the end. The only other entry of any interest was a

number to "my room in Lund." Linda hesitated then dialed the number. A man picked up almost at once.

"Peter here."

"I'd like to speak to Anna. Is she in?"

"I'll check."

Linda waited. She heard music in the background but couldn't remember the name of the singer.

"No, she's not in. Can I take a message?"

"Do you know when she'll be back?"

"I don't even know if she's around. I haven't seen her for a while. But I can ask the others."

She waited again while he asked around.

"No one's seen her here for a couple of days."

She asked him for the address, which he gave and then promptly hung up. She was left holding the receiver to her ear. *No Anna,* she thought. The man called Peter had clearly not been worried and Linda was starting to feel foolish. She thought about herself and her own tendency to take off without leaving messages about where she was going. Her dad had often been on the verge of reporting her when she was younger. *But I always sense when I'm gone too long and I always call in,* she thought. *Why wouldn't Anna do the same?*

Linda rang Zeba and asked her if she had heard from Anna. Zeba said no, there had been no news. They decided to meet for coffee the following day.

As she put the phone down, Linda thought, *I'm staging this as a disappearance so as to have something to do. As soon as I can put my uniform on and actually start working she'll turn up. It's like a game.*

She went out into the kitchen and made herself a cup of tea, then took it with her to Anna's bedroom. She sat down on the side of the bed across from where Anna normally slept. Putting down her cup of tea, she stretched out for a moment, and before she knew it she had fallen asleep.

When she woke up she didn't know where she was at first. She looked at the time—she had been asleep for an hour. The tea was cold. She drank it anyway because her mouth was dry, then stood up and straightened the covers. That was when she saw it.

The covers. On Anna's side. There was an indentation that was still visible: someone had slept there and not smoothed the bed afterward. That wasn't like Anna. She was the kind of person who never left crumbs on the table.

Linda lifted the covers on impulse and found a T-shirt, size XXL, dark blue with the Virgin Airlines logo. She sniffed carefully and confirmed that it didn't smell like Anna—it had the masculine scent of aftershave or perhaps very strong deodorant soap. She laid the T-shirt out on the bed. Anna preferred nightgowns, and classy ones at that. Linda was willing to bet that she would not have used a Virgin Airlines T-shirt even for one night.

Suddenly the phone in the living room rang. Linda flinched, then walked out and looked at the answering machine. Should she answer it? She stretched out her hand but pulled it back. The machine picked up after the fifth ring. It was Henrietta. *Hi, it's Mom. Your friend Linda—the one who wants to become a policewoman—came by here yesterday looking for you. I just wanted to let you know. Call me when you get back. Bye.*

Linda played the message back. Henrietta's voice sounded calm. There was no unvoiced anxiety between the words, nothing out of the ordinary. She heard the implicit criticism of her choice of careers clearly enough. That bothered her. Did Anna share her mother's dismissive attitude? *To hell with them,* Linda thought. *Anna can carry on her disappearing act without me.* Linda walked around one last time watering the plants, then left the apartment.

By the time Wallander came home around seven o'clock she had cooked and eaten dinner. She heated up the food she had left for him while he changed. She sat in the kitchen while he ate.

"What happened?"

"With the missing woman? Svartman and Grönkvist are in charge of it. Nyberg is examining her apartment. We have decided to take her disappearance seriously. Now we can only wait and see."

"And what do you think?"

Wallander pushed his plate away.

"Something about it still worries me, but I could be wrong."

"What worries you?"

"Certain people shouldn't go missing, that's all. It's not something they do—if it happens it means something is wrong. I guess that's been my experience."

He got up and put on a pot of coffee.

"We had a real-estate agent whose wife went missing about ten years ago. Maybe you remember it? She was religious, something evangelical. They had small children. The moment he came in to notify us she was missing I knew something had happened. And I was right. She had been murdered."

"But Birgitta Medberg is a widow and she doesn't have small children. She's probably not even religious—I certainly can't imagine that fat daughter of hers being religious, can you?"

"I don't think you can tell that just by looking at someone. But I'm talking about something else, something unexpected."

Linda told him about her latest discovery in Anna's apartment. She watched her father's face take on a strong look of disapproval.

"You shouldn't be getting yourself mixed up in this," he said. "If anything's happened it's a case for the police."

"I'm almost the police."

"You're a rookie, and the proper line of work for you is breaking up drunken brawls in town."

"I just think it's strange she's gone, that's all."

Wallander brought his plate and his coffee cup over to the sink.

"If you're genuinely concerned, you should go to the police."

He left the kitchen. Linda stayed behind. His condescending tone irritated her, not least because he was right.

She sulked in the kitchen until she felt ready to see her dad again. He was in the living room, asleep in a chair. Linda shook his arm when he started to snore. He jerked awake and raised his arms as if to ward off an attack. *Just like me*, she thought. *That's another thing we have in common.* He went to the bathroom, then got ready for bed. Linda watched a film on TV without really concentrating. Shortly before midnight she went to bed. She dreamed about her ex-boyfriend, Herman Mboya, who was back in Kenya and had opened his own practice.

The buzzing of the cell phone woke her up. It vibrated next to the lamp on the bedside table. She answered it at the same time that she checked her alarm clock. Three fifteen. There was no voice on the other end, just breathing. Then the line went dead. Linda knew it had something to do with Anna, whoever had made the call. It was a kind of message, even if it only consisted of a few breaths. It had to mean something.

Linda never managed to fall back asleep. Her father got up at a quarter past six. She let him shower and change in peace, but when he started making noise in the kitchen she joined him. He was surprised to see her up and dressed at that hour.

"I'm coming with you."

"Why?"

"I thought about what you said, that if I was worried about Anna I should raise the matter with the police. Well, I *am* worried and I'm going to report her disappearance. I think something is seriously wrong."

14

Linda had never learned to predict when her dad would fall into one of his sudden rages. She remembered with painful clarity how she and her mother would cringe when he got like this. Her grandfather was the only one who simply shrugged it off or gave as good as he got. By now she had learned to look for certain signs: the telltale red patch on the forehead, the nervous pacing.

But this morning she was once more taken by surprise at the vehemence of his reaction to her decision to report Anna's disappearance. Her dad started by throwing a stack of napkins to the floor. There was a comical element in this gesture, since the anticipated violence of the crash never came, and the white papers fluttered softly across the kitchen floor. But it was enough to kindle Linda's childhood fear. She recalled what Mona had said after the divorce: *He can't see it himself. He doesn't know how intimidating it is to be met with a raging temper when you least expect it. Others probably think of him as a friendly, slightly eccentric perhaps, but capable policeman, which is probably a fair assessment of him in the workplace. But at home he let his temper run loose like a wild animal. He became a terrorist in my eyes. I feared him, and I also grew to hate him.*

Linda thought of her mother's words as she sat across from her giant of a father, still furious, now kicking at the napkins on the floor.

"Why don't you listen to me?" he was saying. "How are you ever going to be a respected police officer if you think a crime has been committed every time one of your friends doesn't pick up the phone?"

"Dad, it's not like that."

He swept the rest of the napkins off the table. *A child*, Linda thought. *A big child throwing all his toys on the ground.*

"Don't interrupt me! Didn't they teach you anything at the academy?"

"I learned to take things seriously."

"You're going to be laughed out of the force."

"So be it. But Anna has disappeared."

His rage died down as suddenly as it had started. There were still a few drops of sweat on his cheek. *That was a short one,* Linda thought. *And not as furious as I remember. Maybe he's more afraid of me now, or else he's getting old. I bet he even apologizes this time.*

"I'm sorry."

Linda didn't answer. She picked up a few napkins from the floor and threw them into the trash. Her heart was still pounding with fear. *I'll always feel this way when he gets angry,* she thought.

"I don't know what gets into me."

Linda stared at him, waiting to speak until he actually looked at her.

"You just need to get a little action."

He flinched as if she had struck him, then he blushed.

"You know I'm right," she continued. "Anyway, you should get going. I'll walk so you don't have to be embarrassed."

"I was planning to walk myself, actually."

"Do it tomorrow. I don't like it when you scream and yell. I need some space."

Wallander set off meekly as instructed. Linda changed her top since she was drenched in sweat. She reconsidered her decision to report Anna's disappearance and had still not made up her mind by the time she left the apartment.

The sun was shining and there was a brisk breeze. Linda paused out on the street, unsure of what to do next. She prided herself on being a decisive person as a rule, but sometimes being around her father sapped her of willpower. She thought angrily that she couldn't wait until she was allowed to move into her apartment behind Mariakyrkan. She couldn't stand living with him much longer.

Finally she turned toward the police station. If something had really happened to Anna she would never forgive herself for not following through on reporting it. Her career as a police officer would be over before it had begun.

She walked past the People's Park and thought about a magician she had seen there as a child when she had been out with her dad. The magician had taken gold coins out of children's ears. This memory gave rise to another, one that had to do with a fight between her parents. She had woken up in her room at the sound of their angry voices. They had been arguing about money, some money that should have been in the account, that was gone, that had been frittered away. When Linda had carefully tiptoed to her door and peeked into the living room, she had seen her mother with blood coming out of her nose. Her dad had been looking out of the window, his face sweaty and flushed. She immediately realized that he had hit her mother, on account of the money that wasn't there.

Linda stopped walking and squinted up at the sun. The back of her throat was starting to constrict. She remembered looking at her parents, thinking that she was the only one who could solve their problems. She didn't want Mona to have a bloody nose. She had gone into her bedroom and taken out her piggy bank. Then she walked out into the living room and put it on the table. The room fell silent.

She kept squinting up at the sun but the tears came anyway. She rubbed her eyes and changed direction, as if this would force her mind to change track. She turned onto Industrigatan and decided to postpone reporting Anna's disappearance. Instead she would swing by the apartment one last time. *If anyone's been there since last night I'll know,* she thought. She rang the doorbell—no answer. When she opened the front door her whole body tensed up, all of her antennae out. But there was nothing.

She walked around in the apartment, looking at the bed where she had lain the night before. She sat down in the living room and went through what had happened. Anna had now been missing for three days, if she really was missing.

Linda shook her head angrily and walked back into the bedroom. She apologized to the air and started looking through the diary again. She flipped back about thirty days. Nothing. The most notable occurrence was a toothache on August 7 and 8 and a resulting appointment with Dr. Sivertsson. Linda remembered those days and furrowed her brow. On August 8, she, Zeba, and Anna had taken a long walk out at Kåseberga. They had taken Anna's car. Zeba's boy was cooperative for once, and they had all taken turns carrying him when he was too tired to walk.

But a toothache?

Linda again had the feeling that there was a strange kind of double-language in Anna's diary, perhaps a code. But why? And what could an entry about a toothache possibly signify?

She kept reading and looked closely at the handwriting itself. Anna frequently changed her pen, even in the middle of a sentence. Perhaps she was interrupted by the phone and couldn't find the same pen when she was done. Linda put the journal down and went to get a glass of water from the kitchen.

When she turned the next page she drew a breath. At first she was sure she was getting it confused. But no, there it was: on August 13, Anna had written *Letter from Birgitta Medberg.*

Linda read it again, this time by the window with the sun on the page. Birgitta Medberg was not a common name. She put the diary down on the windowsill and picked up the phone book. It only took her a few minutes to confirm that there was only one Birgitta Medberg in this area of southern Sweden. She called information and asked about Birgitta Medbergs in the rest of the country; there were only a few other individuals with that name. And there was only one who was listed as a cultural geographer in Skåne.

Linda returned to the journal and read the rest of the text with impatience. She finally reached the strange message at the end: *myth fear, myth fear.* But there was no other reference to Birgitta Medberg.

Anna disappears, she thought. *A few weeks earlier she receives a letter from Birgitta Medberg, who has also gone missing. In the middle of all this is Anna's father, whom she thinks has just reappeared on a street in Malmö after a twenty-four-year absence.*

Linda looked through the apartment for Birgitta Medberg's letter. She no longer felt guilty for violating Anna's privacy. She found a number of letters over the next three hours. Unfortunately, the letter from Medberg wasn't one of them.

Linda left the apartment with Anna's car keys. She drove herself down to the Harbor Café and had a sandwich and a cup of tea. A man her own age in oil-spattered overalls smiled at her as she was getting ready to leave. It took her a while to recognize him as a classmate from high school. She stopped and they said hello. Linda struggled in vain to remember his name. He stretched out his hand after first wiping it clean.

"I'm sailing," he said. "I have an old boat with a dud motor. That's why I'm covered in grease."

"I've only just moved back to town," Linda said.

"What do you do?"

Linda hesitated without even knowing why.

"I've just graduated from the police academy."

His name suddenly came back to her: Torbjörn. He smiled at her again.

"I thought you were into old furniture."

"I was, but I changed my mind."

He stretched out his hand again.

"Ystad is pretty small. I'm sure I'll see you around."

Linda hurried up to the car, parked behind the old theater. *I wonder what they'll think,* she thought. *I wonder if they'll be surprised that Linda became a cop.*

She drove out to Skurup, parked on the main square, and then walked over to the house where Birgitta Medberg lived. There was a strong smell of cooking in the stairwell. She rang the doorbell; there was no answer. She listened, then called through the mail slot. When she was sure no one was there, she took out her pass keys and opened the door. *I'm starting my career in law enforcement by breaking and entering,* she thought. She was sweating and her heart was thumping. Alert for any noise, she carefully made her way through the whole apartment, constantly afraid that someone would come in. She didn't know exactly what she was looking for here, just something that would confirm the connection between Anna and Birgitta Medberg.

She was about to give up when she found a paper under the green writing pad on the desk. It was a photocopy of an old surveyor's map on which the lines and words were hard to make out.

Linda turned on the desk lamp and was finally able to make out the writing on the bottom of the page: Rannesholm Estate. She recognized the name, but where was it exactly? She had seen a map of southern Sweden in the bookcase. She took it out and managed to find Rannesholm, which only lay a few miles north of Skurup. Linda looked at the older map again. Even though it was a poor copy, she thought she could see the outlines of some notes and arrows. She tucked both maps into her coat, turned off the light, and checked for noise through the mail slot before leaving.

It was four o'clock by the time she reached a public parking lot by the nature reserve at Rannesholm. *What am I doing here?* she asked herself. *Am I just playing a game to pass the time?* She locked the car and walked down to the lake. A pair of swans were out in the middle of the lake where the wind sent ripples across the surface of the water. It looked like rain clouds were moving in from the west. She zipped up her jacket. It was still summer, but there was the unmistakable feeling of fall in the air. She looked back at the parking lot. It was empty except for Anna's car. She tossed a few pebbles into the lake. *There is a connection between Medberg and Anna,* she thought. *But what could they have in common?* She threw another stone into the water. *The only thing I can think of that links them is the fact that both of them have disappeared. The police are investigating one case, but not the other.*

The rain came sooner than she had expected. Linda ducked under a tall oak tree next to the parking lot. Raindrops started to fall all around her and suddenly the whole situation seemed completely idiotic. She was about to brace herself for a run through the rain to the car when she saw something glittering between the wet branches of a nearby bush. At first she thought it was a discarded beer can. She poked at one of the branches and saw a black tire. She started pulling the branches away with both hands and her heart beat faster. Then she ran to the car and grabbed her phone. For once her dad had his cell phone with him and turned on.

"Where are you?" he asked.

His voice was unusually gentle. She could tell he was still trying to make up for the morning.

"I'm at Rannesholm Manor," she said. "In the parking lot."

"What are you doing up there?"

"Dad, there's something you need to see."

"I can't. We're about to have a meeting about crazy new directives from Stockholm."

"Skip it. Just get over here—I've found something."

"What?"

"Birgitta Medberg's Vespa."

She heard her father's sharp intake of breath on the other end.

"Are you sure?"

"Yes."

"And how did this happen?"

"I'll tell you everything when you get here."

There was a noise on the line and the connection was broken, but Linda didn't bother calling him again. She knew he was on his way.

15

It was raining even harder now. Linda saw something flashing through the windshield and turned on the wipers. It was her father's car. He parked, ducked out, and jumped into the passenger seat next to her. He was impatient, clearly in a hurry.

"Let's hear it."

His impatience made her nervous.

"Do you have the journal with you?" he interrupted.

"No. Why? I've given you the text word for word."

He had no more questions and she continued her account. When she had finished, he sat and stared out into the rain.

"A strange story," he said.

"You always say to watch for the unexpected."

He nodded, then looked her over.

"Did you bring a raincoat?"

"No."

"I have one you can borrow."

He popped the door open and ran back to his car. Linda was amazed to see her large, heavyset dad move so quickly, with such agility. She followed him out into the rain. He stood at the back of the car putting on his gear. When he saw her he handed her a raincoat that fell all the way down to her feet. Then he fished out a baseball cap with the logo of a local car-repair shop and pushed it down over her head. He stared up at the sky. The rain poured down over his face.

"It's Noah and the flood all over again," he said. "I don't remember rain like this since I was a child."

"It rained a lot when I was young," Linda said.

He nudged her on and she led the way over to the oak tree and pushed the bushes away so he could see. Wallander took out his cell phone and she heard him call the police station. He grumbled when they didn't pick up right away. Wallander read out the license-plate number and waited for confirmaton. It was her Vespa. Wallander put the phone back in his pocket.

The rain stopped at that exact moment. It happened so fast it took them a while to register what had happened. It was like rain on a movie set being turned off after the take.

"God has decided to take pity on us," Wallander said. "You've found Birgitta Medberg's Vespa."

He looked around.

"But no Birgitta Medberg."

Linda hesitated, then pulled out the photocopy of the old map that she had found in Birgitta Medberg's apartment. She regretted it as soon as she had taken it out, but it was too late.

"What's that?"

"A map of the area."

"Where did you find it?"

"Here on the ground."

He took the dry piece of paper from her and gave her a searching look. *Here comes the question I won't be able to answer,* she thought.

But he didn't ask. Instead he studied the map, looked down to the lake and the road, at the parking lot and the various paths that branched out from it.

"She came here," he said. "But this is a big park."

He studied the area right around the Vespa. Linda watched him, trying to read his mind.

Suddenly he looked at her.

"What's the first question we should be asking?"

"If she hid the Vespa deliberately, or was only trying to protect it from being stolen."

He nodded.

"There's a third alternative, of course."

Linda understood what he was getting at. She should have thought of it right away.

"That someone else hid it."

"Exactly."

A dog came running out from one of the paths. It was white with little black spots; Linda couldn't remember what that kind was called. Then another and finally a third dog appeared out of the forest, followed by a woman dressed in rain gear from head to toe. She was walking briskly and put all three of the dogs on leashes when she caught sight of Linda and Wallander. She was in her forties, tall, blond, and attractive. Linda saw her father react instinctively to the presence of a good-looking woman: he stood up straight, pulled up his head to make his throat appear less wrinkled, and held in his stomach.

"Excuse me," he said. "My name is Wallander and I'm with the Ystad police."

The woman looked at him skeptically.

"May I see your identification?"

Wallander dug out his wallet, then presented his ID card, which she studied closely.

"Has anything happened?"

"No. Do you often walk your dogs in this area?"

"Twice a day, actually."

"That must mean you know these paths very well."

"Yes, I would say I do. Why?"

He ignored her last question.

"Do you meet many people in the forest?"

"Not during the fall. Spring and summer there are a fair number of people in the park, but soon it will only be dog owners who make the effort. That's always a relief. Then I can let the dogs off the leash."

"But aren't they supposed to stay on the leash year-round? That's what the sign says."

He pointed at a sign a few feet away. She raised her eyebrows.

"Is that why you're here? To catch women who let their dogs run loose?"

"No. There's something I'd like to show you."

The dogs strained impatiently on their leashes while Wallander lifted away some of the undergrowth to reveal the Vespa.

"Have you ever seen this scooter before? It belongs to a woman in her sixties by the name of Birgitta Medberg."

The dogs immediately wanted to pull forward and sniff it, but they were firmly restrained by their owner. Her voice was steady and without hesitation.

"Yes," she said. "I've seen both the Vespa and the woman. Quite a few times."

"When did you see her last?"

She thought about it.

"Yesterday."

Wallander threw a quick glance at Linda, who was standing to one side, listening.

"Are you sure?"

"No, not completely. But I think it was yesterday."

"Why can't you be sure?"

"I've seen her so often over the last few weeks."

"The last few weeks? Can you be more precise?"

She thought about it again before answering.

"I suppose all through July, perhaps the last week of June. That was when I first saw her. She was walking on a path on the other side of the lake and we stopped and chatted for a bit. She told me she was mapping old walking trails around Rannesholm. I saw her again from time to time after that. She had many interesting stories to tell. Neither I nor my husband had any idea that there were pilgrim trails on our property. We live in the manor," she added, "My husband manages an investment fund. My name is Anita Tademan."

She looked at the Vespa again and her expression became anxious.

"Is something wrong?"

"We don't know. I have one last question for you. When you last saw her, which path was she on?"

Anita Tademan pointed back over her shoulder.

"That one I was just on. It's a good one when it rains because the canopy is so thick. She found a completely overgrown path in there that starts about five hundred meters into the forest next to a fallen beech tree. That was where I last saw her."

"Then I have no more questions for you," Wallander said.

"Can't you tell me what this is all about?"

"She may have disappeared. We're still not sure."

"How awful. That nice woman."

"Was she always on her own?" Linda asked.

The question flew out of her mouth before she had a chance to stop herself. Wallander looked over at her with surprise but did not look angry.

"I never saw her with anyone," Anita Tademan said. "And if that's all your questions I must be on my way."

She let the dogs off their leashes and started walking up the road that led up to the castle. Linda and her father stood watching her for a while.

"A beauty."

"Snobby and rich," Linda said. "Hardly your type."

"Never say never," he said. "I know how to behave in polite society. Both your mother and your aunt have taught me well."

He looked down at his watch and then up at the sky.

"We'll go five hundred meters and see if we find anything."

He started down the path at a quick pace. She followed him and was forced to half-run in order to keep up with him. A strong scent of wet earth rose up from the forest floor. The path wound around boulders and the exposed roots of old trees. They heard a pigeon fly up from a branch, and then another.

Linda was the one who spotted it. Wallander was walking so fast he didn't see where a thin path branched off to one side. She shouted out to him and he backtracked.

"I was counting," she said. "This is about four hundred fifty meters in."

"The woman said five hundred."

"If you don't count every step, five hundred can feel like four or six hundred meters, depending."

"I know how to judge distances," he said, irritated.

They started following the new path that was only barely visible. But both of them noted soft imprints. *One pair of boots,* Linda thought. *One person.*

The path led them deep into a part of the forest that looked untouched. They stopped at the edge of a shallow ravine that cut through the forest. Wallander crouched down and picked at the moss with his finger.

They made their way carefully into the ravine. At one point

Linda's foot was caught in some roots and she fell. A branch broke and sounded like a gunshot. They heard birds fly up all around them although they couldn't see them.

"Are you all right?"

Linda brushed the mud from her clothes.

"I'm fine."

Wallander made his way through the brush and Linda followed closely. He parted a few of the branches in front of them and suddenly she saw a small hut. It was like something out of a fairy tale, the house of a witch, the shack leaned up against the rock face. A broken pail lay half-buried in the earth outside the door. Both of them listened attentively for sounds, but there were none. Only the occasional tap of a raindrop.

"Wait here," Wallander said and walked up to the door.

Wallander opened the door and looked in, flinched, and stepped back. Linda caught up with him and pushed past him to peer inside. At first she didn't know what she was looking at.

Then she realized that they had found Birgitta Medberg.

Or, more precisely, what remained of her.

PART II

the void

16

What Linda saw through the open door, that which had caused her father to flinch and stumble backward, resembled something she had once seen as a child. The image flickered to life in her mind; she had seen it in a book Mona had inherited from her mother, the other grandmother Linda had never met. It was a large book with old-fashioned type, a book of Bible stories. She remembered the full-page illustrations, protected by a translucent sheet of tissue paper. One of the pictures depicted the scene she was now witnessing firsthand, with only one difference. In the book the picture had shown a man's head with closed eyes, placed on a gleaming tray, a woman dancing in the background. Salome with her veils. That picture had made an almost unbearably strong impression on her.

Perhaps it was only now, when the picture had escaped from the page, the memory resurrected in the guise of a woman, that the moment of childhood horror was fully replaced. Linda stared at Birgitta Medberg's severed head on the earth floor. Her clasped hands lay close by, but that was all. The rest of her body was missing. Linda heard her father groan in the background, then she felt his hands on her back as he dragged her away.

"Don't look!" he shouted. "You shouldn't see this. Turn back."

He slammed the door shut. Linda was so scared she was shaking. She scuttled back up the side of the ravine, ripping her pants in the process. Her father was at her heels. They ran until they reached the main path.

"What is going on?" she heard him mutter under his breath. "What's happened?"

He called the station and gave the alarm, using code words that

she knew were meant to slip under the noses of journalists and curious amateurs listening in on police radio communications. Then
they returned to the parking lot and waited. Fourteen minutes went
by until they heard the first sirens in the distance. They had said
nothing to each other during their wait. Linda was shaken and
wanted to be with her father but he turned his back and took a few
steps away. Linda had trouble making sense of what she had seen.
At the same time another fear was mounting, a fear that this was
somehow connected with Anna. *What if there is a connection,* she
thought despairingly. *And now one of them is dead, butchered.* She interrupted her train of thought and crouched down on the ground,
suddenly faint. Her father looked over at her and started to walk
over. She forced herself to stand and shook her head at him as if to
say it was nothing, a momentary weakness.

Now she was the one who turned her back to him. She tried to
think clearly—slowly, deliberately, but above all clearly. *An officer
who can't think clearly can't do her job.* She had written this statement
on a piece of paper and pinned it to the wall next to her bed. She
knew she always had to keep her cool, but how was she supposed
to do that when right now she felt like bursting into tears? There
was no trace of calm in her mind, only terrible flashes of the
severed head and clasped hands. And even worse, the question
of what had happened to Anna. She couldn't keep new images
from forming in her mind: Anna's head, Anna's hands. John the
Baptist's head on a plate and Anna's hands, Anna's head and Birgitta Medberg's hands.

The rain had started again. Linda ran over to her father and showered his chest with blows.

"Now do you believe me? Don't you realize something must
have happened to Anna?"

Wallander grabbed her shoulders, trying to keep her at arm's
length.

"Calm down. That was Birgitta Medberg in there, not Anna."

"But Anna wrote in her diary that she knew her. And now Anna
is gone. Don't you get it?"

"You have to calm down. That's all."

Linda slowly regained control of herself, or rather, felt a paralysis settle over her. Three, then four police cars came slipping and sliding into the muddy parking lot. The police officers got out and gathered around Wallander after quickly having thrown on the rain gear that they all seemed to keep stashed in the backs of their cars. Linda stood outside the circle, but no one tried to stop her when she eventually joined them. Martinsson was the only one who acknowledged her, with a nod, but even he never asked her what she was doing there. At that moment, in the rainy parking lot by Rannesholm Manor, Linda cut the cord to her life at the police academy. She fell in line behind the others and followed them in their long train into the forest. When a crime scene technician dropped a light stand, she picked it up and carried it for him.

She stayed there while day turned into dusk and finally evening. Rain clouds came and went, the ground was saturated with moisture, the lights erected around the site cast strong shadows. The crime scene technicians painstakingly marked out a working path to the hut. Linda took care not to get in their way, and she never put her foot down without placing it in someone else's footprint. Sometimes her father met her gaze, but it was as if he could not really see her. Ann-Britt Höglund was always at his side. Linda had bumped into her from time to time since she came back to Ystad, but Linda had never liked her. In fact, she felt her father would do best to stay away from her. Höglund had barely greeted her today, and Linda sensed she would not be an easy person to work with, if that ever became the case. Of course, Höglund was a full-fledged detective inspector, while Linda was a rookie who hadn't even started working yet and who would be busy breaking up street fights before she even had the opportunity to apply for a more specialized line of work.

She watched her future colleagues go about their business, noting the order and discipline that always seemed to be on the verge of giving way to sheer chaos. From time to time someone raised his voice, especially the irritable Nyberg, who often swore at his team for not watching where they put their feet. Three hours after they had arrived the human remains were removed from the scene, enclosed in thick plastic. Everyone stopped working as they were carried away. Linda could see the contours of Birgitta Medberg's head and hands through the plastic casing.

Then they all resumed their work. Nyberg and his technicians crawled around on hands and knees, someone was sawing off branches and clearing away the underbrush, others were setting up lamps or repairing generators. People came and went, phones rang, and in the middle of all this her father stood rooted to one spot as if restrained by invisible cords. Linda felt sorry for him; he looked so lonely standing there, always available to answer a steady stream of questions, making snap decisions so that the investigation could proceed smoothly. *He's walking a tightrope,* Linda thought. *That's how I see him. A nervous tightrope walker who should go on a diet and address the issue of his loneliness once and for all.*

It was only much later that Wallander realized she was still there. He finished talking to someone on the phone, then turned to Nyberg, who was holding out an object for him to look at. He held it in the beam of one of the strong lights that attracted insects and burned them to death. Linda took a step closer to see what it was. Nyberg handed Wallander a pair of rubber gloves that he pulled onto his big hands with some difficulty.

"What's this?"

"If you weren't completely blind you would see it was a Bible."

Wallander didn't seem to take any notice of Nyberg's tone.

"A Bible," Nyberg repeated. "It was on the ground next to the hands. There are bloody fingerprints. But they could belong to someone else, of course."

"The murderer?"

"Possibly. It's a gory scene in there. The whole hut is spattered with blood. Whoever did this must have been completely drenched."

"No weapons?"

"Nothing at this point. But this Bible is worth a closer look, even apart from the fingerprints."

Linda took yet another step closer as her father put on his glasses.

"Open it to the Book of Revelations," Nyberg said.

"I don't know my way around this thing. Just tell me what's in there."

But Nyberg would not let himself be hurried.

"Who knows their Bible anymore? But the Book of Revelations is an important chapter, or whatever those parts are called."

He threw a hasty glance at Linda.

"Do you know? In the Bible, is it called a chapter?"

Linda gave a start.

"No idea."

"You see, the young are no better than we. Whatever. The thing is that someone has written comments between the lines. See?"

Nyberg pointed to a page. Wallander held it up closer to his eyes.

"I see some gray smudges. Is that what you mean?"

Nyberg called out to someone called Rosén. A man with mud up to his chest came clomping over with a magnifying glass. Wallander tried again.

"Yes, someone has been writing between the lines. What does it say?"

"I've made out two of the lines," Nyberg said. "It seems as if whoever wrote in here wasn't happy with the original. Someone has taken it upon themselves to improve on the word of God."

Wallander removed his glasses.

"What does that mean, anyway, 'the word of God'? Can you try to be more specific?"

"I thought the Bible *was* the word of God. How much more specific do I have to be? I just think it's interesting that someone should rewrite passages in the Bible. Is that something a normal person does? A person in basic possession of his or her senses?"

"A lunatic, then. What is this hut, anyway? A place where someone was living, or a temporary hideout?"

Nyberg shook his head.

"Too early to say. But can't they be the same thing for someone who wants to stay out of the public eye?"

Nyberg gestured out to the forest, which was impenetrably dark beyond the spotlights.

"We've had dogs search the area and I think they're still out. The units claim the terrain is all but impassable. If you needed a hideout you couldn't pick a better place."

"Any idea who it might belong to?"

Nyberg shook his head.

"There are no personal effects, no clothes. We can't even determine if it was a man or a woman living here."

A dog started barking somewhere in the darkness as a light rain began to fall. Höglund, Martinsson, and Svartman emerged from various directions and gathered around Wallander. Linda hovered in the background, part participant, part spectator.

"Give me a scenario," Wallander said. "What happened here? We know a repulsive murder took place—but why? Who did it? Why did Medberg come here? Did she plan to meet someone? Was she even killed here? Where is the rest of the body? Tell me."

The rain continued to fall. Nyberg sneezed. One of the spotlights went out. Nyberg kicked the light over, then helped set it up again.

"A picture of what happened," Wallander said.

"I've seen a lot of things that qualify as repulsive," Martinsson said. "But nothing like this. Whoever did this was truly fucked up. Where's the rest of the body? Who used this hut? We don't know yet."

"Nyberg found a Bible," Wallander said. "We'll run prints on everything, of course, but it turns out someone's written new text between the lines in the book. What does that tell us? We have to see if the Tademans ever visited this place. We may have to go door-to-door for answers. We'll maintain an investigation with a broad front, working around the clock."

No one spoke.

"We have to get this psycho," Wallander said. "The sooner the better. I don't know what this is all about, but I'm scared."

Linda stepped into the light. It was like stepping onto the stage without having learned your lines.

"I'm scared too."

Wet, tired faces turned to her. Only her father looked tense. *He's going to explode,* she thought. But she had to do this.

"I'm scared too," she repeated. And then she told them about Anna. She made a point of not looking at her father as she spoke. She tried to remember all the details—omitting the parts about her intuitive fears—and present all the facts.

"We'll look into it," her father said when she had finished. His voice was ice-cold.

Linda instantly regretted what she had done. *I didn't want to,* she thought. *I did it for Anna's sake, not to get back at you.*

"I know," she said. "I'm going home now. There's no reason for me to be here."

"You found the Vespa, didn't you?" Martinsson asked. "Isn't that right?"

Wallander nodded and turned to Nyberg.

"Can you spare someone who can escort Linda to her car?"

"I'll do it," Nyberg said. "I have to use the bathroom up there anyway. Can't do my business in the forest—the dogs' noses are far too sensitive."

Linda clambered up out of the ravine, only now realizing how tired and hungry she was. Nyberg's strong flashlight lit up the path for her. They ran into a canine unit on the way, the dog's tail drooping behind him. Other lights glimmered among the trees. *Night orienteering,* Linda thought. *Police officers hunting for clues in the dark.* Nyberg muttered something unintelligible when they reached the parking lot, and then he was gone. Linda got into Anna's car, someone lifted the yellow tape to let her past, and she was out on the main road. There were onlookers all along the road to the highway, people in parked cars waiting for something to happen, to see something. She felt as if her invisible uniform was back on. *Go home!* she thought. *There's a brutal murder to be solved and you're getting in the way of our work.* But then she shook the thoughts away. She wasn't a policewoman, not quite yet.

After a while she noticed she was driving too fast and slowed down. A hare sprang out onto the road. For a brief moment his eye was frozen in her headlights. She slammed on the brakes. Her heart was beating hard. She took a few deep breaths. Lights from other cars came at her and she decided to turn into a parking lot. She turned off the lights first, then the engine. Darkness settled in all around her. She got out her cell phone, but it rang before she had a chance to dial the number. It was her dad. He was furious.

"Do you know what you did back there? You were telling me I didn't know how to do my job."

"I didn't say anything about you," she said. "I'm just afraid that something's happened to Anna."

"Don't you ever do anything like that again. Ever. If you do, I'll make sure your stint in Ystad is over before you know it."

She didn't have a chance to answer. He hung up. *He's right,* she thought. *I didn't think, I just started to talk.* She was about to dial his number to apologize or at least explain herself, but then she realized there was no point. He was still angry and it would take a couple of hours before he'd be ready to hear her out.

Linda needed to talk to someone and dialed Zeba's number. The line was busy. She slowly counted to fifty and dialed again. Still busy. Without knowing why she dialed Anna's number. Busy. Linda was startled and tried again. It was still busy. A huge wave of relief came over her. *Anna's back,* she thought. She started the engine, turned on the headlights and swung back out onto the highway. *Good God,* she thought. *I'll have to tell her everything that happened just because she didn't show up that night.*

17

Linda got out of the car and stared up at the windows of Anna's apartment. They were dark. Her fear returned; the phone had been busy. Linda called Zeba again. Zeba picked up right away as if she had been waiting by the phone. Linda talked in a hurry, stumbling over her words.

"It's me. Were you talking to Anna just now?"

"No."

"Are you sure?"

"Of course I'm sure! Have you been trying to call? I was explaining to my brother why I'm not going to lend him any money. He's a spendthrift. I have four thousand kronor in the bank and that's the full extent of my fortune. He wants to borrow the whole thing to buy a share in a trucking venture involving cargo transports to Bulgaria. . . ."

"To hell with him," Linda interrupted. "Anna's disappeared. She's never stood me up before."

"Well, sometime has to be the first."

"That's what my dad says too, but I think something's happened. Anna's been away for three days."

"Maybe she's in Lund."

"No. It doesn't even matter where she is. It's just not like her to be gone like this. Has she ever done this to you—not shown up on time or not been at home when she had invited you over?"

Zeba thought it over.

"Actually, no."

"See?"

"Why are you so worked up over this?"

Linda almost told her about the severed head and hands. But that would mean breaking her professional code of secrecy.

"I don't know. You're right: I'm worked up over nothing."

"Come over."

"I don't have time."

"I think you're going crazy with all this free time on your hands. But I have something for you, a mystery that needs solving."

"What is it?"

"A door I can't get to open."

"Can't do it, sorry. Call the property manager."

"You need to slow down."

"I will. See you."

Linda rang the doorbell in the hopes that the windows were dark because Anna was asleep. But the apartment was still empty and the bed untouched. Linda looked at the phone. The receiver was in place and the message light wasn't blinking. She sat down and thought about everything that had happened over the past couple of days. Every time an image of the severed head flashed through her mind she felt sick. Or were the hands even worse? What kind of a maniac would cut a person's hands off? Cutting a person's head off was a way to kill them. But their hands? She wondered if the forensic team would be able to determine if Birgitta Medberg's hands had been cut off before or after she died. And where was the rest of the body? Suddenly her nausea got the better of her. She only just made it to the toilet before she threw up. Afterward she lay down on the bathroom floor. A little yellow rubber ducky was stuck under the bathtub. Linda stretched out her hand to touch it, remembering when Anna had gotten the duck.

It was a long time ago. They had been maybe twelve or thirteen. She couldn't remember whose idea it was, but between them they had decided to go to Copenhagen together. It was spring and both of them were bored and restless at school. They covered for each other when one of them cut class, which happened more and more frequently. Mona had given her permission, but her dad wouldn't hear of it. She heard him describe Copenhagen as a den of sin and iniquity, a beast waiting to consume two very young girls who knew nothing about life. In the end Anna and Linda had gone anyway. Linda knew there would be trouble waiting for her when she returned, so, as a kind of advance revenge, she lifted a hundred kronor from her dad's wallet before she left. They took the train to Malmö and the ferry to Copenhagen. To Linda it seemed like their first serious excursion into the adult world.

It had been breezy but sunny, a happy, giggly day. Anna won the rubber ducky at an amusement stand at the Tivoli, and at first all of their experiences were transparent, joyous ones. They had their freedom, their adventure. Invisible walls crumbled around them wherever they went. Then the image darkened. Something happened that day that was the first real blow to their friendship. *We were sitting on a green bench,* Linda remembered. *Anna had been borrowing money from me all day because she was broke. She had to go to the bathroom and asked me to hold her purse. Somewhere in the background a Tivoli orchestra was playing. The trumpet was out of tune.*

Linda was thinking of all this while she lay on the bathroom floor. The warmth from the heating system installed under the tile felt good against her back.

It was a green bench and a black bag. After all these years she couldn't say what had made her open the purse. There had been two crisp hundred-kronor notes inside, not even crumpled or hidden inside a secret compartment. She had stared at the money and felt a stab of betrayal. She closed the purse and decided she wouldn't say anything, but when Anna came back and asked if Linda would buy her a soda, something exploded inside her. They stood there shouting at each other. Linda had forgotten what Anna had said in her defense, but they had gone their separate ways and had sat apart on the return trip to Malmö. It took them a long time to start speaking to each other again. They never talked about what had happened in Copenhagen, but eventually they had managed to resume their friendship.

Linda sat up. *There are lies at the heart of this,* she thought. *I'm sure Henrietta concealed something from me when I was there, and I know Anna is capable of lying. I discovered that in Copenhagen and I've found her out on later occasions as well. But with her at least I know her so well that I can tell when she's telling the truth. The story she told me about seeing her father—or a doppelgänger—in Malmö is true. But what's behind all this? What didn't she tell me? Sometimes the part that's left out is the biggest part of the lie.*

Her cell phone rang. She knew it was her father. She got to her feet to steel herself in case he was still angry, but the tone of his voice only told her that he was tense and tired. Her father had more voices than other people, it seemed to her.

"Where are you?" he asked.

"In Anna's apartment."

He was silent. She could hear that he was still out in the forest. There were voices of people walking past, the scrape of walkie-talkies, and a dog barking sharply.

"What are you doing there?" he asked after a while.

"I'm more afraid now than I was before."

To her surprise he said:

"I know. That's why I'm calling. I'm on my way over. I need to hear about this in more detail. There's no reason for you to worry, of course, but I'm taking this matter seriously now."

"How could I not worry? It's not natural for her to be gone like this, that's what I've been trying to tell you all along. If you don't understand that, then you can't possibly know why I'm afraid. Also, her phone line was busy, but then when I got here she wasn't in. Someone was here, I'm sure of it."

"I'll get the full report when I get there. What's the address?"

Linda gave it to him.

"How is it going?" she asked.

"I've never seen anything like this."

"Have you found the body?"

"Not yet. We haven't found anything, least of all clues to what actually happened here. I'll honk when I arrive."

Linda bent over the bathroom sink and rinsed her mouth out. In order to freshen her breath she brushed her teeth with one of Anna's toothbrushes. She was about to leave the bathroom when she impulsively opened the bathroom cabinet. She saw something that surprised her. *This is just like leaving the journal behind,* she thought.

From time to time Anna developed eczema on her throat. She had talked about it only a few weeks earlier when they were all over at Zeba's place, talking about their dream vacations. Anna had said that the first thing she would pack was the prescription-strength cream that kept her eczema under control. Linda remembered her saying she only bought this cream one tube at a time in order to keep it as fresh as possible. And yet here it was, sitting among the other bottles and toothbrushes on the shelf. Anna had a thing about toothbrushes. Linda counted nineteen brushes in the cabinet, eleven of which had never been used. She looked at the cream again. *Anna would never have left this behind,* Linda thought. *Not willingly. Neither this cream nor her diary.* She closed the bathroom cabinet and left the bathroom. What could have happened? There were no signs that Anna had been removed by force, at least not from the apartment itself. Perhaps something had happened on the street. She could have been knocked over or forced into a car.

Linda stood by the window and waited for her father. She felt tired and cheated. Her time at the academy had in no way prepared her for what she had been through this day. She could never have imagined that she could one day find herself looking at a severed gray-haired female head and a pair of clasped hands cut off at the wrists.

Not simply clasped, she thought. *Hands knit together in prayer before they were cut.* She shook her head. What happened in those last moments, in the dramatic pause while the axe was lifted above those hands? What had Birgitta Medberg seen? Had she looked into another person's eyes and understood what was about to happen? Or had she been spared that dreadful knowledge? Linda stared out at a streetlamp swaying in the wind. She sensed what must have happened: hands clasped together pleading for mercy. The executioner denies the plea. *She must have known,* Linda thought. *She knew what was coming and she pleaded for her life.*

Headlights suddenly lit up the side of the building. Her father honked his horn once, parked the car, then got out and looked around for the right entryway until he saw Linda in the window gesturing to him. She threw the keys down to the street and heard him come up the stairs. *He's going to wake up all the neighbors,* she thought. *I have a father who thunders his way through life like an infantry battalion.* He was sweaty and tired, his clothes soaked through.

"Is there anything to eat?"

"I think so."

"And a towel?"

"The bathroom is over there. There are towels on the bottom shelf."

When he came back to the kitchen he had removed all his clothes except his undershirt and briefs. The wet clothes were hanging on the hot pipes in the bathroom. Linda had set the table with all the food she could find in the refrigerator. She knew he wanted to eat in peace. When she was growing up it had been forbidden to talk or make noise around the table at breakfast. His silence had driven Mona up the wall—she always waited to have her breakfast until after he had left for work. But Linda had often sat there sharing the silence with him. Sometimes he lowered the paper, usually the *Ystad Allehanda,* and winked at her. Silence at breakfast was sacred.

"I should never have brought you along," he said suddenly, a sandwich halfway to his mouth. "There's no excuse for it. You should never have had to see what was in that hut."

"How is it going?"

"We have no clues, no explanations for what happened."

"But what about the rest of the body?"

"There's no sign of it. The dogs can't pick up a scent. We know Birgitta Medberg was mapping trails in that part of the forest, so it seems reasonable to assume she stumbled onto the hut by accident. But who was hiding out there? Why this brutal murder, why mutilate the body and dispose of it in this way?"

Wallander finished the sandwich, made a new one and left it half-eaten.

"So tell me. Anna Westin, this friend of yours, what does she do? She's a student—but of what exactly?"

"Medicine. You know that."

"I never rely on my memory. You had arranged to meet her, you said. Was that here?"

"Yes."

"And she wasn't home when you came over?"

"No."

"Is there any possibility of a misunderstanding?"

"No."

"Tell me the part about her father again. He's been gone for twenty-four years and has never once communicated with her in any way. And then she's in a hotel and sees him through a window?"

Linda told him everything in as much detail as she could muster. He was quiet when she finished.

"We have one person who turns up after being missing for years," he said finally. "And the following day the person who saw that person goes missing herself. One appears, the other disappears."

He shook his head. Linda told him about the journal and the neck cream, and about her visit to Henrietta. He listened attentively to everything.

"What makes you think she was lying?"

"If Anna thought she saw her father on a regular basis she would have told me long before now."

"How can you be so sure?"

"I know her."

"People change. You can never know everything about them, even friends."

"Is that true for me too?"

"For me, for you, your mother, Anna, everyone. Then, of course, there are people who are totally incomprehensible. My father was an outstanding example of the latter."

"I knew him."

"You think you did."

"Just because the two of you didn't get along doesn't mean I felt the same way. And we were talking about Anna."

"I heard you never reported it."

"I followed your advice."

"For once."

"Oh shit, give me a break."

"Show me the journal."

Linda went to get it, and opened it to the page where Anna had written about the letter from Birgitta Medberg.

"Did she ever mention her name to you?" Wallander asked.

"Not that I can remember."

"Did you ask her mother if she had any connection to Medberg?"

"I saw Henrietta before I knew about this."

Wallander went to the bathroom to get his notepad from his jacket.

"I'll have someone talk to her again tomorrow."

"I can do it."

Wallander sat down.

"No," he said sternly. "You can't do it. You're not a police officer yet. I'll get Svartman or someone else to do it. You aren't going to be doing any more investigating on your own."

"Do you always have to sound so pissed-off?"

"I'm not pissed-off, I'm tired. And worried. I don't know why what happened in that hut happened, only that it was horrifying. And I don't know if it marks an end or a beginning."

He looked at his watch and got up again.

"I have to go back there," he said.

Then he stopped in the middle of the kitchen, indecisively.

"I have trouble believing it was just a coincidence," he said. "That Medberg simply had the misfortune to run into the wicked witch who lives in the gingerbread house. I can't see that you'd get murdered for knocking on the wrong door. There are no monsters in Swedish forests. Not even trolls. She should have stuck with but-terflies."

Wallander walked back to the bathroom and put his clothes back on. Linda tagged along. What was it he had said? The door to the bathroom was slightly ajar.

"What was it you said?"

"No monsters live in Swedish forests."

"After that."

"I didn't."

"You did. After the monsters and trolls and all that. The last thing?"

"She should have stuck to butterflies and not started mapping ancient trails."

"What butterflies?"

"Höglund talked to the daughter—someone had to inform the

relatives. The daughter said Medberg had had a large butterfly collection. She sold it a few years ago to help Vanya and her kids buy an apartment. Vanya always felt guilty about it because she thought her mother missed the butterflies. People often have these kinds of reactions when someone dies. I was the same way when Dad died. I could start blubbering at the thought of how he used to wear mismatched socks."

Linda held her breath. He noticed something was up.

"What is it?"

"Come with me."

They walked out into the living room. Linda turned on a lamp and pointed to the wall.

"I've tried to keep an eye out for things that are different, I've already told you that. But I forgot to say that something was missing."

"What?"

"A butterfly case. You know, a butterfly in a frame. It disappeared the day after Anna went missing."

Wallander frowned.

"Are you sure?"

"Yes," she said. "And the butterfly was blue."

18

It seemed to Linda that it took a blue butterfly to convince her father to take her seriously. She wasn't just a kid anymore, not just an officer-in-training with potential, but a full-fledged adult with judgment and keen powers of observation.

She was sure of herself. The butterfly had been removed at the same time or shortly after Anna's disappearance. That settled it. Wallander called his team in the field and asked Höglund to come to the apartment. He asked how things were going at the crime scene. Linda heard Nyberg's irritated voice in the background, then Martinsson, who was sneezing violently, and finally Lisa Holgersson, the chief of police. Wallander put the phone down.

"I want Ann-Britt to be here," he said. "I'm so tired I'm not sure I can trust my own judgment any more. Are you sure you've told me all the relevant facts?"

"I think so."

Wallander shook his head.

"It seems too much of a coincidence."

"A few days ago you said one always has to be prepared for the unexpected."

"I say a lot of crap," he said thoughtfully. "Is there any coffee in the house?"

The water had just boiled when Höglund honked her horn down on the street.

"She drives too fast," Wallander said. "She has two young children—what is she thinking? Throw her the keys, will you?"

Höglund caught the keys in one hand and walked briskly up the stairs. Linda noted she had a hole in her sock but her face was made up—heavily made up. When did she have time to do that? Did she sleep with her makeup on?

"Would you like some coffee?"

"Please."

Linda thought her father would be the one to talk, but when she came in with the coffee cup and put it on the table in front of Höglund, Wallander nodded at her to begin.

"It's better for her to hear it from the horse's mouth," he said. "Don't leave out any details, you can count on Inspector Höglund to be a good listener."

Linda picked up her story with both hands and unfolded it as carefully as she was able, all in the right order. Then she showed Höglund the journal with the page that mentioned Birgitta Medberg. Wallander only broke in when she started talking about the butterfly. Then he took over, changing her story to something that would perhaps form the basis of an investigative narrative. He got up off the sofa and tapped the wall where the butterfly had been hanging.

"This is where the lines intersect," he said. "Two points, or perhaps three. Birgitta Medberg's name is in Anna's journal and they exchange at least one letter, although we haven't found it. Butterflies figure in both of their lives, although we don't know yet what the significance of this is. And then there is the most important similarity: they're both missing."

Someone outside started shouting in Polish or Russian, most likely a drunk.

"It's certainly a strange coincidence," Höglund said. "Who knows Anna best?"

"I don't know."

"Does she have a boyfriend?"

"Not right now."

"But she's had one?"

"Doesn't everyone? I think probably her mother knows her best."

Höglund yawned and ruffled her hair.

"What about all this business with her father? Why did he disappear? Had he done something?"

"Anna's mother seems to think he was running away."

"From what?"

"Responsibility."

"And now he's back and Anna disappears. And Medberg is murdered."

"No," Wallander broke in. " 'Murdered' isn't an adequate description of it. She was slaughtered, butchered. Hands clasped as in prayer, head severed, torso and limbs missing. Martinsson has tracked down the Tademans, by the way. Mr. Tademan was extremely intoxicated, according to Martinsson, which is interesting. Anita Tademan—whom Linda and I met—seems to have been much easier to talk to. They haven't seen any unusual persons in the area, no one knew about the hideout in the forest. She called someone she knows who often hunts around there, but he hadn't seen any hut or even the ravine, strangely enough. Whoever used the place knew how to keep a low profile while remaining in relatively close proximity to people. I sense this is an important point, that he was invisible but close by."

"Close to what, or whom?"

"We don't know."

"We'll have to start with the mother," Höglund said. "Should we call her right now or wait until morning?"

"Wait until morning," Wallander said after hesitating. "We have our hands full right now as it is."

Linda felt her face flush.

"What if something happens to Anna in the meantime?"

"What if her mother forgets to tell us something important because we got her out of bed in the middle of the night? We'll scare her half to death."

He walked to the door.

"That's how it's going to be. Go home and get some sleep. But you'll be coming with us to see Anna's mother tomorrow morning."

Höglund and Wallander put on their boots and rain gear and left. Linda watched them from the window. The wind was blowing harder, coming in strong gusts from the east and south. She washed the cups and thought about the fact that she needed to sleep. But how was she supposed to do that? Anna was gone, Henrietta had lied, Birgitta Medberg's name was inscribed in the journal. Linda started to look through the apartment again. Why couldn't she find Medberg's letter?

She searched more energetically this time, pulling bookshelves from the wall and backings from paintings to make sure nothing was hidden inside them. She continued with this until the doorbell rang. Linda stopped. It was after one o'clock in the morning. Who rang a doorbell in the middle of the night? She opened the door and found a man outside in thick glasses, a brown robe, and worn pink slippers on his feet. He said his name was August Brogren.

"There's a great deal of noise coming from this apartment," he said angrily. "Would you be so kind as to keep it down, Miss Westin?"

"I'm sorry," Linda said. "I'll be quiet from now on."

August Brogren took a step closer.

"You don't sound like Miss Westin," he said. "You aren't Miss Westin at all, in fact. Who are you?"

"A friend."

"When one has bad eyesight one learns to differentiate people's voices," Brogren explained sternly. "Miss Westin has a gentle voice, but yours is hard and rasping. It is like the difference between soft white bread and hardtack."

Brogren fumbled his way back to the handrail of the staircase and started walking back down. Linda thought about Anna's voice and understood Brogren's description. She closed the door and got ready to leave. Suddenly she was close to tears. *Anna is dead,* she thought. But then she shook her head. She didn't want to believe that, didn't want to imagine a world without Anna. She put the car keys on the kitchen table, locked the door, and walked home through the deserted streets. When she got home she wrapped herself up in a blanket and curled up on her bed.

Linda woke up with a start. The hands on the alarm clock glowed in the dark and showed a quarter to three. She had hardly been asleep for more than an hour. What had caused her to wake up? She had dreamed something, sensed a danger approaching from afar like an invisible bird diving soundlessly toward her head. A bird with a beak as sharp as a razor. The bird had woken her up.

Even though she had slept so briefly, she felt clearheaded. She thought about the investigators still out at the crime scene, people moving back and forth in the strong spotlights, insects swarming in the light beams and burning themselves on the bulbs. It seemed to her that she had woken up because she didn't have time to sleep. Was Anna calling out to her? She listened, but the voice was gone. Had it been there in her dreams? She looked at the time. It was now three minutes to three. *Anna called out to me,* she thought again. And she knew what she was going to do. She put on her shoes, took her coat, and ran down the stairs.

The car keys were still lying on Anna's kitchen table. When she drove out of town it was twenty minutes past three. She swung north and ended up parking on a small overgrown road that lay out of sight of Henrietta's house. Stepping out of the car, she listened for any noise, then gently closed the car door. It was chilly. She pulled her coat tightly around her body and chastised herself for not having brought a flashlight.

She started walking along the small road, taking care not to trip. She didn't know exactly what she was planning to do, but Anna had called out to her and she felt compelled to respond. She followed the dirt road until she came to the path leading to the back of Henrietta's house. Three windows were lit. *The living room,* she thought. *Henrietta is still up—although she could have gone to bed and left the lights on.*

Linda walked toward the light, giving a wide berth to a rusty harrow and getting closer to the garden. She stopped and listened. Was Henrietta in the middle of composing? She made it to the fence and climbed over it. *The dog,* she thought. *Henrietta's dog. What am I going to do if it starts barking? And what am I doing out here in the first place? Dad, Höglund, and I are coming back here in a couple of hours. What is it I think I can find out on my own now?* But it wasn't really about that. It was about waking up from a nightmare that seemed like a cry for help from a friend.

She approached the lighted windows, then stopped short. Voices.

At first she couldn't determine where they were coming from, but then she saw that one of the windows was pushed open. Anna's neighbor had said that her voice was gentle. But this wasn't Anna's voice, it was Henrietta's. Henrietta and a man. Linda listened, trying to will her ears to send out invisible antennae. She walked even closer and was now able to see through the glass. Henrietta sat in profile, the man was on the sofa with his back to the window. Linda couldn't hear what the man was saying. Henrietta was talking about a composition, something about twelve violins and a lone cello, something about a last communion and apostolic music. Linda didn't understand what she was talking about. She tried to be absolutely quiet. The dog was in there somewhere. She tried to figure out who Henrietta was talking to, and why they were talking in the middle of the night.

Suddenly, very slowly, Henrietta turned her head and looked straight at the window. Linda jumped. It seemed like Henrietta was looking directly into her eyes. *She can't have seen me,* Linda thought. *It's impossible*. But there was something about the woman's gaze that frightened her. She turned and ran, accidentally stepping on the edge of the water pump, causing a clang from within the pump structure. The dog started to bark.

Linda ran back the way she had come. She tripped and fell, got up and stumbled on. She heard a door open somewhere behind her as she threw herself over the fence and ran down the path, trying to make her way back to the car. At some point she took a wrong turn. She didn't know where she was. She stopped, gasping for air, and listened. Henrietta had not set the dog loose. It would have found her by now. She listened again. There was no one there, but she was still so scared she was shaking. After a while she cautiously started making her way back to the path, but she couldn't see where she was going because it was so dark. The darkness frightened her, making shadows into trees and trees into shadows. She stumbled and fell.

When she stood up she felt a searing pain in her left leg. She felt as if she had been stabbed with a knife. She screamed and tried to get away from the pain, but she couldn't move. It was as if an animal had sunk its teeth into her, except that this animal didn't breathe or make any noise. Linda groped down her leg until her hand hit something cold and metallic connected to a chain. Then she understood. She was caught in a hunter's trap.

Her hand was wet with blood. She continued to cry out, but no one heard her, no one came.

19

Linda tried to free herself from the trap. She didn't like the idea of calling her father, but the trap was impossible to budge. She took out her cell phone and dialed his number. She explained where she was and that she needed help.

"What's happened?"

"I'm caught in a trap."

"What on earth are you talking about?"

"I have a steel trap around my leg."

"I'm on my way."

Linda waited, shivering. It felt like an eternity before she saw the headlights from a car in the distance. Linda called out. The front door opened and the dog barked. She called and called. They walked over in the dark, a flashlight lighting their way. It was her father, Henrietta, and the dog. There was a third person with them but he hung back.

"You're caught in an old fox trap. Who is responsible for putting this here?"

"Not me," said Henrietta. "It must be the man who owns the land around here."

"We'll have a word with him." Wallander forced the trap open.

"We'd better get you to the hospital," he said.

Linda tried to put some weight on the foot. It hurt, but she was able to steady herself with it. The man in the shadows now came closer.

"This is a colleague you haven't met yet," Wallander said. "Stefan Lindman. He started with us a couple of weeks ago."

Linda looked at him. His face was partly lit by the flashlight and she liked what she saw.

"What are you doing here?" Henrietta asked.

"I can explain," Lindman said.

He spoke with some kind of dialect. But which was it? She asked her father later when they were driving back to Ystad.

"He's from western Götaland," Wallander said. "A strange language. They have trouble commanding respect, as do people from eastern Götaland and the island of Gotland. The ones who command the most respect are northerners, apparently. I don't know why."

"How is he going to account for me being out there tonight?"

"He'll think of something. But maybe you can tell me what you thought you were doing."

"I had a dream about Anna."

"What sort of dream?"

"She called out to me. I woke up and drove out here. I didn't know what I was planning to do. I saw Henrietta inside talking to a man. Then she looked over in my direction and I ran and then I got caught in that trap."

"Now at least I know you're not sneaking out for secret assignations."

"Don't you understand that this is serious?" she screamed. "Anna is missing!"

"Of course I take you seriously. I take her disappearance seriously. I take my whole life and yours seriously. The butterfly was the clincher."

"What are you doing about it?"

"Everything that can and should be done. We're turning every stone, chasing every lead. And now we're not going to discuss this further until we've had your leg checked out at the hospital."

It was an hour before anyone could deal with her. Wallander dozed in an uncomfortable chair. And the process of cleaning the wound and bandaging it seemed to take forever. Just as they were finally leaving, Stefan Lindman walked in. Linda now saw he had closely cropped hair and blue eyes.

"I said you had terrible night vision," he said cheerfully. "It doesn't make a lot of sense but it will have to suffice as an explanation for what you were doing wandering around out there."

"I saw a man in the house with her," Linda said.

"Henrietta Westin told me she had a visit from a man who wants her to set music to some dramatic verse. It didn't sound suspicious."

Linda put her jacket on against the morning cold. She regretted having yelled at her father in the car. It was a sign of weakness. *Never scream, always keep your cool.* But she had done something stupid and had needed to turn the spotlight on someone else's shortcomings. She also felt a huge wave of relief. Anna's disappearance was no longer a figment of her imagination. A blue butterfly had made all the difference. The price was a painful ache in her leg.

"Stefan will take you home. I have to get back to the station."

Linda went into the ladies' room and combed her hair. Lindman was waiting for her in the corridor. He was wearing a black leather jacket and was sloppily shaven on one side of his face, which Linda didn't like. She chose to walk on his good side.

"How does it feel?"

"What do you think?"

"It must hurt. I know something about that."

"What do you mean?"

"Pain."

"Have you ever had your leg caught in a bear trap?"

"It was a fox trap. But no, I haven't."

"Then you don't know how it feels."

He held the door open for her. She was still irritated by his unshaven cheek and didn't say anything else. They came out into a parking lot at the back of the hospital. It was broad daylight. He pointed to a rusty Ford. As he was unlocking the door, an ambulance driver came over and demanded to know what he meant by blocking the emergency entrance.

"I came to pick up a wounded police officer," Lindman said, nodding in Linda's direction.

The ambulance driver accepted this and left. Linda maneuvered herself into the passenger side.

"Your dad said you live on Mariagatan. Where is that?"

Linda explained, and wondered silently about the strong smell in the car.

"It's paint," Lindman said. "I'm fixing up a house out in Knickarp."

They turned onto Mariagatan and Linda pointed out her doorway. He got out and opened the car door for her.

"It was nice to meet you," he said. "And the reason I know what it's like to be in pain is that I've had cancer. Steel trap or a tumor—it's all the same."

Linda watched his car drive off. She had forgotten his last name.

She let herself into the apartment and felt fatigue set in. She was about to collapse onto the sofa when the phone rang.

It was her dad.

"I heard you made it home."

"What was the name of the guy who drove me home?"

"Stefan."

"No—the last name."

"Lindman. He's from Borås, I think. Or else it was Skövde. It's time you got some rest."

"I want to know what Henrietta said to you."

"I don't have time to go into that right now."

"You have to. Just give me the highlights."

"Wait a minute."

His voice broke off. Linda sensed he was at the station, but on his way out. She heard doors closing, phones ringing, and then the sound of an engine starting up.

He came back on the line, his voice tense.

"Are you there?"

"I'm here."

"OK, I'll make this quick. Henrietta said she didn't know where Anna was. She hadn't heard from her recently. Nothing to suggest that Anna is depressed. She had apparently not said anything about seeing her father. On the other hand, Henrietta claims that this happened all the time when Anna was growing up. So it's the mother's word against yours. She couldn't give us any leads, nor did she know anything about Medberg. So as you see it wasn't very productive."

"Did you notice that she was lying?"

"How would I have noticed that?"

"You always say all you have to do is breathe on someone to know if they're telling the truth or not."

"I didn't get the impression she was lying."

"She's lying."

"I have to go now. But Lindman—the one who gave you the ride—is working on the connection between Medberg and Anna. We've sent out missing persons reports on her, by the way. That's all we can do for the moment."

He hung up. Linda didn't feel like being alone, so she called Zeba. She was in luck: Zeba's son was at her cousin Titchka's house and Zeba had nothing lined up. She agreed to come over.

"Buy some breakfast on the way," Linda said. "I'm hungry. The Chinese restaurant by the main square, for example. I know it's out of your way but I'll make it up to you the next time you find yourself stuck in a steel trap."

Linda told Zeba what had happened. Zeba had heard the news on the radio about the severed head that had been found, but she still had trouble believing that anything bad might have happened to Anna.

"If I were a crook I'd think twice before picking on Anna. Don't you know she did martial arts? I can't remember which kind, but I think it's one where everything is allowed—short of actually killing someone, of course. No one messes with Anna and gets away with it."

Linda regretted having brought it up in the first place. Zeba stayed for another hour before it was time for her to pick up her son.

Linda woke up when the doorbell rang. At first she was going to ignore it, but she changed her mind and limped out into the hallway. Stefan Lindman was standing outside the door.

"I'm sorry if I woke you up."

"I wasn't sleeping."

Then she looked at herself in the hall mirror. Her hair was standing on end.

"Actually I *was* sleeping," she said. "I don't know why I said that. My leg hurts."

"I need the keys to Anna Westin's apartment," he said. "I heard you tell your father you had a spare set of keys."

"I'll come along."

He seemed surprised by this.

"I thought you were in pain."

"I thought that too. What are you going to do over there?"

"Try to create a picture for myself."

"If it's a picture of Anna, then I'm the person you should be talking to."

"I'd like to have a look by myself first. Then we can talk."

Linda pointed to a set of keys on a table. The keyring had a profile of an Egyptian pharaoh.

Linda hesitated.

"What was that about you having cancer?"

"I had cancer of the tongue if you can believe it. Things looked bad for a while, but I survived and there's been no recurrence."

He looked her in the eye for the first time.

"I still have my tongue, of course; I wouldn't be able to speak without it. But my hair has never recovered."

He tapped his neck with a finger.

"Soon it'll all be gone."

He walked down the stairs and Linda returned to bed.

Cancer of the tongue. She shuddered at the thought. Her fear of death came and went, though right now her life force was strong. But she had never forgotten what had gone through her mind while she was balancing on the edge of the bridge. Life wasn't just something that took care of itself. There were big black holes you could fall into with long sharp spikes at the bottom, monstrous traps.

She turned over on her side and tried to sleep. Right now she didn't have the energy to think about black holes. Then she was startled out of her half-awake state. It was something to do with Lindman. She sat up. She had finally caught hold of the thought that had been bugging her. She dialed a number on her cell phone. Busy. On the third try her father finally picked up.

"It's me."

"How do you feel?"

"Better. There was something I wanted to ask about the man who was at Henrietta's house last night. The one who was said to be commissioning a composition. Did she say what he looked like?"

"Why would I have asked her that? She only gave me his name. I made a note of the address. Why?"

"Do me a favor. Call her and ask about his hair."

"Why would I do that?"

"Because that's what I saw."

"I will, but I really don't have the time for this. We're drowning in rain over here."

"Will you call back?"

"If I get ahold of her."

He called her back nineteen minutes later.

"Peter Stigström—the man who wants Henrietta to set his verse to music—has shoulder-length dark hair with a few gray streaks. Will that do?"

"That will do just fine."

"Are you going to explain yourself now or when I get home?"

"That depends on when you were planning to come home."

"Pretty soon. I have to get out of these clothes."

"Do you want something to eat?"

"No, we've been taken care of, in fact. There are some enterprising Kosovo immigrants out here who make a living out of putting up food stands around crime scenes and fires. I have no idea how they hear about our work, but there's probably a leak at the station who gets a commission. I'll be home in an hour."

When the conversation was over, Linda sat staring down at the phone for a few minutes. The man she had seen through the window, the back of the head that had been turned toward her, had not had shoulder-length dark hair with a few gray streaks. His hair had been short and neatly trimmed.

20

Wallander came bounding in, his clothes soaked, his boots covered in mud, but with the happy news that the weather was about to clear up. Nyberg had called the air-control tower at Sturup, he said, and had received the report that the next forty-eight hours would be free of rain. Wallander changed his clothes, declined Linda's offers of food, and fixed himself an omelet.

Linda waited for the right moment to tell him about the conflicting descriptions of Henrietta's visitor. She didn't know exactly why she was waiting. Was it a lingering childhood fear of his temper? She didn't know, she just waited. And then, when he pushed away his plate and she plopped into the chair across from him and was about to launch into her story, he started talking.

"I've been thinking about your grandfather," he said.

"What about?"

"What he was like, what he wasn't like. I think you and I knew him in different ways. That's as it should be. I was always looking for bits of myself in him, worried about what I would find. I've grown more and more like him the older I get. If I live as long as he did maybe I'll find myself a ramshackle, leaky house and start painting pictures of wood grouse and sunsets."

"It'll never happen."

"Don't be too sure."

Linda broke in at this point and told him about the man she had seen whose close-cropped head didn't match Henrietta's description. He listened attentively, and when she stopped he didn't ask her if she was sure of what she had seen. He reached for the phone and dialed a number from memory—first incorrectly, then getting it right. Lindman picked up. Wallander told him succinctly that in light of what Linda had observed they had to make another visit to Henrietta Westin.

"We have no time for lies," he said. "No lies, half-truths, or incomplete answers."

Then he put the phone down and looked at her.

"This is unorthodox at best," he said. "Not even necessary, strictly speaking, but I'm still going to ask you to come along. If you feel up to it, that is."

Linda felt a surge of pleasure.

"I'll do it."

"How's the leg?'

"Fine."

She saw that he didn't believe her.

"Does Henrietta know why I was there last night?" she asked. "She can hardly have believed what Stefan told her."

"All we want to know is who was there with her last night. We have a witness; we don't have to tell her it's you."

They walked down to the street and waited for Lindman. The air-traffic controllers had been right; the weather was changing. Drier winds were blowing in from the south.

"When will it snow?" Linda asked.

He looked at her in amusement.

"Not for a while, I hope. Why do you ask?"

"I can't remember when it comes, even though I was born and raised here. I don't remember the snow."

Stefan Lindman pulled up in his car. Linda climbed into the back seat, her father sat in the front. His seat belt was caught on something and he had trouble getting it on.

They drove toward Malmö and Linda saw the sea shimmering to her left. *I don't want to die here,* she thought. The thought came out of nowhere. *I don't only want to exist. Not like Zeba. And not be a single mother like her, or thousands of others whose lives become one long damned struggle to pay the rent and the babysitters and getting someplace on time. I don't want to be like Dad, who can never find the right house and the right dog and the wife he needs.*

"What was that?" Wallander asked.

"Nothing."

"That's funny. It sounded like you were swearing."

"I didn't say anything."

"I have a strange daughter," Wallander said to Lindman. "She curses without even knowing it."

They turned onto the road that led to Henrietta's house. The memory of being caught in the steel trap made Linda's leg throb. She asked what would happen to the man who had set the trap.

"He went a little pale in the face when I told him he had snared a police cadet. I'm assuming he'll have to pay a hefty fine."

"I have a good friend in Östersund," Stefan Lindman said. "A policeman. Giuseppe Larsson is his name."

"He sounds Italian."

"No, he's from Östersund. But he has a connection of sorts with an Italian lounge singer."

"What's that supposed to mean?" Linda leaned forward between the seats. She had a sudden urge to touch Lindman's face.

"His mother had a dream that his father was not her husband but an Italian singer she had heard perform at an outdoor concert. It's not just us men who have these fantasies."

"I wonder if Mona has ever had the same thoughts," Wallander said. "In your case it would be a black dream father, Linda, since she worshipped Hosh White."

"Josh," Lindman said. "Not Hosh."

Linda wondered vaguely what it would have been like to have a black father.

"Anyway," Lindman said. "My friend has an old bear trap on the wall at his place. It looks like an instrument of torture from the Middle Ages. He always said that if a person ever got caught in one, the steel teeth would cut all the way through the bone. The animals that get trapped in them have been known to gnaw their own legs off in desperation."

Lindman stopped the car and they climbed out. The wind was gusty. They walked up to the house, in which several of the windows were lit up. When they entered the front yard, all three of them wondered why the dog hadn't started to bark. Lindman knocked on the door, but no one answered. Wallander peeked in through a window. Lindman felt the door. It was unlocked.

"We can say we thought we heard someone call 'Come in!'" he said tentatively.

They walked in. Linda's view was blocked by the broad backs of the two men. She tried standing on tiptoe to see past them but winced with pain.

"Anybody home?" Wallander called out.

"Doesn't look like it," Lindman said.

They proceeded through the house. It looked much as it had when Linda was there last. Papers, sheet music, newspapers, and coffee cups were scattered all over. But she recognized that this superficial impression of disarray only disguised a home comfortably arranged to meet Henrietta's every need.

"The door was unlocked," Lindman said, "and her dog is gone. She must be out on an evening walk. Let's give her a quarter of an hour. If we leave the door open she'll know someone's inside."

"She may call the police if she thinks the house is being burgled," Linda said.

"Burglars don't leave the front door wide open for everyone to see," her father said.

He sat down in the most comfortable armchair, folded his hands over his chest, and closed his eyes. Lindman put his boot in the front door to keep it open. Linda picked up a photo album that Henrietta had left lying on the piano. The first pictures were from the early 1970s. The colors were starting to fade. Anna sat on the ground surrounded by chickens and a yawning cat. Anna had told Linda about the commune outside Markaryd where she had spent the first years of her life. Henrietta was holding her in another picture from that time, in baggy clothes, clogs, and a Palestinian shawl around her neck. *Who is holding the camera?* Linda wondered. *Probably Eric Westin, the man who was about to disappear without a trace.*

Lindman walked over to her and she pointed to the pictures, explaining what she knew about them: the commune, the green wave, the sandal maker who vanished into thin air.

"It sounds like something out of a story," he said. "Like *A*

Thousand and One Nights. I mean the part about the Sandal Maker Who Vanished into Thin Air."

They kept turning the pages.

"Is there a picture of him?"

"I've seen a few at Anna's place, but that was a long time ago. I have no idea where they would be."

Pictures of life in the commune gave way to images of an Ystad apartment. Gray concrete, a wintry playground. Anna was a few years older.

"By this time he had been gone for several years," Linda said. "The person taking the pictures is closer to Anna than before. Pictures in the commune are always taken from a greater distance."

"Her father took those pictures and now Henrietta is the one taking them. Is that what you mean?"

"Yes."

They flipped through to the end of the album, but there was no picture of Westin. One of the last pictures was of Anna's high school graduation. Zeba was included at the edge of the frame. Linda had been there too, but she wasn't shown.

Linda was about to turn the page when the lights flickered and went out. The house was plunged into darkness and Wallander woke up with a start. They heard a dog barking outside. Linda sensed the presence of people out there in the night, people who did not intend to show their faces, but rather shied away from the light and were retreating even farther into the world of shadows.

21

He only felt secure in total darkness. He had never understood why there was always this talk of light in connection with mercy, eternity, images of God. Why couldn't a miracle take place in total darkness? Wasn't it harder for the Devil and his demons to find you in the shadows than on a bright expanse where white figures moved as slowly as froth on the crest of a wave? For him God had always manifested Himself as an enveloping, deeply comforting darkness.

He felt the same way now as he stood outside the house with the brightly lit windows. He saw people moving around inside. When all the lights suddenly went out and the last door of darkness was sealed he took it as a sign from God. *I am his servant in the darkness,* he thought. *No light escapes from here but I shall send out holy shadows to fill the void in the souls of the lost. I shall open their eyes and teach them the truth of the images that reside in the shadow-world.* He thought about the lines in John's second epistle: "For many deceivers are entered into the world, who confess not that Jesus Christ is come in the flesh. This is a deceiver and an antichrist." It was the holiest key to his understanding of God's Word.

After the terrible events in the jungles of Guyana he could recognize a false prophet: a man with smooth black hair and even white teeth, who surrounded himself with light. Jim Jones had feared the dark. He had cursed himself countless times for not seeing through the guise of this false prophet who would lead them so astray—to their deaths. All of them except himself. This had been the first task God had assigned him: to survive in order to tell the world about the false prophet. He was to preach about the kingdom of darkness, which would become the fifth gospel that he would write to complete the holy writings of the Bible. This too was fore-told at the end of John's letter: "Having many things to write unto you, I would not write with paper and ink: but I trust to come unto you, and speak face to face, that our joy may be complete."

This particular evening he had been thinking about all the years that had gone by since he was last here. Twenty-four years, a large part of his life. When he left he was still a young man. Now age had started to claim his body. He took care of himself, ate sensibly, kept himself in constant motion, but the process of growing old had be-gun. No one could escape it. *God lets us age in order for us to under-stand that we are completely in his hands. He gives us this remarkable life, but as a tragedy so that we will understand that only he has the power to grant us mercy.*

He stood in the darkness and thought back to all that had hap-pened. Everything had been what he had dreamed of until he fol-lowed Jim Jones to Guyana. Even though he missed those he had left behind, in the end he had been convinced by Jim that this loss was necessary to prepare him for the higher purpose God held in store for him. He had listened to Jim, and sometimes he had not thought about his wife and his child for weeks at a time. It was only after the massacre, when the whole community lay rotting on the fields, that they returned to his consciousness. But by then it was too late. The void created by the God that Jim had killed in him was so devastating that he could not think of anyone but himself.

He had retrieved the money and papers he had stored in Cara-cas, then took the bus to Colombia, to the city of Barranquilla. He remembered the long night he spent in the border station between Venezuela and Colombia, the city of Puerto Paez, where armed guards watched over the travelers like hawks. Somehow he had managed to convince these guards that he was John Clifton, as his documents stated, and he even managed to convince them that he didn't have any money left. He had slept with his head on the shoulder of an old Native woman who carried a small cage with two chickens on her lap. They had not exchanged any words, just a look, and she had seen his exhaustion and suffering and offered him her shoulder and wrinkled neck to rest his head. That night he dreamed about those he had left behind. He woke up drenched in sweat. The old woman was awake. She looked at him and he dropped back against her shoulder. When he woke up in the morning she was gone. He felt inside his shirt and touched the thick wad of dollar bills. It was still there. He wanted her back again, the old woman who had let him sleep. He wanted to lean his head against her shoulder and neck and stay there for the rest of his life.

From Barranquilla he took a plane to Mexico City. He washed off the worst of his filth in a public restroom. He bought a new shirt and a small Bible. It had been confusing to see the rushing crowds again, this life that he had left behind when he followed Jim. He walked past the newsstands and saw that what had happened had made the front-page headlines. Everyone was dead, he read. No one was thought to have survived. That meant they must think he was dead too. He existed but he had stopped living, since he was presumed to be one of the bloated bodies found in the jungle.

He still didn't have a clear plan. He had $3,000 left after paying for the fare to Mexico City, and if he was frugal he could get by on that for quite a while. But where should he go? Where could he find the first step back to God, out of this unbearable emptiness? He didn't know. He stayed in Mexico City, in a small hostel, and spent his days attending various churches. He deliberately avoided the large cathedrals as well as the neon-lit tabernacles run by greedy and power-hungry clergy. Instead he sought out the small congregations where the love and the passion were palpable, where the ministers were hard to tell apart from those who came to listen to their sermons. That was the way he had to find for himself. *Jim hid himself in the light,* he thought. *Now I want to find the God who can lead me to the holy darkness.*

One day he woke up with the overwhelming feeling that he had to leave. He took a bus going north the same day. To make the journey as cheap as possible, he took local buses. On certain stretches he hitched rides with truck drivers. He crossed the border into Texas at Laredo, where he checked into the cheapest motel he could find. He spent a week at the public library catching up on everything he could find that had been written about the catastrophe. To his consternation he found that there were former members of the People's

Temple who were accusing the FBI and CIA and the American government of fostering hostility toward Jim Jones and his movement, thereby inciting the mass suicide. He started to sweat. How could they defend the false prophet?

During the long sleepless nights it occurred to him that he should write about what had happened. He was the only living witness. He bought a notebook and started to write, but he was overcome with doubt. If he were going to tell the real story he would have to reveal his true identity: not John Clifton, as his documents claimed, but another man with another nationality and name altogether. Did he want that? He hesitated.

Then he read an interview with a woman named Mary-Sue Legrande in the *Houston Chronicle*. There was a photo of her: a woman in her forties with dark hair and a thin, almost pointed face. She talked about Jim Jones and claimed to know his secrets. In the interview she presented herself as a distant spiritual relative of Jim. She had known him at the time he had the series of visions that would later lead him to found his church, the People's Temple.

I know Jim's secrets, said Mary-Sue Legrande. But what were they? She didn't say. He stared at the photograph. Mary-Sue seemed to be looking right back at him. She was divorced with a grown son and now owned a small mail-order company in Cleveland. Her company sold something called "manuals for self-actualization."

He put the newspaper back on the shelf, nodding to the friendly librarian before walking out onto the street. It was an unusually mild day in December, shortly before Christmas. He stopped in the shade of a tree. *If Mary-Sue Legrande can tell me Jim Jones's secrets I will understand why I was taken in by him. Then I will never suffer this same weakness again.*

He stepped off the train in Cleveland on Christmas Eve. His trip had taken more than thirty hours. He found a cheap hotel close to the railway station and ate some dinner at a Chinese restaurant before he went back to his room. There was a green plastic Christmas tree with flashing lights in the lobby of the hotel. He lay down on the bed in the dark hotel room. *Right now I'm nothing more than the person who is registered for this hotel room,* he thought. *If I were to die now, or disappear, no one would miss me. They would find enough money in my sock to cover the costs of this room and a funeral—that is, unless someone stole the money and they had to dump me in a pauper's grave. Perhaps someone would discover that I was not John Clifton. But the case would probably be put on the back burner, like a piece of paper you save without knowing why. That would be the extent of it. Right now I'm nothing more than a guest in a hotel room, and I can't even remember the name of the hotel.*

Snow fell over the city of Cleveland on Christmas Day. He ate warm noodles, fried vegetables, and rice at the Chinese restaurant and then returned to lie motionless on his bed. The following day, December 26, the snowy weather had passed. A thin white powder had dusted the streets and sidewalks and it was three degrees below zero Celsius. There was no wind, and the water on Lake Erie was calm. He had located Mary-Sue Legrande with the help of a phone book and a map. She lived in a neighborhood in southwestern Cleveland. He thought it was God's intention that he meet her this day. He washed carefully, shaved, and put on the clothes he had bought in a secondhand store in Laredo. *What will she see when she opens her door and sees my face?* he thought. *A man who hasn't given up, a man who has suffered greatly.* He shook his head at his reflection in the mirror. *I don't inspire fear,* he thought. *Perhaps pity.*

He left his hotel and took a bus along the lakeshore. Mary-Sue Legrande lived on 1024 Madison, in a stone house partially hidden behind tall trees. He hesitated before he walked up the path and rang the doorbell. Mary-Sue Legrande looked exactly like her photograph in the *Houston Chronicle*, except that she was even thinner. She looked suspiciously at him, ready to slam the door in his face.

"I survived," he said. "Not everyone died in Guyana. I survived. I've come because I want to know Jim Jones's secrets. I want to know why he betrayed us."

She looked at him for a long time before answering. When she did, she didn't show any sign of surprise, or of any emotion whatsoever.

"I knew it," she said finally. "I knew someone would come."

She opened the door wide and stepped aside. He followed her in and stayed in her house for almost twenty years. It was with her help that he got to know the real Jim Jones, the man he had not been able to see through. Mary-Sue told him in her mild voice about Jim Jones's dark secret. He was not the messenger of God he had given himself out to be; he had taken God's place. Mary-Sue claimed that Jim Jones knew deep down that his vanity would one day be the destruction of everything he had built. But he had never been able to overcome his flaw and change course.

"Was he insane?" he had asked.

No, Mary-Sue insisted, far from it. Jim Jones had meant well; he had genuinely wanted to start a Christian awakening around the world. It was his vanity and pride that had prevented him from succeeding, that had turned his love into hate. But someone needed to take up where he left off, she told him. Someone who was strong enough to resist the pitfall of pride but could also be merciless when needed. The Christian awakening would only come to pass through bloodshed.

He stayed and helped her run the mail-order business she called God's Keys. She had written all the self-help manuals herself, with their blend of vague suggestions and inaccurate Bible quotations, and he soon realized that she understood Jim Jones so well because she was a kind of charlatan herself. But he stayed with her, since she let him. He needed time to plan what would become his life's mission. He was going to be the one to take over where Jim Jones had gone astray. He would sidestep the pitfalls of pride and vanity but never forget that the Christian rebirth would demand sacrifice and blood.

The mail-order company did well, especially with a product she called "The Aching Heart Package" priced at forty-nine dollars without tax and shipping. They started to get rich, and left the house on Madison for a large house in Middleburg Heights. Mary-Sue's son Richard returned after completing his studies in Minneapolis and settled in a house nearby. He was a loner but always friendly when they saw each other. It was as if he was relieved not to have to take on his mother's loneliness.

The end arrived quickly and unexpectedly. One day Mary-Sue came back from a trip into Cleveland and sat down across from him at his desk. He thought she had been running errands.

"I have cancer and I'm going to die," she announced. She said the words with a strange air of relief, as if telling the truth lifted a great burden from her shoulders.

She died on the eighty-seventh day after she came back from the doctor with the news. It was in the spring of 1999. Richard inherited all her assets, since she had never remarried. They drove out to Lake Erie for a walk the evening after the funeral. Richard wanted him to stay. He suggested that they continue running the mail-order business and share the profits. But he had already made up his mind. The void in him had been assuaged by living with Mary-Sue, but he had a mission to complete. His thinking and his plans had matured over the years. He didn't say any of this to Richard. He simply asked him for some money—only as much as Richard could comfortably part with. Then he would make his preparations. Richard asked no questions.

He left Cleveland on May 19, 2001, flying to Copenhagen via New York. He arrived in Helsingborg on the south coast of Sweden late on the evening of the twenty-first. He paused for a moment after stepping onto Swedish soil. It was as if he had left all his memories of Jim Jones behind at last.

22

Wallander was looking for the number to the power company when the electricity came back on. A few seconds later they all gave a start as Henrietta and the dog walked in. The dog jumped up on Wallander with its muddy paws. Henrietta ordered him to his basket and he obeyed. She then threw his leash aside with fury and turned to Linda.

"I don't know what gives you the right to enter my house when I'm not home. I don't like people sneaking around."

"If the power hadn't gone out we would have walked right out again," Wallander said. Linda could tell he was losing his temper.

"That's not an answer to my question," Henrietta said. "Why did you enter in the first place?"

"We just want to know where Anna is," Linda jumped in.

Henrietta didn't seem to listen to her. She walked around the room, looking carefully at her things.

"I hope you didn't touch anything,"

"We haven't touched anything," Wallander said. "We simply have a few questions to ask and then we'll be on our way."

Henrietta stopped and stared at him.

"What is it you need to know? Please tell me."

"Should we sit down?"

"No."

This is when he explodes, Linda thought and closed her eyes. But her father managed to control himself, perhaps because she was there.

"We need to be in touch with Anna. She's not in her apartment. Can you tell us where she is?"

"No, I can't."

"Is there anyone who would know?"

"Linda is one of her friends; have you asked her? Or maybe she doesn't have time to talk to you since she spends all her time spying on me."

This sent Wallander over the edge. He yelled so loudly even the dog sat up. *I know all about that voice,* Linda thought, *the yelling. God knows, it's one of the earliest memories I have.*

"You will answer my questions clearly and honestly. If you refuse to cooperate, we will bring you down to the station. We need to locate your daughter because she may have some information regarding Birgitta Medberg."

Wallander made a short pause before continuing.

"We also need to assure ourselves that nothing has happened to her."

"And what could possibly have happened to her? Anna studies in Lund. Linda knows that. Why don't you talk to her housemates?"

"We will. Is there anyplace else she could be, in your opinion?"

"No."

"Then we'll move on to the question of the man who was in your house last night."

"Peter Stigström?"

"Could you describe his hair for us?"

"I already have."

"We can call on Peter Stigström in person, but perhaps you could humor us."

"He has long hair, about shoulder-length. It's dark brown, with some gray streaks. Will that do?"

"Can you describe his neck?"

"Good grief—if you have shoulder-length hair it covers your neck. How would I know what it looks like?"

"You're sure of this?"

"Of course I'm sure."

"Then I'll thank you for your time."

He got up and left, slamming the door behind him. Lindman hurried out after him. Linda was confused. Why hadn't he confronted Henrietta with the fact that she had seen a man with short hair? As she got ready to leave, Henrietta blocked her path.

"I don't want anyone coming in here when I'm gone. I don't want to feel I have to lock the door every time I take the dog out. Is that clear?"

"Yes."

Henrietta turned her back to her.

"How is your leg?"

"Better, thanks."

"Maybe sometime you'll tell me what you were doing out there."

Linda left the house. Now she understood why Henrietta wasn't worried about Anna, even though a terrible murder had been committed that intersected in some way with her daughter's life. Henrietta wasn't worried because she knew very well where Anna was.

Lindman and Wallander were waiting in the car.

"What is it she does?" Lindman asked. "All that sheet music. Does she write popular stuff?"

"She composes the kind of music no one wants to hear," Wallander said.

He turned to Linda.

"Isn't that right?"

"Something like that."

A cell phone rang. They all clutched at their pockets. It was Wallander's phone. He listened to the caller and checked his watch.

"I'll be right there."

"We're heading out to Rannesholm," he said. "Apparently new information has come in about individuals sighted in the area over the past few days. We'll take you home first."

Linda asked him why he hadn't confronted Henrietta about the conflicting descriptions of Peter Stigström's hair.

"I decided to sit on it," he said. "Sometimes these things need time to ripen."

Then they talked about Henrietta's apparent lack of concern for her daughter's safety.

"She knows where Anna is," Wallander said. "There's no other way to account for it. Why she's lying is a mystery, though I expect we'll find the answer sooner or later if we keep trying. But it's not a top priority for us at this point."

They drove on in silence. Linda wanted to ask about the investigation out at Rannesholm but felt it would be wiser to wait. They stopped outside the apartment on Mariagatan.

"Could you turn off the engine for a minute?" Wallander turned around so he could see Linda. "Let me repeat what I just said. I'm satisfied that no harm has come to Anna. Her mother knows where she is and why she's staying away. We don't have the manpower to investigate this any further. But there is nothing to stop you from going to Lund and talking to her friends there. Just do me a favor and don't pretend to be a police officer."

Linda got out and waved them off. It was only as she was opening the front door that she thought of something that Anna had said. Was it the last time before she disappeared? Linda scoured her memory but couldn't put her finger on what it was.

The next day Linda got up early. The apartment was empty and her father had clearly not been home at all since the day before. She left shortly after eight. The sun was shining and it was unusually warm. Because she had plenty of time, she decided to take the coastal highway toward Trelleborg and turn up north to Lund once she got to Anderslöv. She listened to the news on the radio but there was nothing about Birgitta Medberg.

Then her cell phone rang. It was her dad.

"Where are you?"

"On my way to Lund. Why are you calling?"

"I just wanted to see if I needed to wake you up."

"You didn't have to do that. By the way, I saw you never made it home last night."

"I slept a while at the manor. We've staked out a few rooms for the time being."

"How is it going?"

"I'll tell you later. Bye."

She put the phone back in her pocket. She found the right street in inner-city Lund, found a place to park the car, and bought herself an ice cream. Why had her father called? *He's trying to control me,* she thought.

The house Anna shared was a two-story wooden building with a small garden in front. The gate was rusty and about to fall off its hinges. Linda rang the doorbell, but no one answered. She rang again and strained her ears. She didn't hear a ringing on the inside, so she started to knock loudly. Finally a shadow appeared on the other side of the glass inlay. The man who opened the door was in his twenties, his face covered in acne. He was wearing jeans, an undershirt, and a large brown robe with big holes. He reeked of sweat.

"I'm looking for Anna Westin," Linda said.

"She's not in."

"But she lives here?"

The man stepped aside so Linda could enter. She felt his eyes on the back of her head when she walked past him.

"She has the room behind the kitchen," he said.

They walked into the kitchen, which was a mess of dirty dishes and leftover food. *How can she live in this shit?* Linda thought.

She reluctantly stretched out her hand to shake his, shuddering at his limp and clammy handshake.

"Zacharias," he said. "I don't think her door's locked, but she doesn't like anyone to go in there."

"I'm one of her closest friends. If she hadn't wanted me to go in, she would have locked the door."

"How am I supposed to know you're her friend?"

Linda felt like pushing him out of the kitchen, but pulled herself together.

"When did you see her last?"

He stepped back.

"What is this—a cross-examination?"

"Not at all. I've been trying to get in touch with her and she hasn't gotten back to me."

Zacharias kept staring at her.

"Let's go into the living room," he said.

She followed him into a room full of shabby, mismatched furniture. A torn poster of Che Guevara's face hung on one wall, a tapestry embroidered with some words about the joys of home on the other. Zacharias sat down at a table with a chess set. Linda sat across from him, which was as far away as she could get.

"What do you study?" she asked.

"I don't. I play chess."

"And you make a living from that?"

"I don't know. I just know I can't live any other way."

"I don't even know how all the pieces move."

"I can show you, if you like."

Not a chance, Linda thought. *I'm getting out of here as soon as I can.*

"How many of you live here?"

"It depends. Right now there's four of us: Margareta Olsson, who studies economics, me, Peter Engbom, who is supposed to be majoring in physics but is currently mired in the history of religion, and then Anna."

"Who is studying medicine," Linda filled in.

The facial movement was almost imperceptible, but she caught it. His face had registered surprise. At the same time she caught hold of the thought she had had the night before.

"When did you see her last?"

"I don't have a good memory for these things. It may have been yesterday or a week ago. I'm in the middle of a study of Capablanca's most accomplished endgames. Sometimes I think it should be possible to transcribe chess moves like music. In which case Capablanca's games would be fugues or enormous masses."

Another nut interested in unplayable music, she thought.

"That sounds interesting," she said and got up. "Is anyone else home right now?"

"No, just me."

Linda walked back to the kitchen, with Zacharias at her heels.

"I'm going in now, whatever you say."

"Anna won't like it."

"You can always try to stop me."

He watched her as she opened the door and walked in. Anna's room must at one time have been a kitchen maid's room. It was small and narrow. Linda sat down on the bed and looked around. Zacharias appeared in the doorway. Linda suddenly had the feeling he was going to throw himself on top of her. She got up and he took a step back but kept watching her. It was no use. She wanted to pull out the desk drawers but as long as he was watching she couldn't bring herself to do it.

"When do the others get home?"

"I don't know."

Linda walked out into the kitchen again. He smiled at her, revealing a row of yellow teeth. She was starting to feel sick and decided to leave.

"I can show you all the chess moves," he said.

She opened the front door and paused on the steps.

"If I were you I'd spend some much-needed time in the shower," she said and turned on her heel.

She heard the door slam shut behind her. *What a waste of time,* she thought angrily. The only thing she had managed to do was to demonstrate her weaknesses. She kicked open the gate. It hit the mailbox sitting on a fence post. She stopped and turned around. The front door was closed, and she couldn't see anyone looking out of a window. She opened the mailbox. There were two letters. She picked them up. One was addressed to Margareta Olsson from a travel agency in Gothenburg. The other was addressed by hand, to Anna. Linda hesitated for a moment, then took it with her to the car. *First I read her journal, then I open her mail,* she thought. *But I'm doing it because I'm worried about her.* Inside the envelope was a folded piece of paper. She flinched when she opened it; a dried, pressed spider fell out onto her lap.

The message was short, apparently incomplete, and without a signature.

We're in the new house, in Lestarp, behind the church, first road on the left, a red mark on an old oak tree, back there. Let us never underestimate the power of Satan. And yet we await a mighty angel descending from the heavens in a cloud of glory. . . .

Linda laid the letter on the passenger seat. She thought back to the insight she had had back in the house. It was the one thing she could thank that smelly chess-player for. He had mentioned what everyone who lived in the house studied, as well as their names. But Anna was just Anna. She was studying medicine ostensibly to become a physician. But what had Anna said when she told Linda about seeing her father in Malmö? She had seen a woman who had collapsed in the street, someone who needed help. And she had said that she couldn't stand the sight of blood. Linda was now struck by the incongruity of this statement coming from someone who professed to want to be a doctor.

She looked at the letter beside her. What did it mean? *We await a mighty angel descending from the heavens in a cloud of glory.*

The sun was strong. It was the beginning of September, but it was one of the warmest days of the summer. She took a map of Skåne out of the glove compartment. Lestarp was between Lund and Sjöbo. Linda pushed down the sun visor. *It's so childish,* she thought. *This business with the dried spider, the kind that falls out of lamp shades. But Anna is missing. This childishness exists alongside the reality, the reality of a little gingerbread house in the forest. Hands at prayer and a severed head.*

It was as if she only now fully understood what she had seen in the hut that day. And Anna was no longer the person she thought she knew. *Maybe she isn't even studying medicine. Maybe this is the day I realize I know nothing about Anna Westin. She's dissolving in an unfathomable fog.*

Linda was not aware of formulating a conscious plan as such; she just started driving toward Lestarp. It was almost thirty degrees Celsius in the shade.

23

Linda parked outside the church in Lestarp. She could see that it had been recently renovated. The newly painted doors gleamed. A small black-and-gold plaque above them was inscribed 1851. Linda remembered her grandfather saying something about his own grandfather drowning in a storm at sea that very year. She thought about him as she looked for a bathroom in the vestibule. It was located in the crypt. The cool air felt good to her after the heat outside. *I only remember important years,* her grandfather had said. *A year when someone drowns in a terrible accident, or when someone, like you, is born.*

When she had finished, she washed her hands thoroughly as if she were washing off the remains of the chess-playing Zacharias's limp handshake. She looked at her face in the mirror. It passed muster, she decided. Her mouth was stern as always, her nose a little big, but her eyes were arresting and her teeth were good. She shuddered at the thought of the chess-player trying to kiss her, and hurried back up the stairs. An old man was walking in carrying a box of candles. She held the doors open. He put the box down and then placed his hands on his back.

"You would think God could spare his devoted servant from the trials of back pain," he said in a low voice. Linda realized he was keeping his voice down because someone was sitting in the pews. She thought at first it was a man, then saw she was mistaken.

"Gudrun lost two children," the old man whispered. "She comes here every single day."

"What happened?"

"They were run over by a train, a terrible tragedy. One of the ambulance drivers who took care of their remains lost his mind."

He picked up the box again and continued up the aisle. Linda walked back out into the sun. *Death is all around me,* she thought, *calling out to me and trying to deceive me. I don't like churches, or the sight of women crying. How does that mesh with wanting to become a police officer? Does it make any more sense than Anna not being able to stand the sight of blood or of people collapsing in the street? Maybe you can want to become a doctor or a police officer for the same reason: to see if you have what it takes.*

Linda wandered into the little cemetery attached to the church. Walking along the row of headstones was like perusing the shelves of a library. Every headstone was like a folder or the cover of a book. Here, for example, lay the householder Johan Ludde and his wife Linnea. They had been buried for ninety-six years, but he was seventy-six when he died, and she was only forty-one. There was a story here, in this poorly tended grave. She kept browsing the headstones, wondering what her own would look like. A headstone that was overgrown caught her eye. She crouched down and cleared moss and earth from its face. SOFIA 1854–1869. Fifteen years old. Had she too teetered on a bridge railing, but with no one to help her?

She left the car parked where it was and followed the narrow road that led to the back of the church on foot. She came upon the tree with the red mark almost immediately and turned onto a road that led down a small hill. The house was old and worn, the main part whitewashed stone with a slate roof, an addition built of rustic red-painted wood. Linda stopped and looked around. It was absolutely quiet. A rusty, overgrown tractor stood to one side, by some apple trees. Then the front door opened and a woman in white clothes started walking out to greet Linda, who didn't understand how she had been spotted. She hadn't seen anyone and she was still partly hidden by the trees. But the woman was making her way briskly straight for her, smiling. She was about Linda's age.

"I saw that you needed help," she said when she was close enough. She spoke a mixture of Danish and English.

"I'm looking for a friend of mine," Linda said. "Anna Westin."

The woman smiled.

"We have no use for names here. Come with me. You may find this friend you are looking for."

The mildness of her voice made Linda suspicious. Was she walking into a trap? She followed the woman into the cool interior of the main house. It took some time for Linda to see clearly. The slowness of her eyes to adjust from bright outdoor light to dim interiors was one of her few physical weaknesses, one she had discovered during her time at the academy.

All of the walls on the inside were also whitewashed, with no rugs on the bare, broad planks of the floor. There was no furniture, but a large black wooden cross hung between two arched windows. People sat along the walls, directly on the floor. Many with their arms wrapped around their knees, all silent. They were of all ages and in different styles of dress. One man with short hair was wearing a dark suit and tie; by his side was an older woman in very simple clothes. Linda looked all around but could not pick out Anna among them. The woman who had come out to greet her looked inquiringly at her, but Linda shook her head.

"There's one more room," the woman said.

Linda followed. The wooden walls of the next room were also painted white. These windows were far less elaborate. Here too people sat along the walls, but Linda did not see anyone who looked like Anna. What was going on in this house? What had the letter said? *A mighty angel in a cloud of glory?*

"Let us go out again," said the woman.

She led Linda across the lawn, around the side of the house to a group of stone furniture in the shadow of a beech tree. Linda's curiosity was now fully engaged. Somehow these people had something to do with Anna. She decided to come clean.

"The friend I'm looking for is missing. I found a letter in her mailbox that described this place."

"Can you tell me what she looks like?"

I don't like this, Linda thought. *Her smile, her calm. It's completely disingenuous and makes my skin crawl. Like when I shook that chess-player's hand.*

Linda gave her Anna's description. The woman's smile never wavered.

"I don't think I've seen her," she said. "Do you have the letter with you?"

"I left it in the car."

"And where is the car?"

"I parked it over by the church. It's a red VW Golf. The letter is lying on the front seat. I left the car unlocked, actually, which I know is careless of me."

The woman was silent. Linda felt uncomfortable.

"What do you do here?"

"Your friend must have told you. Everyone who is here has the mission of bringing others to our temple."

"This is a temple?"

"What else would it be?"

Of course, Linda thought sarcastically. *What was I thinking? This is clearly a temple and not simply the somewhat dilapidated remains of a humble Swedish farmstead where the owners once struggled to put food on the table.*

"What is the name of your organization?"

"We don't use names. Our community comes from within, through the air we share and breathe."

"That sounds very deep."

"The self-evident is always the most mysterious. The smallest crack in a musical instrument alters its timbre completely. If a whole panel falls out, the music ceases. It is the same with human beings. We cannot fully live without a higher purpose."

Linda did not understand the answers she was getting, and didn't like this feeling. She stopped asking questions.

"I think I'll leave now."

She walked away quickly without turning around, nor did she stop until she reached the car. Instead of leaving right away, she sat and looked out at the trees. The sun was shining through the leaves and into her eyes. Just as she was about to start the engine she saw a man cross the gravel yard in front of the church.

At first she only saw his outline, but when he crossed into the shade of the high trees she felt as if she had just taken a gulp of frigid air. She recognized his neck, and not just that. During the seconds before he walked back out into the blinding sun she heard

Anna's voice reverberate inside her head. The voice was very clear, telling her about the man she had seen through the hotel window. *I am also sitting by a window,* Linda thought. *A car window. And suddenly I'm convinced I've just seen Anna's father. It is completely unreasonable. But that's what I think.*

24

*I*s it completely ridiculous to think you can identify a person by his neck? Linda wondered. What had convinced her so completely about something she had no grounds for knowing? *You can't recognize someone you've never met, let alone someone you've only ever seen in a few snapshots and heard brief descriptions of from a person who in turn hasn't seen him in twenty-four years.*

She shook off the thought and drove back to Lund. It was early afternoon. The sun was still strong, and the heat hung oppressively over the surroundings. She parked outside the house she had visited just a few hours earlier and prepared herself for another meeting with Zacharias the chess-player. But the door was opened by a girl a few years younger than Linda with blue streaks in her hair and a chain suspended from her nostril to her ear. She was wearing black clothes in a combination of leather and vinyl. One of her shoes was black, the other white.

"There are no available rooms," she said brusquely. "If there's still a notice up at the student union it's a mistake."

"I don't need a room. I'm looking for Anna Westin. I'm a friend of hers—my name's Linda."

"I don't think she's here, but you can take a look."

She stepped aside and let Linda pass her. Linda cast a quick glance into the living room. The chess set was still there, but not the player.

"I was here a few hours ago," Linda said. "I talked to the guy who plays chess."

"You can talk to whomever you like."

"Are you Margareta Olsson?"

"That's my assumed name."

Linda was taken aback. Margareta looked amused.

"My real name is Johanna von Lööf, but I prefer a simpler name. That's why I call myself Margareta Olsson. There's only one Johanna von Lööf in this country, but a couple of thousand Margareta Olssons. Who wants to be unique?"

"Beats me. You study law, right?"

"No. Economics."

Margareta pointed to the kitchen.

"Are you going to see if she's in or not?"

"You know she isn't here, don't you?"

"Of course I know. But there's nothing stopping you from checking it out yourself."

"Do you have some time to chat?"

"I have all the time in the world—don't you?"

They sat in the kitchen. Margareta was drinking tea but she didn't offer Linda any.

"Economics. That sounds hard."

Margareta tossed her head with irritation.

"It is hard. Life should be hard. What did you want to know?"

"I'm looking for Anna. She's my friend, and I want to make sure nothing has happened to her. I haven't heard from her for a while, and that's not like her."

"And what can I do for you?"

"You can tell me when you last saw her."

Margareta's answer was caustic.

"I don't like her. I try to have as little to do with her as possible."

Linda had never heard that before—someone not liking Anna. She thought back to their school days. Linda had often fought with her fellow students, but she couldn't remember Anna doing so.

"Why?"

"I think she's stuck-up. I can generally tolerate that in others since I'm just as bad. But not in her case. There's something about her that drives me up the wall."

She got up and rinsed her teacup.

"It probably bothers you to hear me say this about your friend."

"Everyone has a right to their opinion."

Margareta sat down again.

"Then there's another thing. Or two, more precisely. She's stingy and she doesn't tell the truth. You can't trust her. Either what she says or that she won't use all your milk."

"That doesn't sound like Anna."

"Maybe the Anna who lives here is a different person. All I'm saying is I don't like her, she doesn't like me. We cope. I don't eat when she's eating and there are two bathrooms. We rarely bump into each other."

Margareta's cell phone rang. She answered and then left the kitchen. Linda thought about what she had just been told. More and more she was starting to realize that the Anna she had become reacquainted with was not the same Anna she had grown up with. Even though Margareta—or Johanna—didn't make the best impression, Linda instinctively felt that she had been telling the truth. *I have nothing more to do here,* she thought. *Anna is choosing to stay away. She has some reason for it, just as there will turn out to be a reason why she and Birgitta Medberg were in contact.*

Linda got up to leave as Margareta came back into the kitchen.

"Are you angry?"

"Why would I be angry?"

"Because I've told you unflattering things about your friend."

"I'm not angry."

"Then maybe you'd like to hear more?"

They sat down at the table again. Linda felt tense.

"Do you know what she studies?"

"Medicine."

"That's what I thought too; we all did. But then someone told me she had been expelled from the medical school. There were rumors about plagiarism—I don't know if that was true or not. Maybe she simply gave up. But she never said anything to us about it. She pretends that she's still studying medicine, but she's not."

"What does she do?"

"She prays."

"Prays?"

"You heard me," Margareta said. "Prays. What you do when you go to church."

Linda lost her temper.

"Of course I know what it is. Anna prays, you say. But where? When? How? Why?"

Margareta did not react to her outburst. Linda was grudgingly impressed by this display of self-control of a kind that she herself lacked.

"I think it's genuine. She's searching for something. I can understand her in a way. Personally, I'm on a quest for material wealth; other people are looking for the spiritual equivalent."

"How do you know all of this if you don't even talk to her?"

Margareta leaned over the table.

"I snoop, and I eavesdrop. I'm the person who hides behind curtains and hears and sees everything that goes on. I'm not kidding."

"So she has a confidante?"

"That's a strange word, isn't it? 'Confidante'—what does it really mean? I don't have one, and I doubt if Anna Westin does either. To be completely honest, I think she's unusually dim-witted. God forbid I would ever be diagnosed and treated by a physician like her. Anna Westin talks to anyone who will listen. I think all of us here find her conversation a series of naïve and worthless sermons. She's always lecturing us on moral topics. It's enough to drive anyone insane, except perhaps our dear chess-player. He cherishes vain hopes about getting her into bed."

"Any chance?"

"Zilch."

"What do her lectures consist of?"

"She talks about the poverty of our daily existence. That we don't nurture our inner selves. I don't know exactly what she believes in, other than that she's Christian. I tried to discuss Islam with her one time and she went ballistic. She's a conservative Christian. More than that I don't know. But there's something genuine about her when she talks about her religious views. And sometimes I hear her when she's in her room. It sounds real. That's the only time she isn't lying or stealing. She's being herself. Beyond that, I can't say."

Margareta looked at her.

"Has something happened?"

Linda shook her head.

"I don't know. Maybe."

"But you're worried?"

"Yes."

Margareta got up.

"Anna Westin's God will protect her. At least that's what she always brags about. Her God and some earthly angel named Gabriel. I think it was an angel. I can't remember exactly. But with that kind of protection she should be fine."

She stretched out her hand.

"I have to go now. Are you also a student?"

"I'm a police officer. Or will be soon, that is."

Margareta took a closer look at her.

"I'm sure you will, as many questions as you've been asking."

Linda realized she had one more.

"Do you know anyone called Mirre? She left a message on Anna's answering machine."

"No. But I can ask the others."

Linda gave her her phone number and left the house. She was still vaguely envious of Margareta Olsson's poise, her self-confidence. What did she have that Linda didn't?

The following morning, Monday, Linda was awakened by the sound of the front door slamming shut. She sat up in bed. It was six o'clock. She lay down and tried to fall back asleep. Raindrops were spattering against the windowsill. It was a sound she remembered from childhood. Raindrops, Mona's shuffling slippered gait, and her father's firm footsteps. Once upon a time these sounds had been her greatest source of security. She shook off her thoughts and got up. Her father had forgotten to turn the stove off, and he hadn't finished his coffee. *He's nervous and he left in a hurry,* she thought.

She pulled the paper toward her and leafed through it until she saw an article about the latest developments in the Rannesholm case. There was a short interview with her dad. It was early, he had said, and although there were almost no clues, they thought they had some leads, but he was not free to comment further for the time being. She put the paper away and thought about Anna. If Margareta Olsson was right—and she had no reason to doubt she was telling the truth—Anna had turned into a very different person. But why was she staying away, and why did she claim to have seen her father? Why wasn't Henrietta telling the truth? And that man that Linda had seen walk past the front of the church—why was she convinced it was Anna's father?

And the other crucial question: what was the connection between Anna and Birgitta Medberg?

Linda had trouble separating all these thoughts. She heated up the coffee and wrote everything down on a piece of paper. Then she crumpled it up and threw it away. *I have to talk to Zeba,* she thought. *I'll tell her everything. She's smart. She never loses touch with reality. She'll give me some good ideas.* Linda showered, put her clothes on, and then called Zeba. Her answering machine picked up. Linda tried her cell phone but it was out of range. Since it was raining, she could hardly have taken her boy out for a walk. Maybe she was with her cousin.

Linda was impatient and irritated. She thought about calling her father, possibly even her mother, just to have someone to talk to. She decided she didn't want to interrupt her father. And a conversation with Mona could drag on forever. She didn't need that. She pulled on her boots and a rain jacket and walked down to the car. She was getting used to having a car. That was dangerous. When Anna came back, Linda would have to start walking places again. When she couldn't borrow her dad's car. She drove out of the city and stopped at a gas station. A man at the next pump nodded to her. She recognized his face without being able to place him until she was standing in line at the cashier's window. It was Sten Widén, her father's friend who had cancer.

"It's Linda, isn't it?"

His voice was hoarse and weak.

"Yes. Sten, right?"

He laughed, something that seemed to cost him an effort.

"I remember you as a little girl. And suddenly you're all grown. A police officer no less."

"How are the horses?"

He didn't answer until she had finished paying and they were walking back to their cars.

"Your dad has probably told you what's going on," Widén said. "I have cancer and I'm going to die soon. I'm selling the last of the horses next week. That's how it is. Good luck with your life."

He didn't wait for an answer, just got into his muddy Volvo and drove away. Linda watched him leave and could only think one thing: how grateful she was that she wasn't the one selling her last horse.

She drove to Lestarp and parked by the church. *Someone must know,* she thought. *If Anna isn't here, where is she?* Linda pulled up the hood of her yellow rain jacket and hurried down the road behind the church. The yard to the house was deserted. The old tractor was wet and shiny from the rain. She banged on the front door and it swung open. But no one had opened it; it hadn't been properly closed. She called out, but no one answered. The house was empty, abandoned. Nothing was left. She saw that they had taken the black cross on the wall. It felt as if the house had been empty for a long time.

Linda stood in the middle of the room. *The man in the sun,* she thought. *The one I saw yesterday and thought was Anna's father. He came here, and today everyone is gone.*

She left the house and drove to Rannesholm. There she was told that Wallander was up at the manor, conducting a meeting with his closest associates. She walked over in the rain and settled down to wait for him in the big hall. She thought about the last thing Margareta Olsson had said, something about Anna Westin not having to worry about her safety because she had God and an earthly guardian angel named Gabriel for protectors. It seemed important. She just couldn't think how.

25

Linda never stopped being surprised by her father, by his rapid mood changes, that is. When she saw him come through a door in the large hall at Rannesholm manor she expected him to be tired, anxious, and downcast. But he was in good spirits. He sat down next to her and launched into a long-winded story about a time he had a left a pair of gloves at a restaurant and been offered a broken umbrella instead. *Is he going crazy?* she thought. Then he left to go to the bathroom and Martinsson stopped briefly on his way out. He told her that her father had been in a relatively good mood ever since she had moved back to town. Martinsson hurried on when Wallander returned. He sat down so heavily on the old sofa that the springs groaned. She told him about running into Sten Widén at the gas station.

"He's remarkably stoic about his fate," Wallander said. "He reminds me of Rydberg, who had the same calm attitude. I hope that will turn out to be true for me one day, that I'll be stronger than I think."

Some officers carrying cases of equipment walked by. Then the room was silent.

"Are you making progress?" Linda asked.

"Not really, or slowly, I should say. The worse the crime, the more impatient one becomes about solving it, even though in these cases patience is critical. I once knew an officer in Malmö—Birch—who used to compare our investigative work to that of a surgeon facing a complicated operation. The calm, time, and patience needed for such procedures are key ingredients even for us. Birch is dead now, as it happens. He drowned in a little lake. He went swimming, must have suffered a cramp, no one heard him. He should have known better, of course, but now he's dead. I feel as if people are dying all around me, although I know it's irrational. Births and deaths are going on all around us all the time. But the dying seems more pronounced when you reach the front of the line. Now that my father is dead there's no one ahead of me anymore."

Wallander looked down at his hands. Then he turned to her and smiled.

"What was it you asked me?"

"How is the investigation going?"

"We haven't found a single trace of the perpetrator. We have no idea who was living in that hut."

"What do you think?"

"You know you should never ask me that. Never what I think, only what I know or what I suspect."

"I'm curious."

He sighed.

"I'll make an exception. I think Birgitta Medberg came upon the hut accidentally in her search for the pilgrim trail. The person who was there panicked or became enraged and killed her. But the fact that he dismembered the body complicates the picture."

"Have you found the rest of it?"

"We have divers in the lake and a canine unit combing the forest. They haven't found anything yet."

He got ready to get up off the sofa.

"I take it there's something you want to tell me."

Linda told him in great detail about her visit to Anna's house in Lund as well as to the house in Lestarp.

"Too many words," he said when she finished.

"I'm working on it. Did you get the gist?"

"Yes."

"Then it couldn't have been too bad."

"I'd give it a beta query," Wallander said.

"What's a beta query?"

"When I was in school, anything less than a beta query was considered a failing grade."

"So what do you think I should do?"

"Stop worrying. You haven't been listening to me. What happened to Birgitta Medberg was a mishap, one of almost biblical proportions. She took the wrong path. If I'm not mistaken, Birgitta Medberg had excruciatingly bad luck. Therefore there's no longer any reason to think Anna is in any danger. The journal shows there is a connection between the two of them, but it's no longer of concern to us."

Ann-Britt Höglund and Lisa Holgersson came walking by at a brisk clip. Holgersson nodded kindly to Linda. Höglund didn't seem to notice her. Wallander got up.

"Go home now," he said.

"We could have used an extra set of hands," Holgersson said. "I wish the money was there. When is it you start?"

"Next Monday."

"Good."

Linda watched them walking out together, and then she also left the manor. It was raining and getting colder, as if the weather couldn't make up its mind. She walked back to the car. The house behind the church had sparked her curiosity. Why were they all gone? *I can at least find out who the owner of the house is,* she thought. *I don't need a permit or a police uniform for that.* She drove back to Lestarp and parked in her usual spot. The doors to the church were half-open. After hesitating for a moment, she walked in. The old man she had talked to before was in the vestibule. He recognized her.

"Can't stay away from our beautiful church?"

"I came by to ask you something."

"Isn't that why we all come here? To find answers to our questions?"

"That wasn't quite what I meant. I was thinking about the house behind the church. Do you know who owns it?"

"It's been in many different hands. When I was young, a man with one leg shorter than the other lived there. His name was Johannes Pålsson. He worked as a day laborer up at Stigby farmstead and was good at mending china. The last few years he lived alone. He moved the pigs into the living room and the chickens into the kitchen. That kind of thing went on in those days. When he was gone, someone else used the place as storage for grain. Then there was a horse breeder, and after that, sometime in the 1960s, the house was sold to someone whose name I've forgotten."

"You don't know who owns it now?"

"Oh, I've seen people come and go lately. They're peaceful and discreet. Some say they use the house for meditation. They've never bothered us. But I don't know who the owner is. You should be able to find out through the property-tax records."

Linda thought for a moment. What would her father have done?

"Who knows all the gossip in this village?"

He looked at her with a smile.

"That would be me, wouldn't it?"

"But apart from you. If there's anyone who would know who owns the house, who would it be?"

"Maybe Sara Edén, the retired schoolteacher. She lives in the little house next to the car-repair shop. She devotes her time to talking on the phone. She knows everything that's going on, and fills in the rest as needed. She's a good sort, just insatiably curious."

"What will happen if I ring her doorbell?"

"You'll make a lonely old woman's day."

The front door opened wider and the grieving woman walked in. She met Linda's gaze before walking to her regular pew.

"Every day," the old man said. "The same time, the same face, the same grief."

Linda left the church and walked down to the house. It was still empty. She returned to the church, decided to let the car stay where it was, and walked down the hill to Rune's Auto and Tractor. On one side of the shop there was a ramshackle pile of spare car parts; on the other there was a high fence. Linda suspected that the retired schoolteacher didn't care for a view of a car-repair shop. She opened the gate and stepped into a well-tended garden. An elderly woman was kneeling over a flowerbed. She stood up when she heard Linda come in.

"Who are you?" she asked sternly.

"My name is Linda. Do you mind if I ask you some questions?"

Sara Edén came over to where Linda was standing, holding a garden shovel aggressively outstretched. It occurred to Linda that there were people who were the human equivalent of ill-tempered dogs.

"Why would you want to ask me questions?"

"I'm looking for a friend who's disappeared."

Sara Edén looked skeptically at her.

"Isn't that something for the police? Looking for missing persons?"

"I am from the police."

"Then perhaps you'll show me your ID. That's my right, my older brother informed me. He was the headmaster at a school in Stockholm. He lived to be one hundred and one years old despite his bothersome colleagues and even more bothersome students."

"I don't have an ID card yet. I'm still in training."

"I'll have to take your word for it then. Are you strong?"

"Fairly."

Sara Edén pointed to a wheelbarrow that was filled to the brim with discarded plants and weeds.

"There's a compost pile around the back of the house, but my back has been giving me a bit of trouble. I must have slept in a strange position."

Linda took hold of the wheelbarrow. It was very heavy, but she managed to coax it around to the compost pile. When she had finished emptying it, Edén showed a kindlier side. There were some chairs and a table tucked into a little arbor.

"Do you want a cup of coffee?" she asked.

"Yes, please."

"Then you'll have to pick it up yourself from the vending machine by the furniture warehouse on the road out to Ystad. I don't drink coffee—or tea for that matter. But I can offer you a glass of mineral water."

"No, thank you."

They sat down. Linda had no trouble imagining Ms. Edén as a schoolteacher. She probably saw Linda as an unruly schoolgirl.

"Well, tell me what happened."

Linda gave her a brief outline of the events and said she had traced Anna to the house behind the church. She was careful not to let on how worried she was.

"We were supposed to meet," she said. "But something happened."

The old lady looked doubtful.

"And how do you believe that I can be of assistance?"

"I'm trying to find out who owns that house."

"In the olden days, one always knew who was who and who owned what. But in this day and age, there's no way of telling. One day I'll find out I've been living next to an escaped criminal."

"I thought perhaps in such a small town people still knew these things."

"There has been a great number of comings and goings in that house during the past while, but nothing that caused any disturbance. If I have understood it correctly, the people there are involved in some kind of health organization. Since I take good care of myself and am not planning to give my departed brother the satisfaction of dying at a younger age, I watch what I eat and drink, and I am curious about this new so-called alternative medicine. I went up to the house one time and spoke to a very friendly English-speaking lady. She gave me a pamphlet. I don't remember what the organization was called, but they espoused meditation and certain natural juices for promoting health."

"Did you ever go back?"

"The whole thing was far too vague for my tastes."

"Do you still have the pamphlet?"

Edén nodded toward the compost.

"I doubt there's anything left of it by now."

Linda tried to think of something else to ask, but she didn't see the point of pursuing it further. She got up.

"No more questions?"

"No."

They walked back to the front of the house.

"I dread the fall," Sara Edén said. "I'm afraid of the creeping fog and the rain and the noisy crows in their treetops. The only thing that keeps my spirits up is the thought of the spring flowers I'm planting right now."

Linda walked out to the gate.

"There may be something else," the old lady said.

They were now standing on either side of the gate.

"There was a Norwegian," she said. "I sometimes go in to Rune's shop and complain if they're making too much of a racket on a Sunday. I think Rune is a little afraid of me. He's the kind of person who never grows out of the respect he had for his teachers. The noise usually stops. But one day he told me about a Norwegian who had just been by to fill up his car and who paid with a thousand-kronor note. Rune isn't used to bills that big. He said something about the Norwegian owning the house up there."

"So I should ask Rune?"

"Only if you have time on your hands. He's on vacation in Thailand right now. I don't even want to think about what he might be getting up to."

Linda thought for a moment.

"A Norwegian. Did he say what he looked like?"

"No. If I were in your place I would ask the people who most likely handled the sale of the house. That would be the Sparbank real estate division. They have an office in town. They may know."

Linda left. She thought that Sara Edén was a person she would like to know more about. She crossed the street, passed a hair salon, and stepped into the tiny Sparbank office. There was only one person inside; he looked up when she came in. Linda asked him her question and the answer came without his having to consult any binders or notes.

"That's right," he said. "We handled the sale of that house. The seller was a Malmö dentist by the name of Sved. He had used the house as a summer retreat for a while but grown tired of it. We advertised the property online and in the *Ystad Allehanda*. A Norwegian came in and demanded to see the place. I asked one of the Skurup realtors to take care of him. That's fairly normal, since I run the branch by myself and can't always take on the extra responsibility for real-estate sales. Two days later the sale was finalized. As far as I recall, the Norwegian paid cash. They've got money coming out their ears these days."

The last comment revealed his grumbling displeasure at the vibrant Norwegian economy. But Linda was more interested in the Norwegian's name.

"I don't have the papers here, but I can call the Skurup office."

A client walked into the branch, an old man who walked with the help of two canes.

"Please excuse me while I attend to Mr. Alfredsson first," the man behind the counter said.

Linda waited impatiently. It took what seemed like an endless amount of time before the old man was finished. Linda held the door open for him. The man behind the counter placed his call, and after about a minute he received an answer that he wrote down on a piece of paper. He finished the conversation and pushed the note over to Linda. She read: *Torgeir Langas.*

"It's possible he spells the last name with a double 'a,' that would be *Langaas.*"

"What's his address?"

"You only asked me for his name."

Linda nodded.

"If you need more information, you can turn to the Skurup office directly. Do you mind my asking why you so urgently need to contact the owner of the house?"

"I may want to buy it," Linda said and left.

She hurried up to the car. Now she had a name. As soon as she opened the car door, she noticed that something was amiss. A receipt that had been on the dashboard was on the floor, a matchbox had been moved. She had left the car unlocked; someone had been in it while she was gone.

Hardly a thief, she thought. *The car radio is still here. But who's been in the car? Why?*

26

The first thought that ran through Linda's head was completely irrational: *Mom did this. She's been rifling through my stuff again like she used to.* Linda climbed hesitantly into the car. Another thought ran through her like electric current: a bomb. Something was going to explode and tear her to pieces. But of course there was no bomb. A bird had left a big dropping on the windshield, that was all. Now she noticed that the seat had been pushed back. The person who had been here was taller than she was. So tall he or she had to adjust the seat in order to slip behind the wheel. She sniffed for new scents but couldn't pick anything out, no aftershave or perfume. She looked everywhere. Something was different about the black plastic cup of loose change that Anna had taped behind the gearshift, but she couldn't put her finger on it.

Linda's thoughts returned to her mother. The game of cat-and-mouse had gone on for most of her childhood. She couldn't remember the exact moment when she realized that her mother was constantly looking through her things in search of who knows what kind of secrets. Maybe it had started when Linda was eight or nine and noticed when she came home from school that something had changed about her room. At first she had simply thought she must have been wrong. The red cardigan had been lying over the green sweater like that, not the other way around. She had even asked Mona, who had snapped at her. That was when the suspicion had been born and the game of cat-and-mouse started in earnest. She had left traps for Mona among her clothes, toys, and books. But it was as if Mona immediately sensed what was going on. Linda laid increasingly elaborate traps and even noted the exact arrangement of her things in a notebook so that she could catch her mother.

Linda kept looking around the car. *A mom has been here, a mom who may have been either a man or a woman. Snooping in their kids' stuff is more common than you'd think. Most of my friends had at least one parent who did it.* She thought about her dad. He had never looked through her things. Sometimes she had seen him peer in through her half-open door to make sure she was really there. But he never made surreptitious expeditions into her life. That had always been Mona.

She concentrated on the question of what kind of person had been in the car. Taking the radio would have been a simple way to cover his or her tracks. Then Linda would simply assume there had been a normal break-in and chastise herself for being so lazy she didn't even lock the car. *This is not a particularly cunning mom*, she thought.

She didn't get any further. There was no conclusion to be drawn, no answer as to who and why. She readjusted the front seat, got out, and looked around. *A man walked by in the blinding sun. I saw his back and thought it was Anna's father.* Linda shook her head in irritation. Anna had just been imagining things when she said she saw her father in the street. Maybe her acute disappointment was what made her take off for a few days. She had done that before—taken a trip without advance warning. But Zeba had said she always let at least one person know where she was going.

Who did she tell this time? Linda wondered.

She walked back over the gravel yard in front of the church, glancing up at some pigeons circling the bell tower, and then continued down to the house. *A man named Torgeir Langaas bought the house*, she thought. *He paid cash.*

She walked around to the back of the house, looking thoughtfully but absentmindedly at the stone furniture. There were several black and red currant bushes. She picked a few strands of berries and ate them. Her memories of Mona returned. Linda didn't think she had snooped out of sheer curiosity; rather, it seemed that she had been motivated by fear. Why had she been so afraid? *Was she afraid I wasn't who she thought I was? A nine-year-old can play roles and have her secrets, but hardly of a magnitude that requires continuous snooping in order to truly understand her, especially if she is your own child.*

Open warfare had only broken out when Mona started reading Linda's diary. Linda had been thirteen by then and had been hiding her diary behind a loose panel at the back of a closet. At first she had thought it was safe there, but one day she realized that her mother had found her secret hiding spot. The diary had been pushed back a few centimeters too far. She could still remember the rage she had experienced. That time she really hated her mother.

There was an epilogue to that memory. Linda had decided to set another trap for her mother. This time she simply wrote a message on the first blank page in the diary stating that she knew her mother was reading it, that she was snooping in all her things. She put the diary back in its hiding place and started walking to school. About halfway there she slowed down and decided to cut class, since she knew she would not be able to concentrate anyway. She spent the day wandering around in the shops downtown. When she came home she broke out in a cold sweat, but her mother greeted her as if nothing had happened. Late that evening after they had all gone to bed Linda got out of bed, took out the diary, and saw that her mother had written—without apology or explanation—"I won't read it anymore, I promise."

Linda picked a few more berries. *We never talked about it,* she thought. *I think she stopped snooping altogether after that, but I could never be sure. Maybe she got better at covering her tracks, maybe I stopped caring as much. But we never talked about it.*

The real estate agent's name was Ture Magnusson and he was in the middle of a transaction involving the sale of a house in Trunnerup to a retired German couple. Linda skimmed through a folder of houses for sale while she waited. Ture Magnusson spoke German very badly. Finally he got up and walked over to her. He smiled.

"They want a moment alone," he said and introduced himself. "These things tend to take time. What can I do for you?"

Linda gave him her story without playing the policewoman this time. Ture Magnusson nodded before she was even finished. He seemed to remember the deal without having to look it up.

"That house was indeed bought by a Norwegian," he said. "A pleasant sort, very quick to make up his mind. He was what you would call an ideal client, paid in cash, no hesitation, no second thoughts."

"How can I get in touch with him? I'm interested in the house."

Ture Magnusson leaned back and seemed to take stock of her. His chair creaked as he pushed onto the back legs of the chair and balanced up against the wall.

"To be perfectly honest, he paid too much for that house. I shouldn't tell you that, but it's true. I can show you at least three other places in much better condition, in more beautiful surroundings going for less."

"This is the house I want. I'd like to at least ask the owner if he would consider selling."

"Of course. I understand. 'Torgeir Langaas was his name,'" Ture Magnusson said, singing the last sentence. He had a good voice. He went into the next room and soon reappeared with an opened folder.

"Torgeir Langaas," he read. "He spells his last name with a double 'a' at the end. He was born somewhere called Baerum, forty-three years old."

"Where in Norway does he live?"

"Nowhere. He lives in Copenhagen."

Ture Magnusson put the folder down in front of her so she could see. *Nedergade 12.*

"What sort of man would you say he was?"

"Why do you ask?"

"I want to know if there's any point in looking him up, in your opinion."

Ture Magnusson leaned back up against the wall.

"It was clear from the moment I laid eyes on him that Torgeir Langaas meant business. He was very courteous. He had already picked out the house he wanted. We drove out there together and inspected the property; he didn't ask any questions. When we returned he pulled the cash out of his shoulder bag. I don't think that's ever happened to me except on one other occasion. The other was when one of our young tennis stars came with a suitcase full of bank notes and bought a large estate in West Vemmenhög. He's never been there since, as far as I know."

Linda wrote down Langaas's address in Copenhagen and prepared to leave.

"Come to think of it, there was something else I noticed about him."

"What was it?"

Ture Magnusson shook his head slowly.

"It wasn't anything remarkable, just that he turned around a lot, as if he were afraid of running into someone he knew. He also excused himself a number of times, and when he returned from the bathroom the last time, his eyes were glazed over."

"Had he been crying?"

"No, I would almost say he seemed high."

"Alcohol?"

"I would have smelled that on his breath. I guess he could have been drinking vodka."

Linda tried to think of something else to ask.

"But respectful, pleasant," Magnusson said again. "Perhaps he'll sell you the house. Who knows?"

"What did he look like?"

"He had a normal-looking face. What I remember most about him is his eyes, not simply because they were glazed over but because there was something disturbing about them. Some people would perhaps even have found his look menacing."

"And yet his manner struck you as pleasant?"

"Oh, very. An ideal client, as I said. I bought myself a very nice bottle of wine that evening. Just to celebrate such an easy day's work."

Linda left the real-estate office. *This is another step on the way*, she thought. *I can go to Copenhagen and find this Torgeir Langaas. I don't know exactly why—perhaps it helps to diminish my anxieties. I'm treating this as if Anna simply decided to go away without remembering to mention it to me.*

Linda drove toward Malmö. Just before the turnoff to Jägersro and the Öresund Bridge she decided to make an unexpected visit. She pulled up outside the house in Limhamn, parked, and walked in through the gate. A car was pulled into the driveway. She stopped herself as she was about to ring the doorbell; why, she couldn't say. Instead she walked around to the back of the house to the glassed-in porch. The garden was well-tended. The gravel path was even raked. The door to the porch was slightly ajar. She pushed it open farther and listened. It was quiet, but she was sure that someone was home. These people spent far too much time locking doors and checking their alarm system. She walked into the living room, looking at the painting over the sofa. It was a picture she had often looked at as a child, fascinated and disturbed by the brown bear shot through with flames and about to explode. She still found it disturbing. Her dad had won it in a lottery and given it to her mother as a birthday present.

Linda heard a noise in the kitchen and walked to the door. Her "hello" stuck in her throat. Mona was standing at the kitchen counter. She was naked and drinking vodka straight from the bottle.

27

Afterward Linda would think that it had been like staring at an image from her past. An image that reached beyond the reality of her mother standing there naked with a bottle of vodka, to something else, an impression, a memory she only managed to grasp when she drew a deep breath. She had experienced the same thing herself once.

She had been only fourteen years old, in the midst of those terrible teenage years when nothing seems possible or comprehensible, but where everything is also straightforward, easy to see through. All parts of the body vibrate with a new hunger. It had happened during a brief period in her life when not only her father but even her mother disappeared off to work all day, having pulled herself out of an unfulfilling stay-at-home existence to work for a shipping company. This finally enabled Linda to be alone for a few hours after school, or to bring friends home with her. She was happy.

That was the time Torbjörn came into her life. He was her first real boyfriend, one whom Linda imagined looked much like Clint Eastwood would have looked at fifteen. Torbjörn Rackestad was half-Danish, a quarter Swedish, and a quarter Native American, a fact that not only gave him a beautiful face but a tinge of exoticism.

It was with him that Linda started a serious investigation into all that went under the rubric of love. They were slowly approaching the moment of truth, although Linda equivocated. One day, when they were sprawled half-naked on her bed, the door opened. It was Mona. She had had a fight with her boss and left work early. Linda still broke out into a sweat when she remembered the shock she had felt. At the time she had started laughing hysterically. Since she had buried her face in her hands she didn't know exactly how Torbjörn had reacted, but he must have pulled his clothes on and left the apartment soon afterward.

Mona hadn't lingered in the doorway. She had simply shot her a look that Linda could never quite describe. There had been everything in that look from despair to a kind of smug triumph in finally having her worst fears about her daughter's nature confirmed. When Linda eventually went out into the living room, they had had a shouting match. Linda could still recall Mona's repeated war cry: *I don't give a shit what you do as long as you don't get pregnant.* Linda could also hear echoes of her own shouts—their sound, not the words. She remembered the embarrassment, the fury, and the sense of humiliation.

All these thoughts ran through her head as she stared at the nude older woman by the refrigerator. It also occurred to her that she hadn't seen her mother naked since she was a little girl. Mona had gained a lot of weight, the extra flesh spilling out in unappealing bulges. Linda's face registered disgust, a brief unconscious expression but distinct enough for Mona to see it and snap out of her initial shock. She slammed the bottle down on the counter and pulled the refrigerator door open as a kind of shield for her body. Linda couldn't help giggling at the sight of her mother's head sticking up over the door.

"What do you mean by sneaking in like this? Why can't you ring the doorbell?"

"I wanted to surprise you."

"But you can't just barge into a person's house!"

"How else would I find out that my mother spends her days getting pissed?"

Mona slammed the refrigerator door shut.

"I am not a drunk!" she screamed.

"You were swigging vodka straight from the bottle, Mom."

"It's water. I chill it before I drink it."

They both lunged for the bottle at the same time, Mona to hide the truth, Linda to uncover it. Linda got there first and sniffed it.

"This is pure, undiluted vodka. Go and put something on. Have you taken a look at yourself recently? Soon you'll be as big as Dad. But you're all blubber, he's just heavy."

Mona grabbed the bottle out of her hands. Linda didn't fight her. She turned her back to Mona.

"Mom, put your clothes on."

"I can be naked in my own house if I want to."

"It's not yours, it's the banker's house."

"His name is Olof and he happens to be my husband. We own this house together."

"You do not. You have a prenuptial agreement. If you get divorced he keeps the house."

"Who told you that?"

"Grandpa."

"That old bastard. What did he know?"

Linda turned and slapped her in the face.

"Don't say that about him."

Mona took a step back, unbalanced more by the alcohol than the slap.

"You're just like your dad. He hit me too."

"Put some clothes on, for God's sake."

Linda watched as her naked mother took one more long swallow from the bottle. *This isn't happening,* she thought. *Why did I stop by? Why didn't I go straight to Copenhagen?*

Mona tripped and fell. Linda wanted to help her up but got pushed aside. Mona finally pulled herself up into a chair.

Linda went into the bathroom and got a robe, but Mona refused to put it on. Linda started to feel sick to her stomach.

"Can't you put anything on?"

"All my clothes feel too tight."

"Then I'm leaving."

"Can't you at least stay for a cup of coffee?"

"Only if you put something on."

"Olof likes to see me naked. We always walk around naked in the house."

Now I'm becoming a mother to my mother, Linda thought, firmly guiding her mother into the robe. Mona put up no resistance. When she reached for the bottle, Linda moved it away. Then she started to make coffee. Mona followed her movements with dull eyes.

"How is Kurt?"

"He's fine."

"That man has never been fine in his entire life."

"Right now he is. He's never been better."

"Then it must be because he's rid of his old man—who hated him."

Linda held her hand up as if to strike and Mona shut up. She lifted her palms in apology.

"You have no idea how much he misses him. No idea," Linda said.

Mona got up from the chair, swaying but staying on her feet. She disappeared into the bathroom. Linda pressed her ear against the door. She heard a faucet running, but no bottles being taken from a secret stash.

When Mona reappeared she had combed her hair and washed her face. She looked around for the vodka that Linda had poured down the drain, then served the coffee. Linda suddenly felt a wave of pity for her. *I never want to be like her,* she thought. Never this snooping, nervous, clingy woman who never really wanted to leave Dad but was so insecure that she ended up doing the very things she didn't want.

"I'm not usually like this," Mona said.

"Just now I thought you said you and Olof always walk around naked."

"I don't drink as much as you think."

"Mom, you used to drink next to nothing. Now I catch you stark naked in your kitchen, tossing back vodka in the middle of the day."

"I'm not well."

"You mean you're sick?"

Mona started to cry, to Linda's dismay. When had she last seen her mother cry? She would sometimes fall into a nervous, almost restless sobbing if a meal didn't turn out well or if she had forgotten something, and she had cried when she had fought with Linda's father. But these tears were different. Linda decided to wait them out. The sobbing stopped as suddenly as it had started. Mona blew her nose and drank her coffee.

"I'm sorry."

"I'd rather you told me what was bothering you."

"What would that be?"

"Only you know that, not me. But clearly something's on your mind."

"I think Olof has met another woman. He denies it, but if there's one thing life has taught me it's to tell when a man is lying. I learned that from your dad."

Linda immediately felt the need to jump to his defense.

"I don't think he lies more than anyone else. Not any more than I do."

"You don't know the things I could tell you."

"And you don't know how little I care about that."

"Why do you always have to be so mean?"

"I'm just telling you the truth."

"Right now I could do with some plain old-fashioned kindness."

Linda's feelings for Mona had always oscillated between pity and anger, but now they seemed to have reached an unprecedented intensity. *I don't like her,* she thought. *My mother asks for a love I'm incapable of giving to her. I need to get out of here.* She put down her cup.

"Are you leaving already?"

"I'm on my way to Copenhagen."

"What for?"

"I don't have time to go into it."

"I hate Olof for what he's doing."

"I'll come back another time when you're sober."

"Why are you so mean to me?"

"I'm not mean. I'll call you."

"I can't live like this anymore."

"Then leave him. You've done it before."

"You don't need to tell me what I've done."

Her voice was full of hostility again. Linda turned and walked out. She heard Mona's voice behind her: *stay a little longer.* And then, just as she was about to close the door: *all right then—go. But don't you dare show your face here again!*

Linda reached the car drenched in sweat. *Bitch,* she thought. She was furious, but she knew that before she was halfway across the Öresund Bridge her anger would flip over into guilt; she should have been a good daughter and stayed with her mother, listening to her troubles.

———

The guilt had already started to take over as she paid the toll for the bridge, and she wished she were not an only child. *I'm the one who will have to take care of them one day.* She shivered and decided to tell her father what had happened. Maybe he knew if Mona had ever had problems with alcohol in the past, if there was something Linda didn't know about.

She reached Denmark and started to feel better. Her decision to talk to her father made her feel less guilty. Leaving Mona alone was the only thing to she could do until Mona sobered up. If she had stayed, they would only have kept yelling at each other.

Linda drove to a parking lot and got out. She sat down on a bench overlooking the sound, and stared off across the water at the misty outline of Sweden. Over there somewhere were her parents. They had enveloped her whole childhood in a strange mist. *My dad was the worst,* she thought. *The talented but gloomy policeman who had a sense of humor but never let himself laugh. My father who never found a new woman to share his life since he still loves Mona. Baiba tried to explain it to him but he wouldn't listen. Baiba told me he claimed, "Mona belongs to the past." But he hasn't forgotten her, he never will. She is his one great love. Now I've seen her wandering around naked, drinking hard alcohol in the middle of the day. She's also lost in the gloomy fog. I haven't managed to free myself from it and I'm almost thirty.*

Linda kicked angrily at the gravel, picked up a pebble and threw it at a seagull. *The eleventh commandment is the most important,* she thought, *the one that reads "Thou shalt never become like thy parents."* She got up and returned to the car. She stopped in Nyhavn and looked at a tourist map, finally locating Nedergade.

It was already starting to get dark by the time she found Nedergade. It was a street in a shabby neighborhood with rows of tall, identical apartment buildings. Linda immediately felt unsafe and would have preferred to come back in broad daylight, but the bridge toll was too expensive to waste a trip. She locked the car and stamped her foot on the pavement as a way of rousing her courage. Then she tried to make out the names of the people who lived in the building, although it was difficult to see in the dim light. The front door opened, and a man with a scar across his brow walked out. He was startled when he saw her. She caught the door and walked in before it closed behind him. Inside there was another notice board with names, but no one by the name of Langaas, or Torgeir, for that matter. A woman, about Linda's age, walked by carrying a bag of trash. She smiled at her.

"Excuse me," Linda said. "I'm looking for a man by the name of Torgeir Langaas."

The woman stopped and put the bag down.

"Does he live here?"

"He gave this as his address."

"What was his name? Torgeir Langaas? Is he Danish?"

"Norwegian."

She shook her head. It seemed to Linda that she genuinely wanted to help.

"I don't know of any Norwegians around here. We have a couple of Swedes and some people from other countries, but that's all."

The front door opened and a man walked in, dressed in a hooded sweatshirt. The woman with the garbage bag asked him if he knew of a Torgeir Langaas. He shook his head. The hood was pulled up and Linda couldn't see his face.

"Try Mrs. Andersen on the second floor. She knows everything about everyone in this building. I'm sorry I can't help you myself."

Linda thanked her for the tip and started walking up the stairs. Somewhere above her a door was pulled open, and loud Latino music reverberated in the stairwell. Outside Mrs. Andersen's door there was a small stool with an orchid. Linda rang the doorbell. Immediately a dog started to bark on the other side of the door. Mrs. Andersen, shrunken and hunched over, was one of the smallest women Linda had ever seen. The dog, barking by her slippered feet, was also one of the smallest dogs Linda had seen. She asked Mrs. Andersen her question. The old lady pointed to her left ear.

Linda shouted out her question again.

"I may hear badly but there's nothing wrong with my memory," Mrs. Andersen said. "There's no one living here by that name."

"Could he be staying with someone?"

"I know everyone who lives here, whether or not they are on

the lease. It's been forty years, believe it or not, since they built this house. Now there are all kinds of people here, of course."

She leaned closer to Linda and lowered her voice:

"They sell drugs here. And no one does anything about it."

Mrs. Andersen insisted on inviting her in and serving her coffee that she poured from a pot in the narrow kitchen. Linda managed to leave after half an hour. By then she knew all about what a wonderful husband Mr. Andersen had been, a man had who died far too young.

Linda walked down the stairs. The music had stopped. Instead there was the sound of a child wailing. Linda walked out the front door and looked each way before crossing the street. She sensed someone's presence in the shadows and turned her head. It was the man with the hooded sweatshirt. He grabbed her by her hair. She tried to get away but the pain was too great.

"There is no Torgeir," he said through clenched teeth. "No Torgeir Langaas. Drop it."

"Let me go!" she screamed.

He let go of her hair, but punched her hard in the temple. Linda fell headlong into darkness.

28

She was swimming as fast as she could, but the great waves had almost caught up with her. Suddenly she saw rocks in front of her, big black prongs sticking out of the water ready to spear her. Her strength ebbed away and she screamed. Then she opened her eyes.

Linda felt a sharp pain in her head and wondered what was wrong with the bedroom light. Then she saw her father's face looming over her and wondered if she had slept in. But what was she supposed to do today? She had forgotten.

Then she remembered. What caught up with her was not the great waves but the memory of what had happened right before she plunged into darkness. The stairwell, the street, the man who stepped out of the shadows, delivered his threat, and hit her. She winced. Her dad laid a hand on her arm.

"It's OK. Everything's going to be OK."

She looked around the hospital room, the dim lighting, the screens, and the rhythmic hissing of medical equipment.

"I remember now," she said. "But how did I get here? Am I hurt?"

She tried to sit up while at the same time testing all her limbs to make sure nothing was broken. Wallander tried to restrain her.

"They want you to stay lying down. You were knocked unconscious, though there doesn't appear to have been any internal damage, not even a concussion."

"How did you get here?" she asked and closed her eyes. "Tell me."

"If what I've heard so far from my Danish colleagues and one of the emergency-room physicians here at the Rikshospital is correct, you were extremely lucky. A patrol car was driving by and saw a man knock you down. It only took a few minutes for the ambulance to arrive. The officers found your driver's license as well as your ID card from the police academy. They contacted me in half an hour. I drove over as soon as I heard about it. Lindman is also here."

Linda opened her eyes and looked at her dad. She thought in a fuzzy way that she was maybe a little in love with Stefan Lindman even though she had hardly spent any time with him. *Am I delirious? I return to consciousness after some lunatic has knocked me out and the first thing I think about is that I've fallen in love, and much too quickly at that.*

"What are you thinking about?"

"Where's Lindman now?"

"He went to get a bite to eat. I told him to go home, but he wanted to come with me."

"I'm thirsty."

Wallander gave her some water. Linda's head was clearer now; images from the moments before the assault were coming back.

"What happened to the creep who assaulted me?"

"They arrested him."

Linda sat up so quickly that her father couldn't stop her.

"Lie down!"

"He knows where Anna is. Or perhaps he doesn't know that— but he does know something."

"Calm down."

She reluctantly stretched out on the bed again.

"I don't know his name, it could be Torgeir Langaas, but I can't know for sure. But he knows something about Anna."

Her father sat down on a chair beside the bed. She looked at his watch. It was a quarter past three.

"Is it day or night?"

"It's night. You've been sleeping like a baby."

"He grabbed my hair and then he threatened me."

"What I don't understand is what you were doing here in the first place. Why Copenhagen?"

"It'll take too long to explain. But the bastard who attacked me may know where Anna is. Maybe he assaulted her too. Or he may have something to do with Birgitta Medberg."

Wallander shook his head.

"You're tired. The doctor said your memory would come back in bits and pieces, and things may be jumbled for a while."

"Don't you understand what I'm saying?"

"I do. As soon as the doctor checks you again we can go home. Stefan can drive your car home."

The truth was starting to dawn on her.

"You don't believe a word I've told you, do you? That he threatened me?"

"No, I know he threatened you. He's admitted to that."

"Admitted to what, exactly?"

"That he threatened you because he wanted to get the drugs that he assumed you had bought while you were in the apartment building."

Linda stared at her father while her mind was trying to absorb this new information.

"He threatened me and told me to stop asking about Torgeir Langaas. He never said a word about drugs."

"We should be grateful the matter has been cleared up, and that the police were nearby at the time. He's going to be charged with assault and attempted robbery."

"There was no robbery. It's all about the man who owns the house behind the church in Lestarp."

Wallander frowned.

"What house is that?"

"I haven't had time to tell you about this before. I went to Anna's house in Lund and found a lead that pointed to Lestarp and a house behind the church. After I was there asking about Anna, everyone disappeared. The only thing I managed to find out was that the house is owned by a Norwegian by the name of Torgeir Langaas, and his address is in Copenhagen."

Her father looked at her for a long time, then took out his notebook and started reading from one of the pages.

"The man they arrested is one Ulrik Larsen. If my Danish colleague is to be believed, Larsen is hardly the kind of man who owns very many country houses in Sweden."

"Dad, you're not listening to me!"

"I am listening, but what you don't seem to understand is that there's a man who has confessed to trying to steal drugs from you."

Linda shook her head desperately. Her left temple throbbed. Why didn't he understand what she was trying to tell him?

"My mind is completely clear. I know I was knocked out but I'm telling you what actually happened."

"You *think* you are. What I still don't understand is what you were doing in Copenhagen—after barging in on Mona and upsetting her like that."

Linda went cold.

"How do you know about that?"

"She called me. She was in a terrible state. She was crying so hard she couldn't speak clearly, so at first I thought she was drunk."

"She *was* drunk, damn it. What did she say?"

"That you had accused her of all manner of things and complained about both her and me. She's crushed. And that banker husband was apparently not there to comfort her."

"I caught Mom naked in the kitchen with a bottle of vodka in her hand."

"She said you snuck into the house."

"I walked in through the veranda doors, which hardly qualifies as sneaking in. She was as high as a kite, whatever she may have told you on the phone."

"We'll talk about this later."

"Thanks."

"What were you doing in Copenhagen?"

"I've already told you."

Wallander shook his head.

"Can you explain why a man has been arrested for trying to rob you?"

"No. But I also can't explain why you refuse to believe me."

He leaned over.

"Do you understand what I went through when they called me? When they told me you had been admitted to a hospital in Copenhagen after an assault—do you know what that felt like?"

"I'm sorry that you had to worry about me."

"Worry? I was scared out of my mind—more frightened than I've been in years."

Maybe you haven't been so scared since I tried to kill myself, she thought. She knew his greatest fear was that something should happen to her.

"I'm sorry, Dad."

"I wonder what it will be like when you start working, of course," he continued. "If that will turn me into a worried old man who can't sleep when you're working the night shift."

She tried to tell her story again, slowly, with painstaking care, but he still didn't seem to believe her.

She had just finished when Stefan Lindman walked into the room. He had a paper bag with sandwiches. He nodded happily at her when he saw she was awake.

"How are you doing?"

"Fine."

Lindman handed the paper bag to Wallander, who immediately started to eat.

"What kind of car do you have? I'm going to get it for you," Lindman said.

"A red VW Golf. It's parked across the street from the apartment building on Nedergade. I think it's in front of a smoke shop."

He held up the key.

"I took this out of your coat pocket. You were lucky, you know. Desperate drug addicts are about the worst thing you can run into."

"He wasn't a drug addict."

"Tell Lindman what you told me," her father said in between bites.

She proceeded through her account again, calmly and methodically, just as she had been taught.

"This doesn't exactly jibe with what our Danish colleagues reported," Lindman said when she was done. "Nor with what the thug said either."

"But I'm telling you what really happened."

Wallander carefully wiped his hands with a paper napkin.

"Let me put this a different way," he said. "It's unusual for people to confess to crimes they haven't committed. It does happen, admittedly, but not very often, and least of all by convicted drug offenders, since what they fear most is incarceration and the possibility that they will be cut off from their lifeline of drugs. Do you see what I'm saying?"

Linda didn't answer. A physician walked into the room and asked her how she felt.

"You can go home," he said. "But take it easy for a few days, and call a doctor if the headache doesn't subside."

Linda sat up. Something had just occurred to her.

"What does Ulrik Larsen look like?"

Neither Lindman nor her father had seen him.

"I'm not leaving until I know what he looks like."

Her father lost his temper.

"Haven't you caused enough trouble? We are going home—now."

"Surely it can't be hard to get a description of him. Can't you ask one of these Danish colleagues you keep talking about?"

Linda realized she was shouting. A nurse popped her head in and gave them a stern look.

"We need this room for another patient," she said.

There was a bleeding woman lying on a stretcher in the corridor, banging her fist against the wall. A waiting room was empty and they walked in.

"The man who hit me was about one hundred and eighty centimeters tall. I couldn't see his face since he was wearing a sweatshirt with the hood pulled up. The sweatshirt was either black or dark blue. He had dark pants and brown shoes. He was thin. He spoke Danish and had a high-pitched voice. He also smelled of cinnamon."

"Cinnamon?" Lindman said.

"Maybe he had been eating a cinnamon bun, how should I know? Anyway, call your colleagues and find out if the man they have in custody matches this description. If I can just find that out, I'll keep my mouth shut for the time being."

"No," Wallander said. "We're going home."

Linda looked at Lindman. He nodded carefully after Wallander had already turned his back.

The doorbell rang. Linda sat up in a daze and looked at the alarm clock. It was a quarter past eleven. She climbed out of bed and put on her robe. Her head was sore, but the throbbing pain was gone. She opened the front door. It was Lindman.

"I'm sorry if I woke you up."

She let him in.

"Wait in the living room. I'll be right back."

She ran into the bathroom, splashed water on her face, brushed her teeth, and combed her hair. When she returned he was standing in front of the balcony door. It was open.

"How are you feeling today?"

"I feel OK. Would you like some coffee?"

"I don't have time. I just wanted to tell you about a phone call I made about an hour ago."

Linda waited. He must have believed what she told him back at the hospital.

"What did they say?"

"It took a little while to get to the right officer. I had to wake somebody called Ole Hedtoft who had worked all night. He was one of the patrol officers who found you, and who arrested the guy who did it."

Lindman took out a piece of paper from the pocket of his leather jacket and looked at her.

"Give me Ulrik Larsen's description again."

"I don't know if his name really is Ulrik Larsen, but the man who attacked me was one hundred and eighty centimeters, thin, with a black or navy blue hooded sweatshirt, dark pants, and brown shoes."

Lindman nodded and then rubbed the bridge of his nose with his thumb and index finger.

"Ole Hedtoft described the same man. But you may have misunderstood the threat he made."

Linda shook her head.

"That's not possible. He talked about the man I was looking for, Torgeir Langaas."

"Well, somebody must have misunderstood something."

"Why do you keep going on about a misunderstanding? I know what happened, and I'm more afraid than ever that Anna is in danger."

"Report it then. Talk to her mother. Why doesn't she come report her missing?"

"I don't know."

"Shouldn't she be worried?"

"I can't explain why she isn't worried, but I do know Anna may be in danger."

Lindman started walking back to the front door.

"Report it to the police and let us take care of it."

"You haven't done much up to this point."

Lindman stopped dead. He was angry when he answered her.

"We're working around the clock," he said. "We're investigating something that has actually taken place: a homicide, and a repulsive, baffling one at that."

"Then we're in the same situation," she said calmly. "My friend Anna isn't there when I call or knock on her door. And I'm baffled by that too."

She opened the door for him.

"Thanks for at least believing part of what I told you."

"This is between the two of us. There's no need to mention it to your dad."

Lindman ran down the stairs. Linda ate a hasty breakfast, put her clothes on, then called Zeba. She didn't pick up. Linda drove over to Anna's apartment, but this time there were no signs that the place had been disturbed in any way. *Where are you?* Linda called out silently. *You'll have a lot to explain when you get back.*

She opened a window, pulled up a chair, and opened Anna's journal. *There has to be a clue somewhere,* she thought. *Something that can explain what's happened.*

Linda started reading, going back about a month into the past. Suddenly she stopped. There was a name scribbled in the margin, as if a reminder by Anna to herself. Linda frowned. She knew she had seen or heard it recently, but where? She put down the diary. There was a distant rumble of thunder. The heat was oppressive. A name that she had seen or heard, the question was where or from whom. She made herself some coffee and tried to distract herself enough to make her brain relax and shake out the name. Nothing happened.

———

It was only later when she was about to give up that she finally remembered.

She had seen it less than twenty-four hours ago. It was the name of one of the people living in the apartment building on Nedergade.

29

*V*igsten. She knew she was right. She wasn't sure if it was someone living on the street side or in the inner building over the
courtyard, nor if there was a D or an O as a first initial, but she knew
she was right about the surname. *What do I do now?* she thought. *I'm
working on something that is actually starting to hang together. But I'm the
only one who takes it seriously; I haven't managed to convince anyone else. Of
course, I have no idea what is actually going on. Anna thought she saw her
father and then she disappeared. Two disappearances that camouflage each
other, cancel each other out, or complete each other?* Linda felt a sudden
need to talk to someone, and there was no one to turn to except
Zeba. She ran down the stairs of Anna's building and drove to Zeba's
place. Zeba was just on her way out with her son. Linda tagged
along. They went to a nearby playground, where the boy ran off to
the sandbox. There was a bench there, although it was littered with
dirt and chewing gum.

They sat on the edge of the sandbox while the boy threw sand
around and let out whoops of joy. Linda looked at Zeba and felt the
usual sting of envy: Zeba was extravagantly beautiful. There was
something arrogant and inviting about her at the same time, the
kind of woman Linda had once dreamed of becoming. *But I became
a policewoman,* she thought. *A policewoman who hopes she won't turn
out to be a scaredy-cat.*

"I've been trying to reach Anna," Zeba said. "She hasn't been
home. Have you seen her?"

This infuriated Linda.

"Hello? Have you been listening to a single word I've said? About
her being gone, that I'm worried about her, that I think something's
happened to her?"

"But you know what she's like, don't you?"

"Do I? Apparently not. What *is* she like?"

Zeba frowned.

"Why are you so worked up?"

"I'm worried about her."

"What do you think has happened? And what is that bruise on your head, for heaven's sake?"

Linda decided to fill her in on the latest events. Zeba paid attention in silence. The boy played.

"I could have told you that," she said when Linda finished. "The part about Anna being religious."

Linda looked at her.

"Religious?"

"Yes."

"She never said anything to me."

"You only just met up again, after a long gap. And Anna is the kind of person who says different things to different people. She tells a lot of lies."

"Really?"

"I had been meaning to warn you, but I thought it would be best if you discovered it for yourself. Anna is a compulsive liar. She can say just about anything."

"She didn't used to be like that."

"People change, don't they?" Zeba said in a mocking tone. "I'm friends with Anna because of her good qualities. She's cheerful, nice to my son, helpful. But when she starts telling one of her stories, I don't bother to listen. Do you know that she spent last Christmas with you?"

"I was still in Stockholm last winter."

"She said she had been up to see you. Among the many things you did together, apparently, was a trip over to Helsinki on the ferry."

"That's absurd."

"Of course it is. But that's what Anna told me. I don't know why she lies, perhaps it's an illness or else she's just bored."

"Do you think she was lying when she said she had seen her father in Malmö?"

"Of course. It's so typical of her to invent an amazing reappearance like that, even though her father has probably been dead for a long time."

"So you don't think anything has happened to Anna?"

Zeba looked at her with an amused expression.

"What could possibly have happened to her? She's gone off like this many times before. She comes back when she's done, and then she has a fantastic and completely fabricated story about where she's been."

"And nothing of what she says is true?"

"Compulsive liars are only successful if they weave in enough aspects that are true. Then we believe it, then the lie sails by, until we finally realize their whole world is built out of lies."

Linda shook her head in slight bewilderment.

"The medical studies?"

"I don't believe a word of it."

"But where does she get her money? What does she do?"

"I've wondered about that. Sometimes I think she might be a professional con artist, but I really don't have a clue."

Zeba's son called out to her and she joined him in the sandbox. Linda watched her as she walked over. A man walking by on the street also turned around to look at her. Linda thought about what Zeba had said. *It doesn't explain everything,* she thought. *It explains a part of it, and it reduces my anxiety and above all infuriates me, since I now know that Anna has been feeding me lies. I don't like people claiming to have gone to Helsinki with me when it's not true. It explains a lot,* she thought. *But not everything.*

When they had gone their separate ways, Linda walked down into the center of town and withdrew some money from an ATM. She was careful with money since she worried about finding herself without. *I'm like my dad,* she thought. *We're both thrifty to the point of being miserly.*

She walked home, cleaned the apartment, and then called the housing agency. After several tries she managed to reach the man in charge of her case. She asked if she could move into the apartment earlier than planned, but apparently that wasn't possible. She lay on the bed in her room and thought more about the conversation with Zeba. Her concerns for Anna's well-being had been replaced by a feeling of unease over the fact that she hadn't seen through her lies. But what should she have noticed? How did one see through a person who did not concoct remarkable, fantastic stories but lied about everyday events?

Linda got up and called Zeba.

"I never finished talking to you about Anna's religiosity."

"Why don't you ask her about it when she comes back? Anna believes in God."

"Which one?"

"The Christian one. She goes to church occasionally, or she says she does. But she does pray. I know because I've caught her in the act a couple of times. She gets down on her knees."

"Do you know if she belongs to a particular congregation or sect?"

"No. Do you?"

"I don't know. Have the two of you ever talked about it?"

"She's tried to a couple of times but I've always put a stop to it. God and I never got along too well."

Linda heard a howl in the background.

"Oops, he just hurt himself. Bye."

Linda walked back over to the bed and continued staring up at the ceiling. *What do we really know about people?* An image of Anna floated through her mind, but it was like looking at a stranger. Mona was also there, naked, with a bottle in her hand. Linda sat up. *I'm surrounded by a bunch of crazy people,* she thought. *The only normal one is Dad.*

She walked out onto the balcony. It was still a warm day. *I'm going to drop this thing here and now,* she said to herself. *I should concentrate on something important, like enjoying this weather for instance.*

Linda read in the newspaper about the investigation into Birgitta Medberg's murder. Her father was interviewed. She had read the same words many times before. *No definitive leads, the investigation continues on many fronts, results may take time.* She threw the paper down and thought about the name in Anna's diary. *Vigsten.* The second person in her diary after Birgitta Medberg to have crossed Linda's path.

One more time, she thought. *One more trip across the bridge, even though it's expensive. But one day I'll present Anna with a bill for all the needless worrying she's caused.*

This time I'm not going to walk around on Nedergade in the dark, she thought as she drove across the bridge toward Denmark. *I'm going to look up the man—I'm assuming it's a man—whose name is Vigsten and ask him if he knows where Anna is. That's all. Then I'm going to go home and cook dinner for my dad.*

Linda parked in the same spot as before and was hit by a sense of dread when she got out of the car. It was as if she hadn't fully realized it before now: she had been attacked on this street the night before.

She got back into her car and locked the doors. *Take it easy,* she thought. *I'm just going to get out of the car; there's no one who's going to knock me down. I'll walk into that building and find this Vigsten person. And that will be that.*

Linda kept telling herself to remain calm, but she ran across the street. A cyclist veered hard to get out of her way and almost fell over, yelling an obscenity after her. The front door opened when she pushed on it. She saw the name almost immediately. On the fourth floor, F. Vigsten. She hadn't remembered the initial correctly. She started walking up the stairs. *Fredrik Vigsten,* she thought. *It'll be Fredrik if it's a man, that's typically Danish. Or Frederike for a woman.* She stopped and caught her breath once she was on the fourth floor. Then she rang the doorbell, which played a short melody. She waited and counted slowly to ten. Then she rang again, and the door opened at about the same time. An older man with ruffled hair and glasses hanging from a cord around his neck gave her a stern look.

"I can't walk any faster," he said. "Why can't you young people have some patience?"

He stepped aside without asking for her name or why she was there, hurrying her into the hall.

"I sometimes forget when I have a new student," he said. "I don't always make a note of everything as conscientiously as I should. Please feel free to hang up your things. I'll wait in there."

He disappeared down a long corridor with short, almost springy steps. *A student of what?* Linda wondered. She took off her jacket and followed him. It was a large apartment, perhaps the result of knocking down a wall between two smaller ones. In the room farthest in from the door there was a black baby grand piano. The white-haired man was over by the window, leafing through the pages of a monthly planner.

"I can't see an appointment for today," he complained. "What did you say your name was?"

"I'm not a student," Linda said. "I just want to ask you some questions."

"I've been answering questions my whole life," he said. "I've told them why it's so important to sit correctly when playing the piano. I've tried to explain to countless young pianists why not everyone can learn to play Chopin with the right combination of caution and power that is required. Above all I try to get my impatient opera singers to stand properly, and not attempt the hardest pieces without wearing good shoes. Have you got that? Opera singers need good shoes, and pianists need to take care to avoid developing hemorrhoids. What did you say your name was?"

"It's Linda and I'm neither a pianist nor an opera singer. I've come to ask you about something that has nothing to do with music."

"Well, you must have the wrong man because I can only answer questions about music. The world beyond that is incomprehensible to me."

Linda was momentarily confused.

"Your name is Fredrik Vigsten, isn't it?"

"Not Fredrik: Frans. But the last name is right."

He sat down at the piano and began turning over the pages of some music. Linda had the feeling that he had forgotten she was there.

"Your name appears in my friend Anna Westin's diary," she said.

Frans Vigsten tapped his finger on the paper rhythmically and did not seem to hear her.

"Anna Westin," she repeated in a louder voice.

He looked up abruptly.

"Who?"

"Anna Westin. A Swedish girl."

"I've had many Swedish pupils," he said. "Of course, now it is as if everyone has forgotten about me, and—"

He interrupted himself and looked at Linda.

"Did you tell me your name?"

"I'm happy to tell you again. It's Linda."

"And you are not a pupil? Not a pianist? Not an opera singer?"

"No."

"You're asking about someone called Anna?"

"Anna Westin."

"I don't know an Anna Westin. Vest-in. My wife was a vest*al*, but she died thirty-nine years ago. Do you have any idea what it is like to be a widower for almost forty years?"

He stretched out a thin hand with finely etched blue veins and touched her wrist.

"Alone," he said. "It was one thing when I had my day job doing rehearsals at Det Kongelige. But then one day they told me I was too old. Maybe it was that I insisted on doing things the old way. I didn't tolerate sloppiness."

"I found your name in my friend's diary," Linda broke in.

She took his hand. The fingers that grabbed onto hers so hungrily were surprisingly strong.

"Anna Westin, is that right?"

"Yes."

"I've never had a pupil by that name. My memory is not what it once was, but I can still remember all their names. They are the only ones who have given my life any meaning since Mariana was taken by the gods."

Linda didn't know if there was any point in continuing the conversation. There was really only one thing left to ask.

"Do you know anyone by the name of Torgeir Langaas? I'm looking for him."

But Frans Vigsten was lost in dreamland again. He picked out some notes on the piano with his free hand.

"Torgeir Langaas," she repeated. "A Norwegian."

"I have had many Norwegian pupils. The one I remember best

was Trond Ørje. He was from Rauland and a wonderful baritone, but he was so shy he could only pull it off in the recording studio. He was the most remarkable baritone and the most remarkable person I ever met in my life. He cried with consternation when I told him he had talent. A remarkable man. There are others. . . ."

Linda got up. She was never going to get a sensible answer out of him. It also seemed unlikely to her that Anna had had any contact with him.

She left the room without saying good-bye. As she walked to the front door, she heard him start playing on the piano. She glanced into the other rooms on her way out. The apartment was a mess and the air was stale. *A lonely man who only has his music,* she thought. *Just like my grandfather and his painting. What am I going to do when I get old? What about Dad? And what about Mom—the bottle?*

She lifted her jacket from the hook in the hall. Music filled the apartment. She stood motionless and studied the clothes hanging by the door. Vigsten might be a lonely old man, but he had a coat and a pair of shoes that did not belong to an old man. She glanced back into the apartment. There was no one there. But she already knew that Frans Vigsten did not live alone. Fear flooded her so quickly that she jumped. The music stopped, and she listened for any sounds. Then she fled, running across the street to the car, and driving away as fast as she could. She only started to calm down when she was back on the Öresund Bridge heading home.

At the same time that Linda was driving over the bridge, a man broke into the Ystad pet store. He doused the rows of caged birds, hamsters, and mice with gasoline, threw a match on the floor, and left just as the animals caught fire.

PART III

the noose

30

He chose the location for his ceremonies with great care. This was something he had learned as early as during his flight from Jonestown: where could he rest, where would he feel safe? There were no ceremonies as such in his world back then; that came later, when he had reestablished a connection to God that was finally going to help fill the emptiness that threatened to consume him from the inside.

Now it was more important than ever not to make any mistakes in selecting the places where his assistants prepared their assignments. Everything had gone well until now, until the unfortunate incident where a woman accidentally hit upon one of their hideouts and was killed by his disciple, Torgeir.

I never saw Torgeir's weakness for what it was, he thought. *The poor little rich boy that I plucked out of the sewer in Cleveland had a temper I never succeeded in taming. I treated him with infinite patience and listened to him talk. But he carried a powerful rage behind those locked doors.*

He had tried to get Torgeir to explain his actions. Why this senseless fury at a woman stumbling down the wrong path? They had even talked about what they should do in the event that someone chose to follow the abandoned path one day. They always had to remain alert to the possibility that the unexpected could happen. Torgeir had not been able to give him an answer. The plan had always been to meet unexpected visitors in a cordial fashion, then remove themselves from the area as soon as was practical. Torgeir had chosen the opposite approach. A fuse had blown in his brain. Instead of giving the woman a friendly welcome, he had reached for an axe. Why he dismembered her body he couldn't say, nor why he saved the head and posed the hands as if in prayer. Then he had put the remaining body parts in a sack with a heavy rock, removed his clothes, and swum out into the middle of the nearest pond, where he let the whole parcel sink to the bottom.

Torgeir was strong—that had been among his first impressions of the drunk man he encountered in one of Cleveland's worst slums. He was simply going to walk on when he heard the man sprawled in the gutter moan a few slurred words in a language that sounded like Danish or Norwegian. He had stopped and bent down, understanding that God had sent this man his way. Torgeir Langaas had been near death. The physician who later examined him and prepared the rehabilitation program had been very insistent on this point: there was no room left for any more alcohol or drugs in his body. Only his natural strength had saved him. But now his organs were using their last reserves. His brain was damaged and would perhaps never recover large portions of memory that were missing.

It was a moment he would always remember, the day when a homeless Norwegian by the name of Torgeir Langaas looked up at him with eyes so bloodshot they glowed like a rabid dog's. But it wasn't the look that had made such an impression, it was what he said, because in Torgeir's confused mind the face bending down toward him belonged to God. He had grabbed his coat with his massive hands and directed his putrid breath into his redeemer's face.

"Are you God?" Torgeir asked.

In that moment everything that had been unresolved in his life—his failures, dreams, and hopes—were reduced to a single point, and he answered:

"Yes, I am your God."

In the next moment he had been beset with doubts, although there was no reason his first disciple couldn't be one of the lowest. But who was he? How had he ended up here?

He had walked away and left Torgeir there, but his curiosity got the better of him. He returned to the slum the very next day. *It's like stepping down into hell*, he thought, *lost souls everywhere*. In looking for Torgeir he came close to being mugged several times, but at last an old man with an oozing, stinking sore in the place where his left eye should have been told him that there was a Norwegian with large hands who sometimes took shelter behind a rusty bridge pillar. That was where he found him. Torgeir Langaas was sleeping, snoring loudly. His body reeked of sweat and urine and his face was badly cut.

It didn't take more than a couple of sessions under the crumbling bridge to get Torgeir's life story. He had been born in Baerum in 1948, heir to the Langaas shipping enterprise, a company that specialized in oil and cars. His father, Captain Anton Helge Langaas, had studied the shipping industry during his years at sea. Langaas Shipping was an offshoot of the established Refsvold Shipping Company. The parting had not been amicable. Nor was it known where Captain Helge Langaas had initially made the fortune that forced the unwilling board members of the Refsvold Shipping Company to admit him into their midst. Rumors abounded.

Captain Langaas waited to marry until his company was in the black and he was financially secure. In a gesture of contempt for the shipping aristocracy, he chose a wife who was as far from the sea as it was possible to be and still be in Norway, from a village in the forests east of Røros. There he found a woman called Maigrim who delivered mail to the isolated farms of the region. They built a large house in Baerum outside Oslo and had three children one after the other: Torgeir, and then two girls, Anniken and Hege.

Torgeir Langaas sensed what his parents wanted of him from an early age, but realized just as early that he would never be able to live up to their expectations. He never quite understood the role he was supposed to play in life, nor what the play was about, nor why he had been chosen for the starring role. He started rebelling in early adolescence. Captain Langaas fought a battle that was doomed from the outset. Finally he capitulated and realized that Torgeir would never take over his place in the family business. Instead, he turned to his daughters. Hege resembled her father, showed a focused determination even as a child, and retained an executive position within the company at twenty-two years of age. At that point Torgeir had already started his long slide into oblivion with a focused determination of his own. He had already developed several addictions, and

despite Maigrim's best efforts, none of the expensive clinics nor ther-
apists called in to help did any good.

The final breakdown came one Christmas. Torgeir gave his family
presents of rotting meat, old tires, and dirty cobblestones. Afterward
he tried to set fire to himself, his sisters, and his parents. He ran away,
with no intention of ever returning, a considerable amount of money
to his name. When his passport expired and was not renewed, he
was wanted by the International Police, but no one found him in
the Cleveland streets where he was drifting. He kept his financial
assets hidden from those around him, changing his bank, changing
everything except his name. He still had five million Norwegian
crowns to his name when the man he came to see as his savior
turned up in his life.

But I did not take adequate stock of his weakness, he thought again. *The
rage that would lead to uncontrolled violence.* Torgeir was blinded by his
fury and hacked the woman to pieces. But there was also something
of value even in this unexpected reaction and capacity for brutality.
Setting fire to animals was one thing, killing a person quite another.
Apparently Torgeir would not hesitate to commit such an act. Now
that all the necessary animals had been sacrificed, they would proceed to the next level: human sacrifice.

They met at the Ystad train station. Torgeir had taken the train
from Copenhagen, since he sometimes lost his sense of concentration when driving. Torgeir had bathed—that was part of the purifica-
tion process that always preceded the ritual sacrifice. It was important
to be clean. Jesus always washed his feet. He had explained to
Torgeir that everything was there in the Bible. It was their map, their
guide.

Torgeir carried a small black bag in his hand. He knew what was
in it and did not have to ask. Torgeir had long since proved himself to
be reliable—except with regard to the woman in the forest, which
had caused an unnecessary amount of publicity and activity. Newspapers and television stations were still broadcasting the news. The
act they were planning now had already been postponed for two
days, and he had felt it best that Torgeir use his Copenhagen hideout while they lay low and waited it out.

They walked up toward the center of town, turned a corner when they reached the post office, and continued on to the pet store. There were no customers inside. The woman behind the counter was young. She was busy putting cans of cat food on a shelf when they arrived. There were hamsters, kittens, and birds in the cages. Torgeir smiled but said nothing; there was no point in letting her hear his Norwegian accent. While Torgeir walked around the store and made a mental note of how he would carry out his actions, his savior selected and bought a packet of birdseed. Then they left the store and walked down past the theater and toward the harbor. It was a warm day, and a number of sailboats were still coming and going.

That was the second part of their preparations, to be close to the water. Once, they had met by the shores of Lake Erie, and from then on they always sought out a body of water when they had important preparations to make.

"The cages are close together," Torgeir said. "I'll spray with both hands in either direction, light the lighter, and run. Everything will be on fire within a few seconds."

"And then?"

"Then I say: 'The Lord's will be done.'"

"And then?"

"I go to the left, then right. Not too fast, not too slow. I stop on the main square and make sure no one is following me. Then I walk up to the newsstand by the hospital, where you'll be waiting."

They paused their conversation and looked at a small boat on its way into the harbor. The engine was loud and hacking.

"These are the last animals. We have reached our first goal."

Torgeir was about to kneel right then and there on the pier. He dragged him up by his arm.

"*Never* in public."

"I forgot."

"Are you calm?"

"Yes."

"Who am I?"

"My father, my shepherd, my savior, my God."

"Who are you?"

"The first disciple. Found on a street in Cleveland, saved and helped back into life. I am the first apostle."

"What else?"

"The first priest."

Once I made sandals for a living, he thought. *I dreamed of greater things and had to run away to escape my shame, my sense of failure, my sense of having destroyed those dreams by my inability to live up to them. Now I make people in the same way I once cut out soles, insteps, and straps.*

It was four o'clock. They walked around the city and sat on various park benches, remaining silent the whole time. They were past words now. From time to time he looked over at Torgeir. He seemed calm and focused on the task at hand.

I've made him happy, he thought. *A man who grew up spoiled but also stifled and desperately unhappy. Now I bring joy to his life by taking him seriously and giving him a purpose.*

They wandered from bench to bench until it was seven o'clock. The pet store closed at six. Many people were out in the streets in the warm evening. That was to their advantage.

They went their separate ways. He walked up to the main square and turned around. Their plans ticked like a timer in his head. Now Torgeir was breaking down the front door with the crowbar. Now he was inside, closing the broken door behind him, listening for signs of anyone in the store. Now he was dropping the bag, taking out the bottles of gasoline and the lighter.

He heard the boom and thought he saw a flash of light behind the buildings. A plume of smoke rose up into the sky. He turned and started walking away. He heard the first sirens even before he had made it to the appointed meeting place.

It's over, he thought. *We are reviving the Christian faith, the Christian dictates of a righteous life. The long years in the desert have come to an end.*

The simple beast who feels pain but lacks comprehension is no longer our concern.

Now we turn to the human being.

31

When Linda got out of the car at Mariagatan, she smelled something that reminded her of a week-long vacation she had taken with Herman Mboya to Morocco. They had chosen the cheapest package deal and bunked in a cockroach hotel. It was during that week that she had begun to think they didn't have a future together. The following year they had gone their separate ways; Herman had returned to Africa and she had started down the path that finally led her to the police academy.

The smell was what triggered the memory. Mounds of garbage were burned at night in Morocco. *But no one burns their trash in Ystad,* she thought. Then she heard the fire trucks and police sirens. There was a fire in the center of town somewhere. She started to run.

The fire was still raging when she arrived, panting like a housebound old woman. When had she gotten this out of shape? She saw tall flames leap up through the roof. The families that lived in the upper stories had been evacuated. A badly damaged baby carriage had been abandoned in front. Firefighters were busy securing the surrounding buildings. Linda made her way up to the police tape.

Her father was quarreling with Svartman about a witness who had not been interviewed thoroughly, and to top it off had been allowed to disappear.

"We'll never get this madman if we can't even follow the simplest of routines."

"Martinsson was in charge of it."

"And he's told me twice that he delegated it to you. Now you'll have to track down the witness somehow."

Svartman left, clearly feeling wronged. *They're like angry bulls,* Linda thought. *All this time and energy spent marking their territory.*

———

A fire truck that was backing up toward the rescue operation knocked a hose loose, which started whipping around, spraying water. Wallander jumped to the side, and caught sight of Linda at the same time.

"What happened here?" she asked.

"One or more firebombs in the store. Torched animals, same as the swans and the calf."

"Any clues?"

"One witness, but no one seems to know where the person went."

Wallander was so furious he was shaking. *This is how he'll die,* Linda thought suddenly. *Exhausted, outraged by an oversight in a pressing criminal investigation.*

"We have to get these bastards," he said, interrupting her train of thought.

"I think this is different."

"What is it?"

He looked at her as if she knew the answer.

"I don't know. It's as if it were really about something else."

Höglund called out to Wallander.

Linda watched him walk away, a large man with his head pulled down into his shoulders, stepping carefully over the hoses and the smoking remains of what had once been a pet store. Linda's gaze fell on a teary-eyed young woman watching the blaze. *The owner,* she mused. *Or simply someone who loves animals.* There were a number of spectators, all silent. *Burning buildings always inspire dread,* she thought. *A house on fire is a reminder that our own home could one day burn to the ground.*

"Why aren't they asking me questions? I don't get it."

Linda turned around and saw a woman in her twenties pressed up against a nearby wall. She was talking to a friend. A waft of smoke made them both pull back even farther.

"Why don't you just go over and tell them what you saw?" her friend said.

"I'm not going to go out of my way for the police."

The witness, Linda thought and took a step closer.

"What did you see?" she asked.

The woman eyed her suspiciously and Linda saw that she was slightly walleyed.

"Who are you?"

"My name is Linda Wallander. I'm a police officer."

Well, it's almost true, she thought.

"How could someone kill all those animals? And I heard there was a horse in there too. Is that true?"

"No," Linda said. "What did you see?"

"A man."

"What was he doing?"

"He started the fire that burned all those animals. I was walking from the direction of the theater. I was going to mail some letters, which I do several times a week. When I was about halfway to the post office, about a block from the pet store, I noticed someone walking behind me. I was startled because he had been walking almost soundlessly. I let him pass me. Then I started following him, trying to walk as quietly as he did, I don't know why. But after a few feet I realized I had left a letter in the car so I turned around and went back for it."

Linda lifted her hand.

"How long did it take you to go back and get the letter?"

"Three or four minutes. The car was parked by the delivery entrance to the theater."

"What happened when you started back for the post office? Did you see the man again?"

"No."

"And when you walked past the pet store, what did you do?"

"I glanced at the window—but I'm not so interested in hamsters and turtles."

"What did you see?"

"A blue light inside the store. It's always on. It's some kind of heat lamp, I think."

"Then what happened?"

"I mailed my letters and started walking back to the car. It took another three minutes or so."

"And then?"

"Then the store exploded, or it felt that way. I had just walked past it. There was a sharp light all around me. I threw myself down onto the street. Then I saw that the store was in flames. An animal must have gotten loose, and it ran past me with its fur on fire. It was horrible."

"What did you do then?"

"It all happened so fast. But I saw a man standing on the other side of the street. The light was so strong that I was positive; it was the man who had overtaken me on the street. He was carrying a bag in his hand."

"Had he been carrying it before?"

"Yes. I forgot to mention it. A black bag, like an old-fashioned doctor's bag."

Linda knew what they looked like.

"What did you do?"

"I called out to him to help me."

"Were you hurt?"

"I thought so. It was such a loud bang and then that terrible light."

"Did he help you?"

"No, he just looked at me and walked away."

"In what direction?"

"Up toward the main square."

"Had you ever seen him before?"

"Never."

"How would you describe him?"

"He was tall and strong-looking. Maybe bald, or with very short hair. He had a dark blue coat, dark pants. His shoes I had looked at when he walked past and I wondered how he could walk so quietly. They were brown and had thick rubber soles, but they weren't running shoes."

"Do you remember anything else?"

"He shouted something."

"Who was he talking to?"

"I don't know."

"Was there anyone else there?"

"Not that I could see."

"What did he say?"

"It sounded like 'The Lord's will be done.' "

" 'The Lord's will be done'?"

"I'm sure of the word 'Lord,' but the word 'will' sounded like it was pronounced in a foreign language. Danish, maybe. Or Norwegian, more like it. Yes, that's it. The guy sounded like he was speaking Norwegian."

Linda's heart beat a little faster. *It has to be the same guy,* she thought. *Unless there's a Norwegian conspiracy at work. But that seems a little far-fetched.*

"Did he say anything else?"

"No."

"What's your name?"

"Amy Lindberg."

Linda fished a pen out of her pocket and wrote down Amy's phone number on her wrist.

They shook hands.

"Thanks for listening to me," Amy Lindberg said, and she turned to rejoin her friend.

The mysterious Torgeir Langaas, Linda mused. *He keeps cropping up in my life when I least expect it.*

She could see that the firefighting operation had reached a new stage. Workers were moving more slowly, a sign that the blaze would soon be contained. She saw her dad talking to the fire chief. When his head turned in her direction she pulled herself back even farther, although it was impossible for him to see her in the shadows. Stefan Lindman walked by with the young woman she had seen earlier, who had cried as she watched the fire. *It suits him to comfort crying women,* she thought. *I, on the other hand, almost never cry. I stopped all that when I was still little.* She watched Lindman lead the woman over to a patrol car. They said a few words to each other, then he opened the door for her and she climbed in.

The conversation with Amy Lindberg kept coming back to her. *The Lord's will be done. But what exactly did this god want? That a pet store burn to the ground, that some helpless animals die in unimaginable terror and pain? First it was swans,* she thought. *Then the calf: singled out, charred, dead. And now a whole store full of pets. It was clearly the work of the same man, one who had calmly regarded his work and said: The Lord's will be done.*

Linda walked over to Lindman, who looked at her with surprise.

"What are you doing here?"

"I'm just a curious onlooker. But I need to talk to you."

"What about?"

"The fire."

He thought for a moment.

"I have to go home and eat something anyway," he said. "You can come along."

Stefan's apartment was located in one of three high-rises scattered arbitrarily across an area dotted with a few single-family homes and a paper-recycling center.

His was the middle building. The glass in the front door had been smashed and replaced by a piece of cardboard in which someone had also kicked a hole. Linda saw a message scribbled on the wall: LIFE IS FOR SALE. SPREAD THE WORD.

"I read that every day," Stefan said. "Makes you think, doesn't it?"

He unlocked the apartment and handed her a hanger for her coat. They walked into the living room, which was furnished with a few simple pieces, randomly scattered around the room.

"I don't have anything to offer you except water or beer," he said. "This is just a place for me to camp out."

"Where are you moving? You said something about Knickarp."

"I'm renovating a house out there. It has a large garden. I'm looking forward to it."

"I'm still at my dad's," Linda said. "I'm counting the days until I get out of there."

"You have a good father."

She was taken aback.

"What do you mean?"

"Just that. You have a good father. I didn't."

Some newspapers were lying on a side table. She pulled over a copy of the *Borås Daily*.

"I'm not nostalgic," he said. "I subscribe to it because I enjoy reading about everything I've managed to escape."

"It was that awful?"

"I knew I had to leave when it was clear I was going to survive the cancer."

He fell silent. Linda wasn't sure how to change the subject. Then he stood up.

"I'll get the beer and some sandwiches."

He came back with two glasses. Linda declined the sandwich.

She told him how she had overheard the conversation between Amy Lindberg and her friend and subsequently asked her some questions. Stefan listened attentively. She continued to talk, going back to the incident when Anna thought she saw her father in the street in Malmö. The shadowy figure of a Norwegian, who was perhaps named Torgeir Langaas, kept appearing in her account.

"Someone is killing animals," she said in conclusion. "Someone has also killed a person, cut her up into pieces. And Anna has disappeared."

"I understand your concern," Stefan said. "Not only because of the vaguely disturbing possibility of a return by Anna's father. We also have the menacing presence of an unknown person, someone who says 'The Lord's will be done'. Perhaps not aloud, but the intent is there in all his actions. You've also learned that your friend Anna is religious. These random facts are starting to look like pieces of a grotesque puzzle, not least the morbid detail of allowing two severed hands to go on pleading for mercy after death. From everything you've said and from what I already know of the case, it's clear that there's a religious dimension to all of this that we haven't taken as seriously as we perhaps should have."

He drank the last of his beer. There was a rumble of thunder in the distance.

"It's out over Bornholm," Linda said. "There are often thunderstorms out there."

"It's an easterly wind. That means it's on its way here."

"What do you think about what I just told you?"

"That it's true. And that what you've told me will impact our investigation."

"Which investigation?"

"Birgitta Medberg. Anna's disappearance has not been a priority up to this point. I guess that will change now."

"Am I right to be scared?"

He shook his head hesitantly.

"I don't know. I'm going to write down everything you've told me, and it wouldn't be a bad idea for you to do the same. I'll let my colleagues know about this tomorrow."

Linda shivered.

"Dad will be furious that I went to you first and not him."

"Why don't you blame it on the fact that he was so busy with the arson?"

"He keeps saying he's never too busy when it comes to me."

Stefan helped her put on her coat. She thought again that she was genuinely attracted to him. His hands on her shoulders were gentle.

She returned to Mariagatan. Her father was waiting for her at the kitchen table, and she could tell from his face that he was angry. *You bastard,* she thought. *Couldn't you at least have waited until I got home?*

She sat down across from him and braced herself.

"If you're just going to rant and rave I'm going to bed. No, I'll leave. I'll sleep in the car."

"You could at least have talked to me. This amounts to a breach of trust, Linda. A huge breach of trust."

"For Christ's sake—you were in the middle of a pet massacre. A street was going up in flames."

"You shouldn't have taken it upon yourself to talk to that girl. What gave you the right to do that? How many times do I have to tell you this is not your business? You haven't even started working yet."

Linda pulled up her sleeve, and showed him Amy Lindberg's phone number.

"Will that do? I'm going to bed."

"I find it deeply disturbing that you don't even have enough respect for me not to go behind my back."

Linda's eyes widened.

"Go behind your back? Who said anything about going behind your back?"

"You know what I'm saying."

Linda swept a salt shaker and a vase of withered roses to the floor. He had gone too far. She rushed out into the hallway, grabbed her coat, and slammed the front door behind her. *I hate him,* she thought, fumbling in her pocket for the car keys. *I hate his endless nagging. I'm not spending another night in this place.*

She tried to calm herself when she reached the car. *He expects me to feel guilty,* she thought. *He's waiting for me to go back and tell him that little Linda Caroline had a moment of rebellion but takes it all back now.*

"Well, I'm not going back," she said aloud. "I'll stay with Zeba." She was about to start the car when she changed her mind. Zeba would talk, ask questions, discuss the situation. Linda didn't have the energy for that. She drove to Anna's apartment instead. Her dad could sit at the kitchen table and wait until the end of the world as far as she was concerned.

She put the key in the lock and pushed the door open.

Anna was standing in the hall with a smile on her face.

32

I knew it had to be you. No one else would drop by like this, like a thief in the night. You probably intuited I had come back and woke up. Isn't that it?" Anna said cheerfully.

Linda dropped her keys.

"I don't understand. Is it really you?"

"It's me."

"I can't tell you how relieved I am."

Anna frowned.

"Why are you relieved?"

"I've been worried sick about you."

Anna lifted her hands in apology.

"I'm guilty, I know. Do you want me to apologize or tell you what happened?"

"You don't have to do either right now. It's enough that you're here."

They went into the living room. Even though Linda was struggling to come to terms with the fact that Anna was back and sitting in her usual chair, she noticed that the framed blue butterfly was still missing.

"I came over because I had a fight with my dad," Linda said. "I thought I would sleep on your couch since you were away."

"You can still sleep here even though I'm back."

"He made me so mad. My dad and I are like two roosters fighting on a dung heap. The more we struggle, the more we get mired into the muck. We were arguing about you, actually."

"About me?"

Linda stretched out her hand and brushed Anna's arm with her fingertips. Anna was wearing a robe on which the sleeves had been cut off for some reason. Anna's skin was cold. There was no doubt that it really was Anna who had come back and not an impostor. Anna's skin was always cold. Linda could remember that from their childhood when they—with the tingling feeling of exploring forbidden territory—had played dead. The game had made Linda warm and sweaty, but Anna had been cold, so cold in fact that they stopped playing. It had scared them both.

"I was so worried about you," Linda said. "It's not like you to disappear and not be home when we had agreed to meet."

"You have to remember my world was turned upside-down. I thought I had seen my father. I was convinced he had come back."

She paused and looked down at her hands.

"What happened?" Linda asked.

"I went to look for him," she said. "I didn't forget about our plans, but I thought you would understand. I had seen my father for a second and I had to find him again. I was so worked up I was shaking and couldn't drive. I took the train down to Malmö and set out to look for him. It was an absolutely indescribable experience. I walked up and down the streets using all my senses, thinking there had to be a trace of him somewhere, a scent, a sound.

"It took me several hours to get from the station to the hotel where I had seen him. When I walked into the hotel lobby a fat lady was half-sleeping in the chair I had been sitting in. I became furious; she had taken my place! No one had the right to sit in the holy chair where I had seen my father and he had seen me. I walked up to her and shook her arm. I told her she had to move because the furniture was going to be replaced. She did as I asked, although I still don't understand how she could think I was part of the hotel staff in my raincoat and with wet hair stuck to my cheeks. I sat down in the chair when she had left. There was no one outside. But I thought if I just stayed there long enough he would return."

Anna stopped talking and left to go to the bathroom. Thunder rumbled in the distance. She came back and continued:

"I sat in the chair until the receptionists started looking at me suspiciously. I booked a room, but tried to spend as little time as possible there. To conceal my true purpose I pretended to be reading and taking notes. On the second day the fat lady came back. She must have been spying on me and felt that she had found me out because she said 'You thief—you stole my seat!' She was so worked up I thought she was going to hyperventilate. I thought to myself that no one would make up a lie about sitting in a chair in hopes of catching a glimpse of a father they hadn't seen in twenty years. So I told her the truth and she believed me. She sat down in the chair next to me and said she'd be happy to keep me company while I waited. It was crazy. She talked nonstop, mainly about her husband, who was attending a conference in men's hatwear. You can laugh—I didn't, of course—but it was true. She told me all about it in excruciating detail, about the rows of somber men in airless conference rooms meeting to decide which kinds of hats to order for the new season. She talked and talked until I was ready to strangle her. But then her husband appeared. He was as fat as she was, and was wearing a broad-brimmed and probably very expensive hat. She and I had never actually introduced ourselves. As she was about to leave with her husband, she said to him, 'This young lady is waiting for her father. She's been waiting a long time for him.' And the man asked, 'How long?' while he tipped his elegant hat. 'Almost twenty-five years,' she told him. And he looked at me, thoughtfully but also with great respect. And the entire hotel lobby, with its polished, sterile surfaces and strong smell of commercial-grade cleaning agents, was transformed into a church. He said, 'One can never wait too long.' Then he put his hat back on, and I watched them leave the hotel. The whole situation was absurd, almost unbelievably so, but that's what made it so real.

"I stayed in that chair for close to two days before I realized that my father was not going to reappear. I decided to go out and look for him, though I kept the room. There was no master plan to my search. I walked through the parks, along the canals and the various harbors. My father had left me and Henrietta because he sought a freedom he couldn't have while he was with us. Therefore I looked for him in the open spaces. There were times when I thought I had found him. I would get so dizzy I'd have to lean against a wall or a tree, but it was never him. All the longing I had been bottling up for so long finally turned to rage. There I was, still looking for him, still wanting so badly to find him, and he had simply chosen to humiliate me by showing himself to me once and then disappearing again. Naturally I started to doubt myself. How could I be sure that it had been him? Everything spoke against it. The last night I was there, I ended up in Pildamm Park. It was three o'clock in the morning and I called out into the darkness: 'Daddy, where are you?' But no one answered. I stayed in the park until dawn, and then I suddenly felt as though I had been through the final trial in my relationship with him, as though I had been wandering in a fog of delusion, thinking he was going to show himself to me, and when at last I emerged into the light I accepted that he didn't exist. Well, maybe he does exist, maybe he's not actually dead. But for me, from that point on, he was just going to be a mirage, a dream, that I could evoke from time to time at will, nothing more. All of those years I had always believed deep down that he was out there somewhere. Now, at the very moment that I believed he had finally returned, I realized he was never coming back at all. Now that I could no longer hold on to the idea of him as a living, breathing person, to be mad at, to keep waiting for, he was finally gone for real."

The storm clouds had moved on to the west. Anna stopped talking and looked down at her hands. Linda almost had the impression she was making sure none of her fingers were missing. She tried to imagine what it would be like if her own father had disappeared when she was a child. It was an impossible thought. He had always been there, a big enveloping shadow, sometimes warm, sometimes cold, circling her and keeping his eye on her. Linda suddenly wondered if following in his footsteps and becoming a police officer was going to be the greatest mistake of her life. *Why did I do it?* she asked herself. *He's going to crush me with all the kindness, understanding—even jealousy—he should really be giving to another woman and not to his own daughter.*

She pushed her thoughts away. She was being unfair, to him as well as to herself.

Anna looked up from her hands.

"It's over," she said. "It was no more than a reflection in the glass. I can return to my studies. Let's not talk about it anymore. I'm sorry I worried you so much."

Linda wondered if she had heard about the death of Birgitta Medberg. That was still an unanswered question—what connection was there between her and Anna? And what about Vigsten in Copenhagen? Was the name Torgeir Langaas in any of her journals? *I should have plowed through them while I had the chance,* Linda thought callously. *Reading one page or a thousand makes no difference once you've crossed the line.*

Somewhere inside her the sliver of anxiety was still there, gnawing away at her. But she decided that her questions would have to wait until later.

"I went to see your mother," Linda said. "She didn't seem particularly worried. I took that as a sign that she knew where you were. But she didn't seem to want to tell me anything."

"I didn't tell her I thought I saw my dad."

Linda thought about what Henrietta had claimed, that Anna regularly reported sightings of her father. *Who is lying, or not telling the whole truth?* Linda decided it wasn't important for the moment.

"I went to see my mother yesterday," Linda said. "I was going to surprise her, which in fact I did."

"Was she happy?"

"Not particularly. I found her in the kitchen, stark naked, drinking vodka."

"Is she an alcoholic?"

"That remains to be seen. I guess anyone can have a bad day."

"You're right," Anna said. "Well, I need to get some sleep. Do you want me to make up the couch for you?"

"No, I'm going home," Linda said. "Now that I know you're back I can sleep in my own bed, even though I'll probably have another fight with my dad first thing tomorrow morning."

Linda got up and walked out into the hall. Anna remained in the doorway to the living room. The storm had passed.

"I didn't tell you what happened at the end of my trip," Anna said. "I saw someone I wasn't expecting. This morning I was having a cup of coffee at the train station while I waited. Suddenly someone came over to my table. You'll never guess who it was."

"Since I'll never guess, it must have been the fat lady."

"Right. Her husband was standing guard over one of those huge old-fashioned trunks. It must have been full of wonderful hats all set to become the latest fashion. The fat lady was sweating and her cheeks were flushed. She leaned over to me and asked me if I had seen him. I didn't want to disappoint her, so I said yes, I had seen him. Everything had gone well. Her eyes filled with tears, then she said, 'May I tell my husband? We are returning to Halmstad now, and meeting a young woman who has been reunited with her father is a memory to cherish for life.'"

"I'll come by tomorrow," Linda said. "Let's go out like we were planning a week ago."

They agreed to meet around noon. Linda gave Anna the car keys.

"I borrowed your car when I was looking for you. I'll fill it up for you tomorrow."

"There's no need to do that. You shouldn't have to pay for being worried about me."

Linda walked home. The storm clouds were gone but there was a light rain. The wind had died down. Linda stopped and drew in the smell of asphalt and damp earth. *Everything is all right,* she thought. *I was wrong. Nothing has happened.*

But the niggling splinter of anxiety remained. She kept thinking about what Anna had said: *I saw someone I wasn't expecting.*

33

Linda woke up with a start. Her curtains were askew, letting in a ray of sunlight that reflected off the roof of a building across the street. She stretched her arm out into the light. *When does the day start?* she wondered. Every morning she had the feeling that she had a dream right before waking up that told her it was time: the day is about to begin.

She sat up. Anna was back. Linda held her breath for a moment to rule out the suspicion that it had all been a dream. But Anna had really been there in that funny robe with the sleeves cut off. Linda lolled back onto the bed and put her hand back in the ray of sun. *Summer will be over soon,* she thought. *I start work in five days. Then I get a new apartment and my father and I won't rub each other raw anymore. Soon it will be fall, and one morning there will be frost on the ground.* She looked at her arm bathed in sunlight. *We're still in the time before the frost.*

She got up when she heard her father rattling around in the bathroom. She couldn't help laughing—no one else was able to make such a racket in a bathroom. It was as if he were engaged in a fierce battle with the soaps, faucets, and towels. She put on her robe and walked out into the kitchen. It was seven. Her father appeared, drying his hair.

"I'm sorry about last night," he said.

Without waiting for an answer he walked over to her and bent his head.

"Can you tell if I'm losing my hair?"

She flicked through his wet hair.

"There's a little spot right here."

"Damn it. I don't want to go bald."

"Grandpa didn't have much hair either. It must run in the family. You'd look like an American army officer if you cut it all off."

"I don't want to look like an American army officer."

"Anna's back."

Wallander stopped in the middle of filling a pot of water.

"Anna Westin?"

"She's the only Anna I know who's been missing. Yesterday when I left I went over to her place to sleep. And there she was, just standing in her hall."

"What had happened?"

"She had gone to Malmö and stayed in a hotel. She was looking for her dad."

"Did she find him?"

"No. Finally she realized she had imagined the whole thing. Then she came back. That was yesterday."

Wallander sat down.

"She spends a few days in Malmö looking for her father. She checks into a hotel and tells no one—not a friend nor her mother— where she is. Is that right?"

"Yes."

"Do you have any reason to doubt her word?"

"Not really."

"What does that mean? Yes or no?"

"No."

Wallander filled the rest of the pot.

"So I was right. Nothing had happened."

"Birgitta Medberg's name was in her journal. As is Vigsten's. I don't know how much Lindman told you during your gossip session yesterday."

"It was no gossip session. He was very thorough—I think he's going to be the new Martinsson when it comes to making clear, concise reports. I'm going to have Anna come down to the station so she can answer a few questions for us. You can tell her that, but don't mention Medberg, and no more independent investigating from your side, understood?"

"Now you're starting to sound like a patronizing chief inspector," Linda said.

He looked surprised.

"I am an inspector," he said. "In case you didn't know. But I don't think I've ever been accused of being patronizing."

They ate their breakfast in silence, each with a section of the *Ystad Allehanda*. At half past seven Wallander got up to leave, but he changed his mind and sat down again.

"You said something the other day," he said tentatively.

Linda immediately knew what he was thinking of. It amused her to see him so embarrassed.

"You mean what I said about you needing a little action?"

"What did you really mean by that?"

"What do you think? Isn't it self-explanatory?"

"My sex life is my business."

"You don't have a sex life."

"It's still my business."

"Even if it's nonexistent? Anyway, I don't think it's good for you to be alone. For every week that passes, you just gain more weight. All those extra pounds scream out how lonely you are—you might as well hang a sign around your neck saying 'I need to get laid.'"

"You don't have to raise your voice."

"Who could possibly hear us?"

Wallander got up, quickly.

"Forget it," he said. "I'm going."

She watched him as he rinsed out his coffee cup. *Am I too hard on him?* she thought. *But if I don't do it, who will?*

Linda called Anna at around ten o'clock.

"I just want to make sure I didn't dream the whole thing."

"And I realize now how much I worried you. But I called Zeba, so she knows I'm back."

"And Henrietta?"

"I'll talk to her later. Are you still coming over at noon?"

"I'll be there."

Linda didn't put the receiver down right away after they ended the conversation.

That little sliver of anxiety was still inside her somewhere. *It's a message*, she thought. *My body is trying to tell me something, like dreams where everything leads back to you even though it may seem like you're dreaming about someone else. Anna has returned. She's unhurt and everything seems normal, but I keep wondering about two names that appeared in her journal: Birgitta Medberg and Vigsten. And then there's a third person, a Norwegian by the name of Torgeir Langaas. I won't be able to shut the door on these thoughts until I get some answers.*

She went out and sat on the balcony. The air was cool and fresh after the previous night's thunderstorm. The paper had said the rain had caused sewers to overflow in Rydsgård. A dead butterfly lay on the balcony floor. *That's another question I need answered*, Linda thought. *The blue butterfly on the wall.*

She put her legs up on the balcony railing. *Only five more days*, she thought. *Then I'll no longer be in limbo.*

Linda didn't know where the thought had come from, but she went inside and called information. The hotel was run by the Scandic Corporation. She was put through, and a cheerful man's voice picked up. She sensed the trace of a Danish accent.

"I'd like to speak to one of your guests, Anna Westin."

"One moment."

The first lie is easy, she thought. *Then it gets harder.*

The cheerful voice returned.

"I have no one registered under that name."

"Perhaps she's already checked out. I know she was staying at your hotel."

"Anna Westin, you said? Is that W-e-s-t-i-n?"

"Yes."

"One moment."

This time he returned almost immediately.

"There's been no guest by that name in the last two weeks, at least. Are you sure you have the right spelling of the name?"

"She definitely spells it with a 'W.'"

"We've had a Wagner, Werner, Wiktor with a 'W,' Williamsson, Wallander . . ."

Linda squeezed the receiver.

"Excuse me. What was the last name?"

"Williamsson?"

"No, Wallander."

The cheerful voice took on a steely edge.

"I thought you said you were looking for someone by the name of Westin."

"But her husband's name is Wallander. Perhaps she had booked them under his name?"

"Please hold the line for a moment."

It can't be, she thought. *This isn't happening.*

"I'm afraid that isn't right either. The only Wallander we've had was a woman who was staying in a single room."

Linda couldn't speak.

"Hello? Are you still there?"

"Was her first name Linda, by any chance?"

"Yes, it was, actually. I'm sorry I can't do anything more for you. Perhaps your friend was staying elsewhere. We also have a wonderful establishment outside Lund."

"Thank you."

Linda almost slammed the phone down. At first she had felt surprise, but now it was anger. She knew she should speak to her father and not keep working on her own. *Right now this is the only question that matters to me,* she thought. *Why would Anna go to Malmö to look for her father and book a room under my name?*

She tore a piece of paper from a pad lying out on the kitchen table and crossed out the word "asparagus" already written on it. *He doesn't even eat asparagus,* she thought irritably. By the time she was ready to start jotting down all of the names and events associated with Anna's disappearance, she no longer knew where she should begin. Eventually she drew the outline of a butterfly and started filling it in with blue. Then the pen ran out and she got another. One of the wings was blue, the other black. *This is a butterfly that doesn't exist anywhere but in the realm of imagination,* she thought. Just like Anna's dad. Reality is full of other things, such as burning swans, a butchered body in the forest, a mugger in Copenhagen.

At eleven she walked to the harbor, strolled out onto the pier, and sat down on a bollard. She tried to think of a reasonable explanation for Anna using her name. A dead wild duck floated in the turbid water. When Linda finally stood up, she still had not thought of a reasonable explanation. *It must exist,* she thought. *I just can't think of it.*

She rang Anna's doorbell at exactly twelve o'clock. The anxiety she had felt earlier was gone. Now she was simply on her guard.

34

Torgeir Langaas opened his eyes, surprised that he was still alive, as always. His life should have ended in that Cleveland gutter, his body disposed of by the state of Ohio.

He lay still in what had once been the maid's room off the kitchen—a room Vigsten had forgotten all about—and listened to noises issuing from the apartment. A piano tuner was working on the baby grand. He came every Wednesday. Torgeir Langaas had enough of an ear to know that the tuner only needed to make very minor adjustments to the pitch. He imagined old Vigsten sitting on a chair by the window, his eyes following the tuner as he worked. Langaas stretched out. Everything had gone according to plan yesterday evening. The pet store had burned to the ground; not a single mouse or hamster had escaped. Erik had stressed how important this last animal sacrifice was, how crucial it was that nothing go wrong. Erik came back to this point over and over: that God allowed no mistakes.

Every morning Langaas recited the oath that Erik had taught him, first and foremost disciple: "It is my duty to God and my Earthly Master to follow the orders I receive without hesitation and undertake whatever actions necessary to teach the people what will happen to those that turn away from Him. Only by accepting the Lord through the words of his only true prophet will redemption be possible, and with it the mercy of being counted among those who will return after the great transformation."

He folded his hands in prayer and mumbled the verses from Jude that Erik had taught him: "And the Lord, when he had saved his people from Egypt's land, afterward smote those who had not believed in Him." *You can turn every room into a cathedral,* Erik had told him. *The church you seek is here and everywhere.*

Langaas whispered his oath, closed his eyes, and pulled the blankets up to his chin. The piano tuner hit the same high-pitched note again and again. Erik's words were what had sparked the memory of his grandfather who, despite his diminishing comprehension, had spent his last few years alone in his house by Femunden. One of Langaas's sisters had spent a whole week with him without his registering the fact. Langaas had told Erik about his idea and received his cautious blessing. Frans Vigsten had appeared as if from nowhere. Langaas sometimes wondered if Erik had steered Vigsten in his direction. Langaas had been at a café in Nyhavn, testing himself to see if he could resist the multitude of temptations that came his way. The old man had been there drinking wine. Suddenly he had come over to Langaas and asked:

"Could you please tell me where I am?"

Langaas had realized he was senile rather than drunk.

"At a café in Nyhavn."

The old man had lowered himself onto a chair across from him, and after a long silence asked:

"Where is that exactly?"

"Nyhavn? In Copenhagen."

"I can't seem to remember where I live."

They found the address on a piece of paper in Vigsten's wallet. Nedergade.

"My memory comes and goes," he said. "But this may be where I live, where my piano is, and where I receive my students."

Langaas had helped him into a cab, and then accompanied him to Nedergade. Vigsten's name appeared on the list of residents in the entryway. Langaas followed him up into the apartment. Vigsten recognized the smell of stale air.

"This is where I live," he said. "This is what it smells like."

Then he had wandered off into the recesses of the large apartment and appeared to completely forget about the man who had helped him home. Langaas found and pocketed a spare set of keys before he left. A few days later he returned and made the maid's room into another of his temporary residences. Vigsten had still not realized that he served as a host to a man who was waiting to be transported to a higher state. He could tell Vigsten had long since forgotten about their meeting in Nyhavn. Vigsten assumed he was a pupil. When Langaas said he had in fact come to service the radiators, Vigsten had simply turned his back and forgotten about him in that instant.

Langaas looked down at his hands. They were large and strong, and they no longer shook. It had been many years since he had been lifted from the gutter, and he had not had a drop of alcohol or any drugs since then. Erik had always been there, supporting him. Torgeir knew he could never have done it without him. It was through Erik that he had his faith, the strength he needed to continue living.

I am strong, he thought. *I wait in my hiding places for my instructions. I follow them to the letter and return into hiding. Erik never knows exactly where I am, but I can always sense when he needs me.*

I have received this strength from Erik, he thought. *And I have only one small weakness left that I have not been able to shake off.* The fact that he kept a secret from Erik was a source of great shame. The prophet had always spoken openly to him, the man from the gutter. He had not concealed any part of himself, and he had demanded the same from the man who would be his disciple. When Erik had asked him if he was free of all secrets and weaknesses, he had answered yes. But it had been a lie. There was one link to his old existence. For the longest time he had resisted the task that awaited him. But when he woke up this morning, he knew he could no longer put it off. Setting fire to the pet store last night had been the final step before he was lifted to the next level. He could wait no longer. If Erik did not discover his weakness, then surely God would turn his anger on him. This fury would also strike Erik, and that was an unbearable thought.

He got up and dressed. Through the window he saw that it was overcast and windy. He hesitated between the leather jacket and his long coat, then decided on the jacket. He fingered the pigeon and swan feathers that he picked up from the streets when he walked. *Perhaps this collecting is also a form of weakness,* he thought. *But it is a weakness for which God forgives me.* He got off the bus at City Hall, walked over to the train station, and bought the morning paper. News about the Ystad pet store that had burned down was on the front page. A police officer from Ystad had commented, "Only a sick person could do something like this; a sick person with sadistic tendencies."

Erik had taught him to keep his cool, whatever happened. But reading that his actions were regarded as a kind of twisted sadism outraged him. He crumpled up the newspaper and threw it into the trash. As penance for this weakness he gave fifty kronor to a drunk who was asking for spare change. The man stared after him, slack-jawed. *One day I'll come back and beat you to a pulp,* Langaas thought savagely. *I'll crush your face with a single blow, in the name of the Lord, in the name of the Christian uprising. Your blood will be spilled and join the river that will one day lead us to the promised land.*

It was ten o'clock. He went to a café and ate breakfast. Erik had ordered him to lie low this day. His instructions were simply to seek out one of his hiding places and wait. *Maybe Erik knows I still have a weakness,* he thought. *Maybe he's known all along but wants to see if I have the strength to deliver myself of it on my own?*

God makes his plans well, he thought. *God and Erik, his servant, are no dreamers. Erik has explained how God organizes everything down to the very last details of a person's life. This is why this day has been granted to me, in order that I should rid myself of my one remaining weakness, and stand prepared at last.*

Sylvi Rasmussen had come to Denmark in the early 1990s, along with a boatload of other illegal immigrants in a ship that had landed off the west coast of Jutland. At that point she had already undertaken a long and at times terrifying journey from her home in Bulgaria. She had traveled in trucks and in trailers hitched up to tractors, and she had even spent two terrible days sealed in an increasingly airless container. Her name back then wasn't Sylvi Rasmussen, it was Nina Barovska. She borrowed the money for her trip, and when she arrived on that deserted beach in Jutland, two men were waiting for her. They took her to an apartment in Aarhus, where they raped and beat her again and again for a week and then—when they had broken her will—took her to an apartment in Copenhagen where they forced her to work as a prostitute. She had tried to escape after a month, but the two men cut off her little finger from each hand and threatened to do something worse if she ever tried to escape again. She didn't. To make her existence more bearable, she started using drugs and hoped she would not have to live too long.

One day a client whose name was Torgeir Langaas had come in to see her. He became a regular and she would try to talk to him, desperately trying to make the time they spent together more human, less cold. But he always shook his head and mumbled unintelligible responses. Although he was gentle, she would sometimes break into uncontrollable shivers after one of his visits. There was something vaguely threatening about him, something uncanny, even though he was her most loyal and generous client. His large hands always touched her gently, but he still frightened her.

He rang her doorbell at eleven o'clock. He invariably came to see her in the mornings. Since he wanted to spare her the moment of realization that she was to die this day in the beginning of September, he grabbed her from behind as they were on their way into the bedroom. His large hands reached for her forehead and neck and snapped her spine. He put her body on the bed, pulled off her clothes, and tried to make it look like a sex crime. When he was done, he looked around and thought that Sylvi had deserved a better fate. If circumstances had been different, he would have wanted to bring her along to the promised land. But Erik set the rules, and he demanded that his disciples be free of all worldly weakness. And now he had achieved this state. Woman, desire, was finally gone from his life.

He left the apartment. He was ready. Erik was waiting for him. God was waiting.

35

Her grandfather had often complained about difficult people, a category that included almost everyone, and he consequently did his best to minimize contact with other people. However, as he said, one could never avoid them completely. Linda had been particularly struck by the image he had used.

"They're like eels," he said. "You try to keep hold of them, but they wiggle free of your grasp. The thing about eels is also that they swim at night. By that I don't mean you only meet difficult people at night—if anything, they seem most likely to come with their idiotic suggestions in the morning. Their darkness is of a different order; it's something they carry inside. It's their total obliviousness to the difficulty they cause others by their constant meddling. I have never meddled in other people's lives."

That was the biggest lie of his life. He had died without recognizing the extent to which he himself had often meddled in the decisions, dreams, and actions of those around him, trying in particular to bend his two children to his will.

These thoughts about difficult people came unbidden to Linda just as she was about to ring Anna's doorbell. She paused, her finger hovering a few centimeters from the buzzer. *Anna is a difficult person,* she thought. *She doesn't seem to understand the worry she caused, and how her actions affect me.*

When she finally rang the doorbell, Anna opened, smiling, dressed in a white blouse and dark pants. She was barefoot and had pulled her hair back into a loose knot.

Linda had decided to bring it up right away to clear the air. She threw her jacket over a chair and said:

"I have to tell you I read the last few pages of your journal. I only did it to see if there was any explanation for your disappearance."

Anna flinched.

"Then that was what I sensed," she said. "It was almost as if there was a different smell when I opened the pages."

"I'm sorry, but I was so worried. I only read the last couple of pages, nothing more."

We lie to make our half-truths seem more plausible, she thought. *Anna may see through me. The journal will always be between us now. She'll always be asking herself what I did and didn't read.*

They walked into the living room. Anna stood by the window, her back to Linda.

Linda realized she no longer knew Anna. She looked at her friend, who stood with her back turned, thinking she might as well be looking at an enemy.

"There's one question you still need to answer."

Linda waited for her to turn around but she didn't.

"I hate talking to people's backs."

Still no reaction. *You may be a difficult person,* Linda thought. *But sometimes difficult people go too far. Grandpa would have thrown an eel like this into the fire and let it writhe to death in the flames.*

"Why did you check into that hotel under my name?"

Linda tried to interpret Anna's back while she simultaneously wiped the sweat from her neck. *This will be my curse,* she had thought back in the first month of her police training. *There are laughing policemen and crying policemen, but I'm going to be known as the perspiring policewoman.*

Anna burst into laughter and turned around. Linda tried to judge if her laughter was genuine.

"How did you find out?"

"I called the hotel."

"May I ask why?"

"I don't know."

"What did you ask them, exactly?"

"It's not so hard to figure out."

"Tell me."

"I asked if an Anna Westin was still there or if she had checked out. They didn't have an Anna Westin, but they did have a Wallander, they said. It was that simple. But why did you do it?"

"What would you say if I told you I didn't know why I used your name? Maybe I was afraid my father would run away again if he found out I had checked into the hotel where we saw each other. If you want the truth, it's that I don't know."

The phone rang, but Anna made no move to pick it up. The answering machine switched on and then Zeba's chirpy voice filled the room. She was calling for no reason, she informed them happily.

"I love people who call for no reason with so much positive energy," Anna said.

Linda didn't answer. She had no room to think about Zeba.

"I read a name in your diary: Birgitta Medberg. Do you know what's happened to her?"

"No."

"Don't you read the papers?"

"I was looking for my father."

"She's been found murdered."

Anna looked closely at her.

"Why?"

"I don't know why."

"What are you saying?"

"I'm saying she was murdered. The police don't know who did it, but they're going to want to talk to you about her."

Anna shook her head.

"What happened? Who would want to kill her?"

Linda decided not to reveal any details about the murder. She simply sketched out the news in broad brush-strokes. Anna's dismay seemed completely genuine.

"When did this happen?"

"A few days ago."

Anna shook her head again, left the window, and sat down in a chair.

"How did you know her?" Linda asked.

Anna looked narrowly at her.

"Is this a cross-examination?"

"I'm curious."

"We rode horses together. I don't remember the first time we met, but there was someone who had two Norwegian Fjord horses that needed exercising. Birgitta and I both volunteered to ride them. I didn't know her at all. She never said very much. I know she mapped old pilgrimage trails. We also shared an interest in butterflies. But I don't know anything more about her. She wrote to me fairly recently and suggested we buy a horse together. I never replied."

Linda tried to remain alert for any hints that Anna was lying. *I'm not the person who should be doing this,* she thought. *I should be driving a patrol car and picking up drunks. Dad should be talking to Anna, not I. It's just that damn butterfly. It should be hanging on the wall.*

Anna had already followed her gaze and read her mind.

"I took the butterfly with me when I went to look for my dad. I was going to give it to him, but then when I realized it was all my imagination, I threw it into the canal."

It could be true, Linda thought. *Or else she lies so well I can't tell.*

The phone rang again. Ann-Britt Höglund's voice came into the room. Anna looked at Linda, who nodded. Anna picked up the receiver. The conversation was brief and Anna didn't say much. She hung up.

"They want me to come in now," she said.

Linda got up.

"Then you'd better go."

"I want you to come with me."

"Why?"

"I'd feel more secure."

Linda hesitated.

"I'm not sure it's appropriate."

"But I'm not accused of anything. They just want to have a conversation with me, at least that's what the woman said. And you're both a police officer and my friend."

"I'm happy to go down there with you, but I'm not sure they'll let me stay in the room when they talk to you."

Höglund came out into the reception area at the police station to meet Anna. She looked disapprovingly at Linda. *She doesn't like me,* Linda thought. *She's the kind of woman who prefers young men with piercings and an attitude.* Höglund had put on weight. *Soon you'll be dumpy,* Linda thought with satisfaction. *I still wonder what Dad saw in you when he courted you a few years ago.*

"I want Linda to be there," Anna said.

"I don't know if that will be possible," Höglund said. "Why do you want her to be there?"

"I have a tendency to make things more complicated than they are," Anna said. "I just want her there for support, that's all."

Höglund shrugged and looked at Linda.

"You'll have to ask your father if it's OK," she said. "You know where his office is. He's waiting in the small conference room two doors down from there."

Höglund left them and marched off.

"Is this where you'll be working?" Anna asked.

"Hardly. I'll be spending time in the garage and in the front seat of patrol cars."

The door to the small conference room was half open. Wallander was leaning back in his chair, a cup of coffee in his hand. *He's going to break that chair,* Linda thought. *Do cops have to get so fat? I'll have to take early retirement.* She pushed the door open. Wallander didn't seem particularly surprised to see her with Anna. He shook Anna's hand.

"I would like Linda to stay," she said.

"Of course."

Wallander threw a glance behind them into the corridor.

"Where's Höglund?"

"I don't think she wanted to come along," Linda said, seating herself as far away from her father as possible.

That day Linda learned something important about police work from both Anna and her father. Wallander impressed her by steering the conversation with imperceptible yet total control. He never confronted Anna directly; he approached her from the side, listening to her answers, encouraging her even when she contradicted herself. He gave the impression of having all the time in the world, but never let her off the hook.

What Anna taught her was through her lies. She appeared to be trying to keep her lies to a minimum, but without success. Once, when Anna bent down to pick up a pencil that had rolled off the table, Linda and her father exchanged a look.

When it was over and Anna had gone home, Linda sat down at the kitchen table at home and tried to write down the conversation exactly as it had progressed, like a screenplay. What was it Anna had said? Linda started to write, and the exchange slowly reproduced itself on paper.

KW: Thanks for coming. I'm glad that nothing serious happened to you. Linda was very worried, and I was too.

AW: I guess I don't need to tell you about the person I thought I saw in Malmö.

KW: No, you don't. Would you like something to drink?

AW: Juice, please.

KW: I'm afraid we don't have any. There's coffee, tea, or plain water.

AW: I'll pass.

Slowly, but surely, Linda thought. *He has all the time in the world.*

KW: How much do you know about what happened to Birgitta Medberg?

AW: Linda told me she was killed. It's horrible. Incomprehensible. I also know you saw her name in my journal.

KW: Not us. Linda was the one who saw it when she was trying to figure out what had happened to you.

AW: I don't like people reading my journal.

KW: Of course not. But Birgitta's name was there, wasn't it?

AW: Yes.

KW: We're trying to contact all the people she may have known. The conversation we're having is identical to those my colleagues are having with others all around us.

AW: We rode a pair of Norwegian Fjord horses together. They're owned by a man called Jörlander. He lives on a small farm near Charlottenlund. He was a juggler in an earlier life. He has something wrong with his leg and can't ride anymore. We exercised the horses for him.

KW: When did you first meet Birgitta?

AW: Seven years and three months ago.

KW: How come you remember it so precisely?

AW: Because I've thought about it. I knew you would ask me that.

KW: Where did you first meet?

AW: In the stables. She had also heard that Jörlander needed volunteers. We rode two or three times a week. We always talked about the horses, that was all.

KW: You never met each other outside of riding?

AW: I thought she was boring, to be perfectly honest. Except for the butterflies.

KW: Which butterflies? What do you mean?

AW: One day when we were riding, we realized we both had a passion for butterflies. Then we had a new topic of conversation.

KW: Did you ever hear her express any fears?

AW: She always seemed nervous when we had to take the horses across a busy road; I remember that.

KW: And apart from that?

AW: No.

KW: Did she ever have anyone with her?

AW: No, she would always come alone on her little Vespa.

KW: So you had no other contact with each other?

AW: No. Just a letter she wrote to me once. Nothing else.

A slight hesitation, Linda thought as she wrote. *An imperceptible tremor at times, but here she actually stumbled.* What was she hiding? Linda thought about what she had seen in the hut and broke out into a sweat.

KW: When did you last see Birgitta?

AW: Two weeks ago.

KW: In what context was that?

AW: For heaven's sake, how many times do I have to repeat myself? Riding.

KW: This is the last time, I assure you. I just want to make sure I have all the facts straight. What happened in Malmö, by the way? When you were looking for your father?

AW: How do you mean?

KW: I mean, who rode the horses for you? Who filled in for you and Birgitta?

AW: Jörlander has some reserves, young girls mostly. He doesn't like to use them because of their age but he must have had to. You can ask him.

KW: We will. Do you remember if there was anything different the last time you met?

AW: Who? The young girls?

KW: No, I was thinking of Birgitta.

AW: She was her usual self.

KW: Do you remember what you talked about?

AW: I've told you several times now that we didn't talk very much. A little about horses, the weather, butterflies. That was about it.

And right here he had suddenly sat up in his chair, Linda thought, *a tactical maneuver telling Anna to be on her guard.*

KW: We have another name from your diary: Vigsten. He lives on Nedergade in Copenhagen.

Anna had looked over at Linda in surprise, then narrowed her eyes. *There goes that friendship,* Linda had thought at the time. *If it wasn't gone already, that is.*

AW: Clearly someone has read more of my journal than I realized.

KW: That may be. Vigsten. What can you tell me about that name?

AW: Why is this important?

KW: I don't know if it's important.

AW: Does he have anything to do with Birgitta?

KW: Perhaps.

AW: He's a piano teacher. He was my teacher for a while, and we've kept in touch since then.

KW: Is that it?

AW: Yes.

KW: When was he your teacher?

AW: It was during the fall of 1997.

KW: And only then?

AW: Yes.

KW: Dare I ask why you stopped going to him?

AW: I wasn't good enough.

KW: Did he tell you that?

AW: I did. Not to him, to myself.

KW: It must have cost a great deal of money to have a piano teacher in Copenhagen, with all that travel.

AW: It's a matter of setting priorities.

KW: You're going to be a doctor, I understand.

AW: Yes.

KW: How is it going?

AW: What do you mean?

KW: Your studies.

AW: Fine.

At this point Wallander's manner changed. He leaned toward Anna, still friendly, but now he clearly meant business.

KW: Birgitta Medberg was murdered in Rannesholm in an unusually brutal way. Someone severed her head and hands. Can you think of anyone who could do such a thing?

AW: No.

Anna was very calm, Linda thought. *Too calm. Calm in the way that only someone who knows what's coming can be.* But then she retracted her conclusion. It was possible, but she shouldn't make the leap prematurely.

KW: Can you understand how anyone could do this to her?

AW: No.

Then came the abrupt finish. After her last answer his hands came down on the table.

kw: Thank you for your time. You've been very helpful.

aw: But I haven't actually been able to help you with anything.

kw: Oh, I wouldn't say that, Anna. Thank you again. You may hear
more from us at some point.

He had escorted them both back to the reception area. Linda noticed that Anna was tense. *She must be wondering what she said without knowing. My dad is still questioning her, but he's doing it inside her
head, waiting to see what she's going to say.*

Linda pushed the paper away and stretched her back. Then she
called her father on his cell phone.

"I don't have time to talk. I hope you found it instructive."

"Absolutely. But I don't think she was telling the truth."

"I think we can safely assume she wasn't telling us the whole
truth. But the question is why. Do you know what I think?"

"No, tell me."

"I think her father has actually returned. But we can talk more
about that tonight."

Wallander came back to the apartment just after seven o'clock.
Linda had cooked dinner. They sat down at the kitchen table and
he had just started discussing the grounds he had for thinking that
Anna's father had returned when the phone rang.

She could tell from his face that it was something serious.

36

They had arranged to meet in a parking lot between Malmö and Ystad. Even a parking lot could become a cathedral if you chose to see it that way. The balmy September air rose from the ground like pillars for this towering yet invisible church.

He had told them to be there at three, instructing them to wear normal clothes since they would be impersonating tourists from Poland on a shopping trip in Sweden. Alone or in small groups, they would arrive from different directions and receive their final instructions from Erik Westin, who would have Torgeir Langaas at his side.

Westin had spent the last few weeks in a mobile home in a camping area in Höör. He had given up the apartment in Helsingborg and bought a cheap used mobile home in Svedala. His beat-up Volvo had transported it to the camping lot. Apart from his meetings with Langaas and the plans they had carried out together, he had spent all his time in the mobile home, praying and preparing for the task ahead. Every morning he looked into the little mirror on the wall and asked himself if he was staring into the eyes of a madman. *No one could become a prophet without a great deal of inborn humility*, he would think to himself. To be strong was to be able to ask oneself the hardest questions. Even if his commitment to the task God had assigned him never wavered, he still needed to be sure that he was not carried away with pride. But the eyes gazing steadily back at him from the mirror only confirmed what he already knew: that he was the anointed leader of the new age. There was nothing misguided about the great task that lay before them. Everything was already spelled out in the Holy Book. The Christian world had become mired in a bog of misconceptions and had tried God's patience to the point that He had simply given up, waiting for the one who was prepared act as His true servant, to step in and set things right.

"There is only one God," Erik Westin said at the beginning of all his prayers. "One God and his only son, whom we crucified. This cross is the symbol of our only hope. The cross is plainly made—of wood, not gold or precious marble. The truth lies in poverty and simplicity. The emptiness we carry inside can only be filled by the Holy Ghost, not material goods or riches, however tempting they may appear to us."

He had carried on long conversations with God. He had also thought a great deal about Jim Jones, the false prophet, the fallen angel. He thought about the exodus from the United States to Guyana, the initial period of joy and then the terrible betrayal that had led to murder. In his thoughts and prayers there was always a place for those who had died in the jungle. One day they would be set free from the evil that Jim Jones had committed and would be uplifted to the highest realms, where God and the angels awaited them.

During this last little while, he had also felt affirmed and accepted by those he had once left behind. They had not forgotten him. They understood why he had left and why he had now returned. One day when everything was over, he would withdraw from the world and take up the life he had left so long ago: sandal-making. He would have his daughter by his side and all would be fulfilled.

The time had come at last. God had appeared to him in a vision. *All sacrifice is made for the creation of life,* he thought. *No one knows if they have been chosen to live or to die.* He had reinstituted the ritual sacrifices with their origins in the earliest days of Christianity. Life and death went hand in hand; God was both logical and wise. Killing in order to sustain life was an important practice in combating the emptiness that existed inside man. And now the moment was here.

On the morning of the day that they were to meet in the parking lot, Erik Westin went down to the dark lake that still retained some of the summer's heat. He washed himself thoroughly, clipped his nails, and shaved. He was alone in the remote camping area.

After Langaas called, Westin threw his cell phone into the lake. Then he put on his clothes, taking his Bible and money with him to the car and driving a short distance up the road. Then there was only one thing left to take care of. He set fire to the mobile home, and drove away.

Altogether there were twenty-six of them, seventeen men and nine women, and each had a cross tattooed on his or her chest above the heart. The men were from Uganda, France, England, Spain, Hungary, Greece, Italy, and the United States. The women were American and Canadian, with the exception of a British woman who had lived in Denmark for a long time. It had taken Erik four years to build the core group of the Christian army he planned to lead into battle.

Now they were meeting each other for the first time. A light rain fell as they assembled in the parking lot. Westin had parked his car on a hill overlooking the lot. He kept an eye on the proceedings with the help of a telescope. Langaas was there to receive them. He had been instructed to say that he didn't know where Westin was. Westin had often explained to him that secret agreements of this nature could strengthen people's belief in the holy task that awaited them. Westin looked into the telescope. There they were, some in cars, some on foot, two on bikes, one on a motorcycle, and a few more who walked out from a small forested area next to the parking lot as if they had been camping there. Each one carried only a small backpack. Westin had been very strict on this point; no one was to have a large amount of luggage or wear unusual attire. Nothing that would attract attention to God's undercover army.

He trained the lens on Langaas's face. Langaas was leaning against the sign posted on one side of the parking lot. *It would not have been possible without him,* Erik thought. *If I hadn't stumbled across him in that dirty Cleveland street and managed to transform him into an absolutely, ruthlessly devoted disciple, I would not yet be ready to give my army marching orders.*

Langaas turned his head in the direction they had agreed upon. Then he stroked his nose twice with his left index finger. All was ready. Westin packed up his telescope and started walking down to the parking lot. There was a dip beside the road that meant he could walk right up to them without being seen. That way he would seem to appear out of nowhere. When he walked among them everyone stopped what they were doing, but no one talked, as he had instructed.

Langaas had arrived in a truck, into which they now loaded the bicycles and motorcycles, then let the people climb in after them. The cars would have to be left behind. Westin drove and Langaas sat up front with him. They turned off to the right and found their way to Mossby Beach, where they parked. Everyone walked down to the beach. Torgeir carried two large baskets with food. They sat closely pressed together among the sand dunes, like a bunch of tourists who found the weather a little too cold.

Before they started to eat, Westin said the necessary words:

"God demands our presence. He decrees the battle."

They unpacked the baskets and ate. When the food was gone, Westin ordered them to rest. Langaas and Westin walked down to the water's edge. They went through the plan one last time. A large cloudbank moved in, darkening the sky.

"We're getting just what we wanted," Langaas said. "It would be a good night for catching eels."

"We are getting what we need, for we are the righteous and the just," Westin said.

They waited until it was evening, then climbed back into the truck. It was half past seven when Westin swung back onto the road and headed east. He turned north just past Svarte, passing the highway from Malmö to Ystad, and then continued on a road that went west, past Rannesholm Manor. Two kilometers past Hurup he drove onto a small dirt road, turning off the engine and the headlights. Langaas climbed out of the car. In the rearview mirror Erik could see two of the American men climbing off the truck: Peter Buchanan, a former hairdresser from New Jersey, and Edison Lambert, a jack-of-all-trades from Des Moines.

Westin felt his pulse quicken. Was there anything that could go wrong? He regretted even thinking the question. *I'm not crazy,* he thought. *I place my trust in God and his plan.* He started the engine and pulled back out onto the road. One motorcycle overtook him, then another. He continued driving north, throwing a glance at Hurup Church where Langaas and the two Americans were headed. Half a mile north of Hurup he turned left toward Staffanstorp, then turned left again after stopping in front of an abandoned farm for ten minutes. He stepped out of the truck and motioned for those still in the back to follow him.

He checked the time: right on schedule. They walked slowly in order to accommodate the few who were older, or less fit, like the British woman, who had been operated on for cancer six months ago. Westin had debated whether or not to include her, but after consulting with God he received the answer that she had survived her illness precisely so that she could complete her mission. They followed a road that led to the back of Frennestad Church. Westin felt in his pocket for the key that Langaas had made for him. Two weeks ago he had tried it, and it had turned without a single squeak. He stopped them when they reached the churchyard. No one said anything, and all he could hear was breathing. *Only calm breaths,* he noted. *No one is panting, no one seems anxious, not even she who is going to die.*

Westin looked down at his watch again. In forty-three minutes Langaas, Buchanan, and Lambert would set fire to the church in Hurup. They started walking again. The gate opened without a sound. Langaas had oiled it yesterday. They walked single-file up to the church. Westin unlocked the doors. It was cool inside; one person shivered. He turned on the flashlight and looked around. Everyone seated themselves in the front pews, as they had been instructed. The last missive Westin had distributed included 123 detailed instructions that were to be memorized down to the letter. He knew they had done so.

Westin lit the candles that Langaas had placed near the altar. In the dim light he could see Harriet Bolson, the woman from Tulsa, seated on the far right. She was completely calm. *God's ways are inscrutable,* he thought. *But only to those who do not need to understand them.* He looked down at his watch. It was important that the two actions, the burning of Hurup Church and that which was to take place in Frennestad Church, be synchronized. He looked over at

Harriet Bolson again. She had a thin, worn face even though she was only thirty years old. *Perhaps her face shows the traces of her sin,* he thought. *She can only be cleansed through fire.* He turned off the flashlight and walked into the shadows by the pulpit. He reached into his backpack and pulled out the rope that Langaas had bought in a maritime store in Copenhagen. He placed it in front of the altar, then checked his watch again. It was time. He turned and motioned for everyone to stand. He called them up one by one. He handed one end of the rope to the first person.

"We are irrevocably bound together," he said. "From now on, from this day forward, we will never need a rope again. We are bound by our loyalty to God and our task. We cannot tolerate for the Christian world to sink any deeper into degradation. The world will be cleansed through fire, and we must start with ourselves."

While he was uttering the last words he had slowly moved so that he stood in front of Harriet Bolson. At the same moment that he tied the rope around her neck she understood what was about to happen. It was as if her mind went blank from the sudden terror. She didn't scream or struggle. Her eyes closed. *All my years of waiting are finally over.*

The church in Hurup started burning at a quarter past nine. When the fire trucks were on their way they received reports that Frennestad Church was on fire as well.

Langaas and the two Americans had already been picked up. Langaas took Westin's place and drove the truck to the new hideout.

Westin remained behind in the darkness. He sat up on a hill close to Frennestad Church. He watched the firemen try to douse the blaze, in vain. He wondered if the police would make it inside before the roof caved in.

He sat there in the darkness and watched the flames. He thought about how he would one day watch the fires burning with his daughter by his side.

37

That night two churches in roughly the same area, a triangle bounded by Staffanstorp, Anderstorp, and Ystad, burned to the ground. The heat was so intense that at dawn only the bare, smoking skeletons of the buildings remained. The bell tower of Hurup Church collapsed, and those who heard it said it sounded like a howl of bottomless despair.

The warden of Frennestad Church was the first to make it into the burning building, in hopes of saving its unique mass staves dating from the Middle Ages. Instead, he made a gruesome discovery that would haunt him for the rest of his life. A woman in her thirties lay in front of the altar. She had been strangled by a thick rope pulled so tightly it had almost removed her head from her body. He rushed screaming from the scene and fainted on the front steps.

The first fire truck arrived a few minutes later. It had been on its way to Hurup when it had received fresh instructions. None of the firefighters fully understood what had happened, whether the first alarm had been a mistake or if two churches were actually on fire at the same time.

There was a similar state of confusion at the police station during the first few minutes when the two calls came in. When Wallander got up from the dinner table, he was under the impression that he was going to Hurup, where a woman had been reported dead. Since he had drunk some wine with dinner, he asked for a patrol car to pick him up.

It was only as they were leaving Ystad that he learned of the misunderstanding: the church in Hurup was on fire, but the dead woman had been found in Frennestad Church. Martinsson, who was driving, started shouting at the switchboard operator to try to determine once and for all how many damned churches were on fire.

Wallander sat quietly for the duration of the ride, not only because Martinsson was driving with his usual recklessness, but because he sensed that his worst fears were being confirmed. The animals that had been killed were only the beginning. *Lunatics,* he thought, *satanists, fanatics.* As they drove through the darkness he thought he was beginning to discern a logic to the events, if only dimly.

By the time they pulled up outside the burning church in Frennestad, they at least had a clearer idea of the current situation. The two churches had caught fire at almost exactly the same time. In addition there was a dead woman in Frennestad. They sought out the fire chief, Mats Olsson, to whom, it turned out, Martinsson was distantly related. In the midst of the intense heat and chaos, Wallander heard them give greetings to their respective wives. Then they went into the church. Martinsson let Wallander take the lead, as he usually did at a crime scene, and as he was more than willing to do even in the devastating heat. The aisle provided them with a route, and a fireman preceded them with a hose. The dead woman lay in front of the altar with a rope around her neck. Wallander tried to imprint the scene on his memory. It had to be staged. He turned to Mats Olsson.

"How long can we stay?"

"The roof is going to cave. We're not going to be able to put it out in time."

"When?"

"Soon."

"How long?"

"Ten minutes. I can't let you stay any longer."

No technicians would be able to make it to the scene in time. Wallander put on a helmet that someone handed him.

"Go out and see if anyone in the crowd has a camera, or better yet a video camera," he said. "Confiscate it. We're going to need to document this."

Martinsson left. Wallander started to examine the dead woman. The rope was thick, like a ship's hawser. It lay around her neck with the ends outstretched. *Two people pulling in different directions,* he thought. *Like the olden days when criminals were ripped apart by tying them to two horses that were sent off in different directions.*

He glanced at the ceiling. The flames were starting to come through. There were people running all around him carrying objects from the church. An older man in his pajamas was straining to rescue a beautiful old altar cabinet. There was something touching about their struggle. *These people have realized they're losing something precious,* he thought.

Martinsson returned with a video camera.

"Can you figure out how to use it?"

"I think so," Martinsson answered.

"Then you be our photographer. Take full shots, details, from all angles."

"Five minutes," Olsson said. "That's all you have."

Wallander crouched down beside the dead woman's body. She was blond and bore an uncanny resemblance to his sister Kristina. *An execution,* he thought. *First animals, now people. What was it Amy Lindberg thought she heard? "The Lord's will be done?"*

He quickly searched the woman's pockets. Nothing. He looked around. There was no handbag. He was about to give up when he saw a breast pocket on her blouse. Inside was a piece of paper with a name and address: HARRIET BOLSON, 1250 5TH AVENUE, TULSA.

"Time's up," Mats Olsson said. "Let's go."

He rounded up the people left in the church and hurried them out. The body was carried away and Wallander took the hawser.

Martinsson called in to the station.

"We need information on a woman from Tulsa," he said. "All registers, local, European, international. Highest priority."

Linda turned off the TV impatiently. She knew that the spare keys to her dad's car were on the bookshelf in the living room. She picked them up, then headed out the door and jogged down to the police station.

Wallander's car was parked in the corner. Linda recognized the car next to it as Höglund's. Linda fingered the Swiss army knife in her pocket, but this was not a night for slashing tires. She had heard him mention Hurup and Frennestad. She unlocked the car door and drove as far as the water tower. There she pulled over and got out a map. She knew where Frennestad was, but not Hurup. She found it, turned off the light, and headed out of Ystad. Halfway to Hörby she turned left, and after a few kilometers she could see the smoke from Hurup Church. She drove as close as she could, then parked and walked up to the church. Her dad wasn't there. The only police officers were young cadets, and it struck her that if the fire had started only a few days later she could have been one of them. She told them who she was and asked where her father was.

"There's another church on fire," she was told. "Frennestad Church. They have a casualty."

"What's going on?"

"It looks like arson—two churches don't just catch fire at the same time. But we don't know what happened in Frennestad Church, only that there's a body."

Linda nodded and walked away. A sudden noise made her turn around. Parts of the church roof collapsed and a shower of sparks shot up toward the sky. *Who would burn a church?* she wondered. But she couldn't answer that question any more easily than she could imagine what kind of person set fire to swans, cattle, or animals in a pet store.

She got back into the car and drove to Frennestad. There too she saw the burning church from a distance. *Burning churches are something I associate with war,* she thought. *But here there are churches burning in peacetime. Can a country be engaged in an invisible war against an unseen enemy?* She was unable to pursue this thought any further. The road leading up to the church was blocked by cars. When she caught sight of her father in the light of the fire, she stopped. He was talking with a firefighter. She tried to see what he was holding. A hose? She walked closer, pushing past people who were crowded together outside the restricted area. He was holding a rope, she realized finally. A hawser.

Nyberg walked up to Wallander and Martinsson, who were standing outside the church. He looked irritated, as usual.

"I thought you should take a look at this," he said, holding out his hand.

It was a small necklace. Wallander took out his glasses. One side of the frame broke when he put them on. He swore and had to hold the glasses with one hand.

"It looks like a shoe," he said.

"She was wearing it," Nyberg said. "Or had been. The chain broke when the rope was pulled tight. The necklace fell inside her blouse. The doctor found it."

Martinsson took it and turned toward the fire to get more light.

"An unusual motif for a pendant," he said. "Is it really a shoe?"

"It could be a footprint," Nyberg said. "Or the sole of a foot. Once I saw a pendant in the shape of a carrot. A diamond was placed where the greens would have been. That carrot cost four hundred thousand kronor."

"It may help us identify her," Wallander said. "That's what counts right now."

Nyberg walked back over to the low wall next to the graveyard and started yelling at a photographer who was taking pictures of the burning church. Wallander and Martinsson walked down to the barricades.

They saw Linda and waved her over.

"Just couldn't stay away?" her dad said. "You can come with us."

"How is it going?"

"We don't know what we're looking for," Wallander said slowly. "But these churches didn't set fire to themselves, that much is certain."

"They're working on tracing Harriet Bolson," Martinsson said. "They'll let me know the minute they find something."

"I'm trying to understand the significance of the rope," Wallander said. "Why a church, and why an American woman? What does it mean?"

"A few people, at least three but maybe more, come to a church in the middle of the night," Martinsson said.

Wallander stopped him.

"Why more than three? Two who commit the murder and one victim. Isn't that enough?"

"Theoretically, yes. But something tells me there were more, maybe many more. They unlocked the door. There are only two existing keys. The minister has one, and the church warden who fainted has the other. They've both confirmed possession of their keys. Therefore we have to assume these people used a sophisticated pass key or a copy," Martinsson said.

"A group, a society. A band of people who chose this church to execute Harriet Bolson. Is she guilty of something? Did she become victim to a kind of religious extremism? Are we dealing with satanists or some other kind of lunatic fringe? We don't have the answers."

"Another thing," Wallander said. "What about the note I found on her body? Why was it left behind?"

"So that we would be able to identify her. Perhaps it was a message to us."

"We have to confirm her identity," Wallander said. "If she so much as visited a dentist in this country, we'll know."

"They're working on it."

Martinsson sounded affronted.

"I don't mean to get on your case. What's the word?"

"Nothing, as of yet," Martinsson said. "Then there's another thing. Whoever saw a pendant necklace shaped like a shoe or a sandal?"

He shook his head and walked away.

Linda held her breath. Had she heard him correctly?

"What was it he said? What have you found?"

"A note with a name and address."

"Apart from that. Something else?"

"A pendant necklace."

"That looked like something?"

"A footprint. A shoe. Why do you ask?"

She ignored his question.

"What kind of shoe?"

"Maybe a sandal."

The light from the fire grew brighter in spurts as gusts of wind caught the flames.

"May I remind you that Anna's dad was a sandal-maker before he disappeared? That's all."

It took a moment to click in his mind. Then he nodded slowly.

"Good," he said. "Very good. That may just be the opening we need. The question is, where does it leave us?"

38

Wallander had tried to send Linda home to get some sleep, but she had insisted on staying. She had curled up in the back seat of a patrol car and only woke up when he rapped sharply on the window. *He's never learned the art of waking a person gently,* she thought. *My father doesn't simply wake people up, he tears them from their dreams.*

She stepped out of the car and shivered. Shreds of fog drifted over the fields. The church had burned to the ground, and only the gaping, sooty walls remained. Thick smoke still rose from the caved-in roof. Most of the fire trucks were gone; only two crews were needed for the mop-up. Martinsson had left, but she could see Lindman in the distance. He came over to her and handed her a cup of coffee. Her dad was speaking with a journalist on the other side of the police line.

"I've never seen anything like this landscape before," Lindman said. "Not in the west, not up in Härjedalen. Here Sweden simply slopes down into the sea and ends. All this mud and fog. It's very strange. I'm trying to find my feet in a landscape that's completely alien to me."

Linda mumbled that fog was fog, mud was mud. What could possibly be strange about something so ordinary?

"Anything new on the woman?" she asked.

"Not yet. But she's definitely not a Swedish citizen."

"Any reason to think she's not the person named in the note?"

"No. It's far-fetched to think the murderer would leave a false name."

Wallander came walking over. The journalist disappeared down the hill.

"I've talked to Chief Holgersson," he said. "Since you're already involved in the fringes of this investigation, we may as well let you in on the whole thing. I'd better get used to having you around. It'll be a little like having a ball constantly bouncing up and down by my side."

Linda thought he was making fun of her.

"At least I can still bounce. That's more than some people I know."

Lindman laughed. Wallander looked angry, but controlled himself.

"Don't ever have children, Lindman," he said. "You see what I have to deal with."

A car swung onto the road leading up to the church. Nyberg got out.

"He's freshly showered," Wallander noted. "Ready for another day of unpleasantness, no doubt. He'll keel over and die the day he retires and no longer has to be digging in the mud with rainwater up to his knees."

"He acts like a dog," Lindman said in a low voice. "Have you noticed? It's almost as if he's sniffing around, and wishing he could just get down on all fours."

Linda had to agree: Nyberg really did look like an animal intent on picking up a scent.

Nyberg joined their group, seeming not to notice Linda. He smelled strongly of aftershave.

"Do we have any idea how the fires started?" Wallander asked. "I talked to Olsson and he said both churches started burning in several places. The church warden who came on the scene early said that it looked like the fire was burning in a circle, which would imply that it caught in several places at once."

"We haven't found anything yet," Nyberg said. "But it's clearly arson."

"There's a difference between the two cases," Wallander said. "The fire in Hurup seems to have started more in the manner of an explosion. Someone in one of the neighboring houses said it sounded as if a bomb had gone off. The blazes were started in different ways, but synchronized."

"It's a definite pattern," Lindman said. "Starting a fire to distract attention from the murder."

"But why a church?" Wallander asked. "And why would you strangle a person with a hawser?"

He looked over at Linda.

"What do you see in all this?"

She felt herself blushing. The question had come so suddenly that she was unprepared for it.

"The site has been chosen deliberately," she started hesitantly. "Strangling someone with a rope seems akin to torture. But this is also something that has to do with religion, like an eye for an eye, death by stoning, or living burial. Why not strangle someone with a hawser?"

Before anyone had a chance to respond, Lindman's cell phone rang. He listened, then held it out to Wallander.

"We're starting to get information from the States," he said. "Let's go back to Ystad."

"Do you need me?" Nyberg asked.

"I'll call if we do," Wallander said. Then he turned to Linda.

"But you should be there," he said. "Unless you want to go home and sleep first."

"You know there's no need to even ask."

He threw a glance at her.

"I'm trying to be considerate."

"Think of me as a police officer and not your daughter."

They were silent in the car, both from lack of sleep and a fear of saying something that would irritate the other.

Once they had parked in front of the station, Wallander walked off toward the district attorney's office. Lindman caught up with Linda just outside the front door.

"I remember my first day as a police officer," he said. "I was still in Borås and had been to a party with friends the night before. The first thing I did when I walked through the front doors of the station was rush into the restroom and throw up. What do you plan to do?"

"Not that, at any rate," Linda said.

Höglund was standing by the reception desk. She still only barely registered Linda's presence, and Linda decided to treat her the same way from now on.

There was a message for Linda: Chief Holgersson wanted to speak to her.

"Have I done anything wrong?" Linda said.

"I wouldn't think so," Lindman said, then left.

I like him, Linda thought. *More and more, actually.*

Holgersson was on her way out when Linda walked down the corridor to her office.

"Kurt has explained the situation to me," Holgersson said. "We're going to let you sit in on this one. It's a strange coincidence that one of your friends is involved."

"We don't know that for sure," Linda said. "She might be."

The door to the conference room was closed at nine o'clock. Linda sat in the seat her father had pointed out to her. Lindman sat next to her. She looked at her father sitting at the head of the table drinking mineral water. He looked the way she had always imagined him in these situations: thirsty, his hair standing on end, prepared to jump into yet another day of a complicated criminal investigation. But it was an overly romanticized image and therefore a false one, she knew. She shook it off with a grimace.

She had always been under the impression that he was good at his job, a skillful investigator, but today she realized that he had talents she hadn't even imagined. Among other things, she was impressed by his ability to keep so many facts in his head, scrupulously arranged according to time and place. While she listened to him, something stirred in her at a much deeper level. It was as if she only now understood why he had had so little time for her or Mona. There had simply been no room for them. *I have to talk to him about this,* she thought. *When all of the events have been explained and everything is over, we have to talk about the fact that he prioritized work over us.*

Linda stayed behind in the room when the meeting was over. She opened a window and thought about everything that had been said.

Her father had set his bottle of mineral water down and summarized the very unclear situation they were in: "Two women have been murdered. Everything starts with these two. Maybe I'm being too presumptuous in assuming the same perpetrator is responsible for both deaths, since there is no obvious connection, no motive, not even any similarities. Medberg was killed in a hut hidden away deep inside the Rannesholm Forest, and now we find another woman, most probably a foreigner, strangled with a thick rope inside a burning church. The only connections we have found between these events are tenuous, accidental—not really connections at all. On the outskirts of this is another murky series of events. That is why Linda is here."

Wallander slowly picked his way across the terrain that involved everything from swans set on fire to severed hands. It was as if he proceeded with antennae stretched out in every direction at once. It took him one hour and twelve minutes without a break or repetition to reach his conclusion: "We don't know yet what has happened. Behind the two dead women, the burning animals, and the torched churches lies something else that we can't quite put our fingers on. We don't know if what we have here marks the culmination of something, or simply the beginning."

At the words "simply the beginning," Wallander sat down, but continued to speak.

"We're still waiting for information regarding the woman we believe to be named Harriet Bolson. While we wait, I'm going to open this up for general discussion, but before I do I'd like to make a final comment. I have a feeling that the animals weren't burned to satisfy the perverted desires of a sadist. It may have been a form of sacrifice, or an act with its own twisted logic. We have Medberg's praying hands and also a Bible that someone sat and wrote commentary in. And now something that looks like a ritual killing in a church. We have an eyewitness who claims she heard the man who set fire to the pet store shouting the words 'The Lord's will be done' or something in that vein. All of these things may point to a religious message, perhaps the work of a sect or a few crazed individuals. But I doubt the latter. There is an organized quality to this cruelty that speaks against it being the work of a single person. But are we talking about two or a thousand? We don't know. That's why I want us to take the time to discuss the matter without prejudice before we continue our investigation. I think we'll be more effective if we allow ourselves to push everything else aside and concentrate on this point for a moment."

But this discussion was averted by a door opening and a woman announcing that American faxes about Harriet Bolson had started to come in. Martinsson left and returned with a few papers, among them a blurred photograph of a woman. Wallander held his broken glasses in front of his face and nodded. The dead woman was Harriet Bolson.

"My English is not quite what it should be," Martinsson said and passed the papers over to Höglund, who started to read aloud.

Linda had picked up a notebook as she walked into the room. Now she started making notes, without being clear about why she was doing so. She was involved in something without being fully involved, but she sensed that her father had an assignment for her that he would present to her when the time was ripe.

Höglund said the American police seemed to have covered the case thoroughly—but perhaps it hadn't been so hard, since Harriet Jane Bolson had been registered as a missing person since January 12, 1997. That was when her sister, Mary Jane Bolson, had gone to the Tulsa police and filed the report. She had initially tried to reach her sister on the phone for a week without success. Then she had gotten in her car and driven the 300 kilometers to Tulsa, where her sister lived and worked as archivist and secretary to a private art collector. Mary Jane had found her sister's apartment empty. She was also not at her workplace. She seemed in fact to have disappeared without a trace. Mary Jane and all of Harriet's friends had described her as a reserved but conscientious and friendly woman who had had neither a drug addiction nor any other vice that might help explain her disappearance. The police in Tulsa had completed a preliminary investigation and maintained a current file on her case, but during the last four years nothing had turned up. No clues, no sign of life, nothing.

"A police officer by the name of Clark Richardson is eagerly awaiting our reply and confirmation of the fact that the woman we've found really is Harriet. He would like the information as soon as possible."

"Which we can supply him with immediately," Wallander said. "It's her, there's no doubt about it. Is there really no theory about her disappearance?"

Höglund scoured the documents.

"Harriet was unmarried," she said. "She was twenty-six when she disappeared. She and her sister were daughters of a Methodist pastor in Cleveland, Ohio. Prominent, it says. They had a happy childhood, no evidence of trouble, studies at various universities. Harriet had a position in Tulsa with a very good salary. She lived simply with regular habits. She worked hard all week and went to church on Sundays."

"Is that it?" Wallander asked when Höglund finished reading.

"That's it."

He shook his head.

"There has to be something more to her story," he said. "We need to know everything about her. That will be your job. Pour on the charm. Give Officer Richardson the idea that this is the most important murder investigation in Sweden right now. Which it probably is, for that matter."

This was followed by a short period of open discussion. Linda listened attentively. After half an hour her father tapped the table with his pencil and ended the meeting. Everyone except Linda and her father left the room.

"I want you to do me a favor," he said. "Talk to Anna, hang around, but don't ask any questions. Try to figure out why Medberg's name was really in her journal. And Vigsten. I've asked my colleagues to look a little closer at him."

"Not the old man," Linda said. "He's senile. But there was someone else there, someone who kept himself hidden."

"We don't know that for sure," he said impatiently. "Have you understood what I've asked you?"

"Act normal," Linda answered, "but try to get answers to these questions."

He nodded and stood up.

"I'm worried," he said. "I don't know what's happening, and I'm afraid of what's next."

Then he looked at her, stroked her briefly and almost shyly on the cheek, and left the room.

Linda invited Zeba and Anna to join her for coffee down at the harbor the same day. They had just sat down when it started to rain.

39

Zeba's son played happily with a toy car that squeaked because it was missing two of its wheels. Linda looked at him. Sometimes he could be almost unbearably needy and attention-seeking. Other times, like now, he was peaceful, lost in thought about the invisible roads his little yellow car was traveling.

The café was almost empty at this time of day. A few Danish sailors in one corner were hunched over a nautical map. The young woman behind the counter yawned.

"Girl talk," Zeba said suddenly. "Why don't we have more time for that?"

"Talk away," Linda said. "I'm listening."

"What about you?" Zeba asked, turning to Anna. "Are you listening?"

"Of course."

They were quiet. Anna pushed a teaspoon around in her cup, Zeba folded a pinch of snuff into her upper lip. Linda sipped her coffee.

"Is this all there is?" Zeba asked. "In life, I mean."

"What are you thinking of?" Linda asked.

"All our dreams. What became of them?"

"You dreamed of having children," Anna said. "At least that seemed like your main goal."

"You're right. But all the other stuff. I was such a dreamer! Especially when I was drunk out of my mind, you know the way you drink when you're a teenager, when you end up on your hands and knees, throwing up in a bush, having to fight off a guy who's looking to take advantage of the situation. But I never even realized any of my dreams. I drank them away, you could say. When I think of all the things I was going to do: be a fashion designer, rock star—fly a jumbo jet, for God's sake."

"It's not too late," Linda said.

Zeba put her chin on her hands and looked at her.

"Of course it is. Did you really dream about becoming a policewoman?"

"Never. In my dreams, if you can call them that, I was always going to devote my life to theater or refinishing old furniture. Not very exciting."

Zeba turned her head to Anna.

"What about you?"

"I wanted to find a meaning with my life."

"Did you find it?"

"Yes."

"And?"

Anna shook her head.

"It's not the kind of thing you can talk about. You either find it or you don't."

Linda thought Anna seemed to be on her guard. From time to time she looked at Linda as if she was thinking: "I know you're trying to see through me." *But I can't be sure,* Linda thought.

The Danish sailors got up to leave. One of them patted Zeba's boy on the head.

"His existence hung by a thread for a while," Zeba said.

Linda raised her eyebrows.

"What do you mean?"

"I was close to having an abortion. Sometimes I wake up in the middle of the night in a cold sweat and think I really did it, that he doesn't exist."

"I thought you wanted a baby."

"I did. But I was scared. I didn't think I'd be up to it."

"Thank God you didn't do it," Anna said.

Both Zeba and Linda were taken aback by her emphatic declaration. She sounded stern, almost angry. Zeba was immediately put on the defensive.

"Something as abstract as god makes no sense in that context. Maybe you'll understand when you get pregnant one day."

"I'm against abortion," Anna said. "That's just the way it is."

"Having an abortion doesn't mean you're 'for' abortion," Zeba said calmly. "There can be other reasons for it."

"Like what?"

"Like being too young. Or too sick."

"I'm against abortion, period," Anna repeated.

"I'm happy I had my boy," Zeba said. "But I don't regret the abortion I had when I was fifteen."

Linda was taken by surprise, and so was Anna. She seemed to stiffen and stared at Zeba.

"Why are you staring at me like that?" Zeba said. "I was fifteen years old—what would you have done?"

"Probably the same thing," Linda said.

"Not me," Anna said. "It's a sin."

"Now you sound like a priest."

"I'm just telling you what I think."

Zeba shrugged.

"I thought this was girl talk. If I can't talk about my abortion with my friends, who am I supposed to talk to?"

Anna stood up.

"I have to go now," she said. "I forgot about something I have to do."

She disappeared out the door. Linda thought it was strange that she left without even saying good-bye to Zeba's son.

"What got into her?" Zeba said. "It's enough to make you think she had an abortion herself and can't talk about it."

"Maybe she did," Linda said. "You think you know everything about a person, but the truth often comes as a surprise."

Zeba and Linda ended up staying longer than they had planned. With Anna gone, the atmosphere became more lighthearted. They giggled like teenagers. Linda followed Zeba home, and they said good-bye outside Zeba's building.

"What do you think Anna will do?" Zeba asked. "Say that we can't be friends anymore?"

"I think she'll realize she overreacted."

"I'm not sure about that," Zeba said. "But I hope you're right."

Linda went home. She lay down on the bed, closed her eyes, and drifted off. Now she was walking to the lake again, where someone had seen burning swans and called the police. Suddenly she opened her eyes. Martinsson had said they would check the phone log of calls to the station that night. That meant the conversation was preserved on a cassette tape. Linda couldn't recall anyone commenting on what the man had sounded like. *It was a Norwegian by the name of Torgeir Langaas.* Amy Lindberg had also heard someone who spoke either Norwegian or Danish. She got out of bed. *If the man who called in had an accent, we may be able to determine a link between the burning animals and the man who bought the house behind the church in Lestarp.*

She walked out onto the balcony. It was ten o'clock and the air was chilly. *It will be fall soon,* she thought, *the frost is on its way. It will crunch under my feet by the time I become a police officer.*

The phone rang. It was her dad.

"I just wanted to let you know I won't be home for dinner."

"It's ten o'clock, Dad. I ate dinner hours ago."

"Well, I'll be here for another couple of hours."

"Do you have time to talk?"

"What's up?"

"I was thinking of taking a walk down to the station."

"Is it important?"

"Maybe."

"I can't give you more than five minutes."

"I only need two. Correct me if I'm wrong, but don't all emergency calls to the police get recorded and stored?"

"Yes. Why?"

"How long are they kept?"

"For a year. Why are you asking?"

"I'll tell you when I get there."

It was twenty to eleven when Linda walked into the station. Her dad came out into the deserted reception area and met her. His room was full of cigarette smoke.

"Who's been here?"

"Boman."

"Who's that?"

"He's our D.A."

Linda was suddenly reminded of another district attorney.

"Where did she go?"

"Who?"

"The one you were in love with? She was a D.A. back then."

"That was a long time ago. I flubbed my chances."

"How?"

"One's worst embarrassments should be kept to oneself. There are other attorneys here now, and Boman is one of them. I'm the only one who lets him smoke."

"You can't even breathe in here now!"

Linda opened the window.

"What was it you wanted?"

Linda explained.

"You're right," he said when she had finished.

Wallander stood up and motioned for her to follow. They bumped into Lindman in the corridor. He was carrying a stack of folders.

"Put those down and come with us," Wallander said.

They went to the archive where the cassette tapes were stored. Wallander gestured for one of the officers on duty to come over and talk to him.

"The evening of the twenty-first of August," he said. "A man called and reported sighting burning swans at Marebo Lake."

"I wasn't working that night," the officer said after studying a log book. "It was Undersköld and Sundin."

"Call them."

The officer shook his head.

"Undersköld is in Thailand and Sundin is at a satellite intelligence conference in Germany. It'll be hard to get hold of them."

"What about the tape?"

"I'll find it for you."

They gathered around a cassette player. Between a call about a suspected car theft and a drunk man who was calling for help "looking for Mom" was the call about the burning swans. Linda flinched when she heard the voice. It sounded as if he was trying to speak Swedish without an accent, but couldn't disguise his origins. They played the tape several times.

POLICE: Ystad Police Station.

MAN: I would like to report that burning swans are flying over Marebo Lake.

POLICE: Burning swans?

MAN: Yes.

POLICE: Can you repeat that? What is burning?

MAN: Burning swans are flying over Marebo Lake.

That was the end of the call. Wallander was listening through headphones that he then passed to Lindman.

"He has an accent, no doubt about it. I think he sounds Danish."

Or Norwegian, Linda thought. *What's the difference?*

"I'm not sure it's Danish," Lindman said and passed the headphones to Linda.

"The word he uses for 'burning,'" she said. "Is it the same in both Norwegian and Danish?"

"We'll find out," Wallander said. "But it's embarrassing that a police cadet has to be the one to bring this up."

They left the room after Wallander had left instructions about keeping the tape readily available. He led the others to the lunchroom. A group of patrol officers sat around one table, Nyberg and some technicians around another. Wallander poured himself a cup of coffee, then sat down by a phone.

"For some reason I still remember this number," he said.

He held the receiver to his ear. It was a brief conversation. Wallander asked the person he was speaking with to come down to the station as soon as possible. It was clear that this person was resistant to the idea.

"Perhaps you would prefer I order a patrol car with blaring sirens," Wallander said. "And have the officers handcuff you so your neighbors wonder what you've been up to."

He hung up.

"That was Christian Thomassen," he said. "He's first mate on one of the Poland ferries. He's also an alcoholic, though currently dry. He's Norwegian and should be able to give us a positive identification."

Seventeen minutes later, one of the largest men Linda had ever seen entered the station. He had huge feet stuffed into enormous rubber boots, was close to two meters tall, and had a beard down to his chest and a tattoo on his bald pate. When he sat down, Linda discreetly stood up to see the tattoo more clearly. It depicted a compass card. Christian Thomassen smiled at her.

"It's pointing south-southwest," he said. "Straight into the sunset. That way the Grim Reaper will know which way to take me when the time comes."

"This is my daughter," Wallander said. "Do you remember her?"

"Maybe. I don't remember too many people, to be honest. I've survived my drinking, but most of my memories haven't."

He stretched out his hand so she could shake it. Linda was afraid he would squeeze too hard. His accent reminded her of the man on the tape.

"Let's go in," Wallander said. "I want you to listen to a recording for us."

Thomassen listened carefully. He asked to hear the conversation four times, but stopped Lindman when he was about to play it for a fifth time.

"He's Norwegian," Thomassen said. "Not Danish. I was trying to hear where in Norway he's from, but I can't pinpoint it. He's probably been away from Norway for a long time."

"Do you think he's been here a long time?"

"Not necessarily."

"But you're sure that he's Norwegian?"

"Yes. Even if I've lived here for nineteen years and drunk myself silly for eight of those years, I haven't completely forgotten where I came from."

"That's all we needed to know," Wallander said. "Do you need a ride back?"

"I came down on the bike," Thomassen said, smiling. "I can't ride when I've been drinking. I just fall over and hurt myself."

"A remarkable man," Wallander said to Linda after he left. "He has a beautiful bass voice. If he hadn't been so lazy and drunk so heavily he could have been an opera singer. I suspect he would have become world famous, for his sheer size if nothing else."

They went back to Wallander's office.

"So he's Norwegian," Wallander said. "And we know that the man who set fire to the swans was the same as the one who set fire to the pet store, just as we suspected. It will probably turn out to be the same man who set fire to the calf. The question is whether he was the one who was hiding out in the hut in the forest."

"The Bible," Lindman said.

Wallander shook his head.

"Swedish. They've managed to decipher a lot of what's been written in the margins, and it's all in Swedish."

They were quiet. Linda waited. Lindman shook his head.

"I have to sleep," he said. "I can't think clearly anymore."

"Eight o'clock tomorrow," Wallander said.

Lindman's steps died away in the corridor. Wallander yawned.

"You should get some sleep too," Linda said.

He nodded, then stood up.

"You're right. We need to sleep. I need to sleep. It's already midnight."

There was a knock on the door. One of the officers on phone duty looked in.

"This just came," he said, handing a fax to Wallander.

"It's from Copenhagen," the officer said. "Someone called Knud Pedersen."

"I know him," Wallander said.

The officer left. Wallander skimmed the fax, but then sat down at the desk and read it more carefully.

"Strange," he said. "I know from way back that Knud Pedersen is a policeman who keeps his eyes open. They've had a murder there recently, a prostitute by the name of Sylvi Rasmussen. She was found with her neck broken. The unusual thing is that her hands were clasped in prayer—not severed this time, but Pedersen has read about our case and thought we should know about this."

Wallander let the fax fall to the desk.

"Copenhagen again," he said.

Linda was about to ask a question, but he lifted his hand.

"We should get some sleep," he said. "Tired policemen always end up giving the perpetrator a chance to slip away."

———

They left the station. Wallander suggested they go on foot.

"Let's talk about something completely different," he said. "Something to clear our thoughts."

They walked back to Mariagatan without saying a single word.

40

Each time he saw his daughter it was as if the ground disappeared beneath his feet. It could take several minutes before he regained his equilibrium.

Images from his younger life flickered through his mind. Normally he bore his memories with calm; he checked his pulse and it was always steady no matter how upset he felt. "Like the feathered animal, you should shake hate, lies, and anger from your body," God had said to him in a dream. It was only when he met his daughter that he was overcome with weakness. When he saw her face, he also saw the others: Maria and the baby left behind to rot in the steamy jungle that crazy Jim Jones had chosen for his paradise. Sometimes he longed passionately for those who had died, and he also felt guilty that he hadn't been able to save them. *God demanded this sacrifice of me in order to test me*, he thought.

He always varied the times and places he met with his daughter. Now that he had stepped out of his former state of invisibility and shown himself to her, he made sure in turn that she did not disappear from him. He often tried to surprise her. Once, just after they had been reunited, he washed her car. He sent a letter to her Lund address when he had wanted her to come to their hideout behind the church in Lestarp. He had visited her apartment several times without her knowledge, using her phone to make important calls and even once spending the night there.

I left her behind once, he thought. *Now I have to be stronger so that she doesn't do the same to me*. He had prepared himself for the possibility that she wouldn't want to follow him. Then he would have disappeared again. But already after the first three days he decided he would be able to make her one of the chosen. The fact that convinced him was the unexpected coincidence that she knew the woman who Torgeir happened upon and killed in the forest. He had understood then that she had been waiting for him to return all these years.

This time he was going to see her in her apartment. She had placed a flowerpot in the window as a sign that the coast was clear. A few times he had gone in with the set of keys she had given him without waiting for the flowerpot because God told him when it was safe. He had explained to her that it was important to act natural in front of her friends. *Nothing has happened on the surface,* he told her. *Your faith grows deep inside you for now, until the day I call it forth from your body.*

Each time they met, he did something that Jim Jones had taught him—one of the few lessons that was not spoiled by betrayal and hatred. Jones had taught him how to listen to a person's breath, especially those who were new and who perhaps had not yet found the proper humility to put their lives in their leader's hands.

He walked into the apartment. She knelt on the floor of the hall and he laid his hand on her forehead and whispered the words that God demanded he say to her. He reached for a vein in her throat where he could feel her pulse. She trembled but was less afraid now. It was starting to become more familiar to her, all these elements of her new life. He knelt in front of her.

"I am here," he whispered.

"I am here," she replied.

"What does the Lord say?"

"He demands my presence."

He stroked her cheek, then they stood up and walked out into the kitchen. She had put out the food he requested: salad, crispbread, two slices of meat. He ate slowly, in silence. When he was done, she came over with a bowl of water, washed his hands, and gave him a cup of tea. He looked at her and asked her if anything had happened since they had last met. He was interested in hearing about her friends, especially the one who had been looking for her.

He sipped the tea and listened to her first words, noticing that she was nervous. He looked at her and smiled.

"What is troubling you?"

"Nothing."

He grabbed her hand and forced two of her fingers into the hot tea. She flinched but he held her hand there until he was sure she had scalded herself. She started to cry. He let go.

"God demands the truth," he said. "You know I am right when I say that something is troubling you. You have to tell me what it is."

Then she told him what Zeba had said when they were at the café and her little boy was playing under the table. He noticed that she wasn't sure she was doing the right thing. Her friends were still important to her. That wasn't unusual—in fact, he had been surprised at the speed with which he had been able to convert her.

"Telling me about this was the right thing to do," he said when she was finished. "It is also only appropriate that you hesitated in this. Hesitation is a way to prepare to fight for the truth and not take it for granted. Do you understand what I am saying?"

"Yes."

He looked at her for a long time, scrutinizing her. *She is my daughter,* he thought. *She gets her seriousness from me.*

He stayed a while and told her about his life, wanting to bridge the years of his long absence. He would never be able to convince her to follow him if she did not fully understand that his absence had been ordered by God. *It was my time in the desert,* he had said repeatedly. *I was sent out not for thirty days, but twenty-four years.*

When he left her apartment, he was sure she was going to follow him. And even more significantly, she had given him yet another opportunity to punish a sinner.

Langaas was waiting for him at the post office, since they always tried to meet in public. They had a brief conversation, then Langaas leaned forward so his pulse could be checked. It was normal.

Later that same day they met at the parking lot. It was a mild, cloudy evening with rain likely at night. Langaas had replaced the truck with a bus that he had stolen from a company in Malmö, being careful to put on a new license plate. They drove east, passing

Ystad and continuing on minor roads toward Klavestrand, where they stopped at the church. It lay on a hill, approximately four hundred meters from the nearest house. No one would be likely to notice the bus where it was parked. Langaas unlocked the church door with the key that he had copied. They used shielded flashlights as they erected the ladders and covered the windows looking out onto the road with black plastic. Afterward they lit the candles on the altar. Their footsteps made no sounds; all was silent.

Langaas came to see him in the vestry, where he was making his preparations.

"Everything is ready."

"Tonight I will let them wait," Westin said.

He gave the remaining hawser to Langaas.

"Put this on the altar. The hawser inspires fear, fear inspires faith."

Langaas left. Westin sat down at the pastor's table with a candle in front of him. When he closed his eyes, he was back in the jungle. Jim Jones came walking out of his hut, the only one that was supplied with electricity from a small generator. Jim was always so well groomed. His teeth were white, his smile carved into his face. *Jim was beautiful,* he thought, *even if he was a fallen angel. I cannot deny that there were moments with him when I was completely happy. I also cannot deny that what Jim gave me, or what I believed he gave me, is what I am trying to give the people who now follow me. I have seen the fallen angel; I know what to do.*

He folded his arms and let his head come to rest on them. He was going to let them wait for him. The hawser on the altar would be a stimulus of the fear they should feel for him. If the ways of God were inscrutable, so too would be the ways of his servant. He knew Torgeir would not disturb him again. He started to dream. It was like stepping down into the underworld, a world where the heat of the jungle penetrated the cold stone walls of the church. He thought about Maria and the child; he slept.

He woke up with a start at four o'clock in the morning. At first he wasn't sure where he was. He stood up and shook life back into his stiff body. After a few minutes, he walked out into the church.

They were all sitting in the first few pews, frozen, fearful, waiting. He stopped and looked at them before letting them see him. *I could kill them all,* he thought. *I could get them to cut off their hands and eat themselves. Because I too have a weakness. I do not completely trust my followers. I am afraid of the thoughts they think, thoughts I cannot control.* He walked out and stood in front of the altar. This night he was going to tell them about the great task that awaited them, the reason they had made the long journey to Sweden. Tonight he would pronounce the first words of the text that would become the fifth gospel.

He nodded to Langaas, who opened the old-fashioned brown trunk on the floor next to the altar. Langaas walked down the row of people, handing out the death masks. They were white, like masks in a pantomime, devoid of expression, of joy or sorrow.

God has made man in his image, Westin thought. *But no one knows the face of God. Our lives are his breath, but no one knows his face. We have to wear the white masks in order to obliterate the ego and become one with our Creator.*

He watched while they put on the death masks. It always filled him with a sense of power and strength to see them cover their faces.

Finally, Langaas put on a mask. The only one not wearing one was Westin.

He had learned this too from Jim. The disciples always have to know where to find their Master. He is the only one who should not be masked.

He pressed his right thumb against his left wrist. His pulse was normal. Everything was under control. *In the future, this church may become a shrine,* he thought. *The first Christians who died in the catacombs of Rome have returned. The time of the fallen angels is finally over.*

The day he had chosen was the eighth of September. This had come to him in a dream. He had found himself in a deserted factory with puddles of rainwater and dead leaves on the floor. There had been a calendar on the wall. When he woke up, he remembered that the date in the dream was the eighth of September. *That is the day everything ends and everything begins again.*

He stepped closer to them and started to speak.

"The time has come. I had not intended that we should meet before the day that you undertake your great task, but God has spoken to me tonight and told me that yet another sacrifice is necessary. When we meet again, another sinner will die."

He picked up the hawser and held it above his head.

"We know what God demands of us," he intoned. "The old scriptures teach us the law of an eye for an eye and a tooth for a tooth. He who kills must himself be killed. We must remove all doubt from our minds. God's breath is steel and he demands hardness from us in return. We are like the snake who wakes from his winter sleep, we are the lizards who live in the crevices of the rock and change color when threatened. Only through complete devotion and ruthlessness will we conquer the emptiness that exists inside men. The great darkness, the long days of degeneration and impotence are over."

He paused and saw that they understood. He walked along the row and stroked their foreheads, then gave the sign that they were to stand. Together they said the holy words that he told them had come to him in a vision. They did not have to know the truth, that it was something he had read when he was a young man. Or had the words in fact come to him in a dream? He could not be sure, but it was of no importance.

And in our redemption we are lifted high on wings of might
To join him in his power and shine with his holy light.

Later they left the church, locked up, and drove away in the bus. A woman who came in to clean in the afternoon did not notice that anyone had been there at all.

the thirteenth tower

41

The telephone woke her up. She checked the time: a quarter to six.

There were noises coming from the bathroom. Her father was already up but hadn't heard the phone. Linda ran out into the kitchen and picked up.

"May I please speak to Inspector Wallander?" a woman's voice said.

"And who is this?"

"May I please speak to him?"

The woman spoke in a cultured way. *Hardly a cleaning lady at the station,* Linda thought.

"He's busy right now. Who may I say is calling?"

"Anita Tademan from Rannesholm Manor."

"We've met, actually. I'm his daughter."

Anita Tademan ignored her last comment.

"When will I be able to speak to him?"

"As soon as he gets out of the bathroom."

"It's very important."

Linda wrote down the number and put some water on for coffee. The pot had just started to boil when Wallander came into the kitchen. He was so wrapped up in his own thoughts that it did not even strike him as strange to see her up so early.

"Anita Tademan just called," Linda said. "She said it was important."

Wallander looked at his watch.

"It must be, at this hour."

She dialed the number for him and held out the phone.

While he was speaking with Mrs. Tademan, Linda looked through the cupboards and discovered there were no more coffee beans.

Wallander hung up. Linda had heard him agree to a time.

"What did she want?"

"For me to come and talk to her."

"What about?"

"To tell me something she heard from a distant relative who lives in a house on the Rannesholm grounds. She didn't want to elaborate on the phone and insisted I come up to the manor. I'm sure she thinks she's too important to come down to the station like a regular person. But that's when I put my foot down. Maybe you heard that part?"

"No—why?"

Wallander muttered something unintelligible and started to rifle through the cupboard.

"It's all gone," Linda said.

"Do I have to be the only one around here who takes responsibility for keeping coffee in the house?"

That immediately infuriated her.

"You don't understand how incredibly relieved I'll be to move out. I should never have come back here."

He threw out his arms in apology.

"That might have been best. Parents and children shouldn't live on top of each other. But we don't have time to argue about it now."

They drank tea and leafed through their respective parts of the morning paper. Neither one could concentrate on what he or she was reading.

"I want you to come along," he said. "Get dressed."

Linda showered and dressed as quickly as she could. But when she was ready, he had already left. He had jotted something down in the margin of the newspaper. She took that as a sign that he was in a hurry. *He's as impatient as I am,* she thought.

She looked out of the window. The thermometer said it was twenty-two degrees Celsius—still summer. It was raining. She half-ran, half-walked to the station. It was as if she were hurrying to school, with the same anxiety about making it on time.

Wallander was talking on the phone when she came in. She sat down in the chair across from his desk. He put the phone down and stood up.

"Come with me."

They walked into Lindman's office. Höglund was leaning against the wall, a mug of coffee in her hand. For once she acknowledged Linda's presence. *Someone's mentioned it to her,* Linda thought. *Hardly my dad. Maybe Lindman.*

"Where is Martinsson?" Höglund asked.

"He just called," Wallander said. "He has a sick child on his hands, so he'll be in a little later. But he was going to make some calls from home and find out more about this Sylvi Rasmussen."

"Who?" Höglund asked.

"Why are we all crowding around in here, anyway?" Wallander said. "Let's go to the conference room. Does anybody know where Nyberg is?"

"He's still working on the two fires."

"What does he think he's going to find there?"

The last comment came from Höglund. Linda sensed that she was one of those who looked forward to his retirement.

They discussed the case for three hours and ten minutes, until someone knocked on the door and said that an Anita Tademan had arrived to speak with Inspector Wallander. Linda wondered if the discussion had really come to its natural conclusion, but no one made any objections when Wallander stood up. He stopped by her chair on his way out.

"Anna," he said. "Keep talking to her, keep listening to her."

"I don't know what we should talk about. She's going to see through me, that I'm keeping an eye on her."

"Just be yourself."

"Shouldn't you talk to her again?"

"Yes, but not just yet."

Linda left the station. The rain had turned into a thin drizzle. A car honked its horn, so close to her that she jumped. It was Lindman. He pulled over and opened the door.

"Jump in. I'll take you home."

"Thanks."

There was music on. Jazz.

"Do you like this music?" she asked.

"Yes. A lot, actually."

"Jazz?"

"Lars Gullin. A sax player, one of Sweden's best jazz musicians ever. He died much too young."

"I've never heard of him, but I don't like this kind of music."

"In my car I play what I like."

He seemed stung and Linda instantly regretted what she had said. *Unfortunately one of the many things I've inherited from my father is this ability to make thoughtless, hurtful comments.*

"Where are you going?" she asked.

His answer was curt.

"Sjöbo. To see a locksmith."

"Is it going to take long?"

"I don't think so. Why?"

"Maybe I could come along. If you'll have me."

"If you can stand the music."

"From now on I love jazz."

The tension was broken. Lindman laughed and drove north. He drove fast. Linda had the urge to touch him, to run her fingers over his shoulder or his cheek. She felt more desire than she could remember feeling in a long time. She had a silly thought that they should check into a hotel in Sjöbo. Not that there probably even was one. She tried to shake off the thought, but it stayed with her. Rain splattered the windshield. The saxophone poured out some high, insistent, quick notes. Linda tried to pick out the melody line, without success.

"If you're talking to a locksmith in Sjöbo, it must have something to do with the investigation. One of them. How many are there, exactly?"

"Medberg is one. Bolson is another, so are the burned animals, and the two church fires. Your dad wants them all treated under the rubric of one investigation, and the D.A. has agreed. At least for now."

"And the locksmith?"

"His name is Håkan Holmberg. He's not your average dime-store locksmith; he makes copies of very old keys. When he heard that the police were wondering how the arsonists broke into the churches, he remembered that he made two keys a few months ago that could very well have been old church keys. I'm on my way to see if he remembers anything else. His workshop is in the center of Sjöbo. Martinsson had heard of him before. He's won prizes for his craftsmanship. He's also studied philosophy and teaches in the summer."

"In his workshop?"

"In another part of the farmstead. Martinsson has thought about doing it sometime. The students work in the smithy half the day and explore philosophical issues the rest of the time."

"Not something for me," Linda said.

"What about your dad?"

"Even less so."

They arrived in Sjöbo and stopped outside a red brick house with a giant iron key hanging outside the door.

"Maybe I shouldn't go in with you."

"If I understood matters correctly, you've started working."

They walked in. It was very hot. A man working at the forge nodded at them, then took out a piece of glowing iron and started hammering it.

"I need to finish this key," he said. "You can't interrupt this kind of work once you've started. It lets a kind of hesitation into the iron. That happens and the key will never sit well in its lock."

They watched him with fascination. At last the key lay finished on the anvil. Holmberg wiped the sweat from his face and washed his hands. They followed him out into a courtyard with tables and chairs. A coffee pot and some cups had been put out. They shook hands. Linda felt foolishly flattered by Lindman's introducing her as a "colleague." Holmberg served the coffee and put on an old straw hat. He noticed Linda looking at it.

"One of the few crimes I've ever committed," he said. "I take a trip overseas every year. A few years ago I was in Lombardy. One afternoon I was somewhere close to Mantua, where I had spent a few days in honor of the great Virgil, who was born there. I caught sight of a scarecrow out on a field. I don't know what crop he was supposed to be protecting. I stopped and thought that for the first time in my life I wanted to commit a crime, become a dishonest blacksmith, in a word. So I snuck out onto the field and stole his hat. Sometimes in my dreams it isn't a scarecrow at all but a living person. He must have realized I was a harmless coward who would never steal from anyone—that's why he let me take the hat. Perhaps he was the remains of a Franciscan monk hoping to do one last good deed on this earth. In any case, it was an overwhelming, tumultuous experience for me, to commit this crime."

Linda glanced at Lindman and wondered if he knew who Virgil was. And Mantua? Where was that? It had to be Italy, but she had no idea if it was a region or a city. Zeba would have known; she could sit for hours over her maps and books.

"Tell me about the keys," Lindman said.

Holmberg rocked back in his chair and fished a pipe out of the breast pocket of his overalls.

"It happened by accident, in a way," he said after lighting the pipe. "I don't watch or read any kind of news in the summer, as a way to rest my mind. But one of my customers came by to pick up a key. It was the key of an old seaman's chest that had once belonged to a British admiral's ship in the eighteenth century. He told me about the fires and the police suspicion about copied keys. I recalled that I had made two keys a few months ago that looked like church keys. I'm not saying it was definitely the case, but I suspected it was."

"Why?"

"Experience. Church keys often look a certain way. And there aren't very many other doors these days that still use the locks and keys of the old masters. I decided to call the police."

"Who ordered these keys?"

"He said his name was Lukas."

"Lukas—?"

"Mr. Lukas. An extremely well-mannered sort. He was in a hurry and made a generous deposit."

Lindman took a packet out of his pocket, which he unwrapped. Holmberg immediately recognized the contents.

"Those are the keys I made copies of."

He stood up and walked into the smithy.

"This could be something," Lindman said. "A strange old man. But his memory seems good."

Holmberg returned with an old-fashioned ledger in his hand, turning the pages until he found the right one.

"It was the twelfth of June. Mr. Lukas left two keys. He wanted the copies made by the twenty-fifth at the latest. That didn't leave me very long, since I had a lot to do, but he paid well and even I need money, in order to keep up the forge and take my holiday trips."

"What address did he give you?"

"No address."

"Telephone number?"

Holmberg turned the ledger around so that Lindman could see. He dialed the number on his cell phone, listened, then turned it off again.

"That was a florist in Bjärred," he said. "I think we can safely assume that Mr. Lukas doesn't have anything to do with them. What happened after that?"

Holmberg flipped forward a few pages.

"He came to fetch the keys on the twenty-fifth of June. That was all."

"How did he pay?"

"Cash."

"Did you write out a receipt for him?"

"No. I rely on my bookkeeping. I take great pains to pay my share of taxes, even though this kind of situation is ideal for tax evasion."

"How would you describe him?"

"Tall, light hair, maybe losing a little of it in front. Courteous, polite. When he first came in he was dressed in a suit, same when he picked up the keys, though it was a different suit that time."

"How did he get here?"

"I can't see the road from the workshop, but I assume he drove a car."

Linda saw Lindman gather himself for the next question, intuitively sensing what it must be.

"Can you describe the way he spoke?"

"He had an accent."

"What kind of accent?"

"Something Scandinavian. Not Finnish, nor Icelandic. That would leave Danish or Norwegian."

"Do you have anything else to say about him?"

"Not that I can think of."

"Did he say that these keys were for church doors?"

"He said they were keys for some kind of storage facility—in an old manor house, come to think of it."

"Which manor?"

Holmberg knocked some ash out of his pipe and wrinkled his forehead.

"He told me the name, but I've forgotten."

They waited. Holmberg shook his head.

"Could it have been Rannesholm?" Linda asked.

The question simply jumped out of her, like last time.

"Right," Holmberg said. "That was it. Rannesholm. An old brewery at Rannesholm."

Lindman got up, as if he was suddenly in a hurry. He finished the rest of his coffee.

"Thank you," he said. "This has been valuable."

"Working with keys is always meaningful," Holmberg said and smiled. "Locking and opening is, in a sense, man's very purpose on this earth. Key rings rattle throughout history. Each key, each lock has its tale. And now I have yet another to tell."

He followed them out.

"Who was Virgil?" Linda asked.

"Dante's guide," he answered. "And a great poet."

He lifted the old straw hat that was starting to come apart and went back inside. They got in the car.

"So often you meet fearful, angry, shaken people," Lindman said. "But sometimes there are moments of light. Like this man. I'm filing him away in my archive of interesting people I'll remember when I'm old."

They left Sjöbo. Linda saw a sign for a hotel and giggled. He looked at her but didn't ask anything. The cell phone rang. He answered, listened, hung up, and sped up.

"Your dad has finished talking to Anita Tademan," he said. "Apparently something important has come to light."

"Better not tell him that I was with you today," she said. "He had something different in mind for me."

"What?"

"Talking to Anna," she said.

"Maybe you'll have time for both."

Lindman dropped her off in the center of town. When she made it to Anna's apartment and was greeted by her at the door she immediately realized that something was wrong. Anna had tears in her eyes.

"Zeba is gone," she said. "Her boy was screaming so loud that the neighbors were worried. He was home alone. And Zeba was gone."

Linda held her breath. Fear overwhelmed her like a sudden pain. Now she knew she was close to a terrible truth that she should already have grasped.

She looked into Anna's eyes and saw only her own fear.

42

The situation was at once both crystal clear and confusing. Linda knew Zeba would never have abandoned her son of her own free will, or forgotten about him. What had happened? It was something she felt she should know, something that was almost within her grasp and yet eluded her. The big picture. Her father always talked about looking for the way events came together. But she saw nothing.

Since Anna seemed even more confused than she did, Linda forced her to sit down in the kitchen and talk. Anna spoke in unconnected fragments, but it didn't take Linda more than a few minutes to piece together what had happened.

Zeba's neighbor, a woman who often watched the boy for her, had heard him crying through the thin walls. Since he cried for an unusually long time without Zeba seeming to intervene, she went over and rang the doorbell. When there was no answer, she let herself in with the key Zeba had given her and found the boy alone. He stopped crying when he saw her.

This neighbor, whose name was Aina Rosberg, had not seen anything strange in the apartment. It was messy as usual, but there were no signs of commotion. That was the phrase she had used: "no signs of commotion." Aina Rosberg had called one of Zeba's cousins, Titchka, who wasn't home, and then Anna. That's what Zeba had instructed her to do if anything ever happened: first call Titchka, then Anna.

"How long ago did this happen?" Linda asked.

"Two hours ago."

"Has Aina Rosberg called again?"

"I called her back. But Zeba still hadn't returned."

Linda thought for a moment. Most of all she wanted to talk to her dad, but she also knew what he would say. Two hours was not a long time. There was probably a natural explanation for Zeba's absence. But what could it possibly be?

"Let's go over to her apartment," Linda said. "I want to take a look at it."

Anna made no objections. Ten minutes later, Mrs. Rosberg let them in.

"Where can she be?" she said. "This isn't like her. Nobody would leave such a young child alone, least of all her. What would have happened if I hadn't heard him cry?"

"I'm sure she'll be back soon," Linda said. "But it would be best if the boy could stay with you until then."

"Of course he can," Mrs. Rosberg said, and left to go back to her apartment.

When Linda walked into Zeba's apartment, she picked up a strange smell. Her heart grew cold with fear; she knew something serious had happened. Zeba had not left of her own free will.

"Can you smell that?" she asked.

Anna shook her head.

"That sharp smell. Like vinegar."

"I don't smell anything."

Linda sat in the kitchen, Anna in the living room. Linda could see her through the open door. Anna was nervously pinching herself on the arm. Linda tried to think clearly. She walked over to the window and looked out. She tried to imagine Zeba walking out onto the street. Which way had she gone? To the left or to the right? Had she been alone? Linda looked at the little smoke shop that was across the street. A tall, heavily built man was standing in the doorway, smoking. When a customer came by he walked in, then resumed his station at the doorway. Linda thought he was worth a try.

Anna still sat on the couch, lost in thought. Linda patted her on the arm.

"I'm sure she'll turn up," she said. "Probably nothing has

happened. I'm going down to the smoke shop for a few minutes. I'll be back soon."

There was a sign welcoming customers to "Yassar's Shop." Linda bought some gum.

"Do you know Zeba?" she asked. "She lives across the street."

"Zeba? Sure. I give her little one candy when they come in."

"Have you seen her today?"

His answer came without hesitation.

"A few hours ago, around ten o'clock. I was putting up one of the flags that had come down outside. I don't understand how a flag can fall down when there is no wind. . . ."

"Was anyone with her?" Linda interrupted.

"She was with a man."

Linda's heart beat faster.

"Have you seen him before?"

Yassar looked worried. Instead of answering her question, he started asking his own.

"Why do you want to know? Who are you?"

"You must have seen me before. I'm a friend of Zeba's."

"Why are you asking all these questions?"

"I need to know."

"Has anything happened?"

"No. Have you ever seen the man before?"

"No. He had a small gray car, he was tall, and later I thought about how strange it was that Zeba was leaning on him."

"How do you mean 'leaning on him'?"

"Just that. She was leaning, clinging. As if she needed support."

"Can you describe the man?"

"He was tall. That's about it. He had a hat on, a long coat."

"A hat?"

"A gray hat. Or blue. A long gray coat. Or blue. Everything about him was either blue or gray."

"Did you see the license plate?"

"No."

"What about the make of the car?"

"I don't know. Why are you asking all these questions? You

come into my shop and make me as worried as if you were a cop."

"I am a cop," Linda said, and she left.

When she came back to the apartment, Anna was sitting where she had left her. Linda had the same feeling that there was something she should be seeing, realizing, seeing through, although she didn't know what it was. She sat down next to Anna.

"You have to go back to your place, in case Zeba calls. I'm going down to the police station to talk to my dad. You can drop me off there."

Anna grabbed Linda's arm so roughly that Linda jumped. Then, just as abruptly, she let go. It was a strange reaction. Perhaps not the action itself, but the intensity of it.

When Linda walked into the reception area, someone called out to her that her dad was at the D.A.'s office, on the other side. She went over. The outer door was locked, but an assistant who recognized her let her in.

"Are you looking for your father? He's in the small conference room."

She pointed down a corridor. A red light was on outside one of the rooms. Linda sat down outside and waited.

After ten minutes Ann-Britt Höglund came out, saw her, and looked surprised. Then she turned back to the room.

"You have an important visitor," she said and kept going.

Wallander came out with a very young attorney. He introduced Linda and the attorney left. Linda pulled him down in a chair and told him everything that had happened, not even trying to be systematic about the order in which things came out. Wallander was quiet for a long time after she finished. Then he asked a few questions, primarily about Yassar's observations. He returned several times to the issue of Zeba "leaning" on the man.

"Is Zeba the touchy-feely kind?"

"No, I'd say the opposite, actually. It's normally the man who is all over her. She's tough and avoids showing any weakness, although she has several."

"If she was being taken away against her will, why didn't she cry out?"

Linda shook her head. Wallander answered his own question, as he stood up.

"Maybe she wasn't able to."

"And that she had to lean on the man? That she was drugged and would have fallen down if he hadn't held her? That 'leaning on him' could be rephrased as 'propped up by him'?"

"That's exactly what I'm thinking."

He walked quickly to his office. Linda had trouble keeping up. On the way, Wallander knocked on Lindman's door and pushed it open. It was empty. Martinsson walked by carrying a large teddy bear.

"What the hell is that?" Wallander asked irritably.

"It was made in Taiwan. There's a large package of amphetamines inside."

"Get someone else to take care of it."

"I was about to hand it over to Svartman," Martinsson said, not hiding the fact that he too was irritated.

"Try to round everyone up. I want a meeting in half an hour."

Martinsson left.

Wallander sat down behind his desk, then leaned over toward Linda.

"You didn't ask Yassar if he heard the man say anything."

"I forgot."

Wallander handed her the phone.

"Call him."

"I don't know what his number is."

Wallander dialed information for her. Linda asked to be transferred. Yassar answered. He didn't remember the man saying anything.

"I'm starting to worry," Yassar said. "What has happened?"

"Nothing," Linda said. "Thanks for your help."

She put the phone down.

"He didn't hear anything."

Her dad rocked back and forth on his chair and looked at his hands. She heard voices come and go outside in the corridor.

"I don't like it," he said finally. "Her neighbor is right. No one leaves such a young child alone."

"I keep having the feeling that I'm overlooking something,"

Linda said. "Something I should see, something that's staring me in the face. There's a connection, the kind you're always talking about. But I can't think of it."

He looked attentively at her.

"As if part of you already knows what's happened? And why?"

She shook her head.

"It's more as if I've kind of been waiting for this to happen. And as if Zeba isn't the one who's disappeared, but Anna. A second time."

He looked at her for a long time.

"Can you explain what you mean?"

"No."

"We'll give Zeba a few more hours," he said. "If she's not back by then, we'll have to do something. I want you to stay here."

Linda followed him to the conference room. When everyone was gathered and the door was closed, Wallander started by telling everyone about Zeba's disappearance. The tension in the room mounted.

"Too many people are disappearing," Wallander said. "Disappearing, reappearing, disappearing again. By coincidence or because of factors as yet unknown, all this seems to involve my daughter, a fact that makes me like this even less."

He tapped a pencil on the tabletop and continued:

"I talked to Mrs. Tademan. She is not a particularly pleasant woman. In fact, she's about as good an example of an arrogant, conceited Scanian aristocrat I've ever had the misfortune to meet. But she did the right thing in getting in touch with us. A distant cousin who lives on the Rannesholm grounds saw a band of people near the edge of the forest. There were at least twenty of them, and they came and went very quickly. They could have been a group of tourists, but their actions, especially the fact that they were anxious not to attract attention, means they could also have been something else."

"Such as?" Höglund asked.

"We don't know. But keep in mind that we found a hideout in the forest and a woman was murdered there."

"That hut could hardly house twenty people or more."

"I know. Nonetheless, this is important information. We have suspected that there were at least several people involved in the Frennestad Church fire and murder. Now there seem to be indications that there are even more."

"This doesn't make sense," Martinsson said. "Are we dealing with a kind of gang?"

"Or a sect," Lindman said.

"Or both," Wallander said. "That's something we don't know yet. This piece of information may turn out to lead us in the wrong direction, but we're not drawing any conclusions. Not yet, not even provisional ones. Let's put Mrs. Tademan's information aside for the moment."

Lindman reported on his meeting with Håkan Holmberg and his keys. He didn't mention the fact that Linda had been with him.

"The man with an accent," Wallander mused. "Our Norwegian or Norwegian-Danish link. He turns up again. I think we can safely accept Mr. Holmberg's assurance that these were the keys to both the Hurup and Frennestad churches."

"We know that already," Nyberg said. "We've compared them."

The room fell silent.

"A Norwegian orders copies of some church keys," Wallander said. "An American woman is later strangled in the church. By whom and why? That's what we need to find out."

He turned to Höglund.

"What do our Danish colleagues say about Frans Vigsten?"

"He's a piano teacher. He was a rehearsal pianist at Det Kongelige Theater and apparently very much admired as such. Now he's getting increasingly senile and has trouble taking care of himself. But no one has any information indicating that anyone else lives in the apartment, least of all Vigsten himself."

"And Ulrik Larsen?"

"He stands by his confession—and still says he was trying to steal drugs."

Wallander threw a hasty glance at Linda before continuing.

"Let's stay in Denmark for a moment. What about this woman Sylvi Rasmussen? What do we have on her?"

Martinsson rifled through his papers.

"Her original name was something else. She came to Denmark as a refugee after the collapse of Eastern Europe. Drug addict, homeless, the same old story leading to prostitution. She was well-liked by clients and friends. No one has anything bad to say about her. There was nothing else unusual about her life, even the sheer predictable tragedy of it."

Martinsson looked through the papers again before putting them down.

"No one knows who her final client was, but he must be the murderer."

"She kept no written record?"

"No. There are the prints of twelve different people in her apartment. They're being examined, and the Danes will let us know what they find."

Linda noticed that her father was trying to pick up the pace of the meeting. He tried to interpret the information that was brought in, never receiving it passively, always looking for the underlying message.

Finally he opened the floor for general discussion. Linda was the only one who didn't say anything. After half an hour they took a short break. Everyone left to stretch their legs or to get some coffee, except Linda, who was assigned to guard the window.

A gust of wind blew some of Martinsson's papers onto the floor. Linda gathered them up and saw a picture of Sylvi Rasmussen. Linda studied her face, seeing fear in her eyes. She shivered when she thought of her life and fate.

She was about to put the papers back when a detail caught her eye. The pathologist's report stated that Sylvi Rasmussen had had two or three abortions. Linda stared at the paper. She thought of the two Danish sailors who had been sitting in the corner, Zeba's son playing on the floor, and Zeba, telling them about her abortion. She also thought about Anna's unexpected reaction. Linda froze, holding her breath and Sylvi Rasmussen's photograph.

Wallander came back into the room.

"I think I get it," she said.

"Get what?"

"I have one question. That woman from Tulsa."

"What about her?"

Linda shook her head and pointed to the door.

"Close it."

"We're in the middle of a meeting."

"I can't concentrate if everyone comes back in. But I think I'm onto something important."

He saw she meant what she was saying and went to close the door.

43

Wallander put his head out the door and told someone that the rest of the meeting would be postponed a little while. Someone started to protest but he shut the door.

They sat down across from each other.

"What did you want to ask?"

"Did Harriet Bolson ever have an abortion? Did Birgitta Medberg? If I'm correct, the answer will be yes for Bolson, but no for Medberg."

Wallander frowned, at first perplexed, then simply uncomprehending. He pulled his stack of papers over and started looking through them with growing impatience. He tossed the file to the side.

"Nothing about an abortion."

"Are all the facts there?"

"Of course not. A full description of a person's life, however uneventful or uninteresting, still fills a much larger folder than this. Harriet Bolson does not seem to have had a particularly exciting life, and certainly there's nothing as dramatic as an abortion in the material we received from Clark Richardson."

"And Medberg?"

"I don't know, but that information should be easier to get. All we have to do is talk to her unpleasant daughter—although perhaps it's not the kind of thing mothers tell their children? I don't think Mona ever had an abortion. Do you know?"

"No."

"Does that mean that you don't know if she did or that she never had one?"

"Mom never had an abortion. I would know."

"I don't understand what you're getting at. Why is this important?"

Linda tried to clear her head. She could be wrong but every instinct told her she was right.

"Can you find out about the abortions?"

"I'll do it when you've told me why it's important."

Something inside of her burst. Tears started to run down her face and she banged her fists into the table. She hated crying in front of her dad. Not just in front of him, in front of everybody. The only person she had ever been able to cry in front of was her grandfather.

"I'll ask them to do it," Wallander said and stood up. "But I expect you to tell me what this is all about when I get back. People have been murdered, Linda. This isn't an exercise at the police academy."

Linda grabbed an ashtray from the table and threw it at him, hitting him right above the eyebrow. Blood ran down his face and dripped on Harriet Bolson's file.

"I didn't mean to do that."

Wallander pressed a fistful of napkins against the gash.

"I just can't stand it when you needle me," she said.

He left the room. Linda picked up the ashtray from the floor, still trembling with agitation. She knew he was furious with her. Neither of them could stand to be humiliated. But she didn't feel any regret.

He came back after fifteen minutes with a makeshift bandage over his wound and dried blood still smeared across his cheek. Linda expected him to yell at her, but he simply sat down in his chair.

"Does it hurt a lot?" she asked.

He ignored her question.

"Höglund called Vanya Jorner, Medberg's daughter. She found the question deeply insulting and threatened to call the evening papers and complain, but Höglund did establish that she has no knowledge of any abortion."

"That's what I thought," Linda said. "And what about the other one? The one from Tulsa?"

"Höglund is contacting the U.S.," he said. "We're not entirely in agreement about the time difference, but in order to speed things along she's going to call them on the phone rather than send a fax."

Wallander felt the bandage with his fingertips.

"Your turn," he said.

Linda started speaking slowly to keep her voice from wobbling but also so she wouldn't leave anything out.

"There are five women," she said. "Three of them are dead, one of them has disappeared, and the last one disappeared and then returned. I'm starting to see a connection between them, apart from Medberg, who we're assuming was killed because she found herself in the wrong place at the wrong time. But what about the rest? Sylvi Rasmussen was murdered; she had also had two or three abortions. Let's assume that information from Tulsa confirms that Bolson had an abortion. It's also true for the person who's just gone missing: Zeba. She told me only a few days ago that she had one. I think this may be the connection between these women."

Linda paused and drank some water. Wallander tapped his fingers and stared at the wall.

"I still don't get it," he said.

"I'm not finished yet. Zeba didn't just tell me about her abortion, she told Anna too. And Anna had the strangest reaction. She was upset by it in a way I couldn't relate to, nor could Zeba. To say that Anna strongly disapproved of women who had abortions would be an understatement. She walked out on us. And when Anna later found out that Zeba was missing, she clung to my arm and cried. But it was as if she wasn't so much afraid for Zeba as for herself."

Linda stopped. Her dad was still fingering his bandage.

"What do you mean, she was afraid for herself?"

"I'm not sure I know."

"Try."

"I'm telling you all I know."

Wallander gazed absently at the wall. Linda knew that staring at a blank surface was a sign of intense concentration on his part.

"I want you to tell the others," he said.

"I can't."

"Why not?"

"I'll get nervous. I might be wrong. Maybe that woman from Tulsa never had an abortion."

"You have an hour to prepare," Wallander said and stood up. "I'll tell the others."

He walked out and closed the door. Linda had the feeling that she was imprisoned, not physically with a lock and key, but by the imposed time limit. She decided to write down what she was going to say in a notebook, and pulled a pad of paper toward her. When she flipped it open, she was confronted with a bad sketch of a seductively posed naked woman. To her surprise, she saw that it was Martinsson's notepad. *But why should that surprise me?* she thought. *All the men I know spend an enormous amount of mental energy undressing women in their minds.*

She reached for an unused notepad beside the overhead projector and jotted down the five women's names.

After forty-five minutes, the door opened. Everyone marched in like a delegation led by her father. He waved a piece of paper in front of her.

"Harriet Bolson had two abortions."

Wallander sat down, as did everyone else.

"The question of course is why this matters to our investigation. That's what we're here to discuss. Linda is going to present us with her ideas. Over to you, Linda."

Linda drew a deep breath and managed to present her theory without stumbling over her words even once. Wallander took over when she finished.

"I think it's clear that Linda is onto something that may be very important. The terrain is still far from mapped, but there is enough substance here to merit our attention, more substance than we have managed to uncover thus far, in fact, in other facets of the investigation."

The door opened and Lisa Holgersson slipped in. Wallander put his papers down and lifted his hands as if he were about to conduct an orchestra.

"I think we can glimpse the outline of something that we do not yet understand but is there nonetheless."

He stood up and pulled over a large notepad set on an easel, with the words HIGHER WAGES DAMMIT scrawled across it. Chuckles broke out across the room. Even Holgersson laughed. Wallander turned to a clean sheet.

"As usual I ask that you hold your thoughts until I'm done," he said. "Save the rotten tomatoes and catcalls."

"Looks like your daughter's already been taking potshots," Martinsson said. "Blood is seeping through the bandage. You look like the old Döbeln at Jutas, to use a literary analogy."

"Who's that?" Lindman asked.

"A man who stood guard over a bridge in Finland," Martinsson said. "Didn't they teach you anything when you were in school?"

"We had to read that when I was a girl, but you're getting them confused. The man standing guard had a different name. It's a book by some Russian author," Höglund said.

"No, Finnish," Linda heard herself say. "Sibelius, isn't it?"

"For the love of God," Wallander said.

"I'll call my brother Albin," Martinsson said, standing up. "We have to get to the bottom of this."

He left the room.

"I don't think it was Sibelius," Holgersson said after a moment. "He was a composer. But something similar."

Martinsson returned after a few minutes of silence.

"Topelius," he said. "Or possibly Runeberg. And Döbeln did have a large bandage, I was right about that."

"He didn't guard the bridge, though, did he?" Höglund muttered.

"I'm trying to create an overview here," Wallander interrupted, and proceeded to touch on all the known facts of the case.

After the rather lengthy overview, he sat down.

"There's one thing we've neglected to do: why haven't we brought in the real-estate agent in Skurup, Ture Magnusson—the one who sold the house in Lestarp, to listen to the burning-swans tape? We need to take care of that as soon as possible."

Martinsson got up again and left the room. Lindman opened a window.

"Have we talked to Norway about Torgeir Langaas?" Holgersson asked.

Wallander looked at Höglund.

"No word yet," she said.

Wallander looked down at his watch in a way that indicated the meeting was drawing to a close.

"It's too early to arrive at any definitive conclusions," he said. "It's too early, and yet we have to work with two assumptions. Either all this hangs together. Or, it doesn't. And yet the first alternative is compelling. What do we have? Sacrifices, fires, and ritual murder, a Bible in which someone has changed the text. It's easy for us to see this as the work of a madman, but maybe that isn't the case. Maybe we're dealing with a group of very deliberate, methodical people, with a twisted and ruthless agenda. We need to work quickly. There's a gradual increase in tempo in these events, an acceleration. We have to find Zeba, and talk to Anna Westin again."

He turned to Linda.

"I thought you could bring her in. We're going to have a friendly but necessary conversation. We're simply worried about Zeba, that's all you have to say."

"Who's taking care of her son?"

Höglund asked Linda directly, without the superior air she normally adopted.

"Zeba's neighbor."

Wallander hit the table with the flat of his hand marking the end of the meeting.

"Torgeir Langaas," he said as everyone stood. "Lean on our Norwegian colleagues. The rest of us will look for Zeba."

Linda and her dad went to get a cup of coffee without exchanging a single word with each other. When they were done, they went to his office. Martinsson knocked on the door half an hour later, coming in before Wallander answered. He stopped when he saw Linda.

"Sorry," he said.

"What is it?"

"Ture Magnusson is here to listen to the tape."

Wallander jumped out of his chair, grabbing Linda by the arm and pulling her along. Ture Magnusson seemed nervous. Martinsson went to get the tape. Wallander received a call from Nyberg and immediately launched into an argument with him, so Linda was left to take care of Magnusson.

"Have you found the Norwegian?" he asked.

"Not yet."

"I'm not sure I can recognize his voice."

"We'll just hope for the best."

Wallander hung up. At the same time, Martinsson came back with a worried look on his face.

"The tape must still be here," he said. "It's not in the archive."

"Didn't anyone put it back?" Wallander asked with irritation.

"Not me," Martinsson said.

He looked through the shelf behind the tape recorder. Wallander stuck his head into the call center.

"Can we get a little help here?" he shouted. "We're missing a tape!"

Höglund joined them, but no one could find the tape. Linda watched her father get increasingly red in the face. But in the end it was Martinsson who exploded.

"How in the hell are we supposed to do our work when archived tape can go missing like this?"

He picked up a booklet of instructions for the tape recorder and threw it against the wall. They kept looking for the tape. Linda finally had the feeling that the whole police district was looking for the tape, but it didn't turn up. She looked at her dad. He seemed tired, despondent. But she knew it would pass.

"We owe you an apology," Wallander said to Magnusson, "for bringing you down here. The tape appears to be misplaced. There's nothing for you to do."

"I have a suggestion," Linda said.

She had been debating with herself whether or not to suggest this.

"I think I can imitate his voice," she said. "He's a man, I know, but I'd like a shot at it."

Höglund gave her a disapproving look.

"What makes you think you could possibly imitate his voice?"

Linda could have given her a long answer, about how she had discovered a talent for imitation at parties. How her friends had been impressed, and she had assumed it was a one-off success, but how she soon realized she simply had a knack for it. There were voices she couldn't imitate at all, but most of the time she was right on.

"Let me try," she said. "It's not as if we have anything to lose."

Lindman had come back into the room. He nodded encouragingly.

"I guess since we're all here anyway," her father said hesitantly. He waved to Ture Magnusson.

"Turn around. Don't look, just listen. If you have even the slightest doubt, then tell us."

Linda quickly decided on a plan. She was not going to do the voice right away, but work up to it. It would be a test for everyone in the room, not just Magnusson.

"Who remembers what his exact words were?" Lindman asked.

Martinsson had the best memory. He repeated the text. Linda made her voice as deep as possible, and found the right accent.

Magnusson shook his head.

"I'm not sure. I almost think I recognize it, but it's not quite right."

"I'd like to do it again," Linda said. "It didn't come out the way I wanted it to."

No one objected. Again Linda only approximated the right intonation and phrasing. Again, Magnusson shook his head.

"I don't know," he said. "I really couldn't say for sure."

"One last time," Linda said.

This was the time that counted. She took a deep breath and repeated the text, this time getting as close as possible to the original.

"Yes," Magnusson said. "That's what he sounded like. That's his voice."

"But that was on the third try," Höglund said. "What's that worth?"

Linda couldn't quite hide her satisfaction. Her dad saw it at once.

"Why did he only recognize it on the third attempt?" he asked.

"Because the first two times I didn't sound like him," she said. "It was only the third time that I did the voice exactly."

"I didn't hear a difference," Höglund said suspiciously.

"When you imitate someone's voice all the ingredients have to be right," Linda said.

"That's quite something," Wallander said. "Are you serious about this?"

"Yes."

Wallander looked straight at Ture Magnusson.

"Are you sure?"

"Absolutely."

"Then we thank you for taking the trouble of coming in."

Linda was the only one who shook Magnusson's hand. She followed him out.

"Great job," she said. "Thank you for coming in."

"How could you do that so well?" he asked. "It was almost as if I could see him in front of me."

"Anna," Wallander said. "We need to talk to her now."

Linda rang the doorbell to Anna's apartment, but no one answered the door. Anna wasn't home. Linda shivered as she stood outside in the stairwell. She was starting to understand why Anna had decided to disappear again.

44

It had been Langaas's task to pick up Anna by the boarded-up pizzeria in Sandskogen. At first Westin had been planning to get her himself to make sure she was completely willing. But finally he decided that she was so dependent on him she wasn't likely to put up any resistance. Since she had no idea what had happened to Harriet Bolson—he had given Langaas strict instructions not to say anything—she had no reason to try to get away. The only thing he feared was her intuition. He had tried to gauge it and had concluded that it was almost as strong as his own. *Anna is my daughter,* he thought. *She is careful, attentive, constantly receptive to the messages of her subconscious.*

Langaas had been briefed on how to handle the situation, even though it was unlikely that Anna had been frightened by Zeba's disappearance. There was a chance that she would talk to Linda, the girl Westin judged to be her closest confidante, even though he had warned and thereafter forbidden her to have intimate conversations with anyone except himself. It could lead her astray, he had told her, now that she had finally found the right path. He was the one who had been gone for so long, but it was she who was the prodigal son, or daughter. She was the one who was finally coming home, not him. What was happening now was necessary. Her father was the one who was going to hold people responsible for turning their backs on the Lord and for building cathedrals where they worshipped at the altar of their own egos rather than humbling themselves before their true Maker. He had seen the bewitched look in her eye and known that with enough time he would have been able to erase all doubt from her mind. The problem was that he didn't have this time. It was a mistake, he acknowledged to himself. He should have contacted her long before he showed himself to her in Malmö. But he had had all the others to work on, the members of his army who were one day to open the gates and take their place in his plan. Harriet Bolson's death had been their biggest challenge to date. He had told Langaas to watch their reactions over the next few days, in case anyone seemed about to break down or even so much as sway in their conviction. But no one had showed any such signs. To the contrary, Langaas reported a growing sense of impatience among them to undergo the ultimate sacrifice that lay ahead.

Before Langaas went to pick up Anna, Westin had made sure he understood that he was to use force if she did not want to come willingly. That was why he had chosen such a remote area for the meeting. He had watched Langaas's reactions carefully when he mentioned the use of force. Langaas had shown a momentary hesitation; a glimpse of anxiety flickered in his eyes. Westin had made his voice as mild as possible while he leaned forward and placed his hand on Langaas's shoulder. What was it that worried him? Had Westin ever played favorites among his disciples? Had he not plucked Torgeir from the gutters of Cleveland? Why shouldn't his daughter be treated like everyone else? God created a world where everyone was equal, a world that people had turned their backs on and destroyed. Was that not the world they were trying to recover?

If all went well and she showed herself worthy, Anna would one day be his successor. God's New Kingdom on Earth could not be left without a ruler, as in the past. There had to be a leader, and God himself had told him that it was to be a position that would go from father to child.

Sometimes he thought Anna was not the one. In that case, he would have to have more children and select his successor from among them.

Westin wasn't sure how Langaas found these houses that stood empty and unattended, but it was a matter of trust between them. Right now the house Langaas had selected was a villa in Sandhammaren that was conveniently isolated from its neighbors and belonged to a retired sea captain who was in the hospital with a broken leg. This house had the additional advantage of a small room in the basement. The sea captain's house had thick concrete walls, and the room in the basement was well constructed, with a small window in the sturdy door. When Langaas first showed it to him, they agreed that it seemed as if the sea captain had a private jail cell in his home. Langaas had suggested it was perhaps meant as a bomb shelter in the event of a war. But why the thick glass window in the door?

He stopped and listened. In the beginning, when the drugs had worn off, Zeba had screamed, hit the walls, and attacked the bucket that they had put in for her to use as a toilet. Then, when she was quiet, he had peeked in through the window. She had been curled up on the bed. They had put a sandwich and a cup of water on a table, but she hadn't touched it. He hadn't expected her to.

When he looked at her through the window a second time, she was lying on the bed with her back to him, sleeping. He watched her for a long time until he was sure that she was breathing. Then he went back upstairs and sat down on the verandah, waiting for Langaas to arrive with Anna. There was still one problem to be solved, the question of what was to be done about Henrietta. So far, both Anna and Langaas had been able to convince her that all was well, but Henrietta was moody and unreliable. Once upon a time he had loved her, although that time lay wrapped in a haze of unreality. If possible, he would try to spare her life.

He looked out at the sea. People were walking on the beach. One of them had a dog, one was carrying a small child on his shoulders. *I am doing this for your sakes,* he thought. *It is for you that I have gathered the martyrs, for your freedom, to fill the emptiness you may not even realize you carry within yourselves.*

The walkers on the beach vanished beyond his sight. He looked at the water. The waves were almost imperceptible. A faint wind blew from the southeast. He went out into the kitchen and poured himself a glass of water. Langaas and Anna wouldn't arrive for another thirty minutes. He returned to the verandah and watched a ship slowly making its way west on the horizon.

True Christian martyrs were so rare now that people hardly even thought they existed. Some priests had died for the sake of their fellow men in concentration camps during World War II, and there had been other holy men and women. But in general, the act of martyrdom had slipped from Christian culture. Now it was the Muslims who called on the faithful to make the ultimate sacrifice. He had studied their preparations on video, how they documented their intentions to die the death of a martyr. In short, he had learned his craft at the hands of those he hated most, his biggest enemy, the people he had no intention of making room for in the New Kingdom. Ironically, the dramatic events that were about to take place would in all probability be attributed to the work of Muslims. A welcome benefit of this would be to provoke greater hatred of that faith, but it was unfortunate that it would take the world a while to fully understand that the Christian martyrs had returned. This would be no mere isolated phenomenon, no Maranatha, but a wave of true evangelical power that would continue until the New Kingdom of the Lord was fully realized on Earth.

He studied his hands. Sometimes when he contemplated what lay before him they would start to shake. But now they were steady. *For a short while they will see me as a madman,* he thought. *But when the martyrs march forth in row upon row, people will understand that I am the apostle they have been waiting for. I could not have managed this without the help of Jim Jones. He taught me how to overcome my fear of death, of urging others to die for the greater good. He taught me that freedom and redemption only come through bloodshed, through death; that there is no other way and that someone must lead the herd.*

Someone must lead the way. Jesus had done so, but God had forsaken him because he had not gone far enough. *Jesus had a weakness,* he thought. *He did not have the strength I possess. We will complete what he lacked the strength to do.*

Westin scanned the horizon again. The ship he had been watching was gone, and the soft breeze had died down. Soon they would be here. For the rest of the day and night, he would concentrate on her. It had been a big step for her to lie about her relationship to Vigsten, the man in Copenhagen who was Langaas's unwitting host. Anna had never taken a piano lesson in her life, but she had managed to convince the policeman she talked to. Westin again felt irritation at the fact that he had underestimated the time needed to work on her. But it was too late. Everything could not go according to his plan, and the important thing was that the larger events not be altered.

The front door opened. He strained to hear them. During the past long and difficult years, he had trained all of his senses. It was as if he had sharpened the blades of his hearing, sight, and smell. Sometimes he thought of them like finely crafted knives hanging from his belt. He listened to their footsteps. Langaas's feet were heavy, Anna's lighter. She was moving at her own speed, which indicated that he had not had to use force.

They walked out onto the verandah. Westin stood up and embraced Anna. She was anxious, but not so much so that he was unable to comfort her. He asked her to sit while he followed Langaas to the door. They spoke in low tones. The report Langaas gave him was reassuring. The equipment was stored safely, the others were waiting in two separate houses. No one showed any signs of anything except impatience.

"They're hungry now," Langaas said.

"The hour is approaching. Two days and two hours until we come out of hiding and make the first strike."

"She was completely calm when I picked her up. I felt her pulse and it was normal."

His rage appeared as if from nowhere.

"Only I have the right to feel a person's pulse! Not you, never you."

Langaas turned pale.

"I shouldn't have done it."

"No. But there is something you can do for me to make up for it."

"What is it?"

"Anna's friend. The one who has been too curious, too interested. I am going to talk to Anna now. If it turns out that this friend suspects anything, she should disappear."

Langaas nodded.

Westin signaled for him to leave, then quietly returned to the verandah. Anna was sitting in a chair against the wall. *She always keeps her back to the wall,* he thought. He kept watching her. She appeared relaxed, but somewhere inside he had doubts. Suddenly she turned her head in his direction. He drew back behind the door. Had she seen him? It worried him that she was able to unnerve him in this way. *There is one sacrifice I do not want to make,* he thought. *A sacrifice I fear. But I must be prepared even for this. Not even my daughter can expect to go free. No one can expect to do that, except me.*

He walked out to join her. When he sat down, the unexpected suddenly happened. It was the fault of the sea captain, and he cursed him silently. The walls were simply not thick enough. A scream came up through the floor. Anna froze. The scream modulated into something like the roar of a desperate animal chewing its way through the cement.

Zeba's voice, Zeba's scream. Anna stared at him, the man who was her father and so much more. She bit her lower lip so hard it started to bleed.

It would be a long and difficult night. He wasn't sure if Anna had abandoned him or if Zeba's scream had only thrown her off track for a moment.

45

Linda stared at Anna's door, thinking she should kick it open. But why—what was it she thought she would find in there? Not Zeba, who was the only one she cared about right now. Standing outside the door, she broke into a cold sweat as she felt she understood the gist of what was happening, without being able to translate her insight into words. She shoved her hands into her pockets. She had returned all of Anna's keys, except the ones to the car. *But what good will they do me,* she thought. *Where would I go? Is her car even there?* She walked down to the parking lot and saw that it was. Linda tried to think clearly, but fear blocked her thoughts. First she had been worried about Anna. Now it was Zeba who had disappeared. Then she grasped something that had been confusing her. It was about Anna. At first she had been afraid that something had happened to her, but now she was afraid of what she could do.

I'm imagining things, she thought. *What is it I think Anna could do?* She started walking in the direction of Zeba's house, then turned around and hurried back to Anna's car. Normally she would at least write a note, but there was no time for that. She drove to Zeba's house at high speed. The neighbor was out with Zeba's son, but her daughter was home and she gave her the key to Zeba's apartment. Linda let herself in and picked up the strange smell again. *Why is no one testing this?* she thought.

She walked into the middle of the living room, breathing quietly as if hoping to trick the walls into thinking no one was there. *Zeba never locks her door. Someone opens the door and walks right in. Her boy is here but he can't talk. Zeba is drugged and carried away. Her boy starts to cry, and eventually the neighbor comes over to check on him.*

Linda looked around, but she could see no trace of what had

happened. *All I see is an empty apartment, and I can't interpret empti-ness.* She stubbed her toe on the way out. As she was walking to the car, Yassar came out of his store.

"Did you find her?"

"No. Have you thought of anything else?"

Yassar sighed.

"Nothing. My memory is not so good, but I'm sure she was clinging to his arm."

Linda felt a need to defend Zeba.

"She wasn't clinging to him, she was drugged."

Yassar looked worried.

"You may be right," he said. "But do things like that really hap-pen in a town like Ystad?"

Linda only heard a part of what Yassar had to say. She was al-ready on her way to see Henrietta. She had just started the engine when her cell phone rang. It was from the police station, but not her dad's regular office number. She hesitated, then answered. It was Lindman. She was happy to hear his voice.

"Where are you?"

"In a car."

"Your father asked me to call. He wants to know where you are. And where is Anna Westin?"

"I haven't found her."

"What do you mean?"

"What do you mean, what do I mean? I went over to her place and she wasn't there. Now I'm trying to figure out where she could be. When I've found her I'll bring her back to the station."

Why don't I tell him the truth? she wondered. *Is it something I learned because I had two parents who never told me what was going on, who always chose to skirt their way around the truth?*

It was as if he saw through her.

"Is everything all right with you?"

"Apart from the fact that I haven't found Anna—yes."

"Do you need any help?"

"No."

"That didn't sound completely convincing. Just remember you aren't a police officer yet."

"How can I forget when you're always bringing it up?"

She finished the conversation, turned the phone off, and threw it onto the passenger seat. She had only turned one corner when she stopped short and switched the phone back on again. Then she drove straight to Henrietta's house. The wind had picked up and the air was chilly when she got out of the car and walked to the house. She looked toward the place where she had been caught in the animal trap. In the distance, on one of the small dirt roads between the fields, a man was burning trash next to his car. The thin spiral of smoke was torn apart by the gusts of wind.

Fall was just around the corner, the first frost not too far off. She walked into the garden and rang the doorbell. The dog started to bark. She drew a deep breath and shook out her body as if she were about to crouch down into the starting blocks. Henrietta opened the door. She smiled. Linda was immediately suspicious; it seemed as if Henrietta had been expecting her. Linda also noted that she had put on makeup, as if she wanted to make a good impression on someone, or to conceal the fact that she was pale.

"This is unexpected," Henrietta said and stepped aside.

Not true, Linda thought.

"You're always welcome. Please come in."

The dog sniffed her, then returned to his basket. Linda heard a sigh. She looked around, but no one was there. Sighs seemed to emanate from the thick stone walls themselves. Henrietta put out a coffee pot and two mugs.

"What's that sound?" Linda asked.

"I'm playing one of my oldest compositions," Henrietta said. "It's from 1987, a concert for four sighing voices and percussion. Listen!"

Linda heard a single voice sigh, a woman.

"That's Anna. I managed to convince her to participate. She has a melodious sigh, full of sadness and vulnerability. There is always a somewhat hesitant quality to her speaking voice, but never to her sigh."

Henrietta walked over to the tape recorder and turned it off. They sat down. The dog had started snoring, and it was as if this sound drew Linda back to reality.

"Do you know where Anna is?"

Henrietta looked down at her nails, then at Linda, who sensed a moment of doubt in her eyes. *She knows, and she's prepared to deny it.*

"My mistake, then. Each time I think you're here to see me, what you're really after is to find out where my daughter is."

"Do you know where she is?"

"No."

"When did you last talk to her?"

"She called yesterday."

"From where?"

"From her apartment."

"She doesn't have a cell phone?"

"No, she doesn't, as you must know. She resists joining the ranks of those who are always available."

"So she was home last night?'

"Are you interrogating me, Linda?"

"I want to know where Anna is, what she's up to."

"I don't know where she is—what about in Lund? She's in medical school, you know."

No she isn't, Linda thought. Maybe Henrietta didn't know that Anna had taken a break from her studies. *That will be my trump card. But not now—later.*

She chose another route.

"Do you know Zeba?"

"Little Zeba? Yes, of course."

"She's disappeared, just like Anna."

Not a twitch or a quiver betrayed that Henrietta knew anything. Linda felt as if she had been floored by a punch she never saw coming. That had happened during her time at the police academy. She had been in a boxing ring and suddenly found herself facedown on the floor without knowing how she got there.

"And maybe she'll reappear, just like Anna did."

Linda more sensed than saw her opportunity and she rushed in with her fists held high.

"Why didn't you tell me the truth? Why didn't you say you knew where she was?"

It hit the mark. Beads of sweat broke out on Henrietta's forehead.

"Are you saying that I lied to you? If that is the case, I want you to leave right now. I will not be called a liar in my own home. You are poisoning me. I cannot work, the music is dying."

"I *am* saying you lied, and I won't leave until you answer my questions. I have to know where Zeba is because I think she's in danger. Anna is mixed up in this somehow, maybe you are too. One thing is for sure: you know a lot more than you're telling me."

"Go away! I don't know anything!" Henrietta yelled. The dog got up and started to bark.

Henrietta walked over to a window, absently opening it, then closing it, then pushing it slightly ajar. Linda didn't know how to continue, but knew she couldn't let go. Henrietta seemed to have calmed down. She turned around.

"I'm sorry I lost my temper, but I don't like being accused of lying. I don't know where Zeba is, and I have no idea why you seem to think Anna is involved."

Her indignation seemed genuine, or else she was a better actress than Linda imagined. She was still speaking with a raised voice, and she had not sat down again, still standing by the window.

"That night I got caught in the trap," Linda said. "Who were you talking to?"

"Were you spying on me?"

"Call it what you like. Why else would I have been here? I wanted to know why you didn't tell me the truth when I came to ask you about Anna."

"The man who was here had come to talk to me about a composition we are planning together."

"No," Linda said, forcing her voice to remain steady. "It was someone else."

"Are you accusing me of lying again?"

"I know you are."

"I always tell the truth," Henrietta said. "But I prefer not to reveal any part of my private life."

"You lied, Henrietta. I know who was here."

"You know who was here?"

Henrietta's voice was high and shrill again.

"Either it was a man by the name of Torgeir Langaas, or it was Anna's father."

Henrietta flinched.

"Torgeir Langaas," she almost screamed. "I don't know anyone called Torgeir Langaas. And Anna's father has been gone for years. He's dead. Anna is in Lund and I have no idea where Zeba might be."

She went out into the kitchen and returned with a glass of water. She moved some cassette tapes out of the way and sat down on a chair next to Linda, who had to turn her body to look at her. Henrietta smiled. When she spoke again her voice was soft, almost careful.

"I didn't mean to get so carried away."

Linda looked at her, and somewhere inside her head a warning light came on. There was something she should be seeing, but she couldn't think of what it was. She realized that the conversation had been a failure. The only thing she had achieved was to put Henrietta even more on her guard. *An experienced officer should have been in charge of this questioning,* she thought. Now it would be even harder for her father, or whoever it would fall to, to get Henrietta to reveal whatever it was she was hiding.

"Is there anything else you think I've been lying about?"

"I don't think I believe almost anything you say, but I can't force you to stop lying. I just want you to know that I'm asking these questions because I'm worried about Zeba."

"What could possibly have happened to her?"

Linda drew a deep breath.

"I think someone, perhaps more than one person, is killing women who have had abortions. Zeba has had an abortion. So had the woman who was found dead in that church. You've heard about that?"

Henrietta sat absolutely still, which Linda took as a yes.

"What has Anna got to do with all this?"

"I don't know, but it scares me."

"What scares you?"

"The thought that someone might try to kill Zeba. And that Anna is somehow involved."

Something in Henrietta's face changed. Linda couldn't say exactly what it was, but it flickered there for a moment. She decided she wasn't going to get any further and bent down to pick up her jacket from the floor. There was a mirror next to the table. She threw a quick glance at it as she bent over, and she saw Henrietta's face. She was looking past Linda.

Linda grabbed her jacket and sat up. She realized what Henrietta had been looking at: the open window.

She started putting on her jacket and stood up, turning around. There was no one outside, but Linda knew someone had been there. She froze. Henrietta's loud voice, the window that was opened for no reason, her repetitions of the names Linda had given her, and her vehement objections to the accusations. Linda finished putting on her jacket. She didn't dare turn around and look Henrietta in the eye, since she was afraid her realization was spelled out on her face.

Linda quickly made her way to the front door and bent down to pet the dog. Henrietta followed her out.

"I'm sorry I couldn't be of help to you."

"You could have," Linda said. "But you chose not to."

Linda opened the door and walked out. When she reached the end of the path, she turned and looked around. *I don't see anyone,* she thought, *but someone can see me. Someone watched me in the house and— more to the point—heard what we said. Henrietta repeated my questions and the person outside now knows what I know and what I believe and fear.*

She hurried over to the car. She was scared, but she also berated herself for making a mistake. The point at which she was petting the dog and getting ready to leave was the point at which she should have started her questions in earnest. But she had chosen to leave.

Linda kept checking the rearview mirror as she drove away.

46

As Linda walked into the police station, she tripped and split her lip on the hard floor. For a moment she was dizzy, and then she managed to get up and wave away the receptionist, who was on her way over to help her. When she saw blood on her hand she walked to the restroom, wiped off her face with cold water, and waited for the bleeding to stop. When she stepped back out into the reception area she saw Lindman, who was on his way in through the front doors. He looked at her with an amused expression.

"You make quite a pair," he said. "Your father claims he walked into a door. What about you? That pesky door been making trouble for you as well? Maybe we should call you Black Eye and Fat Lip, to save ourselves the trouble of the two of you having the same name."

Linda laughed, which caused the wound to reopen and bleed. She went back into the restroom and got more tissues. Together they walked down the corridor.

"It wasn't a door. I threw an ashtray at him."

They stopped outside Wallander's office.

"Did you find Anna?'

"No, she seems to have disappeared again."

Lindman knocked on the door.

"You'd better go in and tell him."

Wallander had his feet on the desk and was chewing on a pencil. He raised his eyebrows at her.

"I thought you were bringing Anna."

"I thought so too, but I can't find her."

"What do you mean?"

"What do you think I mean? She's not at home."

Wallander didn't manage to conceal his impatience. Linda prepared for the onslaught, but then he noticed her swollen lip.

"What happened to you?"

"I tripped."

He shook his head, then started to laugh. Although Linda appreciated this turn in his mood, she found his laugh hard to take. It sounded like the neigh of a horse and was far too high-pitched. If they were ever out together and he started to laugh, people would actually turn around to see who could possibly be responsible for those sounds.

Wallander threw his pencil down and took his feet off the desk.

"Have you called her place in Lund? Her friends? She has to be somewhere."

"Nowhere that we can reach her, I think."

"You've called her cell phone, at least?"

"She doesn't have one."

He was immediately interested in this piece of information.

"Why not?"

"She doesn't want one."

"Is there any other reason?"

Linda knew that there was a thought process behind these questions, not simply idle curiosity.

"Everyone has a cell phone these days, especially you young folk. But not Anna Westin. How do you explain that?"

"I can't. According to Henrietta, she doesn't want to be reachable at all times."

Wallander thought about this.

"Are you sure she's told you everything? Could she have a phone that she hasn't told you about?"

"How could I know that?"

"Exactly."

Wallander pulled his phone over and dialed Höglund's extension. She came into the office shortly thereafter, looking both tired and scruffy. Linda saw that her hair was messy and her blouse slightly soiled. She was reminded of Vanya Jorner, Medberg's daughter. The only difference between them that she could see was that Höglund was not as fat.

Linda heard her father ask Höglund to see if any cell phone was registered under Anna's name. Linda was irritated that she hadn't thought of it herself.

Before leaving the room, Höglund gave Linda a smile that was more like a forced grimace.

"She doesn't like me."

"If my memory doesn't fail me, you don't care much for her either. It all evens itself out in the end. Even in a small police station like this, people don't always get along."

He stood up.

"Coffee?"

They walked out to the lunchroom, where Wallander was immediately pulled into an evidently exasperating exchange with Nyberg. Linda didn't understand what they were arguing about. Martinsson came in waving a piece of paper.

"Ulrik Larsen," he said. "The one who tried to mug you in Copenhagen."

"Not mug me," Linda said sharply. "The one who threatened me and told me to stop asking questions about a man named Torgeir Langaas."

"That's exactly what I was going to talk to you about," Martinsson said. "Ulrik Larsen has withdrawn his story. The only problem is, he doesn't have a new version. He continues to deny that he threatened you, and he maintains he doesn't know anyone by the name of Langaas. Our Danish colleagues are convinced he's lying, but they can't get him to tell the truth."

"Is that it?"

"Not completely. But I want Kurre to hear the rest."

"Don't call him that," Linda warned. "He hates the nickname 'Kurre.'"

"Tell me about it," Martinsson said. "He likes it about as much as I like being called 'Marta.'"

"Who calls you that?"

"My wife. When she's in a bad mood."

Wallander and Nyberg finished discussing whatever it was that they disagreed about, and Martinsson recounted the information about Ulrik Larsen.

"There's one more thing," he added, "which is the most significant. Our Danish colleagues have naturally run a background check on Larsen, and it turns out that he has no previous criminal record. In fact, it turns out that in all other respects he's a model citizen: thirty-seven years old, married, three children, and with an occupation that doesn't normally lead its practitioners to criminal activity."

"What is it?" Wallander asked.

"He's a minister."

Everyone stared at Martinsson.

"What do you mean, he's a minister?" Lindman asked. "I thought he was a drug addict."

Martinsson looked through his papers.

"Apparently he played the role of a drug addict, but he's a minister in the Danish State church, with a parish in Gentofte. There have been all kinds of headlines over there about the fact that a minister of the church has been accused of assault and robbery."

The room fell quiet.

"It turns up again, then," Wallander said softly. "Religion, the church. This Larsen is important. Someone has to go over and assist our colleagues in their investigation. I want to know how he fits in."

"If he fits in," Lindman said.

"He does," Wallander said. "We just need to know how. Ask Höglund to do it."

Martinsson's telephone rang. He listened and then finished his cup of coffee.

"The Norwegians are stirring," he said. "We've received some information about Torgeir Langaas."

"Let's see it."

Martinsson went to get the faxes. There was a fuzzy version of a photograph.

"This was taken more than twenty years ago," Martinsson said. "He's tall. Over one hundred and ninety centimeters."

They studied the snapshot. *Have I seen this man before?* Linda wondered. But she wasn't sure.

"What do they say?" Wallander asked.

Linda noticed that he was getting more and more impatient.

Just like me, she thought. *The anxiety and impatience go hand in hand.*

"They found our man Langaas as soon as they started to look. It would have come through sooner if the officer in charge hadn't misdirected our urgent query. In other words, the Oslo office is plagued by the same problems we are. Here tapes from the archives go missing, there requests from other stations. But it all got sorted out in the end, and Torgeir Langaas is involved in an old missing-persons case, as it turns out."

"In what way?" Wallander asked.

"You won't believe me when I tell you."

"Try me."

"Torgeir Langaas disappeared from Norway nineteen years ago."

They looked at each other. Linda felt as if the room itself was holding its breath. She saw her dad sit up in his chair as if readying himself to charge.

"Another disappearance," he said. "Somehow all of this is about disappearances."

"And reappearance," Lindman said.

"Or a resurrection," Wallander said.

Martinsson kept reading, slowly, picking his way through the text as if there were land mines hidden between the words: "Torgeir Langaas was the heir of a shipping magnate. His disappearance was unexpected and sudden. No crime was suspected, since he left a letter to his mother, Maigrim Langaas, in which he assured her he was not depressed and had no intentions of committing suicide. He left because he—and I quote—'couldn't stand it any longer.'"

"What was it he couldn't stand?"

It was Wallander who interrupted him again. To Linda it seemed as if his impatience and worry came out of his nostrils like invisible smoke.

"It's not clear from this report, but he left, with quite a stockpile of cash. Several bank accounts. His parents thought he would tire of his rebellion after a while. His parents didn't go to the police until two years had passed. The reason they gave, it says here in the report from January 12, 1984, was that he had stopped writing letters, that they hadn't had any signs of life from him for four months, and that he had emptied all his bank accounts. Since then no one has heard from him."

Martinsson let the page fall to the table.

"There's more, but those are the main points."

Wallander raised his hand.

"Does it say where the last letter was mailed from? And when the bank accounts were emptied?"

Martinsson looked through the papers for these answers, but without success. Wallander picked up the phone.

"What's the number?"

He dialed the number that Martinsson read out. The Norwegian officer's name was Hovard Midstuen. Once they were connected, Wallander asked his two questions, gave him his phone number, and hung up.

"He said it would only take a few minutes," Wallander said. "We'll wait."

Midstuen called back after nineteen minutes. During that time no one had said a word. When the phone rang, Wallander pounced on the receiver, then scrawled a few notes as he listened. He thanked his Norwegian colleague and slammed the phone down triumphantly.

"This might be starting to hang together."

He read from his notes: the last letter Langaas had sent was posted from Cleveland, Ohio. It was also from there that the accounts were emptied and closed.

Not everyone made the connection, but Linda saw what he was getting at.

"The woman who was found dead in Frennestad Church came from Tulsa," he said. "But she was born in Cleveland, Ohio."

Everyone was quiet.

"I still don't understand what's happening," he said. "But there's one thing I know, and that's that Linda's friend Zeba is in danger. It may also be that Linda's other friend Anna Westin is also in danger."

He paused.

"It may also be that Anna Westin is part of this. That's why we need to concentrate on these two and nothing else for the moment."

―――――

It was three o'clock in the afternoon and Linda was scared. All she could think about was Zeba and Anna. A fleeting thought passed through her mind: she would start her real work as a police officer in three days. But how would she feel about that if something happened to either of her friends? She didn't know the answer to that question.

47

When Anna recognized the scream as Zeba's, Westin knew that God was testing him in the same way he had tested Abraham. He perceived all of her reactions even though she had merely flinched and then carefully composed her features to hide her emotions. A moment of doubt, a series of questions—was that some animal or, in fact, a human scream? Could it be Zeba? She was searching for an answer that would satisfy her, and at the same time she was waiting to hear the scream again. What Westin didn't understand was why she didn't simply ask him about it. In a way it was just as well that Zeba had made her presence known. Now there was no turning back. He would soon see if Anna was worthy of being called his daughter. What would he do if it turned out she did not possess the strength he expected of her? It had taken him many years to travel down the road his inner voices had told him to follow. He had to be prepared to sacrifice even that which was most precious to him, and it would be up to God whether Westin too would be granted a stay at the last minute.

I won't talk to her, he thought. *I must preach to her, as I preach to my disciples.* She broke in during a pause. He let her speak, because he knew he could best interpret a person's state of mind at such a moment of vulnerability.

"Once upon a time you were my father. You lived a simple life."

"I had to follow my calling."

"You abandoned me, your daughter."

"I had to. But I never left you in my heart. And I came back to you."

She was tense, he could see that, but still her sudden loss of control surprised him. Her voice rose to a shriek.

"That screaming I heard was Zeba! She's here somewhere below us. What is she doing here? She hasn't done anything."

"You know what she has done. It was you who told me."

"I wish I'd never told you!"

"She who commits a sin and takes the life of another must bear the wrath of God. This is justice, and the word of the Lord."

"Zeba didn't kill anyone. She was only fifteen years old. How could she have cared for a child at that age?"

"She should never have allowed it to happen."

Westin could not manage to calm her, and he felt a wave of impatience. *This is Henrietta,* he thought. *She's too much like her.*

He decided to exert more force.

"Nothing is going to happen to Zeba," he said.

"Then what is she doing in the basement?"

"She is waiting for you to make up your mind. To decide."

This confused her, and Westin smiled inwardly. He had spent many years in Cleveland poring over books about the art of warfare. That work was paying off now. Suddenly she was the one on the defensive.

"I don't understand what you mean. I'm scared."

Anna started to sob, her body shook. He felt a lump in his throat, remembering how he had comforted her as a child when she cried. But he forced the feeling away and asked her to stop.

"What are you scared of?"

"Of you."

"You know I love you. I love Zeba. I have come to join the earthly and the divine in transcendent love."

"I don't understand you when you talk like that!"

Before he had a chance to say anything else, there was a new cry for help from the basement and Anna flew from her chair.

"I'm coming!" she cried, but he grabbed her before she could leave the verandah. She struggled but he was too strong for her. When she continued to struggle, he hit her with an open hand. Once, then again, and finally a third time. She fell to the floor after the third blow, her nose bleeding. Langaas appeared at the French windows, and Westin motioned for him to go down into the basement. Langaas understood and left. Westin pulled Anna up onto a chair and felt her forehead with his fingertips. Her pulse was racing.

His own was only somewhat accelerated. He sat down across from her and waited. Soon he would break her will. These were the last set of defenses. He had surrounded her and was attacking from all sides. He waited.

"I didn't want to do that," he said after a while. "I only do what is necessary. We are about to embark on a war against emptiness, soullessness. It is a war in which it is not always possible to be gentle, nor merciful. I am joined by people who are prepared to give their lives for this cause. I myself may have to give my life."

She didn't say anything.

"Nothing will happen to Zeba," he repeated. "But nothing in this life comes to us for free. Everything has a price."

Now she looked at him with a mixture of fear and anger. The bleeding from her nose had almost stopped. He explained what it was he wanted her to do. She stared at him with wide eyes. He shifted his chair closer to hers and placed his hand over hers. She flinched, but did not pull it away.

"I will give you one hour," he said. "No door will be locked, no guards will watch over you. Think about what I have said, and come to your own decision. I know that if you let God into your heart and mind, you will do what is right. Do not forget that I love you very much."

He stood up, traced a cross on her brow with his finger, and left without a sound.

Langaas was waiting in the hallway.

"She settled down when she saw me. I don't think she'll do it again."

They walked through the garden to an outbuilding that had been used for storing fishing equipment. They stopped outside the door.

"Has everything been prepared?"

"Everything has been prepared," Langaas said.

He pointed to four tents that had been erected next to the shed, then pulled open the flap to one of them. Westin looked in. There were the boxes, piled one on top of the other. He nodded. Langaas pulled the tent flap shut.

"The cars?"

"The ones that will drive the greatest distance are waiting up on the road. The others have been stationed in the positions we discussed."

Erik Westin looked down at his watch. The many, often difficult years he had spent laying the groundwork had seemed endless. Now time was suddenly going too fast. From now on, everything had to work exactly as it should.

"It's time to start the countdown," he said.

He glanced at the sky. Whenever he had thought forward to this moment in the past, he had always imagined that the heavens would mirror its dramatic import, but in Sandhammaren on this day, September 7, 2001, there were no clouds and almost no breeze.

"What is the temperature?" he asked.

Langaas looked at his watch, which had a built-in thermometer, as well as a pedometer and a compass.

"Eight degrees," he said.

They walked into the shed, which still smelled pungently of tar. Those who were waiting for him sat in a semicircle on low wooden benches. Westin had planned to perform the ceremony with the white masks, but now he decided to wait. He still didn't know if the next sacrifice would be Zeba or the policeman's daughter. They would do the ceremony then. Now they only had time for a shorter ritual; God would not accept anyone who arrived late for their appointed task. Not to be mindful of one's time was like denying that even time was a gift of the Lord. Those who needed to travel to their destinations would have to leave shortly. They had calculated how much time was needed for each leg of their journey, and had followed the checklists in the carefully prepared manuals. In short, they had done everything in their power, but there was always the possibility that the dark forces would prevent them from achieving their goals.

When the cars with the three groups who had to travel had left, and the others had returned to their hideouts, Westin remained in the shed. He sat motionless in the dark with the necklace in his hand—the golden sandal that was now as important to him as the cross. Did he have any regrets? That would be blasphemy. He was only an instrument, but one equipped with a free will to comprehend and then dedicate himself to the path of the chosen. He closed his eyes and breathed in the smell of tar. He had spent a summer on the island of Öland as a child visiting a relative who was a fisherman. The memories of that summer, one of the happiest of his childhood, were nestled in the scent of tar. He remembered how he snuck out in the light summer night and ran down to the boat shed in order to draw the smell more deeply into his lungs.

Westin opened his eyes. He was past the point of no return. The time had come. He left the shed and took a circuitous route to the front of the house. He looked out at the verandah from the cover of a large tree. Anna was sitting in the same chair. He tried to interpret her decision from the way she was sitting, but he was too far away.

Suddenly there was a rustling sound behind him. He flinched. It was Langaas. Westin was furious.

"Why are you sneaking around?"

"I didn't mean to."

Westin struck him hard in the face, right below the eye. Langaas accepted the blow and lowered his head. Then Westin stroked his head lightly and they walked over to the house. He made his way soundlessly to the verandah until he was right behind her. She only noticed his presence when he bent over and she felt his breath on the nape of her neck. He sat down across from her, pulling her chair closer until their knees touched.

"Have you made your decision?"

"I will do as you ask."

He had expected that she would say this, but it still came as a relief.

He walked over to a shoulder bag that lay next to the wall and pulled out a small, thin, and extremely sharp knife. He gently lowered it into her hands, as if it were a kitten.

"The moment when she reveals that she knows things she shouldn't, I want you to stab her—not once, but three or four times. Strike her in the chest and force the blade up before you pull it out. Then call Langaas and stay out of sight until we get you. You have six hours to do this, no more. You know I trust you, and love you. Who could love you more than I do?"

She was about to say something, but stopped herself. He knew she had been thinking of Henrietta.

"God," she said.

"I trust you, Anna," he said. "God's love and my love are one and the same. We are living in a time of rebirth. A new kingdom. Do you understand this?"

"Yes."

He looked deep into her eyes. He was still not entirely sure about this, but he had to believe he was doing the right thing.

He followed her out.

"Anna is going home now, Torgeir."

They got into a car that was parked in the front yard. Westin tied the kerchief over her eyes himself to make sure she didn't see anything.

"Drive around a little," he said in a low voice to Langaas. "Make her think it's farther than it really is."

The car came to a stop at five-thirty. Langaas took out Anna's earplugs, then instructed her to keep her eyes closed and count to fifty after he had taken off her blindfold.

"The Lord is watching you, and he will not appreciate it if you peek."

He helped her step out onto the sidewalk. Anna counted to fifty, then opened her eyes. At first she didn't know where she was. Then she realized she was on Mariagatan, outside Linda's apartment.

48

During the afternoon and evening of September 7, Linda once again watched her father try to gather all the threads together and come up with a plan for how they should proceed. Over the course of those hours she became aware that the praise he sometimes received from his colleagues and at times in the press—when they were not chastising him for his dismissive attitude toward them in press conferences—was justified. She realized not only that her father was knowledgeable and experienced but also that he possessed a remarkable ability to focus and inspire his colleagues.

During her time at the police academy, the father of a friend of hers had been an ice-hockey coach for a top team in the second-highest league. She and her friend had once been allowed into the locker room right before a game, during the intermission, and after it was over. This coach had the ability she had just witnessed in her father, an ability to motivate people. After two periods, the team was losing by four goals, but this coach didn't let up. He egged them on, urging them not to let themselves be beaten, and in the last period the players had stormed back onto the ice and almost managed to turn the game around.

Will my dad manage to turn this game around? she wondered. *Will he find Zeba before anything happens to her?* Over the course of the day, during a meeting or press conference when she hovered near the back of the room, she kept rushing out to go to the bathroom. Her stomach had always been her weakest point; fear gave her diarrhea. Her dad, on the other hand, had an iron stomach and sometimes bragged about having the stomach lining of a hyena—apparently their stomach acid was the strongest in all the animal kingdom. His weakness was his head, and sometimes when he was under a great deal of stress he would suffer tension headaches that could last days and only be relieved by taking prescription-strength pills.

Linda was afraid, and she knew she wasn't the only one. There was an unreal quality to the calm and concentration at the police station. She understood something that no one had mentioned at the academy: sometimes the most important task facing a police officer was keeping her own fear in check. If it got out of control, all this concentration and focus would crumble into chaos.

Shortly after four o'clock, Linda saw her father pacing up and down the corridors like a wild animal. The press conference was about to take place. Wallander kept sending in Martinsson to see how many journalists were assembled, and how many television cameras. From time to time he asked Martinsson about individuals by name, and from the tone of his voice it was clear he was hoping they were not present. She watched him walking anxiously to and fro. He was the animal nervously pacing backstage, waiting to be sent into the arena. When Holgersson came to announce that it was time, he lunged into the room. The only thing missing was a roar.

During the thirty-minute-long press conference, Wallander concentrated on Zeba. Photographs were passed around, a slide photograph was projected onto the wall. Where was she? Had anyone seen her? He skillfully sidestepped being pulled into lengthy explanations, keeping his remarks concise and ignoring questions he did not want to answer.

"There is still a dimension here that we do not understand," he said in closing. "The church fires, the two dead women, and the burned animals. We cannot be entirely sure that there is a connection, but what we know is that this young woman may be in danger."

What danger? Who posed this danger? Could he add anything? The room buzzed with dissatisfaction. Linda imagined him lifting an invisible shield and simply letting the questions bounce back unanswered. Chief Holgersson said nothing during the proceedings, except to moderate the question-and-answer session. Svartman mouthed answers to Wallander when there were details that escaped him.

Suddenly it was all over. Wallander stood up as if he couldn't take it any longer, nodded, and left the room. He shook off the reporters that rushed after him. Afterward he left the station without saying another word.

"That's what he always does," Martinsson said. "He takes himself out for some air, as if he were his own dog. Walks around the water tower. Then he comes back."

Twenty minutes later he came storming down the corridor. Pizzas were delivered to the conference room. Wallander told everyone to hurry up, shouted at a young woman from the office who had not provided them with the paper he had asked for, and then slammed the door. Lindman, who was sitting beside her, whispered:

"One day I think he's going to lock the door and throw away the key. We'll turn into pillars of salt. If we're lucky, we'll be excavated a thousand years from now."

Ann-Britt Höglund had just returned from a quick investigative turn in Copenhagen.

"I met this Ulrik Larsen," she said and pushed a photograph over to Linda. She recognized him immediately. He was the one who had warned her not to look for Torgeir Langaas and knocked her down.

"He's evidently changed his mind," Höglund continued. "Now there's no more talk about drugs. He denies having threatened Linda, but he gives no alternate explanation. He is an allegedly controversial minister. His sermons have become increasingly fire-and-brimstone as of late."

Linda saw her father's arm shoot out and interrupt.

"This is important. How do you mean 'fire-and-brimstone,' and specify 'as of late.'"

Höglund flipped through her notebook.

"I was led to believe that 'as of late' means this last year. The fire-and-brimstone is shorthand for the fact that he has started preaching about Judgment Day, the crisis of Christianity, ungodliness, and the punishment that will be meted out to all sinners. He has been admonished both by his own congregation and by the bishop, but he refuses to change the tenor of his sermons."

"I take it you asked the most important question?"

Linda wasn't sure what he meant, and when Höglund answered, Linda felt stupid.

"His views on abortion? I was actually able to ask him myself."

"The answer?"

"There was none. He refused to speak with me. But in some of his sermons he has allegedly stated that abortion is a crime that deserves the severest punishment."

Höglund sat down. Nyberg opened the door at that moment.

"The theologist is here."

Linda looked around the room and saw that only her father knew what Nyberg was talking about.

"Show him in," Wallander said.

Nyberg left and Wallander explained whom they were waiting for.

"Nyberg and I have been trying to make sense of that Bible that was left or deliberately placed in the hut where Medberg was murdered. Someone has gone in and changed the text, notably in the Book of Revelations, Romans, and parts of the Old Testament. But what kind of changes? Is there a logic there? We talked to the state crime people, but they had no experts to send. That's why we contacted the Department of Theology at Lund University and established contact with Professor Hanke, who has come here today."

Professor Hanke, to everyone's surprise, turned out to be a young woman with long blond hair and a pretty face, dressed in black leather pants and a low-cut top. Linda saw that it threw her father. Hanke walked around the room shaking hands and then sat down in the chair that was pulled up next to Lisa Holgersson.

"My name is Sofia Hanke," she said. "I'm a professor at the university and wrote my dissertation on the Christian paradigm shift in Sweden after World War II."

She opened her portfolio and took out the Bible that had been found in the hut.

"This has been fascinating," she said. "But I know that you don't have a lot of time, so I'll try to make it brief. The first thing I want to say is that I believe this is the work of one person, not because of the handwriting, but because there is a kind of logic to what is written here."

She looked in a notebook and continued, "I've chosen an example to illustrate what I mean, from Romans chapter seven. By the way, how many of you know the Bible? Perhaps it's not part of the current curriculum at the police academy?"

Everyone who met her gaze shook his or her head, except Nyberg, who surprised everyone by saying, "I read from the Bible every night. Foolproof way to induce sleep."

Everyone laughed, including Sofia Hanke.

"I can relate to that experience," she said. "I ask mainly because I'm curious. In any case, Romans chapter seven discusses the human tendency to sin. It says, among other things, 'Yes, the good that I wish to do, I do not; but the evil that I do not wish to do, I do.' Between these lines our writer has rearranged good and evil. The new version reads: 'Yes, the evil that I wish to do, I do; but the good that I do not wish to do, I do not do.' St. Paul's message is turned upside down. One of the grounding assumptions of Christianity is the idea that humans want to do what is right, but always find reasons to do evil instead. But the changed version says that humans do not even want to do what is right. This sort of thing happens again and again in the changes. The writer turns texts upside down, seemingly to find new meanings. It would be easy to assume that this is the work of a deranged soul, but I don't think that's what we're dealing with. There is a strained logic to these changes. I think the writer is hunting for a significance he or she believes is concealed in the Bible, something that is not immediately apparent in the words themselves. He or she is looking between the words."

"Logic," Wallander said. "What kind of logic is there in something this absurd?"

"Not everything is absurd; some of it is straightforward. There are also other texts in the margin. Like this quote: 'All the wisdom life has taught me can be summed up in the words 'he who loves God, is blessed.'"

Linda saw that her father was getting impatient.

"Why would someone do this? Why do we find a Bible in a secret hut where a woman has been the victim of a bestial murder?"

"It could be a case of religious fanaticism," Hanke said. Wallander leaned forward.

"Tell me more."

"I normally refer to something I call Preacher Lena's tradition. A long time ago, a milkmaid in Östergötland had mystical visions and started preaching. After a while she was taken to an insane asylum, but these people have always been around: religious fanatics who either choose to live as lone preachers or who try to gather a flock of devotees. Most of these people are honest to the extent that they act out of a genuine belief in their divine inspiration. Of course there have always been con artists, but they are in the minority. Most of these people preach their beliefs and start their sects from a genuine desire to do good. If they commit crimes or evil deeds, they often try to legitimize these acts in the eyes of their God, by interpretation of Bible verses, for example."

The discussion with Sofia Hanke continued, but Linda could already tell that her father was thinking about other things. These scribbles between the lines of the Bible found in the Rannesholm hut hadn't yielded any clues. Or had they? She tried to read his thoughts, something she had been practicing since early childhood. But there was a big difference between being alone with him at home and being in a conference room full of people at the police station, like now.

Nyberg escorted Sofia Hanke out, and Holgersson opened a window. The pizza cartons were starting to empty. Nyberg returned. People walked around, talked on the phone, went to get cups of coffee. Only Linda and her father stayed at the table. He looked at her absently and then retreated into his own thoughts.

When they started their long meeting, Linda was quiet and no one asked her any questions. She sat there like an invited guest. Her father looked at her a few times. If Birgitta Medberg had been a person who mapped old, overgrown paths, then her father was a person who was looking for passable roads to travel. He seemed to have an endless patience, even though he had a clock inside him ticking quickly and loudly. That's what he had told her once when he was in Stockholm and met with Linda and a few of her student friends and told them about his work. During times of enormous pressure, like when he knew a person's life was in danger, he had a feeling that there was a clock ticking away on the right side of his chest, parallel to his heart. Outwardly, however, he was patient, and he only displayed any signs of irritation if anyone started to leave the subject: where was Zeba?

The meeting went on, but from time to time someone made or received a call, or left and returned with some document or a photograph that was immediately worked into the investigation.

Chief Holgersson closed the door at a quarter past eight after a short break. Now no one was allowed to disturb them. Wallander took off his coat, rolled up the sleeves of his dark blue shirt, and walked up to the large pad of paper propped up on the easel. On a blank sheet of paper he wrote Zeba's name and drew a circle around it.

"Let's forget about Medberg for the moment," he said. "I know it may be a fatal mistake, but right now there is no logical connection between her and Harriet Bolson. It may be the same perpetrator or perpetrators, we don't know. But my point is that the motive seems different. If we leave Medberg, we see that it is much easier to find a connection between Bolson and Zeba. Abortion. Let us assume that we are dealing with a number of people—we don't know how many—who with some religious motivation judge and punish women who have had abortions. I use the word *assume* here since we don't know. We only know that people have been murdered, animals killed, and churches burned to the ground. Everything that has happened gives us the impression of systematic and thorough planning."

Wallander looked at the others, then went back to his place at the table and sat down.

"Let us assume everything is part of a ceremony," he said. "Fire is an important symbol in many similar cases. The burning of the animals may have been a sacrifice of some kind. Harriet Bolson was executed in front of the altar in a way that could be interpreted as ritual sacrifice. We found a necklace with a sandal pendant around her neck."

Lindman lifted his hand and interrupted him.

"I've been wondering about that note with her name on it. If it was left there for us, then why?"

"I don't know. What do you think?"

"Doesn't it suggest that we are in fact dealing with a lunatic who challenges us, who wants us to try to catch him?"

"It could be. But that's not the important thing right now. I think these people are planning to do with Zeba what they did to Harriet Bolson."

The room grew quiet.

"This is where we are," he said finally. "We have no suspect, no sure-fire motive, no definite directions. In my opinion, we're at a stalemate."

No one disagreed.

"We have to keep working," he said. "Sooner or later we'll find our way. We have to."

The meeting was over. People left in different directions. Linda felt in the way but had no thoughts of leaving the station. In three days, on Monday the tenth, she would at last be able to pick up her uniform and start working in earnest. But the only thing that meant anything right now was Zeba. Linda went to the bathroom. On her way back, her cell phone rang. It was Anna.

"Where are you?"

"At the station."

"Is Zeba back yet? I called her apartment but there's no answer."

Linda was immediately on her guard.

"She's still missing."

"I'm so worried about her."

"Me too."

She must really be worried, Linda thought. *She can't lie that well.*

"I need to talk," Anna said.

"Not now," said Linda. "I can't get away right now."

"Not even for a few minutes? If I come up to the station?"

"You aren't allowed in."

"But can't you come out? Only a few minutes?"

"Are you sure this can't wait?"

"Of course it can."

Linda heard that Anna was disappointed. She changed her mind.

"A few minutes, then."

"Thanks. I'll be there in ten minutes."

Linda walked down the corridor to her father's office. Everyone seemed to have vanished. She wrote on a note that she left on the desk: *I've gone out for some air and to talk to Anna. Back soon. Linda.*

She put on her jacket and left. The corridor was empty. The only person she passed on the way out was the cleaning woman with her cart. The police officers manning the incoming calls were busy and did not look up. No one saw her walk past the reception area.

The cleaning woman, Lija, who was from Latvia, normally started at the far end of the corridor, where the criminal investigators had their offices. Since several rooms there were occupied, she started with Inspector Wallander's office. There were always loose pieces of paper under his chair that he hadn't managed to throw into the wastebasket. She swept up everything that was under the chair, dusted here and there, and then left the room.

49

Linda waited outside the station. She was cold and pulled the jacket tightly across her body. She walked down to the poorly lit parking lot and spotted her dad's car. She felt her pocket and confirmed that she still had the spare keys. She checked her watch. More than ten minutes had gone by. Why wasn't Anna here?

Linda waited at the entrance to the police station. No one was around. In other parts of the building there were shadows behind the lit-up windows. She walked back over to the parking lot. Suddenly something made her feel ill at ease and she stopped short, looking around, listening. The wind rustled through the trees as if to catch her attention. She turned around quickly, adopting a defensive posture as she did so. It was Anna.

"Why did you sneak up on me like that?"

"I didn't mean to scare you."

"Where did you come from?"

Anna pointed vaguely in the direction of the entrance to the lot.

"I didn't hear your car," Linda said.

"I walked."

Linda was more than ever on her guard. Anna was tense, her face troubled.

"What's so important?"

"I just want to know about Zeba."

"But we talked about that on the phone."

Linda made a gesture up toward the glowing windows of the station.

"Do you know how many people are working in there right now?" she continued. "People with only one thing on their mind:

finding Zeba. You can think what you like, but I'm part of that team and I don't have time to stand here talking to you."

"I'm sorry, I should go."

This doesn't add up, Linda thought. Her whole inner alarm system was ringing. Anna was acting confused. Her sneaking manner and her unconvincing apology didn't match up.

"Don't go," Linda ordered sharply. "Now that you're here, you might as well tell me what's going on."

"I've already told you."

"If you know anything about where Zeba is, you have to tell me."

"I don't know where she is. I just came to ask you if you've found her, or at least have any clues."

"You're lying."

Anna's reaction was so surprising that Linda didn't have time to prepare for it. It was as if Anna underwent a sudden transformation. She shoved Linda in the chest and shouted, "I never lie! But you don't understand what's happening!"

Then she turned and walked away. Linda didn't say anything. She watched—speechless—as Anna walked away. Anna had one hand in her pocket. *She has something in there,* Linda thought. *Something she's clinging to like a life vest. But why is she so upset?* Linda wondered if she should run after her, but Anna was already far away.

She walked back up to the front doors of the police station, but something stopped her. She tried to think fast. She shouldn't have let Anna go. If it was true, as she thought, that Anna was acting strange, then she should have brought her into the station and asked someone else to talk to her. She had been given the task of staying close to Anna. Now she had made a mistake and brushed her away far too soon.

Linda tried to make a decision. She wavered between going back in and trying to stop Anna. She chose the latter and decided to borrow the car, since that would be faster. She drove the way that Anna should have walked, but without spotting her. She drove back the same way but saw nothing. There was an alternate route—same result. Had Anna disappeared again? Linda drove to her apartment building and stopped. The lights were on in the apartment. On her way to the front door, Linda saw a bicycle. The tires were wet, and the water-splashed frame had not yet dried. It wasn't raining, but the streets were full of puddles. Linda shook her head. Something warned her against ringing the doorbell. Instead she returned to the car and backed it up until it was in shadow.

She felt that she needed to consult with someone, so she dialed her father's cell phone. No answer. *He must have misplaced it again,* she thought. She dialed the number to Lindman's phone. Busy, just like Martinsson's, which she tried next. Linda was about to try all three again when a car turned onto the street and stopped outside Anna's door. It was dark blue or black, maybe a Saab. The light in Anna's apartment was turned off. Linda's whole body was tense; her hands holding the cell phone were sweaty. Anna appeared and climbed into the back seat, then they drove away. Linda followed. She tried to call her dad, but he still didn't answer. On Österleden she was overtaken by a speeding truck. Linda stayed behind the truck but pulled out from time to time to make sure the dark car didn't disappear. It turned onto the road to Kåseberga.

Linda kept as great a distance between herself and the other car as she dared. She tried to make another call but only managed to drop the cell phone between the seats. They passed the road to Kåseberga Harbor and kept driving east. It was only when they reached Sandhammaren that the car in front of her made a right turn. The move seemed to come out of nowhere, as the driver had not used the turn signal. Linda continued past the place where it had turned and only stopped when she had gone over a hill and around a corner. She found a bus stop and turned around, then drove back, although she didn't dare take the same turn.

Instead she chose a small dirt road to the left. It came to an end by a broken gate and a rusty harvester. Linda climbed out of the car. There was a stronger wind down here by the sea. She looked around for her father's black knit watch cap. When she pulled it over her head, she felt as if it made her invisible. She wondered if she should try to call again, but when she saw that her phone's battery was running low she put it in her pocket without calling and started walking back the way she had come. It was only a few hundred meters back to the other road. She walked so fast that she broke into a sweat. The road was dark. She stopped and listened, but only heard the wind and the roar of the sea.

She searched among the houses scattered over the area for

about forty-five minutes and had almost given up when she suddenly spotted the dark blue car parked between some trees. There was no house nearby. She listened, but everything was quiet. She shielded the flashlight with her hand to hide the light, then shone it into the car. There were a scarf and some earplugs in the backseat where Anna had been. Then she directed the beam of light onto the ground. There were paths leading in several directions, but one had a multitude of footprints.

Linda thought again about calling her dad but changed her mind when she reminded herself about the battery being low. Instead she sent him a text message: *With Anna. Will call later.* She turned off the light and started following the sandy path. She was surprised that she wasn't scared even though she was breaking the golden rule often repeated during her schooling: Never work alone, never go into the field alone. She stopped, hesitating. Perhaps she should turn back. *I'm just like Dad,* she thought, and inside she felt a gnawing suspicion that this was about showing him she was good enough.

Suddenly she caught sight of a light between the trees and the sand dunes up ahead. She listened. There were still only the sounds of the wind and the sea. She took a few steps in the direction of the light. There were several lit windows. It was a house set off from others, without neighbors. There was a fence and a gate. She turned off her flashlight when she was close enough that the light from the house illuminated the ground in front of her. The garden was large, and she knew the sea must be close by, although she couldn't see it. She wondered who had such a large house near the shore and what Anna was doing there, if that's where she was. Then her phone rang. She was startled and dropped the flashlight, but answered it quickly. It was one of her fellow students from the academy, Hans Rosquist, who now worked in Eskilstuna. They hadn't talked since the graduation ball.

"Is this is a bad time?" he said.

Linda could hear music, the clinking of glasses and bottles in the background.

"Sort of," she said. "Call me tomorrow. I'm working."

"You can't talk even for a few minutes?"

"No. Let's chat tomorrow."

She hung up and kept a finger on the off button in case he called again. When she had waited for two minutes without anything happening, she tucked the phone back into her pocket. Cautiously she climbed over the fence. There were more cars parked in front of the house, and there were also a few tents on the lawn.

Someone opened a window close to where she was. She flinched and crouched down. There was a shadow behind a curtain and the sound of voices. She waited. Then she noiselessly made her way up to the window. The voices had stopped. The feeling that there were eyes out here in the darkness was very strong. *I should run away from this place,* she thought, her heart pounding. *I shouldn't be here, at least not alone.* A door opened, she couldn't see exactly where, but she saw the long patch of light it cast onto the grass. Linda held her breath. Now she caught the whiff of tobacco smoke on the wind. *Someone is standing in the doorway, smoking,* she thought. At the same time, the voices through the window started up again.

The patch of light on the grass disappeared and the unseen door closed. The voices became clearer. It took a few minutes for her to realize that there was actually only one speaker, a man. But the pitch of his voice varied so much that she had at first thought it was several speakers. He spoke in short sentences, paused, and then continued. She strained to hear what language he was using. It was English.

At first she didn't understand what he was talking about, it was simply an incoherent jumble of words. He was giving the names of people, of cities: Luleå, Västerås, Karlstad. It was part of a briefing, she realized. Something was set to happen in these places. A time and a date were repeated over and over. Linda made the calculation in her head. Whatever it was, it would happen in twenty-six hours. The voice spoke methodically and slowly and could occasionally become sharp, almost shrill, and then drop down to a mild tone again.

Linda tried to imagine what the man looked like. She was very tempted to stand up on tiptoe and try to peek into the room, but she stayed in her uncomfortable position crouched next to the wall. Suddenly the voice inside started to talk about God. Linda felt her stomach contract.

Linda didn't have to think about what the alternatives were. She knew she should make her way back and contact the station. Perhaps they were even wondering where she had gone. But she also felt she couldn't leave just yet, not while the voice was talking about God and the thing that was to happen in twenty-six hours. What was the message between the lines of what he was saying? He talked about a special grace that awaited the martyrs. Martyrs? What was he talking about? There were too many questions and not enough room in her head. What was going on, and why was his voice so mild?

How long did she listen until she grasped what he was saying? It might have been half an hour or just a few minutes. The terrifying truth slowly dawned on her and she started to sweat, even though it was cold. Here in a house in Sandhammaren a group of people were preparing a terrible attack—no, thirteen attacks, and a few of those who would set the catastrophe in motion had already left.

She heard a few repeated phrases: *located by the altars and towers*. Also: *the explosives*, and *at the corners of the structures*. Linda was suddenly reminded of her father's irritation when someone tried to inform him of an unusually large dynamite theft. Could there be a connection to what she was hearing through the window? The man inside started to talk about how important it was to attack the foremost symbols of the false prophets, and that that was why he had chosen the thirteen cathedrals as targets.

Linda was sweating, but she was also cold. Her legs were stiff, her knees ached, and she realized she had to get away immediately. What she had heard, what she now knew was true, was so terrifying that she couldn't really get it into her head. *This isn't really happening*, she thought. *These kinds of things happen far away*.

She carefully straightened her back. It was quiet inside. He started to talk again just as she was about to leave. She stiffened. The man who was speaking now said *all is ready*, only that: *all is ready*. But he wasn't speaking a true Swedish, it was as if she were hearing a voice inside herself and on the tape that had disappeared from the police call-center archive. She shivered and waited for Torgeir Langaas to say something else, but the room was quiet. Linda carefully felt her way over to the fence and climbed over. She didn't dare turn on her flashlight. She walked into branches and stumbled over rocks.

After a while she realized she was lost. She couldn't find the path and she had ended up in some sand dunes. Wherever she turned she couldn't see any light except from a ship far out to sea. She took off her hat and stuffed it into her pocket, as if her bare head would help her find her way. She tried to figure out where she was from her position in relation to the sea and the direction of the wind. Then she started to walk, pulling out the hat and putting it on again.

Time was of the essence. She couldn't keep wandering around in circles in these sand dunes. She had to make a call. But the phone wasn't in her pocket. She felt through all her pockets. *The hat,* she thought. *It must have fallen out when I took out the hat. It fell onto the sand and I didn't hear it.* She started crawling around in her own tracks with the flashlight on but she didn't find it. *I'm so incompetent,* she thought furiously. *Here I am crawling around without a clue.* But she forced herself to regain her composure. Again she tried to determine the right direction. From time to time she stopped and let the flashlight cut through the dark.

At last she found the path she had walked in on. The house with the brightly lit windows was on her left. She veered as far away as she could, then broke into a run toward the dark blue car. It was a moment accompanied by a rush of relief. She looked down at her watch: a quarter past eleven. The time had flown by.

The arm came out of the darkness from behind, and it gripped her tightly. She couldn't move; the force holding her was too great. She felt his breath against her cheek. The arm turned her around and a flashlight shone into her face. Without him saying a word she knew that the man looking at her was Torgeir Langaas.

50

Dawn came as a slowly creeping shade of gray. The blindfold over Linda's eyes let in some light and she knew the night was coming to an end. But what would the day bring? It was quiet all around her. Oddly enough, her bowels had held up. It was a stupid thought, but when Langaas had grabbed her it had sped through her mind like a little sentry, screaming: *Before you kill me you have to let me go to the bathroom. If there isn't one around, then leave me for a minute. I'll crouch in the sand, I always have toilet paper in my pocket, and then I'll kick the sand over my shit like a cat.*

But of course she hadn't said anything. Langaas had breathed on her, the flashlight had blinded her eyes. Then he had pushed her aside, put the blindfold over her eyes, and tightened it. She had hit her head when he forced her into the car. Her fear was so great it could only be compared to the terror she felt when she was balancing on the edge of the bridge and arrived at the surprising insight that she didn't want to die. It had been quiet all around her, just the wind and the roar of the sea.

Was Langaas still there by the car? She didn't know, nor did she know how much time passed before the doors to the car were opened. But she deduced from the motion of the car that two people had climbed in, one behind the wheel and the other on the passenger side. The car jerked into action. The person driving was careless and nervous, or simply in a hurry.

She tried to sense where they were driving. They came out on the main road and turned left, toward Ystad. She also thought she felt them drive through Ystad, but at some point on the road to Malmö she lost control of her inner map. The car turned around, changed direction several times, asphalt gave way to gravel which in turn gave way to asphalt. The car stopped, but no doors opened. It was still quiet. She didn't know how long she sat there, but it was toward the end of this phase of waiting that the gray light of morning started to trickle in through her blindfold.

Suddenly the peace was broken by the sound of the car doors being thrown open, and someone pulled her out of the car. She was led along a paved road and then onto a sandy path. She was ushered up four stone steps, noting that the edges were uneven. She imagined that the steps were old. Then she was surrounded by cool air, an echoing coolness. She immediately realized she was in a church. The fear that had grown numb during the night returned with full force. She saw in her mind's eye what she had only heard about: Harriet Bolson strangled in front of the altar.

Steps echoed on the stone floor, a door was opened, and she tripped over a doorjamb. Her blindfold was removed. She blinked in the gray light and saw Langaas's back as he walked out and locked the door behind him. A lamp in the room was lit. She was in a vestry with oil portraits of stern ministers from the past. Shutters were closed over the windows. Linda looked around for a door to a toilet, but there was none. Her bowels were still calm, but her bladder was about to burst. There were some tall goblets on a table. She thought God would forgive her and used one of them as a chamber pot. She looked down at her watch: a quarter to seven, Saturday, the eighth of September. She heard a plane coming in to land passing right over the church.

Linda cursed the cell phone she had managed to lose during the night. There was no phone in the vestry. She searched the cupboards and drawers. Then she started to work on the windows. They opened, but the shutters were tightly sealed and locked. She looked through the vestry one more time but didn't find any tools.

The door opened and a man walked in. Linda recognized him at once, even though he was thinner than in the pictures Anna had showed her, the pictures she had kept hidden in her bureau. He was dressed in a suit with a dark blue shirt buttoned all the way up. His hair was combed back and long at the neck. His eyes were light blue, just like Anna's, and it was even more clear than from the photographs how much they looked like each other. He stopped in the shadows by the door and smiled at her.

"Don't be afraid," he said kindly and approached her with his arms outstretched, as if he wanted to demonstrate that he was unarmed and did not intend to attack.

A thought flashed through Linda's head when she saw his open, outstretched arms. *Anna must have had a weapon in her coat pocket. That's why she came down to the station. To kill me. But she couldn't.* The thought made Linda weak in the knees. She staggered to one side and Erik Westin helped her sit down.

"Don't be afraid," he repeated. "I'm sorry I was forced to let you wait blindfolded in the car. I am also sorry that I am forced to detain you for a few more hours. Then you will be free to go."

"Where am I?"

"That I cannot tell you. The only thing that is important is that you should not be afraid. I also need you to answer one question."

His tone was still concerned, the smile seemed genuine. Linda was confused.

"You have to tell me what you know," Westin said.

"About what?"

He fixed her with his gaze, still smiling.

"That wasn't very convincing," he said softly. "I could ask my question more directly, but that won't be necessary, since you understand full well what I mean. You followed Anna last night and you found your way to a house by the sea."

The majority of what I tell him has to be true, she thought quickly, *otherwise he'll see through me. There is no alternative,* she thought, giving herself more time by blowing her nose.

"I never made it to a house," she said. "I found a parked car under the trees. But I was looking for Anna."

Westin seemed lost in thought, but Linda knew he was weighing her answer. She recognized his voice now. He was the one who had been preaching to an invisible audience in the house by the beach. Although his voice and presence made an impression of a gentle calm, she could not forget what he had said during the night.

He looked at her again.

"You did not find your way to a house?"

"No."

"Why were you looking for Anna?"

No more lies, Linda thought.

"I was worried about Zeba."

"Who is that?"

Now he was the one who was lying and she the one trying to conceal the fact that she saw through it.

"Zeba is a friend we have in common. I think she's been abducted."

"Why would Anna know where she is?"

"She has seemed awfully tense lately."

He nodded.

"You may be telling the truth," he said. "Time will tell."

He stood up without taking his eyes off her.

"Do you believe in God."

No, Linda thought. *But I know the answer you're looking for.*

"I believe in God."

"We shall soon see the measure of your faith," he said. "It is as it is written in the Bible: *Soon our enemies will be destroyed and their excesses consumed by fire.*"

He walked over to the door and opened it.

"You won't have to wait by yourself."

Zeba came in, followed by Anna. The door closed behind Westin and a key turned in the lock. Linda stared at Zeba, then Anna.

"What are you doing?" Linda asked.

"Only what needs to be done."

Anna's voice was steady, but forced and hostile.

"She's crazy," said Zeba, who had collapsed onto a chair. "Out of her mind."

"No, a person who kills an innocent child is crazy. It is a crime that must be punished."

Zeba rushed up from her chair and grabbed Linda's arm.

"She's crazy," she shouted. "She's saying I should be punished because of the abortion."

"Let me talk to her," Linda said.

"You can't reason with crazy people."

"I don't believe she's crazy," Linda said as calmly as she could.

She walked over to Anna and looked her straight in the eye, feverishly trying to order her thoughts. Why had Westin left Anna in the same room as her and Zeba?

"Don't tell me you're part of this," Linda said.

"My father has returned. He has restored the hope I had lost."

"What kind of hope?"

"That there is a meaning to life, that God has a meaning for each of us."

That's not true, Linda thought. She saw the same thing in Anna's eyes that she had seen in Zeba's: fear. Anna had turned her body so that she could see the door. *She's afraid it will open,* Linda thought. *She's terrified of her father.*

"What is he threatening you with?" she asked in a low tone, almost a whisper.

"He hasn't threatened me."

Anna had also lowered her voice to a whisper. *It can only mean she's listening,* Linda thought. *That gives us a possibility.*

"You have to stop telling lies, Anna. We can get out of this if you'll just stop lying."

"I'm not lying."

Time was short. She didn't launch into an argument with Anna. If she didn't want to answer a question, or answered with a lie, Linda could only go on.

"Believe what you like," she said. "But you won't make me responsible for people being murdered. Don't you understand what's going on?"

"My father came back to get me. A great task awaits us."

"I know what task you're talking about. Is that really what you want? Do you really want more people to die, more churches to burn?"

Linda saw that Anna was near the breaking point. She had to keep going, not relax her grip.

"And if Zeba is punished, as you call it, you will have her son's face in front of you for all eternity, an accusation that you will never be able to escape. Is that what you want?"

They heard the sound of the key in the lock. They had run out of time. But just before the door opened Anna pulled a cell phone out of her pocket and passed it to Linda. Erik Westin appeared in the doorway.

"Have you said good-bye?" he asked.

"Yes," Anna said. "I've said good-bye."

Westin stroked her forehead with his fingertips. He turned to Zeba and then to Linda.

"Only a little while longer," he said. "An hour or so."

Zeba lunged at the door. Linda grabbed her and forced her down in the chair. She kept her there until Zeba started to calm herself.

"I have a phone now," Linda whispered. "We'll get through this."

"They're going to kill me."

Linda pressed her hand over Zeba's mouth.

"If I'm going to get us out of this, you have to help me by being quiet."

Zeba did as she was told. Linda was shaking so hard she dialed the wrong number twice. The phone rang again and again without her dad picking up. She was just going to hang up when he answered. When he heard her voice he started to shout. Where was she? Didn't she understand how worried he was?

"We don't have time," she whispered. "Listen."

"Where are you?"

"Be quiet and listen."

She told him what had happened after she left the station, first leaving a note on his desk. He interrupted.

"There's no note. I stayed there the whole night waiting for you to call."

"Then it must have gotten lost. We don't have time, you have to listen."

She was about to cry. He didn't interrupt her again, only breathing heavily as if each breath were a difficult question he needed to find an answer to, an important decision that needed to be made.

"Is this true?" he asked.

"Every word. I heard them."

"They're completely mad," he said.

"No," Linda objected. "It's something else. They believe in what they're doing. They don't think it's crazy."

"Whatever it is, we'll alert all major cities," he said, "I believe we have fifteen cathedrals in this country."

"I only heard mention of thirteen," Linda said. "Thirteen towers. The thirteenth tower is the last one and marks the onset of the great cleansing process. What it all means I don't know."

"You don't know where you are?"

"No. I'm pretty sure we drove through Ystad; the roundabouts matched up. I don't think we could have made it as far as Malmö."

"In what direction?"

"I don't know."

"Did you notice anything else when you were in the car?"

"Different kinds of road. Asphalt, gravel, sometimes dirt roads."

"Did you cross any bridges?"

She thought hard.

"I don't think so."

"Did you hear any sounds?"

She thought of it immediately. *The airplanes passing overhead.* She had heard them several times.

"I've heard airplanes. One was close by."

"What do you mean by close?"

"It was about to land. Or else it was taking off."

"Wait," her dad said.

He called to someone in the room.

"We're getting out a map," he said when he came back on the line. "Can you hear an airplane right now?"

"No."

"Were they big or little planes?"

"Jet planes. Big."

"Then it must be Sturup Airport."

Paper rustled in the background. Linda heard her father tell someone to call the air traffic control tower at Sturup and to patch the call into his line with Linda.

"We have a map here now. Can you hear anything?"

"Airplanes? No, nothing."

"Can you tell me anything more about where you are in relation to the airplanes?"

"Are church towers toward the east or west?"

"How would I know that?"

Wallander shouted out to Martinsson, who answered.

"The tower is always in the west, the altar area in the east. It has to do with the resurrection."

"Then the planes have been coming from the south. If, as I think, I'm facing east, the planes have been coming from the south heading north. Or maybe northwest. They have been passing by almost directly overhead."

There was mumbling and scraping on the other end. Linda felt the sweat running down her body. Zeba sat apathetic, cradling her head in her hands. Wallander came back on the line.

"I'm going to let you talk to a flight controller called Janne Lundwall. I'll be able to hear your conversation and may jump in from time to time. Do you understand?"

"I get it. I'm not stupid, Dad. But you have to hurry."

His voice wavered when he answered.

"I know. But we can't do anything if we don't know where you are."

Janne Lundwall's voice came on.

"Let's see if we can figure out where you are," he said cheerily. "Can you hear any planes right now?"

Linda wondered what her dad had told him. The flight controller's upbeat tone only increased her anxiety.

"I can't hear anything."

"We have a KLM flight due in five minutes. As soon as you hear it, you let me know."

The minutes passed extremely slowly. Finally she heard the faint sound of an approaching plane.

"I can hear it."

"Are you facing east?"

"Yes. The plane is approaching on my right."

"Good. Now tell me when the plane is just above you or in front of you."

There was a noise at the door. Linda turned off the cell phone and shoved it in her pocket. Langaas came in. He stopped, looked at both of them, and then left without saying a word. Zeba sat curled up in her corner. Only when Langaas had left and slammed the door behind him did Linda realize the plane had come and gone.

She dialed the number to her father again. He was clearly upset. *He's just as scared as I am*, Linda thought. *Just as scared and he has as little idea of where I am as I do. We can talk to each other but we can't find each other.*

"What happened?"

"Someone came in. The one called Torgeir Langaas. I had to hang up."

"Good God. Here's Lundwall again."

The next plane was due in four minutes. Lundwall told her it was a charter flight from Las Palmas that was fourteen hours delayed.

"A whole lot of grumpy, pissed-off passengers on their way in for landing," he said smugly. "Sometimes I'm grateful I'm tucked up here in my tower. Can you hear anything?"

Linda told him when she heard the plane.

"Same as before. Tell me when it's above you or right in front."

The plane grew nearer. At the same time the cell phone started to beep. Linda looked at the display. The battery was almost out of power.

"The phone is dying," she said.

"We have to know where you are," her dad shouted.

It's too late, Linda thought. She damned and cursed the phone and pleaded with it not to die on her just yet. The plane came closer and closer, the phone still beeped. Linda called out when the whine of the engines were right between her ears.

"Then we have a pretty good idea where you are," Lundwall said. "Just one more question—"

What he wanted to know, Linda never found out. The phone died. Linda put it in a cupboard with robes and mantles. Did they have enough information to identify the church? She could only hope so. Zeba looked at her.

"It's going to be all right," Linda said. "They know where we are."

Zeba didn't answer. She was glassy-eyed and took hold of Linda's wrist so hard that her nails dug into the skin and drew blood. *We're equally frightened*, Linda thought. *But I'm pretending not to be. I have to keep Zeba calm. If she goes into a panic our waiting period may be cut short.*

What were they waiting for? She didn't know, but if the truth was that Anna had told her father about Zeba's abortion, and if an abortion was the grounds for Harriet Bolson's execution in Frennestad Church, then there was no doubt about what was going to happen.

"It's going to be all right," Linda whispered. "They're on their way."

They waited. It could have been half an hour or more. Then it was as if lightning struck out of nowhere. The door flew open and three men came in and grabbed Zeba. Two more followed and grabbed Linda. They were pulled out of the room. Everything went so fast that it never even occurred to Linda to resist. The arms that held her were too strong. Zeba screamed. It sounded like the howl of an animal. Westin and Langaas were waiting in the church. There were two women and a man in the front pew. Anna was also there, but she sat a little farther back. Linda tried to meet her gaze but Anna's face was like a stiff mask. Or was she wearing a real mask? Linda couldn't tell. The people sitting in the front had something that looked like white masks in their hands.

Linda was filled with a paralyzing fear when she saw the hawser in Westin's hands. *He's going to kill Zeba,* she thought desperately. *He's going to kill her and then he's going to kill me because I've seen too much.* Zeba struggled to free herself.

Then it was as if the walls collapsed. The church doors burst open, while four of the stained glass windows, two on either side of the church, were shattered. Linda heard a voice shouting in a megaphone, and it was her father. He shouted as if he didn't trust the megaphone's amplifying capacity. Everyone inside the church froze.

Westin gave a start, grabbing Anna and using her as a shield. She tried to pull away. He shouted at her to calm down, but she kept writhing. He dragged her with him toward the front doors of the church. Again she tried to get out of his grasp. A shot rang out. Anna jerked and collapsed. Westin had a gun in his hand. He stared in disbelief at his daughter, then ran out of the church. No one dared to stop him.

Wallander and a large number of armed officers—Linda didn't recognize most of them—stormed into the church through the side doors. Langaas started to shoot. Linda pulled Zeba along with her into a pew where they lay down on the floor. The officers were firing back. Linda couldn't see what was happening. Suddenly it grew quiet. She heard Martinsson's voice. He shouted that a man had gone out the front door. *That must be Torgeir Langaas,* she thought.

She felt a hand on her shoulder and flinched. Perhaps she even screamed without realizing. It was her dad.

"You have to get out," he said.

"How is Anna?"

He didn't answer, and Linda knew she was dead. She and Zeba scurried out a door. In the distance she saw the dark blue car disappear down the road, followed by two police cars. Linda and Zeba sat down on the ground on the other side of the cemetery wall.

"It's over," Linda said.

"Nothing is over," Zeba whispered. "I'm going to live with this for the rest of my life. I'm always going to feel something pressing around my throat."

Suddenly there was one more shot, then two more. Linda and Zeba crouched down by the low wall. There were voices, orders, cars that took off at high speed with their sirens going. Then silence.

Linda told Zeba to stay there. She carefully got to her feet and peeked out over the wall. There were a lot of officers surrounding the church, but everyone was still. It was like looking at a painting. She saw her dad and walked over to him. He was pale and grabbed her arm hard.

"Both of them got away," he said. "Westin and Langaas."

He was interrupted by someone who handed him a cell phone. He listened, then handed it back without a word.

"A car loaded with dynamite has just driven right into Lund Cathedral. It drove right through the poles with iron chains and then crashed into the left tower. There's chaos on the scene. No one knows how many are dead. But we seem to have averted attacks against the other cathedrals. Twenty people have been arrested so far."

"Why did they do it?" Linda asked.

Wallander thought for a long time before answering.

"Because they believe in God and love him," he said. "But I don't think their love is reciprocated."

They were silent.

"Was it hard to find us?" Linda asked. "There are a lot of churches in Skåne."

"Not really," he said. "Lundwall was able to locate you almost exactly. We had two churches to choose from."

Silence again. Linda knew they were thinking the same thing. *What would have happened if she hadn't been able to help them figure it out?*

"Whose cell phone?" he asked.

"Anna's. She felt terrible about what she had done."

They walked over to Zeba. A black car had arrived, and Anna's body was carried out.

"I don't think he meant to shoot her," Linda said. "I think the gun went off in his hand."

"We'll catch him," Wallander said. "Then we'll find out."

Zeba stood up as they approached. She was frozen and shivering hard.

"I'll go with her," Linda said. "I did almost everything wrong, I know. I'm sorry."

"I'll be able to relax more when I've got you wearing a uniform and know you're securely seated in a patrol car circling the streets of Ystad," her dad said.

"My cell phone is lost on the dunes somewhere out in Sandhammaren."

"We'll send someone out there to call your number. Maybe the sand will answer."

Svartman was standing by his car. He wrapped a blanket around Zeba and opened the back door and Zeba crawled in and made herself small in the corner.

"I'll stay with her," Linda said.

"How are you doing?"

"I don't know. The only thing I'm sure of is that I'm going to start work on Monday."

"Push it off for a week," her dad said. "There's no hurry."

Linda sat down in the car and they drove away. A plane flew low over their heads, coming in for landing. Linda looked out at the landscape. It was as if her gaze was being sucked into the brown-gray mud and there was the sleep that she needed more than anything else right now. After that she would return one last time to the long wait to start working. But this time the wait would be short. Soon she would be able to throw off her invisible uniform. She thought about asking Svartman if he thought they would catch Erik Westin and Torgeir Langaas, but she didn't say anything. Right now she didn't want to know.

Later, not now. Frost, autumn, and winter—time enough later for thinking. She leaned her head on Zeba's shoulder and closed her eyes. Suddenly she saw Westin's face in front of her eyes. That last moment when Anna slowly fell toward the floor. Now she realized the despair that had been in his face, the vast loneliness. The face of a man who has lost everything.

She looked out over the landscape again. Slowly everything fell away, Erik Westin's face, into the gray clay.

Zeba was asleep by the time they reached her apartment. Linda gently shook her awake.

"We're here," she said. "We're here and everything is over."

51

Monday, the tenth of September, was a cold and blustery day in Skåne. Linda had tossed and turned and only managed to fall asleep at dawn. She was woken up by her father coming in and sitting down on the side of her bed. *Just like when I was little*, she thought. *He was always the one who would sit on the side of my bed, never my mom.*

He asked how she had slept and she told him the truth: poorly, and she had been plagued by nightmares.

The previous evening, Lisa Holgersson had called to say that Linda could wait a week before starting work. But Linda had refused. She didn't want to put it off any longer, even after everything that had happened. They finally agreed that Linda would take one extra day and start work on Tuesday.

Wallander got to his feet.

"I've got to go," he said. "What do you have planned?"

"I'll see Zeba. She needs someone to talk to and so do I."

Linda spent the day with Zeba, whose son was with Mrs. Rosberg. The phone rang off the hook, mostly eager reporters. Finally she and Zeba escaped to Mariagatan. They went over what had happened again and again, especially the part that Anna had played. Could they understand it? Could anyone understand?

"She missed her father her whole life," Linda said. "When he finally turned up, she refused to believe anything except that he was right, whatever he said and did."

Zeba often fell silent. Linda knew what she was thinking, about how close to death she had been and that not only Anna's father but Anna herself had been to blame.

Mid-morning, Wallander called and told her that Henrietta had collapsed and been taken to the hospital. Linda remembered Anna's sighs that Henrietta had woven into one of her compositions. *That's all she has left,* she thought. *Her dead daughter's sighs.*

"There was a letter on her table," Wallander continued, "where she tried to explain what she had done. She didn't tell us about Westin's return because she was afraid. He had threatened her and said that both she and Anna would die if she said anything. There's no reason not to believe her, but she surely could have found a way to let someone know what was going on."

"Did she say anything about my last visit?" Linda asked.

"Langaas was in the garden. She opened the window so he would hear that she didn't reveal anything."

"Westin used Langaas to scare people."

"He knew a lot about people, we shouldn't forget that."

"Is there any trace of them?"

"We should find them, since this matter is top priority all over the world. But maybe they'll find new hiding places, new followers. No one knows how many places Langaas prepared for them, and no one will know for sure until they're found."

"Torgeir Langaas is gone, Erik Westin is gone, but the most gone of all is Anna."

When the conversation was over, Linda and Zeba talked about the fact that maybe Westin was already busy building up a new sect. They knew there were many out there who were prepared to follow him. One such person was Ulrik Larsen, the minister who had threatened and attacked Linda in Copenhagen. He was one of Erik Westin's followers, waiting to be called to action. Linda thought about what her father had said. They couldn't be sure of anything until Westin was caught. One day maybe a new assault would be launched, like the one in Lund.

Afterward, when she had followed Zeba home after first making sure she was feeling up to being on her own with her son, Linda took a walk and sat down on the pier down by the harbor café. It was cold and windy, but she found a sheltered spot out of the wind. She didn't know if she missed Anna or if what she felt was something else. *We never became friends for real,* she thought. *We never got that far. We were really only true friends as children.*

———

That evening, Wallander came home and reported that Torgeir Langaas had been found dead. He had driven into a tree. Everything pointed to suicide. But Erik Westin was still at large. Linda wondered if she would ever find out if it was Westin she had seen in the sunlight outside Lestarp Church. And was he the one who had been her car? These questions remained unanswered.

But there was one question she had found the answer to herself. The puzzling words in Anna's diary: *myth fear, myth fear. It was so simple,* Linda thought *Myth fear—my father, my father. An anagram, that was all.*

Linda and her father sat up and talked for a long time. The police were slowly reconstructing Erik Westin's life and had found a connection to the minister Jim Jones and his sect, who had found death in the jungles of Guyana. Westin was a complicated person whom it would never be possible to fully understand, but it was important to realize that he was a far cry from a madman. His self-image, not least as expressed in the holy pictures he asked his disciples to carry with them, was of a humble person carrying out God's work. He wasn't insane so much as a fanatic, prepared to do whatever it took to realize his beliefs. He was prepared to sacrifice people if need be, kill those who stood in his way, and punish those whom he deemed had committed mortal sins. He sought his justifications in the Bible. He let nothing happen that he did not feel could be justified by the Holy Book.

Westin was also a desperate man who saw only evil and decay around him, not that this in any way justified his actions. But the only hope of preventing something like this in the future, of identifying people prepared to blow themselves up as a chain in something they claimed was a Christian effort, was not to dismiss Westin as a simple madman, Wallander said.

There was not much to add. Those who were to have carried out the well-planned bombings were now awaiting trial. Police all over the world were looking for Westin, and soon fall would come with frosty nights and cold winds from the northeast.

They were about to go to bed when the phone rang. Wallander listened in silence, then asked a few short questions. When he hung up, Linda did not want to ask him what had happened. She saw the glimmer of tears in his eyes, and he told her that Sten Widén had just died. The woman who called was a girlfriend, possibly the last one he had lived with. She had promised Widén to contact Wallander and tell him that everything was over and that it had "gone well."

"What did she mean by that?"

"We used to talk about it when we were younger, Sten and I. That death was something one could face like an opponent in a duel. Even if the outcome was a given, a skillful player could hold off and tire death out so that it only had the power to deliver a single blow. That was how we wanted our deaths to be, something we could take care of so they would 'go well.'"

He was very sad, she could see that.

"Do you want to talk some more?"

"No. This is something I have to work through on my own."

They were quiet for a while, then he stood up and went to bed without a word. Linda didn't manage to sleep many hours that night either. She thought about all the people out there prepared to blow up the churches they hated—and themselves. According to what her father and Lindman had said, and from what she had read in the papers, these people were far from monsters. They spoke of their good intentions, their hopes to pave the road for the true Kingdom of God on Earth.

She was prepared to wait one day, but no longer. Therefore she walked up to the station the morning of September 11. It was a cold, dreary day after a night that had left traces of the first frost. Linda tried on her uniform and signed receipts for her equipment. Then she had a meeting with Martinsson for an hour and received her first shift assignment. She was free for the rest of the day, but she didn't feel like sitting alone at home at Mariagatan and so she stayed at the station.

At three o'clock in the afternoon, she was drinking coffee in the lunchroom, talking to Nyberg, who had sat down at her table of his own accord and was showing his most friendly side. Martinsson came in and, shortly thereafter, her father. Martinsson turned on the TV.

"Something's happened in the U.S.," he said.

"What is it?" Linda asked.

"I don't know," Martinsson said. "We'll have to wait and see."

There was an image of a clock, counting down the seconds to a special news report. More and more people filtered into the room. By the time the news report came on, the room was almost full.

the girl on the roof

The call had come in to the station shortly after seven o'clock on Friday night, November 23, 2001. Linda, who was partnered up with an officer named Ekman that evening, answered the police dispatch department's broadcast. They had just resolved a family conflict in Svarte and were heading back to Ystad. A young woman had climbed onto the roof of an apartment building to the west of the city and was threatening to jump. To make matters worse, she was armed. The head of operations wanted as many patrol cars as possible to get to the scene. Ekman turned on the siren and sped up.

Curious onlookers had already gathered by the time they arrived. Spotlights illuminated the girl, who sat up on the roof with a shotgun in her arms. Ekman and Linda were briefed by Sundin, who was responsible for getting her down. A fire truck with a ladder was also in place, but the girl had threatened to jump if the ladder was driven any closer.

The girl, Maria Larsson, was sixteen years old and had been treated for several episodes of mental illness. She lived with her mother, who was a drug addict. This particular evening something had gone wrong. Maria had rung a neighbor's doorbell, and when the door opened she had rushed in and grabbed a shotgun and some ammunition that she knew were kept in the apartment. The owner of the apartment could count on being in serious trouble, since he had clearly stored both the weapon and the ammunition in an unsecured manner.

But this was about Maria. She had threatened alternately to jump, to shoot herself, and to shoot anyone who tried to approach her. The mother was too high to be of any use, and there was also the chance that she would start to shout at her daughter and incite her to carry out her threats.

Several officers had tried to speak to the girl through a trapdoor located twenty meters from the place by the drainpipe where she was sitting. Right now an old minister was trying to talk to her, but she aimed the weapon at his head and he quickly ducked down. They were feverishly working on locating a close friend of Maria's who would perhaps be able to get through to her. No one doubted that she was desperate enough to do what she had threatened.

Linda borrowed a pair of binoculars and looked at the girl. When the call came through, she had thought of the time she had stood on the bridge railing. When she saw Maria shaking on the roof, her cramped hold on the shotgun, and the tears that had frozen on her face, it was like looking at herself. Behind her she could hear Sundin, Ekman, and the minister talking. No one knew what to do. Linda lowered the binoculars and turned to them.

"Let me talk to her," she said.

Sundin shook his head doubtfully.

"I was once in the same situation," she said. "And she might listen to me since I'm not even that much older than she is."

"I can't let you take that risk. You're not experienced enough to judge what you should and shouldn't say. And her weapon is loaded. She's showing signs of an increasing desperation. Sooner or later she'll use her gun."

"Let her talk to her."

It was the old minister. He sounded very firm.

"I agree," Ekman said.

Sundin wavered.

"Shouldn't you at least call your dad first and talk to him?"

Linda almost lost her composure.

"For goodness' sake, this has nothing to do with him. This is just between me and Maria Larsson. Nothing to do with him."

Sundin agreed. But he made her put on a bulletproof vest and helmet before he let her go up. She kept the vest on, but removed the helmet before sticking up her head through the trapdoor. The girl on the roof heard the creaking of the metal. When Linda peeked out Maria had the gun aimed at her head. She almost ducked her head under again.

"Don't come near me!" the girl shrieked. "I'll shoot and then I'll jump!"

"Take it easy," Linda said. "I'm not going to move an inch. But will you let me talk to you?"

"What do you have to say to me?"

"Why are you doing this?"

"I want to die."

"I wanted to die too, once. That's what I have to say to you."

The girl didn't answer and Linda waited. Then she started to tell her about how she had stood on the bridge railing, what had led up to it, and about the person who had finally been able to talk her down.

Maria listened, but her initial reaction was anger.

"What do you think that has to do with me? My story is going to end down on the street. Go away! Leave me alone!"

Linda wondered what she should do next. She had thought her story would be enough. Now she realized what a naïve assessment that was. *I've watched Anna die,* she thought. *But I've also witnessed Zeba's joy at still being alive.*

She decided to keep talking.

"I want to give you something to live for," she said.

"There is nothing."

"Give me the gun and come here. For my sake."

"You don't know me."

"No, but I've teetered on a bridge railing. Sometimes I have nightmares where I throw myself off."

"When you're dead you don't dream anything. I don't want to live."

The conversation went back and forth. After a while—how long it was Linda couldn't say because time seemed to have been suspended when she first poked her head up out of the roof and faced the barrels of the shotgun—she could tell that the girl was fully engaged in what they were saying. Her voice was calmer, less shrill. This was the first step. Now she held an invisible lifeline of sorts around Maria's body. But nothing was resolved until the moment when Linda had used up all her words and started to cry. And that was when Maria finally gave in.

"All right," she said. "I just want them to turn off all the fucking lights. I don't want to see my mother. I only want to talk to you. And I won't come down right away."

Linda hesitated. What if it was a trap? What if she had decided to jump when the lights were turned off?

"Why won't you come down with me now?"

"I want ten minutes."

"What for?"

"Ten minutes to see what it feels like to have decided to live."

Linda climbed down and all the lights were turned off. Sundin kept an eye on the time. Suddenly it was as if all of the events from the dramatic days at the beginning of September came out of the darkness at her with full force. She had been so grateful for her work, and the new apartment had taken so much of her attention, that she had not yet had the opportunity to slow down enough to take on the full impact of what she had been through. Even more important was the time she had been spending with Stefan Lindman. They had started seeing each other, and sometime in the middle of October Linda had realized that she wasn't alone in having fallen in love. Now, when she stood there trying to pick out the outline of the girl on the roof who had decided to live, it was as if the moment had arrived for a kind of resolution to all that had happened.

Linda stamped her feet to stay warm and looked up again at the roof. Had Maria changed her mind? Sundin mumbled that there was only a minute left. Then the time ran out. The ladder truck drove up to the edge of the building. Two firemen helped the girl down, a third went up and collected the weapon. Linda had told Sundin and the others what she had promised, and she insisted that her side of the bargain be upheld. Therefore she was the only one there when Maria reached the bottom of the ladder. Linda hugged her and suddenly both of them started to sob. Linda had the strange feeling that she was hugging herself.

An ambulance was on the scene. Linda helped Maria over to it and waited until it drove away, the gravel crunching under its wheels. The frost had arrived; the air was already below freezing. Officers, the old minister, the firemen: everyone came up and shook her hand.

Linda and Ekman stayed until the fire trucks and patrol cars had left, the yellow tape had been taken down, and the crowd had dispersed. Then there was a broadcast about a suspected drunk driver on Österleden. Ekman started the engine. They left, and Linda swore under her breath. Most of all she would have liked to go back to the station for a cup of coffee.

But that would have to wait, like so many other things. She leaned against Ekman to read the thermometer for the outside temperature.

Minus three degrees Celsius. Winter had arrived in Skåne.